SUNTOUCHED

A Dark Comedy on a Greek Island

Theresa Nicholas

Pen Press

First published in Great Britain by Pen Press

All paper used in the printing of this book has been made from wood grown in managed, sustainable forests.

ISBN13: 978-1-907499-84-5

Printed and bound in the UK
Pen Press is an imprint of
Indepenpress Publishing Limited
25 Eastern Place
Brighton
BN2 1GJ

A catalogue record of this book is available from
the British Library

Cover artwork by Theresa Nicholas
Cover design by Jacqueline Abromeit

Dedication

In memory of Virginia Parsons, artist, author, illustrator –
in gratitude.

PART I

From the cold windy deck, I watch the coastline of England recede without regret. I've done it again. Done what? Escaped. As if to emphasize my defection, whenever I try to leave my country of origin, there is a strike. If I am going by train it will be the engine drivers; by plane, the air traffic controllers, or the baggage handlers. This time, because I am driving a tiny Fiat 500 Cinquecento and leaving by ferry, it is 'a proposed strike of port officials'. It makes the country that fashioned me into that dubious concoction of inhibitions labelled 'British' a cage or trap, and quite spoils the pleasure I might have in the good things it offers, such as hot baths, kippers and sausages.

Father leaned on the garden gate to watch me drive resolutely away to Dover, leaving him – a widower – in a village containing 38 widows. Since mother died, he has become part of the trap. Waiting for me to get 'this thing' out of my system and finally settle for the middle-class values and comforts. If they don't let me on to that ferry, I shall bloody well swim, dragging the Fiat with my teeth.

On the other side of the Channel, the sun is shining even though it is October. How is that possible? I fling back the sunroof, the smell of *Gauloises* and garlic is reassuringly un-British. The Customs Official, with the features of a weasel under the hard round French hat, smiles down at me perkily as he hands back my papers. "*Bon voyage, Mad'moiselle!*" I am free to take *toutes directions* – but which is the one South…? – to *him*…? *Does he really exist?* Or is he something I made up to escape from England and father? No, the proof is in those telegrams the post office could make little sense of. The telegraph boy apologized, "They're querying the text, Miss…" But they were perfectly understandable to me. "*Small mix last night.* [He had a fight] *Broke my head. Don't worry I fix the Baster. Com back*

1

quick as impossible. Your love Tasso." His letters are equally unreadable except by the Eye of Love. *Come back quick as impossible!* That is what I am trying to do with the migratory urge of a bird......south...south...

The roads have the consistency of glue. Italians driving their own *Cinquecentos* as if they were Ferraris pass me at speed, only to slow down to a crawl, forcing me to overtake them, while they leer at me through the windows, and do it all over again. *Basters!* His word for them. He's right. Brindisi, a non-place of ticket offices and touts: "You go Grecia? Here please! Special price!" A limbo – or is it a purgatory? – between the two worlds of Italy and Greece, where one thing comes to an end before the other has begun. The ferry doesn't leave till 10 pm. On board, I find myself talking with an American girl, who is amazed at my driving across Europe.

"Alone? Without a radio? I'd get to talking to myself."

"I did. I sang too. I would never have got here otherwise."
"Why are you going to Greece?"

The answer to that question is: "To escape an island set in dirty washing up water where you must always say 'sorry' – for an island set in emerald and turquoise, where nobody does anything properly, and never apologizes." Why do I also feel obliged to mention that Tasso is married and can't divorce?

"You mean you can't marry him ever?"

"Divorce is against the law in Greece."

"But don't you want children?"

"NO! All I want is him." She looks thoughtful.

"I had a Greek boyfriend once...back in the States. I really felt good with him...but they can be vicious, yer know..."

*

In the gold of a new-minted morning, the island harbour seems to spin around the ship as it turns to back up to the quay; a waltz of stucco houses with wrought iron balconies and beige tiled roofs. This is the moment '*which happiness itself will not equal*'.

2

He won't be on the quay – useless to expect it. He has his own rituals for receiving me, but until my eyes are blasted by the reality of him, I can't be sure he really exists. As I prepare to drive off the ship, Yannis comes on board looking for me, pokes his head through the car window. "*Tasso einai exo!*" (Tasso is outside) he says, pointing toward the Harbour Café. So he does exist! Relief floods through me. I drive over to the customs building where the tiresome little men in official uniforms ask too many questions and look at me with boot-button eyes full of sex and suspicion. The small office is crammed with men, all Greeks trying to get away with something by shouting and gesticulating. At the bottom of the scrum is the man at the desk. By the time I get to him, he is banging his rubber stamp onto anything and shouting "*Figé!*" Go!

I put my foot on the accelerator and aim for the Harbour Café. I am brought to a halt at the harbour gate by a young guard raising his hand. What the hell now? In slow motion he takes a packet of cigarettes from his shirt pocket and, with the stub of a pencil, writes down the number of my car. I can hear the juke box from the café where *he* is, blasting the early morning air with ethnic music. The vibrations probe to the very core of my being, representing everything I embraced when I embraced him. The young guard puts away the packet and the pencil slowly, regarding me all the while with the sexual curiosity they give to foreign females, and waves me through the gate.

Tasso is standing in the doorway of the café, a very physical presence, handsome and singular, iron-grey wire wool hair, a cut over one eye making him look 'well-done', even over-done – a man well-baked in the oven of life, wearing his old shirt and trousers, though it is Sunday. It tells the world he lives by his own standards and whatever personality can get away with. This spells out the right message to me.

I bring the car to a stop in front of him. Without greeting me, he looks at the car I have been to England to get.

"So small?"

"Were you expecting a Rolls Royce?" His lips twitch. I have hit the mark. Taking a small dark red carnation from the pocket of his shirt, he hands it to me.

"We don't need more," he says.

On an island with only ten cars, a Fiat 500 *is* a Rolls Royce. Having anticipated this opening bout of our relationship, I feel myself rising to it with a wild exhilaration – and despair.

We are together again.

Giant cypresses like green flames lead to the house among the orange trees; two rooms above a cow-byre, a table, two chairs, and a bed – £5 a month, no mod cons, sublime view. "We don't need more," he says.

The first year there wasn't even a cold water tap in the kitchen. A tin tank hung from a nail over the stone sink. I carried buckets of water up from the well to fill it; we flushed the loo with a bucket.

From our balcony, I look down on chickens scratching about; the bantam cock strutting neatly, tail feathers listing like a ship under sail. Maria's two children play in the dust by the well watched over by the grandmother dressed in perpetual black. Maria and her husband show their backs like dolphins among the vegetable they grow for the market. Three huge cows are pegged out on the rough grass by the lagoon. When the sun sets behind the contrapuntal hills, the water of the lagoon takes on the flush of apricot. But if this is The Simple Life – it is not simple at all. England has made me forget the heaviness of water in a bucket rather than a tap. "What's the matter with you?" he asks, returning from work in the afternoon.

"Nothing."

"Then why you have your face like a shoe?"

"Water comes out of taps in England...hot and cold."

"Oh, I know that," he says, though he has never been there. "In four days you forget all that. What other thing bothers you?"

His instinct is unerring. It is not that water does not come out of taps...it is the man standing in the field looking up at our windows. He was there most days before I went away – just standing in the field staring at the house. He appears only when Tasso is at work.

I saw him this morning; I have been back only two days. I tell Tasso about the man.

"I know who is him," he says. "He owns this property. Him a stupid. I will tell Maria to tell him to be careful – I don't joke. If he don't want to understand that way, I fix him myself." He has the habit of hitting any man who loiters near me. It was rather shocking at first.

"Why are you always hitting people?"

"Because it is the only language the *Basters* understand!" When I suggest he is probably a *Baster* too, he says, "Of course – this is the reason to know the others." Greek logic. "You must to remember, the people here is very thirsty of the sex, and our story is a little bit different." That is an understatement. Our story is a lot different. "We are a Big *Skandal*," he says; in which I have difficulty in recognising myself. "You must to be careful. The rest I fix." The man did not come anymore. And I forgot about water coming out of taps, hot and cold, as he predicted, in just four days.

*

He goes to his job with the Electrical Company at six in the morning, spending hours at the top of a pole fixing lines, or manhandling transformers up the hillsides to remote villages which are only now getting electricity. He enjoys physical work, he has always worked with his body; the surprising thing is that he should be making the pen and ink sketches he sells to the tourists. "Very help!" he says, "I make more money that way than from my job!"

I used to sit watching him drawing out the sketches, first in pencil and then in pen and ink. When he had disappeared on one of his mysterious errands, I took up the pen and carefully traced the pencil lines in with the ink. When he came back, he just said, "Good idea! Do more. That way we have more to sell." Soon I could make a passable forgery; now, when he goes to work, I go to work. At least I earn my keep. He signs the pictures. In a community with little conception of Art, he must remain that mysterious thing: 'The Artist' – "or we lose the battle," he says.

He does the shopping every morning in the market; it's the man's prerogative. As their Folk Wisdom defines it: a man doesn't want his wife to touch his money, or the butcher to touch his wife. He does the shopping for his kids as well, sending it to the house by one of the boys who hang about the market ready to do anything for a few drachmas. He leaves our shopping at the wine shop. I drive to town to collect it. The wine shop is an 'Everything shop', selling wine from the barrel, loose honey from the huge tin, sheep's cheese, ham, cooked pork, wines, spirits, beers and boiled sweets. It has four tables for customers to sit and take a coffee, an ouzo, or a glass of wine with Kyria Roula's cheese pies, parcels of *filo* pastry filled with feta cheese, quickly fried in the little galley alongside the counter. She and her elderly husband, Mr Sotiris, keep the shop from 8.30 in the morning till midnight. They have one daughter of ten years old, who comes in from school and does her homework at one of the tables, before playing hopscotch on the stone flagged floor. This is where I collect the shopping, and my post. This is the one place in town where I can sit alone with a glass of wine, waiting for him to turn up and reclaim me. Women in this society do not sit in cafés or taverns or drink wine.

This is also where I meet Pooter. "Ah," he says at the sight of me, "I wondered if I should find you here" – giving the impression he is on urgent business and can only spare you a minute of his time. "How was England?" he asks, not really wishing to know, as he is dying to tell me all that has been happening on the island in my absence. A retired civil-servant – you could wonder how he comes to be this far south of Croydon, still carrying a briefcase in which he puts his shopping. In winter, he wears a Burberry, but he has one gift so un-British as to be almost a flaw: he speaks fluent Greek, as well as French, German, Italian, Hungarian, Serbo-Croat and "just a smidgeon of Russian". The Greeks automatically classify him as "A Spy". Pooter enjoys the projected image, licking his lips like a lizard, smiling complacently. In his colourless way he could be the secret agent on a park bench in Munich, or in a bus queue in London.

He arrived on the island about the same time as I did. He understands the rules, and at first did not attempt to speak to me, restricting himself to a polite nod when he saw me sitting in the corner of the wine shop. Then one day, when Tasso was standing at the counter, he asked formal permission to sit with me and offer a glass of wine. Tasso consented at once. "The Greeks don't like you to sit down with their ladies, but if you go about it the right way, they cannot refuse," Pooter explained complacently. "Let me say at once" – as if to waive any reservations he might have about my irregular relationship – "Tasso is quite the best sort of Greek. Intelligent, charming and genuine. A splendid fellow!"

After that, our social hour in the wine shop became a regular event. He is a rich source of gossip about the few English who choose to live here – all eccentric, "though I try not to say anything malicious about them just because it is amusing," he asserts, but I can see he has some special news he is dying to impart. "I don't suppose you have had time to be aware of our newest 'arrival' on the island? The Honourable Mrs Tinker-Smith. The title, as you no doubt know, means she is the daughter of a Duke." He says he is not a snob – that he *used* to be one. "Does she look like a Praying Mantis?" As I walked up the street to wine shop, I had seen a tall figure of an elderly woman in a hat, who could only be English.

Pooter smirks. "I must admit that does describe her perfectly."

"What is she doing here?"

"She has come to live here – because someone told her it's as beautiful as the South of France and much cheaper. Unfortunately, the Lady was not prepared for the Greeks. She finds them rather…dare I say… You know, I myself am devoted to Greeks, but you could say they haven't the *'je ne sais quoi'* of the French."

"Why doesn't she go back there?"

"That is the problem. Foolishly, she's sent all her belongings here, without knowing if she would really like the place. Now she can't afford to go back. She is quite alone. She *has* been very rich – her father had a diamond mine in Africa. What is left of her fortune comes from there – there are difficulties there now. I feel sorry for her, so I have taken her under my wing, as it were – introducing her to the trades people, showing her ways and means, £100 a month is *ample* to live on here… I myself live on a *very* small pension, and lack nothing. No need to go without the little luxuries…if you know the way." He says this not without a certain smug pride in his economical management.

At that moment, the lady herself appeared in the shop doorway, balanced on high heels at one end and topped off with a little '*chapeau*' at the other; the elongated body in an out-of-date Dior suit with a flared hemline making her look like one of those vintage cars with an extra long chassis – a Lagonda, or a Huispana Suiza. On seeing Pooter she cries out, "I've been looking for you *everywhere*!" Pooter punctiliously rises to his feet. His attempt to introduce me is ignored; her eyes stop short of contact like the needle of a dial fixed not to go beyond a certain point. She has the face of a tortoise, though in her youth, she may have been handsome.

"I want you to come to the Carpenter with me. I MUST have a shoebox made. I have *simply nowhere* to put my shoes…" Pooter defends himself with his carefully cultivated self-importance.

"I cannot possibly accompany you today, my dear lady…I am giving an English lesson this morning."

"I thought you were retired?"

"I am retired in the English conception of the word, but here in Greece I am kept very busy teaching English to the Police Force, and I am late as it is." He looks at his watch. "Tomorrow, dear lady, I will be at your service, but now, good day!" He pays for his wine at the counter and disappears into the street. Without a glance in my direction, she goes too.

3.

In the evenings the wine shop has its habitués – Mr Babbi sits near the door with his glass of cognac, spelt with a K (*Koniak*), eyeing with insatiable curiosity everyone who comes in to get a bottle filled, discussing afterwards with Mr Sotiris to whom they must be related. Family history and scandal are communal and a source of perpetual examination. The Music Master comes in for his supper. He prefers my corner table. His face registers disapproval when he sees me occupying it. A young woman's place is not in a wine shop. Tasso secures me this fragile perch in a man's world; because of him, my presence is politely ignored. The music master loosens his muffler to eat his meal of boiled greens, feta cheese and olives, but keeps his hat on; it is winter. His lips are clamped in a thin line, his shoulders hunched into his overcoat; doctors, lawyers, teachers adopt this desiccated dignity as a cultural distinction, together with the ill-fitting black suit and the tie.

Tasso collects me at nine o'clock. When we have quit the place, they probably talk about us. Long ago Tasso earned the title of '*Bohème*'...a *Bohemian* – adopted straight from the French, no word for it in Greek. Tasso surveys the wet, windy street, deserted except for a solitary figure under a large black umbrella.

"Where I going to find money tonight? We are Ab-so-lutely broke. But…" tapping the side of his nose, "I smell something…" I smell only mutton fat where a man tends the sizzling sticks of meat on a charcoal brazier outside a tavern; the smoke drifts across the lamplight. "I saw foreigners in town this morning…" he goes on musing aloud. "We must to find them…" Foreigners in winter? A few drift through the island like migrating birds en route to the archaeological sites of Delphi, and Olympia. They gravitate to the cleanest looking bar or restaurant, where they hope to find the cleanest toilet, and quickly fall prey to the few locals with a smattering of English/French/German – Tasso predominant among them. All Greeks are opportunists; it is a spontaneous reaction so that foreigners find themselves being treated to wine and food and musical entertainment, quite unaware what battles are being fought over their persons.

We go first to the Old Tavern with the barrels stacked against the wall resting on sturdy racks; the spigots dripping onto the stone floor leave trails of what looks like blood, as if a murder had been committed there. A fat lady with red arms and face tends a primitive charcoal cooking range, with a huge canopy over it to contain the smoke. He orders two retsinas at the counter.

A short flight of steps past a smelly lavatory leads up into an inner room with several tables. From here comes the sound of the guitar, a tenor tuning up and men's voices wrangling over what to sing next. That's Costa, the carpenter, trying out the top register of his light tenor voice, and Panayoti on the guitar, the lorry driver is the baritone; Petros, the "iron-chested", is the bass. This group – no women – spend their evenings making harmony like drunken bees, or wasps in a bottle, with a repertoire of local folksongs, Venetian *cantathas*, *Rebetika*, and Italian Opera. No television yet, and the radio is a 'wireless' enshrined on the wooden counter under a chintz cover specially made for it.

This is just the place foreigners get sucked into – this was the first taverna he brought me to – *that* night. My first and best memories are connected with this place.

But there are no foreigners here tonight. He tosses back his retsina. We leave.

4.

We go on up the street until we arrive in front of an arched doorway filled by a cobweb of wrought iron depicting a salamander over flames. It has started to rain; he taps on the inner glass of the door. A patter of footsteps, the door opens a chink, and Madame Ellie's guttural voice says, "Ooo…Tass-oo…*Chéri*…come in quickly – it is so co-o-old…" At the sight of me: "You here again? Even when it rains? *Mon dieu* – you must be in love…" Madame Ellie: small, middle-aged (though her age is a secret – she could be as old as the Sphinx), large nose, shapeless body, neat ankles and feet. Stories about her abound; her marriages, divorces, her appetites. She has the reputation of a Lucrezia Borgia on this tittle-tattle island. After spending most of her life in Paris and Switzerland, she returned to the island after the war, and opened a bar to have somewhere to go in the evenings. In front of its blazing log fire are the foreigners he is looking for – I might have guessed they would be women. In no time at all, he is sitting with them

"Look at him!" Madame Ellie cries. "Why do you sit here alone…why you don't go there?"

To go there would be to stake my claim on him. Anyway, I know him. When the girls begin to wonder what his motives are, he will produce me like a certificate of hygiene, and they will be more intrigued.

"Darr-ling!" *The moment has arrived.* That endearment lost its fragrance very early. It never characterized our relationship, which is based on polarity; now it serves only to alert me to the fact that he is flirting, though he has no designs on them, except to sell them one of the pen sketches to pay for our evening.

"You're British?" Their eyes widen, visibly reshuffling their impression of him. (*You mean he's not a bastard?*) They are young Americans on a sabbatical, doing Europe and the Near East: "Boy, have we had some experiences…" they chant, embracing the opportunity to unload them on someone who understands their language.

"We got this lift with a taxi on the Pello-po-naze...right? He seemed a *real* nice guy. I sat in front. Lynn went to sleep on the back seat... Suddenly – on a really lonely bit of road – this guy..." (Tasso has gone back to the bar) "...stops the car, turns to me and says, '*Erotá?*' I thought he wanted to go the bathroom, but then the word clicked: *erotá*...erotic? Yeah? So I shook my head. Then he looks over at Lynn on the back seat. '*Erotá?*' 'No, she doesn't want it either...' So he just shrugs his shoulders and drives on. When we stop for lunch he insists of paying for everything and doesn't charge anything for a 50-mile taxi ride. *What's with these guys?* They can be so nice, but they seem to think foreign women are only looking for sex. It's kinda disappointing – you can't be *friends* with them."

I've noticed that.

Tasso comes back. "I have so nice idea...to take the girls to the Paradeisos Night Club." They trust him now and cheerfully pack themselves into the *Cinquecento*.

"What kind of car is this? I never saw one so small..."

We arrive at the cottage 'night club', set in a garden of orange trees, a simple room with eight sturdy tables, walls painted in ox blood, and a jukebox. "This is a *night club?*" Incredulous. "We *gotta* write home about this..."

Tasso orders macaroni, wine and salad, goes to the jukebox, thumbs the buttons, selecting the chorus from the Opera *Nabucco*, Little Richard's "*I'm just a lonely boy*" and a *Zembekiko*.

The macaroni, when it arrives, resembles the inner tubes of bicycle wheels swimming in tomato sauce. The girls are hungry and undaunted by it.

"What do you say for *bon appétit?*"

"*Kali Orexi.*"

The tables fill up with people who know all about each other and us. From the old portfolio he always takes with him wherever he goes, Tasso pulls out the pictures of sun and shadow and, propping them up on the empty chairs, makes his gallery.

"You're an artist!" the girls exclaim, and look at each other. "Didn't we say he looks like Picasso *with hair!*"

A bull-mooing comes from the jukebox as it regurgitates the rhythms of an ethnic Zembekiko, like an animal in labour. It pulls him away from the table into the small area reserved for dancing, where he begins to perform the strange solo dance of the Greek male, an arcane dance like a primordial bird's. When he dances, he exudes a powerful emotional magnetism, yet it is a private dance, a poetic expression of personality and experience. He never looks at his audience. Tracing a pattern on the floor with his feet, pausing – listening to what the music is saying – stretching his arms wide like wings, he crouches and rises in a slow, controlled turn; snapping his fingers like pistol shots, he leans into the music, his face contorted with grief which passes into a triumphant egotism.

"I don't usually go for this masculine display stuff…" says one of the girls, wiping the tomato sauce from her lips.

"Nor me…" says the other. "But he's kinda impressive."

I explain that originally the Zembekiko was danced in the company of men – no women would be present. It was not entertainment – more a sort of primitive therapy for the male soul. With these simple movements and gestures, a man confronts the limitations of his joys, defies his burdens and sorrows, and underwrites his individuality. "No one applauds. Needless to say, it has now become a valuable touristic asset."

"Oh, boy – I can imagine." Suddenly, turning their eyes on me, they ask, "How long have you been with him?"

"Five years…"

"Gee…that's long time with a man like that…"

So how did I get here?

5

It was the spring after Mother died, and Dad had decided a holiday would do us both good.

"What about a Greek island?"

Was he mad? He hated foreign travel and refused to fly anywhere. What had made him choose this obscure Greek island? In the big atlas it was shaped like a mutton chop. Yet the ordeal of Mother's death had burned my youthful expectations of Life to nothing. If the sun shone on this mutton chop island, why not pander to a father's whim.

On a grey Monday morning, we stood in front of a board marked "Boat Train" at Victoria Station. Commuters with pale faces, limp hair and lacklustre eyes seethed past in the morning rush-hour to joyless occupations. This morning, I was not one of them.

In the queue behind us a voice said, "Have you been abroad before?" to the person next to him; the answer was in the negative. "Ooo…you'll find there's noothing to it… noothing to it at all…" he replied reassuringly.

Father's white hair and distinguished appearance got us the services of a porter. From the window of the first-class carriage (father believed in travelling in style), he watched other people struggling with their baggage. "If I had to carry my bag," he said thoughtfully, "I would stay at home."

The train started with a series of jerks before settling down to a steady nationalized pace. It took a long time to leave behind the neat little houses with little gardens in orderly rows; cars parked along the curb; an old lady walking her dog in the park, an old man on a bench feeding pigeons in a huge expanse of cemetery. Finally, green fields and trees, then houses again, until we reached the flat, grey-green sea at Dover. It was a French boat so the life-jackets were *corsets de sauvetage.* A woman leaning on the rail, gazing at the White Cliffs, turned to her friend, saying, "Oh, I *am* disappointed. I thought they'd be *shining* white!"

At Calais, the French smell – *Gauloises and garlic*. Dad was amazed at the indifference of the porters. At the Gare du Nord, Thomas Cook's representative failed to show up. "I've paid for it!" Dad fumed. We had an anxious time looking for our sleeping cars but found them at last. Oh, the romance of those mahogany cubicles! The ingenuity of the gadgets which pulled out, pushed in, lifted up…it was all worth it.

I lay on my bunk rattling through a foreign darkness, shaking gently like a jelly on a plate, thinking Life must, after all, have something to offer. The banging of doors, the halts, the lighted stations, the shouting in foreign languages. Raising the blind in the middle of the night revealed mountains with snow on them. When I looked again, a landscape unmistakably Italian was bathed in the golden light of the sun: white oxen drawing carts, swags of vines between pollarded willows, and an angel on the dome of a church that held up its arms to the glory of the morning. Dad admitted it was picturesque but lacking the crispness of an English morning, and he was dismayed at there being no buffet car.

Finally a boy with a leather bag under his arm came onto the train, and squeezed a thin jet of coffee into paper cups.

"I've never had coffee from a bagpipes before…" Dad mused, as if it confirmed all his ideas about foreigners. He himself was a Welshman.

At Trieste we transferred to a small Yugoslav ship that took us down the Adriatic, calling at ports on the way, before putting us off at our destination. The passengers were German, English and American; the steward steered the English to one table, the Germans to another, and put the two American women with the English Lord and Lady.

The sun shone every day as the ship ploughed south. Early mornings with no horizon, fishing boats suspended in air; sea hours passed in a half-wakeful dream with the weight of the sun on my skin. Was I feeling the sun, or the sun feeling me? The American women stretched their lean bodies in bikinis over the forward hatch. The Lord and Lady sat reading newspapers in deckchairs set apart from the rest of the passengers.

16

The bare Yugoslavian mountains looked like people huddling under a tarpaulin – not inspiring. In drab little ports, we strolled about the harbours, where photography was forbidden and there was nothing to see except *Hamlet* by 'Wiljem Sekspira'.

"I hope they realise he's English," said Dad.

Sibernick, a warren of small streets, ascending and descending steps; Dubrovnik, a serenity of biscuit-coloured stone, swifts screaming through the blue sky, canaries singing in their cages.

The boat went on its way resolutely south, past a lighthouse on a little rock, with a fat woman in a rowing boat, fishing. The steward came to the rail to wave a napkin at her. She stood up and waved back. "My sister," he said, "she is the lighthouse keeper." The wash caught the little boat, the fat lady abruptly sat down.

In the evening on deck in the warm darkness pricked with stars and the occasional probing finger of a lighthouse, I thought a lot about the steward's sister in her lighthouse.

"It's all very well for a fortnight's holiday," Dad said, as if reading my thoughts, "but you couldn't do it all the time – you'd get bored with it."

I supposed so. Was it an incipient disloyalty to our own grey skies that made it necessary to think this way?

At Brindisi we took a horse-drawn carriage to see the town. Dad was afraid of fleas in the upholstery. We saw the railway station, a church, and the end of the Appian Way where Virgil died. Dad said it wasn't worth catching a flea for. Small boys climbed onto the carriage begging for alms, and were beaten off by the driver. Rattling back to the harbour, a policeman on traffic duty groaned audibly at the sight of my bare arm on the edge of the carriage. Dad glanced sharply at me. I was wearing a perfectly respectable sleeveless dress.

We had reached the South – a new experience for both of us.

I read aloud the phrases from the Greek guidebook. *"How are you?" "I am very ill!" "So much the better!" "Bravo!" "Long Live Greece!"* and *"If you please me, I will pay you more…"*

We reached the island at midnight on a very dark night. An official came on board to check our passports, using the inch-long nail of his little finger to sort through the card index he brought

17

with him. Having no previous convictions in the country, we were allowed down the gangway into the night, where Thomas Cook's representative, an elderly man with tortoise features hunched between the lapels of his overcoat, was waiting for us on the quayside. He guided us to a waiting taxi, which looked like something out of a Chicago gangster movie of the '30s. It carried us slowly through the dark town into the darker countryside. There were very few lights.

"Hardly a lively resort," said Dad. It seemed a long way. "Where is this damned hotel?" he fumed, convinced we had been kidnapped.

"It is komming...it is komming..." was all the information the Thomas Cook's man would give, probably all the English he had.

At last the taxi turned into a drive bordered with oleanders, and drew up in front of a building which might have been a clinic or a canning factory. Even without a classical education, this was disappointing.

The receptionist, a large Homeric man, came forward to greet us. Father immediately expressed his dissatisfaction. "For God's sake, it isn't even warm!"

The Homeric man opened his hands palm upwards and said, "Ah...in the morning you will see how beautiful it is."

6

In the morning we saw how beautiful it was. The hotel stood in a garden of olive trees overlooking a sparkling sea, clear as gin. An ancient Chevrolet bus stood by the gate of the hotel. If we had understood the receptionist rightly, it went to the town; there could be no harm in getting on it.

The bus lurched and juddered over the potholed road. The driver, an old man in a cloth cap, hardly glanced at the road, screwing his head round continuously to talk with the passengers behind him. It didn't matter, there wasn't any other traffic. He stopped anywhere for anybody; fat peasant women with large bosoms, baskets and bunches of flowers were hauled onto the bus by the conductor.

When the bus reached the town, it stopped beside a large open space containing nothing but gravel, with neat paving all round, out of which grew a double line of trees and some Victorian lamp-posts. The bus went no further, everybody got off. A handsome arcade confronted the gravelled space with cafés, the tables and chairs set out under the arches and the acacia trees.

"Just the place for a beer – if they understand the word for beer…"

We sat down in one of the cafés. A waiter appeared, an elderly man with white hair distinguished enough for a bank manager.

"Goot morning!" he cried enthusiastically, shaking hands with us. "Ow are yew? What you like to 'ave…?"

"Beer, please."

"Verry goot! One beer? Two beer?"

"Two beers, please."

"Two beer! Verry goot!" Satisfied, he went away and did not come back.

It was 11 o'clock on a week day morning but there was no sign of business activity. Men sat at the café tables with nothing but a tiny cup of coffee and glass of water.

"I wonder if they work?" said Dad. "And I wonder what the purpose of that space is. Is it a car park?"

"There aren't any cars," I pointed out. "Perhaps it's a parade ground?" I added as we watched an army officer stroll across it carrying a beach bag.

A man in a blue and white striped T-shirt, looking like a gondolier, came out of the café behind us, crossed to the yellow kiosk selling newspapers, cigarettes, toothpaste and razorblades; bought a packet of cigarettes and came back towards us, calling out to someone and laughing; laughter that suggested a vigorous enjoyment of life. As he passed us again, he looked straight at us and disappeared into the café.

The Bank Manager returned, depositing the two beers and the glasses onto our table with a swing and bang. "Goot?"

"Yes, thank you…"

"Please!" said the Bank Manager, which seemed to finish the business for him, but left a loose end for us.

The man in the blue striped T-shirt appeared again, stopped by our table, "You British, Sir?" he asked. Dad admitted the fact – recognizing that in foreign countries the English are not always admired. But this man said, "Goot!" and sat down with us. We were interested in local colour, but for a bit of it to break off and sit down at our table was more than we'd bargained for.

"You be enjoying here, Sir?"

"We only arrived last night."

"Oh, then you have the time to be enjoy," which seemed a curious thing to say, like 'please' instead of 'thank you'.

He was about forty, iron-grey hair crisp as wire wool; physically strong and rather brigandish, but not sinister; his eyes, brown and glossy as a dog's, seemed full of wit and humour; his hands were small and neat. He spoke English fluently and incorrectly – making it a language of his own, more like painting with words.

Dad took this chance to satisfy his curiosity. "Now you can tell me, my boy – what is that space in front of us? Is it a parade ground?"

"It is the cricket pitch."

This astonished him. "You play cricket here?"

"Yes, of course…we have many British customs here."

Dad asked the Greek's name. "Tassos, Sir."

"Do you work, Tassos?"

"Of course yes! I fix the lights. I am electrician – but I also painting…"

"House painting?"

"No…no…Streets." Dad was baffled as a dog now. "Come – I show you…"

Leading us inside the café, he pointed to a framed picture on the wall; a pen and ink sketch of a street scene. "This is what I do…"

"Oh, you're an artist." Dad took out his other spectacles. "I am an artist myself. Do you sell these?"

"Of course."

"Where do you sell them?"

"Anywhere. Is not a problem. The tourists buy very meny of my pictures…and when I have money of my paintings, I don't care for anything. I have good time. I spend all. Next morning I broke again." He laughed his laugh again. "That life I make!"

"You know how to enjoy it, obviously…"

"What else except that?"

His words hit me in the solar plexus. What else except *to enjoy life?* It perplexed me, just as the way they had of saying please instead of thank you.

"But tell me, Tasso, if you are an electrician, how is it you can sit down with us in the middle of the morning. Are you on holiday?"

Tassos laughed again. "Ah! That is nice idea! No, I am working now. I must to take the bills around the town. My boss, he trust me. 'Do your job, Tasso,' he says, 'the rest belong to you'."

21

One minute he was with us, the next he had gone. Dad made a signal at the waiter to bring the bill. The Bank Manager bowed before us. "There is nothing to pay, Sir."

"But we had two beers."

"Mr Tassos have pay everything, Sir. Thank yew verry mutz."

"This is extraordinary!" Dad was quite put out, convinced that the chap had been out to cadge a drink. He tried to insist on paying, but the Bank Manager would not take his money, just shook hands with us instead and bowed us off the premises.

We took the rattle-trap bus back to the hotel for lunch. The waiter at our table was called Socrates. Dad suspected the thin slivers of meat to be goat.

"It is the Balkans, after all… Socrates, is this meat goat?"

"Goot! Goot!" said Socrates, doling out the *pomme vapeur.*

"Oh, my God," groaned father and didn't eat much.

He decided next morning we must supplement our diet with fresh oranges. And we needed a corkscrew. "The bar prices in this hotel exceed the Ritz." The first evening we had watched the foreign guests coming to the bar just to take away tonic water or soda, to drink with their duty-free in their rooms. "We'll do the same. I'll be taken for a fool, but not for a bloody fool – as your mother used to say…"

The quest for a corkscrew took us down the alleys in the town, into dim shops selling everything in enamel, tin and pottery. Dad mimed the opening of a bottle, the man understood, and mimed back that he didn't have one; but, beckoning us to follow him out of the shop, he led us through more alleyways to another shop selling a different assortment of things: nails, mousetraps, funnels and wine measures, all suspended from hooks in the wooden beams. The owner glanced up from his newspaper but took no notice as our man rummaged through the drawers in the counter until he held up a corkscrew.

"Yes! That's what we want! Marvellous!" Father held out his hand full of coins, the man selected a minimal amount, held it up, and threw it on the counter where the shop owner hardly glanced at it.

"It's a funny way of going on, but I must say they're very obliging."

On the way back we paused in front of a greengrocer's under a Venetian arch, the fruit and vegetables piled up in heaps of colour. As we were debating whether a kilo of oranges would be too much or too little, Tasso appeared like a genie out of a bottle and took over the transaction, even cutting open an orange to show that it was "full of meat". Again it proved impossible to pay.

"Is this your shop?" I asked.

"Me – keep a shop!" Tasso laughed, crossing himself. "For God-ni-say! No…is the shop of a good friend of me." Again Dad was not allowed to pay. "Your money is no use here, Sir," said Tasso.

Dad was really quite put out at this not being allowed to pay for anything. "What an extraordinary way of going on!"

"It is our way, Sir," said Tasso, and instantly disappeared again.

7

The sun shone. I sat in it, acquiring a tan for the office. Dad kept to the shade. "Thank God, there are no ruins to look at." We had only enough initiative to take the Chevrolet bus to the town every morning for the 'two beer'. Tasso would suddenly appear where there had been only sunlight and shadow, his brigandish, unshaven face smiling at us, a glass of wine in his hand. Dad never succeeded in buying him a drink.

"Today you find me rich!" he said one morning. "Last night I meet some Germans of your same hotel. We finish four o'clock in the morning. Pó! Pó! I singing, I dancing, I drinking much, and I sell all of my paintings! Ah, you miss something nice!"

So life was lived in a higher key by night – not that we were likely to experience it. Well, I had expected nothing of this holiday so I could not be disappointed.

"Don't you be tired to stay all the time in that hotel?" He was talking to father, but speaking to me. "You must to be enjoy a little!"

"Late nights are not for me, my boy…I'm an old man."

But I am not an old woman…

I take no part in the conversation, I contemplate the play of light and shade under the acacias; but when I turn my head, the brown eyes with the diamond highlights are waiting; to meet those eyes is to have a sense of encounter.

"I have a nice idea," he is saying, "I wait you tonight at the night club just by your foots…" – meaning near the hotel. "Just to see Something! You can stay that much you like. I wait you there nine o'clock."

He is gone before Dad can say anything.

*

At nine o'clock, Dad said, "Damn it! That chap is waiting for us at that night club." 'Night club' has an ominous sound; it must be swallowed whole or not at all. I said nothing. "Oh, well, we might go for half an hour. I don't want to hurt his feelings. He's been very kind."

We groped down the ill-lit steps to the road. It was dark and empty. All we could see was the dark olive grove, no lights, no sounds, nothing to suggest the presence of a night club, yet Tasso had described the place as being 'at your foots exactly'.

Then I noticed a tin sign under a dim light on a post across the road, and went to look at it. It said:

RESTAURANT-DANCIN<u>K</u>.

"This must be it."

"It can't be," said father hopefully.

"I'll just go and look…"

I followed the little path up to a cottage with steps up to a veranda straggled with a sagging vine. The door had a glass panel in it. Cautiously peering in, I could see people sitting at tables; suddenly the roar of the jukebox left no doubt – this was the place. I did not want to go back to the hotel. I signalled to Dad to come up, then opened the door and walked in.

Immediately a man jumped up from the nearest table. It was Tasso. I hardly recognised him. He had shaved and was wearing a black corduroy jacket.

The threat of 'night club' was instantly lifted at the sight of the sturdy wooden tables, covered in well-darned cloths, a floor of worn, patterned tiles, and walls painted in ox blood. A grey-haired lady sat in the corner writing out bills; a curly-headed waiter crashed in and out of the kitchen carrying plates of spaghetti, while a fat chromium jukebox in the corner automatically selected and played the records inside its glass bosom; strange music, loud , melodious and appealing… *Would Dad like it?*

"What music is this, Tasso?"

"Greek music, Sir."

The wine tasted of apples and honey. *Would Dad drink it?*

"What wine is this, Tasso?"

"Greek wine, Sir."

Dad drank it.

At the next table, I recognised the German woman we saw every morning at breakfast with her frail elderly husband. She was alone.

Tasso spoke English to us, German to the woman at the next table, and Greek with everybody else in the room, of which he was the focal point as he propped his sketches on the empty chairs, creating an impromptu art gallery.

"Excuse me one minute," he apologized, "but you see I make the business now" – and sold two as we watched.

"There's no flies on him!" Dad said.

Returning to us, he said, with an egoism not for his art, but for himself, "I am not Picasso – but I know how to sell!"

A strong bull-mooing came from the jukebox. Tasso flung back his head and bellowed the words in a throaty voice, which made the vein in his neck swell up. He got up and, placing himself in the centre of the small area between the tables, began to dance. To us it was odd for a man to get up and dance by himself. In England he would have to be drunk. He was not drunk. In this country, presumably, it was a man's right to get up and dance solo.

It was a curious private dance, not graceful yet full of grace. He danced for himself, never looking at the audience. When the music stopped, nobody clapped except the German woman. He came back to our table, coughing.

"That was absolutely marvellous!" I heard myself saying, but our admiration meant nothing to him, it was as natural for him to dance as to breathe.

"What sort of dance is that, Tasso?"

"A Greek dance, Sir," he said, still coughing. "We call it *Zembekiko*. When I dance that, I feel much. I dance my Life…"

"The music is very sad, but you Greeks seem to know how to enjoy life."

"For sure we enjoy! We sing, we dance, we fight – specially me!" He took off his jacket. "This make in England. Very good, but is too dam hot." And he flung it over a chair.

The music took possession of him again, he grabbed my arm. "Come – I teach you to dance Greek."

I stood up readily; then, realising we would be alone on the floor, said, "I can't" and sat down. It was a mistake. He turned to the German woman, and she came to his hand like a cork out of a bottle. She was coarse and over forty, in a black dress with red roses all over it, unspeakably vulgar. He manipulated her around the confined space with the bravura of an Apache.

The music had now changed to a tango. He threw off his shirt; he had tattoos on both biceps. She pranced around, clapping her hands; he went down on his knees, arching his body back until his head almost touched the floor, springing up just as the music finished, then grabbing her and biting her neck. He handed her back to her table, and disappeared into the kitchen. The waiter came to retrieve his shirt and jacket. When he returned he was properly dressed again.

Dad decided it had been interesting enough for one evening, and wanted to pay. "It is my hospitality, Sir." Dad protested, really quite cross about it, but it was useless. We shook hands. *No unspoken conversation in his eye now as he shook my hand, and said goodnight.* As we left, he went to sit with the German woman.

"He's certainly a lively character," Dad said, as we groped our way up the dark steps to the hotel. "Does he do that every night? I wonder what his wife thinks of it…"

I said nothing.

8.

Tasso did not appear at the café next morning. In the evening, I watched the German woman leave the hotel alone. It was the end of the holiday that was 'to do us both good'. The days had slipped by with the flow of sand in an hour-glass that you may not turn over. Father was to take the boat back up the Adriatic, which meant he would leave a day earlier than me. I had to be back in my job on Monday morning, so I would fly via Athens the day after, which would give me twenty-four hours on the island alone.

"If I were you…" (It never occurred to him that he was not me) "…I would get an earlier flight to Athens and see the Acropolis, or something." I agreed.

Tasso had not shown up at the café for two days. It seemed unlikely that we would see him again, even to say goodbye, but on father's last evening, we found him making his 'exposition' in the hotel foyer just before dinner. Trade was brisk; by the time we had finished dinner, he pronounced himself rich and wanted to take us down to the Cottage Night Club again.

"I have a journey tomorrow, my boy…I must have an early night," Dad said, and went over to the reception to settle his bill.

Tasso looked at me. "And you, mademoiselle…you also go so early to the bed?" I said I didn't have to. "Do you like to take a glass of wine with me?"

I thought he meant in the hotel. There was nothing to stop me, but could I say to Dad: "I'm just going to have a drink with Tasso" at ten o'clock at night in a foreign land? It would give him a sleepless night before his journey.

"I'll come back," I heard myself say. Tasso understood perfectly; he understood more than I did.

I followed father upstairs, wondering how I could slip into collusion with a foreign stranger to deceive an innocent, amiable parent. I waited five minutes in my room, listening to Dad settling down in his. Then, instinctively, I pushed my towel over the balcony into the garden below; one form of deception instantly generates another. I closed my door quietly and went down the stairs.

But Tasso wasn't at reception, he wasn't in the bar or the lounge, or on the terrace. *He hadn't waited!* Anger and relief welled up in me. With the receptionist watching me, I went into the garden to retrieve my towel, and went back upstairs with it draped over my shoulder.

Well! Thank God, he hadn't waited. How absurd! How ridiculous! The holiday was over. Tomorrow I would take an early flight and go and see the Acropolis or something. *But why hadn't he waited?*

I didn't sleep at all, turning like a chicken on a spit. In the morning, my watch had gained two hours.

*

The ship sailed with Dad standing at the rail, waving his hat, getting smaller and smaller. It was a new experience to be alone in a foreign land – my last day in the sun! With a sense of liberation as well as nervous excitement, I walked back along the harbour crowded with brightly painted boats with graceful lines, unloading fish, fruit and vegetables; even a couple of sheep being loaded onto waiting horse-carts. Sheep bleated, men shouted – noise – colour – *real* life. I passed through hot slices of sunshine and cool angular shadows in the back streets, under hanging washing dangling like acrobats, and sheets billowing like sails. From a church came a nasal intoning and the scent of incense and beeswax. Candles winked on the brass stand by the door where I stopped, challenged by a gaze of icons from the Iconostasis.

I found the small airline office: tall windows with wrought iron fanlights, some ugly plastic armchairs, a coffee table with an ashtray on it. Behind the counter sat a girl with fat eyes like eggs, and a man who spoke incessantly on the telephone. A porter struggled in and out carrying packages. I asked about the afternoon plane. The girl said she didn't know, and asked the man, who said he didn't know, and to come back at 2.30.

I walked back to the café, where the Bank Manager appeared at once. "'Ow are yew? Goot morning!" he beamed, shaking me by the hand. "Where iss your Fader?"

"He's gone."

"He goin'? Where he goin'?"

"Up the Adriatic on a boat."

"And yew staying…alone?" This with disapproval.

"I leave this afternoon."

"Ah! You going. Okay. I bring you one beer?" still suspicious as to the fate of my father.

An hour passed, no sign of Tasso. Another half-hour. I had finished my one beer and dared not risk the disapproval of the Bank Manager by asking for another. There was nothing for it but to collect my bag from the hotel and return to the airline office to wait for a seat on the afternoon plane.

Sitting on the bus waiting for it to start, I suddenly saw him walking across the cricket pitch towards the bar. Next thing, I was off the bus, running towards him, shouting "Tasso!"

He put out his arms to stop me. He wasn't surprised at all. "I only finish now my job," he said, as if he knew I had been waiting for him.

"I only wanted to say goodbye!" I told him about the plane.

"Okay, come on."

"Come where?"

"To drink something, and eat something. I am terrible hungry. And to hear a little music."

"But I have to be at the airline office by 2.30."

"Okay – we have time." *In Greece they have Time.*

I followed him like a sheep through the small back streets.

"Can I buy a record of that music you dance to?"

"Of course!"

Opening a door into a tiny music shop, we saw a cubicle where a man sat behind a wooden counter with a small record player on it, and a few records in a wooden rack behind him.

30

Tasso told him to play something. The music erupted over us like arterial blood. Tasso began to dance in the narrow space.

"Are you always dancing?"

"Yes, when I hear that music."

I bought two small records with unreadable labels.

Further down the street he opened another door. As all the signs were unreadable, what a door revealed when opened was a surprise. This time it was a café, with tables covered with bright patterned plastic. It was empty. A waiter popped out from behind a curtain like a puppet in a theatre. On Tasso's orders, he brought two small cylindrical glasses of something looking like liquid boot polish, and disappeared again. Nobody came in.

"What is this stuff?"

"Koniak." Cognac, spelt with a K, unlike anything by the name elsewhere; unforgettable as everything in Greece is unforgettable, even when you don't want to remember it. Taking a sip, I wondered what to do with it. Swallowing it, I felt it course through my system like a trail of saltpetre in a Victorian card where it kills the pheasant in the top left corner. My left kidney seemed to be the target. What did it taste of? Each glass is an individual experience. After two, your head buzzes like a hive of bees and you want to go out and gather honey.

Before I could taste it again, he kissed me.

It was only a second but seemed an hour, like being knocked down by a wave and wondering if your breath will hold out. When I came to the surface, the landscape had changed. The tables, the bright plastic, the chairs had taken on a new dimensional value as in a surrealist painting. I wasn't sure if they were friend or foe. As he was going to do it again, I stopped him, my hand fusing with his like melting metal. It required an effort of will to pull mine away.

"Why?" he queried. "You are not angry."

I wasn't angry, I was thinking. "What about the German woman?"

He laughed outright. "You notice that!" he said, crossing himself.

I finished my koniak in one gulp, it made me shudder from head to foot.

"I must go," I said, getting up.

"Go where?" I explained again about the afternoon plane. "But you have a ticket for tomorrow." *He knew that?*

"Yes. But I must go today." I sat down, the koniak had got to my knees.

"You *want* to go?" Puzzled.

"No. I *must* go." I tried getting up again.

He scratched his head, baffled. "You must be a very strong British one."

"Tasso, please get me a taxi."

"Okay, but we must to find a telefon."

We left the café, turned a corner, he opened another door. We were in another café, a long narrow place with doors onto different streets. If you knew your way as he did, you could circulate the town via its taverns, entering by one door and leaving by another.

The man behind the wooden counter immediately filled two glasses with a pale yellowish liquid.

"What's this?"

"Retsina."

A plate containing a bit of cheese, a slice of tomato, a cube of stewed meat and a cold chip impaled by a toothpick was put on the counter in front of us.

"I know you are hungry," Tasso said.

How? How did he know anything about me? Yet of the two of us, he seemed to have the greater knowledge about me.

"Tasso…please…get me a taxi."

He went to a telephone on a little wooden bracket. In no time at all, a taxi slid to a halt outside and hooted.

"How do I tell him where to go?" I said, forgetting that when they speak to each other it is a form of communication.

"He knows."

The taxi drove off with me in it. So this was the end – and we still had not said goodbye.

At the hotel, I explained to the receptionist that I was not sure of a seat on the afternoon plane, so please keep the room for me. He listened politely and said, "You go or not?" I said that was precisely what I couldn't tell him. "Okay," he shrugged, "no problem", and crossed my name out of the ledger. Now if I didn't get the plane, I wouldn't have the room either.

The taxi took me back to the town. Just before the airline office, the driver stopped and hooted like a night bird. Tasso appeared. "Come to take a drink."

"But it's already 2.30!" I couldn't hide my exasperation.

"Take a coffee then."

It was impossible to make anybody understand what I was trying to do. I wasn't sure myself. When I said nothing, he shrugged and signalled the taxi on. I had an acute sense of loss.

We still had not said goodbye.

At the airline office, I hurried over to the counter. I wanted to be picked up by the machinery of departure and whisked away. The girl with fat eyes said, "You must to wait." Wait for what? Why couldn't she tell me simply yes or no? There were no other people waiting for this plane. She didn't explain. Greeks don't explain; when they do, it only adds to the confusion. Baffled, I sat down on the plastic settee.

Tasso appeared again. "You go or not?" he demanded, thrusting a box of Turkish Delight at me, heavy as lead.

"I don't know!"

"I must to go back to my job!" Frustrated too. Taking back the box, he wrote a number on it. "If you no go, call me at this number." He went. We still had not said goodbye.

I sat for half-an-hour. I went to the desk again. The girl merely raised her eyes heavenward, and clicked her tongue in the oriental negative. "You must to wait more."

Why? Whose decision were we waiting for – the gods on Mount Olympus? Was that why they called the airline Olympic Airways?

After I had achieved a hollow patience, my mind finally settling in the eternal Now, there was a scraping of chairs in the room above. Had 'they' come to a decision? The telephone rang. The girl picked it up, listened, put it down. I watched as she came towards me, banging her ample hip on the side of the counter as she passed. I listened as she explained that *because of tail winds, they could not take an extra passenger.* But there seemed to be no passengers at all.

I tried to ignore the bubble of joy bursting inside me. What should I do now? I looked at the numbers written on the box in funny writing with a bar across the 7 and a long hook on the 9. How to use a Greek telephone? I went over to the girl again. Could she get me this number? She did.

"Yia sou, Tasso," she said into the phone. She knew him! "Mr Tassos for you." And she handed the receiver to me with the proper detachment of a messenger of the gods.

"You no go?" His kippered voice burst on my ear.

"There isn't an extra seat," I corrected him.

"Good! Meet me, can you? At the bar – eight o'clock. I wait you. Okay?"

"Okay," I heard myself say.

9

At eight o'clock a transparent blue haze hung over the town, the lights were on, and a steady stream of people moved up and down the street. It was the hour of the '*voltá*'. He was waiting for me inside the bar, looking very fresh in light blue shirt and trousers, with a grey pullover. He handed me a tiny red carnation smelling of cloves. A bowl of the same stood on the counter.

"You took it from there!"

"I know" unabashed. "But I try to have the best."

The night was warm, the cafés full of life, buzzing like a swarm of bees.

"I've been here ten days and I've seen nothing of this!' I cried in astonishment.

"Now," he said conclusively, "you must to see everything. Follow me."

We plunged into the stream of people, cutting through them to gain the back alleys, which he always preferred. One alley led into the vegetable market with the shops still open, fruit and vegetables heaped under the Venetian arches, making rich daubs of colour under the electric light. Had I ever seen so much colour all at once before? Even the fish on the wet marble slabs at the fish booths were bright red and pearly pink; one had rainbow colours in mosaic all over its body.

We came out at the harbour, quiet now, the boats packed flank-to-flank, colours subdued but not extinguished. A white trawler with a swordfish prow lay over its own image like a sleeping swan.

"Beautiful, yes?" he murmured.

"Oh beautiful, yes!" I was falling into his idiom, which already seemed the language of poetry.

At the end of the harbour was a place calling itself Kaffee Bar.

"We begin the night here." It looked dirty and unattractive. "I know is tramp place – but you don't have to be worry because I am the King of the Tramps."

We went in. At the jukebox, called The Giant Wurlizter, he punched the buttons with a dedicated air. The machinery began to whir.

"We start the night with a concert," he said, calling up two wines. "This is the reason to come here."

The Giant Wurlitzer belched and shuddered in giving birth to Beethoven's Egmont Overture.

"I don't want Beethoven!" I protested. I want to see you dance."

"Later you see me to dance. Now I like to have Beethoven. Every night I come here for that. I like verry much."

Smoking a cigarette, he leaned against the counter absorbing the music until, like a chameleon, he began to look like Beethoven. The mighty sound swirled through the tawdry place, over the heads of the backgammon players, and escaped through the door like a cat into the night. It ended with a click and whirring sound as another record dropped onto the turntable – Greek music, thick as blood. Tasso began to dance, the waiter adroitly moving round him with his tray of coffees and drinks.

"The words of this record are nice…" he murmured, translating them as he danced. *"Our destiny is written… One road we must take…. We must to make our life sweet… Because for us there is no other dawn… Two doors has the Life… We go from the one to the other…"*

The stark philosophy of Beowulf, yet they seemed to bear up under it with more gaiety than despair.

It was quite dark when we left the Kaffee Bar. The way he took was uneven under foot and had few lights.

"Where are we going?"

"*I know*," he states with Greek logic. "Anyway, never mind to ask. You already trust me."

I did not ask again.

In the narrow streets of the old town, cats sang piercing songs in the dark corners; high up in a lozenge of light, a woman leaned out to haul in her washing strung across the narrow alley. The pulleys squeaked, then the lozenge of light disappeared as she drew the shutters together with a slight clash.

We continued under hanging washing, down flights of steps until the sound of a tenor singing and the strumming of a guitar came from somewhere nearby. He stopped by what looked like a garage door, though no car could have penetrated the alley. The sounds came from behind it.

"Wait here," he said with an air of mystery.

Smoke drifted across the light at the end of the alley; he disappeared into it, leaving me alone. I heard his unmistakable voice behind the door mixed with shouting and laughter. Putting my eye to the chink, I could see men sitting at a table, and the back of Tasso's head. *Why must I stay outside?* I wondered.

He came back carrying a tin table, followed by a boy bringing two chairs. In stages the boy brought forks, bread, wine, paper napkins, and a grilled steak.

"Why are we eating in the street?"

"More better."

Remarks were being addressed to him through the garage door; what he shouted back, evoked roars of laughter.

"What are they saying?"

"*I know.*"

"I know you know – I asked what."

"We joking with each other, that's all...nothing bad..."

"Why can't we go inside?"

"Later. *I* know the time." Creating his own mystery.

The music began again. Suddenly the door beside us flew open. A shaft of light fell across the alley, into it stepped the tenor in full spate of song, followed by the guitarist. The little street reverberated with passionate singing. At the end of it, there were shouts and applause from inside. Tasso, annoyed at their stealing a march on him, ordered them back inside with the authority of a stage director. They bowed and obeyed. The door was closed again.

37

Tasso methodically cleaned the steak bone with his teeth before throwing it to a waiting cat. "Come," he said.

We passed through the haze of smoke where the boy was fanning the charcoal brazier by the front door. The interior was simply furnished with a wooden counter supporting bottles of all sizes, a pre-war 'wireless' and an alarm clock with two bells. The proprietor greeted Tasso by putting two glasses on the counter and filling them. The cooking range, fired by charcoal with a huge canopy over it to contain the smoke, was tended by a fat lady with red hands and face, and the glazed eyes of a fish.

Big barrels stood against the wall on a sturdy wooden rack. The stone flagged floor, stained with the drips from the spigots, might suggest to the imagination that a murder had been committed there. Three steps beside a boxed-in, smelly WC led up into the back room where the men were singing. Apart from the woman tending the cooking pots, I was the only other female.

"These are all very-good-friends of me," Tasso said, introducing me to the company. Costa the tenor, Panayoti the guitarist, Yanni – "we call him Melon Head." It was shaped rather like a soccer ball. Recognising the reference to his head, Yanni scratched it. Panayoti had a low brow and a wide tartar mouth; he guffawed and talked incessantly with a rasping voice, but played his guitar with delicacy and skill. "And Stavros," – a gaunt-faced man who did not smile readily. "Him a hundred time worse than me," Tasso said, meaning it as a compliment. "Don't be worry at all, I am the boss here!" Tasso reassured me.

Whatever he said to them in Greek made them bang their knees with laughter. He seemed to be the boss wherever he went by rule of natural authority. There seemed such good feeling in their laughter and talk, I wasn't disconcerted by it.

Costa the tenor – "him a carpenter" – with the light, lyrical tenor voice, his features more refined and his temperament as highly strung as a prima donna's, was urging Panayoti to stop talking and take up his guitar. In his frustration he let off top notes at random like a demented rooster. "*Tum -tum- tee-ta-AAA!*"

Panayoti took a slug of wine, slung his guitar into his lap and began picking out an accompaniment to an Italian aria. The tenor sang like a canary, his eyes closed except when Panayoti indulged in a cadenza of his own, leaving Costa in mid-air like a trapeze artist. He opened his eyes wide in indignation and reproof. But all ended happily. They were embraced by the company. The wine was poured again and again, and so it went on – talk, laughter, wine and song.

"What are they saying?"

"Stories…just stories…I have no the words to explain all."

Greek songs were followed by Italian arias and local cantathes. The carpenter soared off into space, Petros, 'the man of iron', plumbed the depths with a sonorous bass from his iron chest, while the others wove their own harmonies. Tasso was somewhere in the middle with a unique Byzantine voice, neither tenor nor baritone.

It was beautiful – the singing – and stirred me to the depths. When the carpenter started 'Santa Lucia', something I had been holding back for years burst inside me, and my voice came out pure and true as a nightingale's from a dark bush. The carpenter opened his eyes, our voices blended perfectly. He nodded approval, and looks of wonder passed from eye to eye.

The policeman came in; they put their fingers to their lips, forbidding him to interrupt. He pointed to a notice that must have said "no singing after 11pm". It was after midnight. He leaned against the wall, listening as the carpenter and I finished with a painfully sweet diminuendo. The company went wild. I was patted on the back and shaken by the hand. I was one of the company, a moment rare in life and almost never repeated.

Tasso looked at me. "Why you not tell me you could sing?" he scolded, and told Yanni to take his hand off my shoulder. The policeman pointed again to the notice and went away.

I took a deep breath and another mouthful of wine. The joy of Life! At last! Already greedy, I wanted more of this!

"Tomorrow I will be in London!" I wailed.

"But tonight, you are here."

The carpenter was humming again. Panayoti took up the guitar. They sang softly at first because of the policeman's warning, but it gathered momentum. Costa stalked into the centre of room, followed by Panayoti. They faced each other, tenor with hand raised in poetic gesture, Panayoti writhing over his guitar, building up sound under his fingers. They were like two flames guttering in the wind. With a final flourish, Panayoti twirled his guitar above his head.

"Come," said Tasso, "it is time to go." Everybody protested, but I was firmly extracted from the company. We shook hands all round like brothers. Nothing like it had ever happened to me before.

*

On leaving the tavern, he was no longer in a hurry and sat down on some steps to smoke a cigarette. Was it very late – or very early? I wasn't tired. There was so much I did not know about him.

"Tell me about yourself, Tasso," I urged, adding daringly, "The truth, if possible…"

"The true, of course – what else except that." He did not take offence.

Drawing on his cigarette, he was silent for a long time before beginning. "Perhaps it was the mistake of my mother to make me…she call me *O pónos mou*, her pain. She love me very much, but afraid much for me. It is true I have the hell inside me from the time I be out of her body. My father was a lofty, pretty man, he come of good family, and was a officer in the army. He want me to go in the army, but I make a big fight when I was seventeen and they put me in the jail. I was not of bad character, but nothing control me when the blood arrive to my head.

"Then begins the war in Europe. I sent to the navy, but when the Germans come here, we sink our ship – we have no more ammunitions. No more Greek Navy. I am free."

"What did you do then?"

"I do many things…too many." He waved his hand in a circular movement, which, in Greek, has many interpretations. "Here was no food, no electricity, everything broke. First we have the Italians, then the Germans. I was in Athens. One night in a taverna I notice a man who looks from far to be English. I go to tell him 'Be careful, the Germans use this place'. He didn't care. 'Have a drink,' he say. He ask me questions, where I from, if I speak German. He tell me to come back here to the island and keep my eyes and ears open, to report anything I notice to him. I say 'Where I going to find you?' but him not so stupid to tell me where I going to find him. 'You find me…' he say. How I loved that man! Him a good fighter. He one of the British they drop by parachute to organize the resistance – you know that?"

"Did you find him?"

"Of course, yes! He was over there in the mountains." Indicating the mainland. "But was no easy to get there. I must to get across the water. You know what I do? The Germans control everything – so I use the Germans to take me there! I tell them lies, always they take me. Oh, so many stories I have on me…"

"After the war – what happened?"

"We have the war of the communists. Another salad! I don`t mix in that shit."

"How did you become an electrician?"

He gave a short hard laugh. "I married! After that, life was another thing." Getting up, he pulled me to my feet. "Come, we must to put you back in the hotel."

There was one antiquated taxi parked in the square, black and cumbersome as a hearse, the sort of car Chicago gangsters drive in old movies. No driver. "Then we must to walk," he said.

The asphalt seems soft underfoot, the sky full of stars overhead. Fireflies flash in galaxies under the olive trees on either side of the road, the call of a tiny owl pierces the stillness with a single fluty note. I float along like a balloon, I could walk beside him into infinity.

"I will kiss you every 50 metres," he says. I raise my face. "It is not yet 50 metres." We laugh; in laughter we recognise each other.

Came the moment. I stopped him with my hands against his chest. "Why don't you want…?" I was seeing the German woman

41

leaving the hotel alone, and knowing who she was going to meet. "I am not the German woman."

I had taken him by surprise, but what sort of victory was it?

"You...you British for sure!" he said, gently kissing me, "*Bon*! You are not *comme les autres*..."

With our arms about each other we walked on. At the hotel, we clung together passionately without kissing. I turned and ran, pressing the night bell desperately to be let in; when I dared to look back, there was nothing in the soft inscrutable darkness but the call of the little owl. A single fluty note: *tzook!*

10

Next morning, I went to the café. He appeared early. The reality of him came as a shock after a night thinking about him. He laid a rose on the table between us.

"What time the plane leaving?"

"Five o'clock."

"Good – the day belong to us! I have be to my doctor." He pronounced it 'dog-tor'.

"Are you ill?"

"No! But him is a good friend of me. I save the matchboxes from the foreigners for him. He like to make a collection. That way he give me the day off my job when I need. You see how much help is a matchbox," he said, picking it up and laying it down again.

We drifted through the hours like plankton under the sea, from jukebox bar to dim taverna, where the sunlight lay like an ingot of gold on the stone floor.

We didn't talk, we understood each other without searching for words like a light switch in the dark. Picking up my hand to kiss it, he sniffed it instead: "Nice soap. Send me some nice soap from England…no…soap is un-lucky.'

He took out his wallet, searching its contents of snapshots, cards and addresses of foreigners (mostly women). He selected a photo of himself and gave it to me.

"A very nice pirate," I said, giving it back.

"Keep it – is for you!"

"I don't want it."

"Why not?" I had surprised him again.

"Because *I must forget you quickly.*"

This was deviating from the norm. "Go on – take it!" he insisted.

"Keep it for the next woman," I said, laughing.

"You!" Searching his vocabulary. "You...*British* for sure!" And he put the photo carefully back into his pocket book.

By four o'clock we had gravitated to a sailors' bar in the harbour close to the airline office. Over the counter hung a notice: "IN GOD WE TRUST ALL OTHERS PAY CASH. One Sandwige 60c". The jukebox was playing *"Bee-ooutiful, bee-ooutiful brown eyes – I'll never love blue eyes again."* Or was it the other way round? I couldn't be sure of anything anymore.

"I don't want to see you go..." he said, putting his head on his arms on the table, missing the siesta. I left him there, lightly touching the wire wool hair, the sensation staying on my fingers as I walked out into the scalding sunlight, surprised how happy I felt in spite of this being the end. I would never see him again.

I had to get into the airport bus immediately this time. As I waited among the passengers in the tiny airport lounge, the ground hostess approached to tell me somebody wanted to speak to me outside. It was Yannis, the melon head. He held out a rose, saying, "Tassos". It was the rose we had been carrying around all day. I took it, feeling foolish.

Just as we were about to board the small Dakota aircraft, he appeared beside me, again saying, "Tassos", pointing to the perimeter fence where a figure on a bicycle was waving.

As the engine revved, the little plane trembled like a cat about to pounce, and roared off into the sky; as we banked over the blue sea, the happiness was still there. It was with me all the way to London.

It snuffed out as I entered my bedsit in Earl's Court, made more dismal by the twilight of a spring evening. A black bird on a chimney pot facing a topaz sky I could not see sang with heart-rending purity.

How we had sung – the carpenter and I... Was it only two nights ago – or already two nights ago? For an instant the toot of a train whistle from the Underground recalled the little owl.

As I took off my jacket, I felt something in the pocket – a piece of card. I pulled it out. His photograph! How had it got into my pocket when I had refused it? On the back was written 'A very nice Pirate'. I propped it up on the mantel over the gas fire, saying out loud as I did so, "I must forget you quickly…"

11.

At the office I bashed my typewriter in a torpid state. A patch of watery sunlight on the carpet could throw me into a reverie which made my boss remark that holidays were disruptive of office routine. In the evening I took the Underground back to my small bedsit, clutching a piece of chicken and some frozen veg, drank too much cheap wine, made a dull meal, and played my Greek records. Music from another planet.

One lunch hour I went into a bookshop, bought a book on the French Impressionists. Writing his name with the café as the address and posting it gave the day an exotic, useless glamour. I didn't expect him to write back. Could he write English?

Two weeks later, a strange envelope lay on the second step of the stairs when I came home. My letters were left on the second step. I approached slowly. The envelope had exotic stamps. Could it be for me? I stood looking down at it, not even picking it up. I could just make out my name in the queer writing. I carried it upstairs like an unexploded bomb and looked at it for a long time before daring to open it. When I did, I found a scrap of paper with a few words I could not understand until I recalled his way of speaking.

"Theng you very mutz for the book. I laike mutz." (He had sold it to the bookshop straight away.) *"Sun verry hot. Meny tourist. Meny womans, bat I no pay attention. Love Tassos"*

Under his name were two wild flowers stuck down with sellotape. On another scrap of paper he had drawn our route from tavern to tavern, an aeroplane flying off, and a figure in a striped vest with his head on his arms at the table beside two glasses of wine.

It was like being stabbed in the heart, the pain was so intense I could hardly bear it. I drank too much wine, played my two Greek records, didn't eat any supper. Taking a piece of paper, I wrote in capital letters, three times: HOW MUCH I WANT TO COME BACK!, sealed it in an envelope and next morning pushed it into the mouth of a letterbox. After that, life returned to its utterly predictable norm.

Fifteen days later another envelope with strange stamps lay on the second step of the stair. The statement it contained blew everything to bits.

"*Yes. Come bak darling. I look after you. Love Tassos.*"

A dialogue opened in my head: *Why not?...Why not what?... Go back...It's impossible...Why is it? I have the money for the ticket...You can't spend it on that!...Why not? What's money for?... Not for that. It's for 'rainy days'...It's always raining! ...For security...What's security for?... For ideas like going back to Greece to be impossible!... To live a death rather than die one? If you accept security, it enters your blood like embalming fluid...You must Work!...At a boring job...You have to Work. Everybody does!...To pay the rent, the gas, the electricity! And what's left? Not enough to Be Enjoy!*

No answer to that. Hah! So what am I doing, supporting an armchair, a table, a few pots and pans, a carpet inherited from the last tenants that grows like fungus on the floor – lifeless objects – until I become one myself? I thought they would give me independence. They don't give me anything! I do not possess them, these things possess me. I am not free.

The doorbell rang. I was not expecting anyone at seven o'clock at night, there was no one to expect. I opened the door with some apprehension. A young man stood there holding a bunch of flowers, asking for Mary.

"She doesn't live here..."

"Oh, I'm terribly sorry..." he mutters, nearly falling down the stairs in his embarrassment. Well, I wouldn't relish an evening with him. There seems to be a shortage of pirates around the Cromwell Road at this period in time.

I closed the door with relief, but niggled by my failure to achieve the creative existence even the smallest bird or worm has by simply being alive. It doesn't work that way with people. It isn't enough to be alive. I *want to live*.

Going into the kitchen where the dishes from last night are piled in the sink, I stare at the ancient gas cooker, realising that the day might come when I put my head in its greasy oven and turn the tap. No! The answer has to be to fling myself on destiny and ride it till I fall off or am consumed. It seems a dangerously fine idea.

And what about your father? Well – what about him? He's hale and hearty, loves his food and wine, he's had a good life and will live for years – *but will I? If I put my head into that oven, he'll have to do without me.*

With this devastating logic, Dad's image shrank to a disposable size – the answer had to be – *Go.*

I fell into bed and slept on it.

When I woke in the morning, my decision was still there, it had taken over in a coup d'état. Without giving a hint to anyone, I set about detaching myself from my existence, ridding myself of my possessions for a few pounds, chucking the rest at the junk men. It was like ballooning, jettisoning sandbags, getting lighter and lighter, more and more buoyant. A ruthless feeling of pure joy possessed me; I wanted to sing all the time, even in the street. Dad attributed my high spirits to the holiday which had done us both good.

I bought my air ticket to Athens for the night of my birthday, choosing the date deliberately as a symbol of rebirth. In my letter to father I chose my words with care, applying weight to all the pressure points. In a fit of compassion I put:

PREPARE FOR SHOCK.

Dear Dad,

By the time you read this I shall be back with Tasso…. I've been hating my life for too long. If I don't do something drastic, I'll put my head in the gas oven. Don't worry about me. I'll be fine. I have money. I'm not a teenager. Remember – it's what you did, when you ran away from schoolteaching in South Wales to London, with only £6 in your pocket, and two pairs of braces! I know now how you felt!

To my brother I gave only the bare details. We had never been close.

12.

Sitting on the airport bus, on the night of the Great Escape, I fumed at how slowly the driver climbed into his seat, chatting all the time with a chap called Fred. Only when he said, "Okay, Fred – right-you-are!" did he start the engine and swing the coach out into the traffic of the Cromwell Road. As we passed the top of my street, I could see the launderette, the church spire and my bathroom window above the railway line. I gazed at it without a pang.

At the airport I thrust my letters into the mouth of a postbox, and offered myself calmly to the mechanism of departure, percolating to the Departure Lounge. I was trying to read my book, which seemed to have been written in Urdu, when an announcement like so many pieces of sliced bread froze me to the PVC settee.

"*The flight to Athens and Nicosia will be delayed by one hour. Thenk yew.*" Click.

Waiting was intolerable. My letters had been posted. I sat through the next hour rigid with anxiety as people all around got up in response to exotic announcements to disperse to the ends of the earth. I was listening so hard, I nearly missed the announcement when it came: "*All passengers for Athens and Nicosia, please proceed to Gate B. Thenk yew.*" Click.

Gate B? I could see A, C and D, but not B. As I got to my feet with the surge of other people, a flight to Manchester was announced at the same time. I tried to divine the destination of the man in front; surely he couldn't be going to Athens, he was just the sort of person to be going to Manchester.

Walking the interminable corridors, my legs seemed to get shorter and shorter, heavier and heavier, until I could hardly drag myself into the waiting bus. The bus drove a long way through a menagerie of aeroplanes being groomed like racehorses, until finally it drew up beside the jet for Athens. I found my seat quickly, and steamed with impatience as the other fools fumbled into theirs, sat on their seatbelts and had to get up again.

50

At last the engines whined to their extremist pitch. Quickly I said goodbye to everything in my life, even childhood, as the ground dropped away and the ugly agglomeration of 'the London Area' became a necklace of diamonds on the dark velvet throat of the night.

The friendly girl next to me, wanting to chat, asked, "Where are you going?"

"To a Greek island."

The way I said it made her ask curiously, "For a holiday – or forever?"

"Forever," I said, adding mentally: *I hope.*

I didn't want to talk. The mystery of re-birth was upon me. I wanted to participate fully this time. I was glad when she fell asleep, yet how could one sleep on a night flight to Athens, when the whole of Europe was bathed in the light of the full moon. The British Channel was beaten pewter, rivers glistened like sacred snakes, the fangs of the Alps bayed at the moon. How calm I felt, how natural it seemed, as if taking a plane from London to Athens was nothing more than a bus trip from Piccadilly to Marble Arch.

The moon stared in at my window with an expression of mild anxiety, reminding me of Dad. I stared back.

Wynken, Blynken and Nod one night
sailed off in a wooden shoe,
sailed on a river of crystal light
into a sea of dew.
"Where are you going, and what do you wish?"
the old moon asked the three…

I knew what I wanted, and what I must do; I was the little dog balancing on the horse's rump, the moon was my paper hoop. I was about to jump right through that paper hoop.

The plane landed in Athens at three o'clock in the morning. The warmth of the air and the bareness of landscape made me think I had been deposited on another planet. The moon had

51

resumed its customary place above my head and no longer took any interest in me. I felt bereft, like a new arrival at a boarding school. I was alone in a strange place at a strange hour. I had leapt a continent.

What next? For the moment I could still follow the person in front, but at the customs desk the machinery of arrival fizzled out and with it went the last glimmers of euphoria like the ignominious descent of a little ball dancing on a jet of water when the water is turned off. I stood glued to my suitcases. Why had I brought so much? I summoned up the resource to accost a man to ask where I should go to get the plane to the island. He took me to a little window, knocked on it. It was opened in the irritable way all such windows are opened. I asked my question again. "Domestic Services building," the man said. "It is no opening till 6.30…" He slammed the window shut.

Three and a half hours… Domestic Services? What a funny thing to call it… I had struggled only a few yards with my suitcases when a porter took them from me without a word. I followed him like a child, not knowing where he was taking them. He hadn't asked me where I wanted to go. He took me over to some tables on a veranda, made me sit down, pointed to another building, then at his watch, indicating he would return at the right time. I wanted a coffee, but the waiter cleaning the table-tops took no notice of me even when he slammed an ashtray in front of me.

The view from this veranda was of a deserted road, some oleander bushes and a huge expanse of sky. A whistling insect sound vibrating in the air seemed to confirm my arrival on another planet. The sky began to lighten imperceptibly at first, then rapidly, passing through tints of pink, lilac, topaz, orange and yellow as the sun came sounding up the sky like a brass trumpet.

*

The little plane swung in over the island with the sea jade green and blue all around it. The journey was over, the consequences about to begin.

52

13

What of Tasso? Was he aware of the depth and significance of the English girl's madness? He had been chosen by Fate, hadn't he? He would not fail to play his part. Messages had passed between us as brief and practical as telegrams, but there was no-one resembling him among those watching the plane's turn-out. I had said I would meet him at the bar at the usual time – 12 o'clock.

A man detaching himself from the onlookers came toward me. It was not Tasso. It was not Yannis. For a moment I wondered what Tasso looked like. Had I forgotten? This was a much older man; he shook my hand in a fatherly way, extracted the baggage ticket from my fingers, put me and my luggage into his old blue taxi, and drove off with me – where to, I could not ask or guess. I sat in the back of the taxi squinting at the bright light and colour.

The taxi drew up outside a pretty pink cottage with flowers growing in pots and whitewashed petrol tins. At the sound of the horn, a plump young woman rushed out to greet me with instant affection. The driver carried my bags into the house. When I tried to pay, he said, "Tassos", shook me by the hand and left. So there really was a Tassos.

The cheerful young woman ushered me proudly into her dining room, containing a table in glossy veneer, a dresser covered with doilies and knick-knacks and family snapshots in cheap metal frames, and a divan in one corner. She rushed over to this, stripping off the cover to indicate that this was where I would sleep. She showed me the rest of the house; her own bedroom filled with a great brass bedstead. Icons and a mahogany case containing wedding crowns gave a pious atmosphere to conjugality.

She took special pride in showing me the bathroom, though it had no bath – only a lavatory and a small washbasin with one tap. She fingered the lavatory chain with special emphasis. I smiled, she smiled; we continued to smile at each other, unable to exchange an intelligent word. It didn't matter. Her gestures were as vivid as mime. Pointing to herself, she said carefully, "Evang-el-ia." Her name was Evangelia. She indicated that she thought me "young" – though I was probably older than she was – and "pretty". She fingered the cloth of my jacket – indicating "very good" quality. Everything about me was "*Oréa...poly oréa*". She kept saying it over and over again.

Two small children stood in the doorway staring. She hustled them in to be presented, a fat girl of around seven with olive skin and almond eyes, called Marianthi, and a boy of about five, thin dark and fidgety, called Dimitri. The two pairs of unblinking brown eyes stuck on me like toffees. I wondered when I would be left to myself. I had travelled more than miles. I needed to be alone.

At last, with smiles revealing strong white teeth, she hustled the children out of the room. I shut the door, and quickly tugged off my stockings – though it seemed odd to be undressing in a stranger's dining room. I pulled on a cotton dress and sandals and slipped out of the front door before Evangelia could catch me again with her kindness.

I knew the direction to take and walked along in a calm, irresponsible manner, telling myself I had done a shocking thing – I had escaped. Far away in London my typewriter had its cover on. At this very moment they would be asking where I was, if I were ill – had anyone heard? My letter would be in the morning post. There should be a word for giving oneself the sack – voluntary dismissal? When they read it, would they think I had gone mad? Had I gone mad? Or had I gone sane? Anyway – it was delightful.

It was not so easy to dismiss my father with the same complacency. I thrust the thought of him aside, and walked on with invisible cicadas trilling deafeningly in the trees, the sea sparkling with diamond points, until I reached the town.

In a narrow street adjoining the main square, I saw a sign I could read, propped up in the window of a little cafenion. FRIED EGGS HERE. Suddenly I knew I needed food.

The place was empty. I went in. An old man shuffled out of a tiny galley and looked at me. "Fried eggs?" I said hopefully. No reaction in the old man's face. The same sign was propped up on the wooden counter; I pointed to it. He looked lugubriously at it; once he must have known what it meant. Then an idea occurred to him; he shuffled into the galley, came out with two eggs, and held them up. I nodded, smiling enthusiastically. He did not smile, he just indicated a table. I sat down. A sound of sizzling from the galley confirmed success. With infinitely slow movements, he brought to the table a tiny knife and fork which might have been part of a doll's set, and a paper napkin but not the eggs, though the sizzling had stopped.

I was so hungry now. Why didn't he bring the eggs? When he approached the table with the plate of eggs, they lay in puddle of olive oil, quite cold; he had been waiting for them to be cool enough to eat. Cold eggs in olive oil mopped up with a sweet bun was a new experience, but that is just what I had come to Greece for: *new experiences*. It gave me a sense of achievement to have fed myself in a foreign land. Perhaps I would survive.

At noon precisely I walked towards the café under the arcades, my knees like jelly. The Bank Manager recognised me at once, and rushed forward to shake my hand in a fierce grip. "'Ow are yew! Wel-kommin...Wel-kommin!" He had the tact not to ask about my father.

There was no sign of Tasso. I dared not turn my head to look for him, convinced that everybody around me knew what I had done, yet I felt him nearby like an animal in the jungle. When I was no longer sure of anything, the Bank Manager – his name was Vassili, I had now discovered – banged two glasses of retsina on the table, and Tasso stepped through the glass doors behind me and sat down.

The reality of him was somewhat different from the version I had been nourishing in the West Cromwell Road...the hair on his forearms?

He didn't say anything, staring into the space beyond the acacia trees, whistling softly through his teeth.

"You okay?" he said at last. "You like the place I find for you?"

I said I did, and before I could drink my retsina, he said, "Come – we go!" Like 'please' instead of 'thank you'.

He took the same way through the back streets to the same bar, ordered the same koniaks, the same plate of bits bristling with

55

toothpicks, selected the same nerve-tingling music on the jukebox, but something was missing, and the koniaks were making me sleepy.

"You need to sleep," he said, looking at me.

"I'm okay!"

"You must to go sleep a bit."

"Are you trying to get rid of me?" He laughed. Then I knew what I had been missing – his laughter.

"I tell you," as if talking to a child, "you need to sleep because tonight we must to go all over the University."

"The university?" I was puzzled.

"*The* University! The whole World!" Exasperated.

"Oh, the *Universe!*" I was laughing now.

"Why you laugh?"

"Your English."

"What's the matter with my Engliss?"

"It's unique!"

"So?" Not doubting he was unique.

"Are you glad I'm here?" I asked suddenly.

"Of course I glad."

"Only *of course? That's not enough!*"

"What more you want? Anyway – later you will see. Now I must to phone a taxi to take you back in Evangelia's house."

Once again a taxi slid to the door. He put me into it; it knew where to go, no money required, all done by magic.

It was the middle of the afternoon now, the house was very quiet. I went to the dining room, fell on the hard bed in the corner, with a pillow like a stone; briefly recollecting that I had done what I had done, and reached my destination, I slept instantly.

14

I am still asleep when he comes to fetch me. I sit up, hardly knowing where I am, or what his presence signifies. It is seven o'clock in the evening. While I dress, he sits on the veranda with Evangelia plying him with the questions she has been frustrated in asking me. He is relieved when I appear ready to go.

"She ask too many questions."

"What questions?"

"How old you are, if you have childrens, if you be married…"

Surely that is the wrong way round? "What did you say?" I am curious to know.

"I say I never ask these questions." It is true. He doesn't know anything about me.

"Is this your scooter?" A red moped is parked by the gate.

"No, I rent for the evening to have the transportation we need."

"To go all over the University?"

"Exactly."

He has to exert a good deal of force to get it to start. I climb on behind, holding his portfolio of pictures – his 'ammunitions'.

"I never go to battle without the ammunitions."

I have never ridden a scooter before; it seems the ideal way to travel through the warm perfumed air of a luminous Mediterranean twilight. The road away from the town is broken at the edges, pitted with deep potholes, and it twists and turns like a snake. The western sky flushes deep apricot, against which the undulating landscape rises and falls in deepening tones like the harmonic themes in a fugue. In the east, a pink moon climbs in a lilac sky.

He took all the bends on the wrong side, but was there a right side? He sang, the sound vibrating through his chest. It was a long way before he turned onto a rough dirt track and bounced along it toward some lights among the olive trees. We had come to a bay cradled between the furry paws of two peninsulas, with a strip of pebble beach, a little wooden jetty with a painted boat resting on a sea as clear as gin. He parked the bike against the wall of the small pink taverna, with its tables and chairs set out under the olive trees. An electric light bulb hung among the grapes on the pergola, and a jukebox offered its fat emotional melodies to the scented darkness. Strangely enough the sound of mortal music did not affect the serenity.

"How are you going to sell your paintings here?" I was puzzled.

"Wait and you see!" There was an eager anticipation about him like a dog on the scent.

It is instantly justified. Two elderly women at one of the tables near the sea are waving their hands to him. "Tassos! *Chéri!*" He goes over to them at once.

I walk out onto the little jetty. The moon, the only witness to my adventurous flight the night before, offers no recognition now as it carves a glistening path towards me across the sea. He is sitting with the French ladies now. Does he understand what I had done?

"Come here – darrling…" he calls. "I find very-good-friends of me from Paris…" Already arranging the empty chairs into a semi-circle under the light in the tree, and drawing the pictures out of the battered portfolio, he creates his gallery. Reluctantly I move toward the table. The women greet me with a lilting "*Bon soir*" and a perspicacious look that takes in my one-dimensional Englishness. Having 'done' French at school, I am unable to speak it; so much for education. Tasso can be charming in four languages with a minimal vocabulary in each. There are degrees of charm and motives for charming; it can be viscous as treacle, false as counterfeit money. His charm is as effortless as a spring – full of wit, originality and invention. He knows he has it, he knows how to use it, but he doesn't know what it is anymore than we who are fascinated by it. The ladies are enjoying it. I am not so sure about myself.

"*Ça c'est très jolie!*" the French women squeak. "*Formidable! Mais oui!*" It draws other people over to look. The French ladies choose two pictures, and another person buys one. The pink bank notes slide into his pocket.

Young people are tramping along the beach toward the other taverns strung like beads around the neck of the bay. Bronze flesh glows in the lamplight; arms about each other, they take kisses like sustenance on the march. They are the young French from 'Le Club' on the peninsular – French is being bandied about like a beach ball, only I fail to catch it.

How long will he stay with these women? I have flung myself across Europe to "Be Enjoy". The French ladies draw his attention to my ill-concealed boredom, positively ordering him to take me away and give me some pleasure. They speak affectionately of *'l'amour'*. It offends my sensibility, convinced as I am that my attitude, being British, is superior to theirs

"*Allez vous! Mes enfants…dancez!*" To my horror he wants to take them with us to the next place on the beach.

"*Non! Non!*" They are laughing and waving their sparkling rings. They have known 'the life' – now for them, only the wine, the moon on the water …nothing more.

"*Allez vous!*" As we leave, he calls to the waiter to take them another bottle of wine.

We tramp through the dark olive grove toward the next taverna. I am silent. He notices. "But – darrling…if I no find the money – how we going to Be Enjoy?"

Money. Preoccupied with my own emotional currency, I had forgotten about Money. Can there really be no magic without money? The scooter, the wines, even the jukebox.

"It make me tired too talking with those old womans, but they don't buy without that! They old now – they need that stuff…" Compassion, cynicism, and egotism. "You think anybody can make what I do?"

There is so much I don't know about him – the delicate machinery of his finances, making pictures to sell for marginal profit requires all his charm, personality and Will. He enjoys it, but he is not doing it for pleasure, it is business. Life is business.

"To make the people to pay attention to my poor paintings…they bull-shit! I know that!" He is ready to throw the whole portfolio into the sea. I put out my hand to stop him.

"I am a Tramp, darrling!" His eyes glow in the dark like a dog's as, sorry for himself, he has won me back to admiration.

"A SUPER TRAMP!" I cry with British enthusiasm, throwing my arms round him. Thus entwined with each other and the portfolio, we tramp on to the next night spot.

"This place is the best place," he says, preparing to enter the Beach Restaurant where a band is playing on a dais under the olive trees with a singer holding the microphone to his mouth. I stop like a donkey.

"I don't want to go in there! I don't like it – it's not Greek!" – wanting the old tavern, the singing and the guitar. The island has changed its face in the three months I have been away.

"What you talking about – of course is Greek. This is the best place!" He drags me through the hedge and straight onto the dance floor. Wriggling like a jar of tadpoles, the young French entwine naked limbs, lipping and nibbling at each other.

"Now we have to Be Enjoy!" he says, but my body in his arms is as stiff as a post.

"You don't know to dance?" He is surprised.

"Of course I can dance! I don't like the place!"

"What's the matter with you?" he demands, shaking me. "Why you *thinking* all the time!"

A damning accusation. I have come all this way to surrender the Me in me, but it is stuck like a cork in a bottle *thinking. To think – or to Be.* I let myself go and cling to *him. Total immersion, nothing else will do.* Moulded to his body, mine becomes flexible again.

"That's better! I want a woman with me – not a potato."

On the dark sea, beyond the tables, a boat with a lamp in the stern passes slowly with the boatman standing at the oars, peering into the water, preoccupied with the silent world under the surface where octopus entwine their naked limbs.

I am just beginning to like the place when I hear the la-di-da English voices of my compatriots. I have run away from them, how have they got here? To have them near me on this particular night of all nights is even worse than the French ladies.

"I don't want to be English anymore."

"But you are. No man can hide behind his finger."

"Did Socrates say that – or you?"

"Both! Anyway, is very Greek." *Very Greek* is beginning to have a significance of its own.

Suddenly Yannis appears at Tasso's elbow and whispers something that makes Tasso look towards a table where a girl is sitting alone. He drags me off the dance floor. Now he wants to leave the place?

"But I'm enjoying myself now."

"Never mind, we have other ways to be enjoy." Yes, but for the moment I've just begun to enjoy this way. Fears will have to be overcome again.

"Let's stay a bit longer."

But he won't, leading the way back through the hedge, forgetting the "ammunitions". He does not go back for them.

At the Pink Taverna, he is no longer in a hurry, and orders another drink. The warm, sweet-smelling darkness, the grapes dangling overhead with the naked light bulb among the leaves; the same fisherman rowing back slowly across the bay. "*This* is Greek!"

We climb onto the scooter and head back to town, passing through warm and chill patches on the empty road. Without the portfolio, I can entwine my arms about his chest and press my face against his back and feel the vibration of his singing. Life is simple after all. Or is it?

Evangelia has left the door unlatched. He follows me into the dining room with the glossy veneered furniture, the doilies, the family photos in cheap metal frames, the knickknacks with the bed in the corner – an odd place for the first magic, entering into the mystery, surrendering to this before becoming two solid bodies again, united and separate. I wish I was more sure of him, he mustn't escape me.

Afterwards, he lights a cigarette. I seem to feel the rasp of the match on my skin. He leaves by the French window into the garden, dropping lightly and silently over the garden wall.

I have travelled many miles in the last twenty-four hours, but I know I have not arrived where I wanted to be.

15

The bright light forcing its way through the shutters woke me. I thought it was electric light but, of course – it was the sun. I jumped off the bed, threw open the shutters, marvelling at the brilliance. It was already hot. What time was it? He had told me to meet him at the café as early as 'impossible'.

There was a tap at the door. Evangelia entered, bringing my breakfast: a cup of tea and a rusk. She sat down at the table to watch me eat. The tea had a funny taste, and the rusk was like concrete. The children came in as well; three pairs of brown eyes watched me struggle with it, perhaps wondering why I didn't dunk it in the tea to soften it. I gave up, rubbing my stomach to indicate I wasn't hungry. Evangelia, interpreting this as 'pain in stomach', was all anxiety. I shook my head vigorously to reassure her. She pointed outside, making swimming movements. I nodded. Tassos? I nodded. Making a tulip shape with her fingers, she indicated something 'good', and placed her tuliped fingertips against her heart: Tassos – good. This kind of conversation has great charm but is more tiring than words. In desperation I went to the bathroom. When I came back, they had gone; I was able to dress and go.

Tasso was working up another set of sketches at a table under the Acacia trees. As I approached, he threw up his arms and started to sing; the doubts I harboured as to the value of the gift of my total self blew away like dandelion clocks.

I sat down at the next table. His brushes and pens were in a French soap box; he sharpened his bamboo pen with a razor-blade, drying it out occasionally with a match. A glass of koniak stood beside the painting water, an upturned saucer acted as the palette for the inks. Sparrows hopped about picking up crumbs from under the tables, cats stalked the sparrows. The strong light filtered through the thick canopy of leaves in which the invisible cicadas kept up an incessant din.

"What will we do today?"

"Wait and you see – anyway we going to have adventures…" He suddenly chucks the painting water at a cat. "I hate the cats to catch the sparrows…"

After an hour he is ready 'for action'. Yannis appears; Tassos tells him to sit with me while he goes to the paper shop to fix the pictures.

Yannis, taking the opportunity to practise his English, says, *"Will-yew-kom-to-my-partee…howabsolootelee marvell-us.* Iss goot my Engliss?"

"Terrific!" I am now almost helpless with laughter, until I see Tasso a few yards away at the corner of the arcade, talking with a girl – nice face, short hair, long slender legs –obviously foreign, but not English… *There is something between them – he is asking her to forgive him – she loves him.* I can read more from a distance than close to.

At the sound of my laughter, he turns his head, her eyes follow his…for the duration of a second, a cobweb of recognition is woven between us. Loyal Yannis summons up every gram of English to divert my attention.

Returning to the table, Tasso says, "Why you laughing so much with him?" and sends Yannis away. I do not ask about the girl. He is ready to go now. With him cradling the newly hatched pictures in the portfolio under his arm, we walk through the town. It is hot walking.

"Where's the scooter?"

"Today we are poor, we must to go by the foots."

At the edge of the town where the road to the north began, he told me to sit in the shade of a monastery wall, and hold the "ammunitions", while he stood in the road waiting for a car to pass. No cars passed.

"What are we doing?"

He pressed down on the air with his hand, signalling, "Wait and you see".

He recognised the driver of the first car to come along. "Him a friend of me – he will take us." The friend stopped readily, but only to apologise for having no space. The car bulged with his mother-in-law in her ample skirts and wimple, and two Calor gas bottles. The next car did not stop. "Him a baster and don't like me anyway."

The third car had foreign number plates, driven by a lone female. "Here we are! We have nice transportation..." He flagged her down.

She stopped. He spoke to her in French. She leaned across to open the door for him, then he pointed to me. And a curious thing happened. She slammed the car into gear and drove off. He turned to me, making the sign of the cross as a statement.

"You know what she say?" I was curious. "I take you if you be alone."

Slow to digest the full implication of this, when I did, I was downright indignant. "Woomans!" His idioms being better than mine on the tongue.

We got a lift at last, in a van, climbing into the back under the awning among the cargo of polished green water melons like 100lb bombs, and huge fat round loaves of bread like cushions with a hole in the middle. I was tempted to sit on one, but Tasso frowned; bread is still sacred in Greece.

We couldn't see anything except the road unravelling behind us, flickering in sun and shadow like an early cinema film. As the van charged round endless bends, we had to keep out of the way of the melons rolling from side to side.

We stopped in a mediaeval village with sun-bleached walls of ochre and apricot, with nothing but the paraphernalia of a rustic life. Tasso disappeared into a little tavern; hearing a shrill peal of feminine laughter, I followed, stepping into an interior of cerulean blue and burnt sienna paintwork against whitewashed walls. It was another 'Everything' shop with tables and chairs, barrels of wine, sacks of lentils and beans, salamis drooping from the beams alongside candles hanging by their wicks. The painted wooden shelves contained bottles of liquids glowing like jewels – ruby, topaz, amber, bright orange and dark amethyst – and looked as if they might explode during the course of time. A Breughelesque female poured out two glasses of 'blue' wine from a wicker demijohn; but before we could drink it, the van hooted. We tossed off the heavy wine, and climbed back into the van. The bread had disappeared, but the melons remained. In the privacy of the van, Tasso kissed off the horns of wine on my lips.

When the van stopped again, we had arrived at a rock-bound bay with a crescent beach. After the blindness of the van, I was stunned by the colour of the sea – Reckitt's blue and emerald green, clear as crystal. Olive trees stood at the edge of the shingle beach with a very modest guest house at one end and a ramshackle taverna at the other. On the cliffy headland, like a bull's brow, nestled a cream and white monastery.

Tasso makes straight for the ramshackle taverna with the benches and wooden tables. He sets out his pens and brushes and begins to work again like a forger printing his own money. I change into my swimsuit in the smelly lavatory.

The rock-bound bay like a goblet holds the kingfisher blue water to the lip of the pebble beach. So cold to the flesh, so transparent that swimming becomes flying over the iridescent depths where fish cruise in their own silence.

Lying on the hot stones, the orange fire of the sun piercing my closed eyelids, it is so quiet I can hear the scrape of his bamboo pen on the paper. Happiness! Happiness! I have found myself. No, I've found him, but finding him is finding the piece of the jigsaw into which I fit – even if the picture remains to be seen. That's what it's all about, isn't it?

Before long I notice I am not hearing the scrape of his pen any more. The sun is so hot, it requires an effort to throw it off and sit up, dizzy with it, seeing sparks and blobs. I stagger to my feet under the weight of the sun. His things are still on the table. Where has he gone? I see him walking towards the hotel at the other end of the beach. Why didn't he call me? His independence fills me with dread; whatever he does I want to do too. I must not go after him, I have my pride. But I will not be where he expects to find me when he comes back.

I wander into the olive grove; it is cooler and the shade is a relief. The grass and flowers are dried to biscuit, no birds sing, only the incessant grating of the cicadas. A hint of blue leads me to another little bay, another shingle beach, another tavern with a painted boat lolling on the transparent water. How many times can they achieve this combination? But without him as the activating principle, it is just a picture postcard. As I have no money on me to buy a drink at the taverna, my independence is exhausted in ten minutes.

Turning away, I see him coming through the olive grove looking for me. It has worked.

"Why you go away? I find one British General and his family, we talking much – come back to sit with them a bit."

"I don't want to sit with a British General!"

"Honestly – is so nice people. You know how much I trust the British."

"Well, I don't." I didn't come to Greece to sit down with the British. "I want a drink at that tavern over there."

"Okay," he concedes.

My triumph is short-lived. At our approach, three women, seeing him, start waving and calling, in Greek, "*Kyrie* Tassos! *Kyrie* Tassos!"

"Do you know them?"

"No, but they know me," he says, going to them. I stalk down to the beach and throw myself into the water again, dangling over my own shadow suspended over rocks and rainbow reflections. I thought love would be like this…

I crawl out and sit moodily on the beach in full sun which is now too hot. I hear their voices on the terrace above. How naive to think the world would consist of me and him! He calls to me to come up. I don't answer. He comes down to the beach with a sunhat borrowed from one of the women.

"You going to be crazy if you stay in sun."

"I *am* crazy!"

He goes back to them. Later he comes down again to offer me a pink carnation picked from one of the pots. Am I a child that needs placating? I take it and pound it to pieces with a stone.

"Don't broke the poor flower. You better to break me." So he knows. Carefully gathering up the broken petals, he puts them in his pocket book, as if he has betrayed them, not me. "This is the

67

reason I never make compliments to the woomans," he says, and returns to the terrace above.

Hugging my knees under the stupid hat he has put on my head, I notice my ring – my gold signet ring – has gone. I wade up and down in the shallow water, which is so clear. Surely I will see it.

"What happens?" he calls down, alerted by my sudden movement.

"I've lost a gold ring."

Gold! The loss of gold excites the women to come down onto the beach to wade up and down, clucking like hens. Tasso borrows a snorkel mask from a German and swims up and down. Surely in water as clear as this he will see it. No, it has gone to be sea-changed.

The women gather round me as if I have received a physical wound; to lose gold – ill-luck has struck at me out of the bright light. Their compassion sticking to me like glue, they almost carry me like ants up to the terrace of the taverna. I do feel as if a part of me has been wrenched away, but I can accept the loss. It isn't that important. What I fear is, having risked so much, I *may not be going to win after all*!

Tasso disappears into the kitchen of the tavern and comes back carrying a lump of burning charcoal in a spoon. Placing a glass of water directly in front me, he drops the charcoal into the water; it sizzles viciously.

"What's that for?" I'm alarmed that I might be made to drink it.

"To put off the Evil Eye."

The women nod in confirmation, patting and stroking me reassuringly. I wish they wouldn't. One of them has some English and thinks she has more.

"It is the fault of you to swimmin' wiss the ring on zee fin-geer. Zee feen-ger bekom thinny and the reeng going away of zee feen-ger…"

When emotions have returned to normal – whatever that is – we go back to the ramshackle taverna at the corner of the beach, where the long wooden tables have filled up with people eating lunch. He orders spaghetti and brown wine. An English family hover at the edge of the crowded taverna, and are about to go away when Tasso calls out "Here you are, Sir! I make a place for you", moving everybody up a bit until there is space for the four of them to sit down.

"We are most awfully grateful," says the pink-faced Englishman.

"We wouldn't have got any lunch without your help," says the wife, and the children chorus, "Thanks *aw*-fully!"

They order lobster. The waiter brings a live crayfish straight from the pen, and pinches its eye to make it kick, before bearing it away to the kitchen to be brutally boiled.

The proximity of my own species makes me nervous and irritable again. I open my mouth only to put in the spaghetti. When Tasso speaks to me in English, the wife, surprised, says, "Oh, are you English?" I admit to it out of natural cowardice. "Are you on holiday?"

"Sort of," I mumble, unable to tell the truth or the lie. What was the truth? What was I on?

"How lovely!" Her eyes rest speculatively on Tasso, she asks no more questions. Tasso talks; they hang on his words, murmuring, "How interesting…"

No barriers between him and them – only between them and me.

Having finished our meal, he says, "Now I must to make the siesta." We leave them. "So good people!" he is saying. "Him a General for sure…" Useless to suggest he is probably a bank manager.

He looks for the deepest shade; it lies under a fig tree. "No good to sleep under that tree."

"Why?"

"It make you bad dreams." But as there is no other, he settles down in a professional way, cradling his head on one arm, and is instantly asleep.

I can't imagine sleeping in the bright vibrating light, dense heat and insect noise. I sit beside him, studying his features while they present no immediate challenge. This is the man I have crossed a continent to be with. His head would look good in bronze, the deeply incised flexible lines on the cheeks, the aggressive nose, subtle mouth suggesting daring and humorous adventures, the capacity to survive and even flourish with ingenuity, wit and cunning... to sing, dance, fight...kill? To act decisively and spontaneously within the element of life and even make a little poetry with it, if that is what a man does when he causes women to be in love with him forever, or hate him forever, which comes to the same thing. Is this what they call A Real Man? Anyway, it is at his feet the load of my pent-up emotions has been delivered like the contents of a hydraulic truck, *and there is no taking it back. If I can't make him love me – what am I going to do?*

He opens one dog-like brown eye. "Now we go to swimming," he declares, taking his shirt from the tree where he has hung it up.

I follow him down to the beach where he does a deal with a boatman and pushes the painted boat onto the glassy surface of the water shimmering in its depths with viridian and purple lights. He rows the boat through a gothic arch of rock into a deep cave with a little beach at the end. Abandoning the oars, he pulls me roughly to him.

"No! I don't want it like that!"

"What you want then?" *Not that way, there is too much at stake.*

"Who was that girl in town this morning?"

This surprises him. He laughs, but is angry. I grab the oars and row us out into the bright light again; he dog-dives overboard and swims ashore.

With the boat in my power, I row for the open sea, beyond the gateway of the bay. The oars creak against the thole pins, the sun pours down, but I am shaded from its force by a cotton awning, and the breeze is strong. I laugh when I notice his wallet on the seat, containing his money – what he has of it. Outside the bay the coastline is all rocks, and the wind much stronger – too strong. I have to untie the cotton awning and row hard for the protection of the bay again; to draw him after me would be a victory, but to have to be rescued would be a defeat.

Back inside the portals of the bay, I turn my head and see a boat coming out from the beach with Tasso lunging at the oars, and the boatman sitting in the stern smoking a cigarette. As the boats come together, "You crazy!" he shouts. "Don't you know the wind is danger out there!", and he dog-dives overboard, twisting to hit the water with his shoulder to send up a fountain of water that drenches me. Drawing himself up easily into my boat, he picks up the towel.

"Were you worried about your money?"

He throws the towel at me, I throw it back, it goes in the water. He grabs it out, throws it again – hard. The wet towel hurts. I throw it back with all my strength. We are drifting in towards the beach, people watch us with amusement. We are making a spectacle of ourselves. He quits, "Okay, *Morgen! You win this time.*"

"Morgen is German, not English."

"Morgen was one hundred per cent British!"

"Who?"

"Morgen! Him a British Sergeant Major – he drinking two bottle of ouzo a day. Nobody joking with him!"

"Is that a compliment, then?"

"It is a SUPER compliment."

"I thought you never made compliments to the *woomans*."

He is ready to throw the towel again, but tosses it onto the seat. "You!"

*

The sun began to lose its fierce power, the intense blue of the sea draining away, leaving the water of the bay tranquil and colourless. People drifted away from the beach, taking their children and their toys with them, as the huge glowing disc of the sun sank into the sea and disappeared.

71

A coach-load of volatile young French from The Club have taken over the ramshackle tavern, lit now by paraffin lamps. Tasso goes over to them, I think he is going to join them, but he returns, saying "They make Lobster Party now, we have to wait till to be finish. But is okay – we have nice transportation. The coach is the only way we be away from here tonight, that's the reason to talking with them."

He orders some more spaghetti and wine. The moths fluttering helplessly around the lamp make me think of Love, the mystery of attraction. In its light, he looks like a Tartar Prince. I tell him so.

"And you a princess."

"I don't feel like a princess…and you are *not* a prince… "

"Never mind not to be – I am Me. Is no necessary to be anything else."

I ponder why it is so simple for him to be himself – so difficult for me to be Me. Isn't that why I am seeking the answer to me in him? Is that what Love is?

When the coach departs after midnight, we are on it, climbing away from the rocky bay, with its cargo of sea-salted, sun-tanned young people singing those French songs that have so many words and so little tune.

"I hope Michaeli have a room free – or tonight we sleep in the trees."

At the Pink Taverna, a row of old peasant cottages offers cell-like accommodation of beguiling simplicity; an iron bedstead, a hook for clothes, a little mirror hanging by a red cotton string, and 'outside facilities'.

Lying together on the creaking bed, I'm still not sure of him. "It's not British to submit like this!"

"Why not?"

"Because you don't *love* me!"

"Never mind. Love is pains in the neck."

The door scrapes on the sandy cement floor as we leave the room at five o'clock in the morning. "I must to be in my job at six…"

It is the moment when the earth, refreshed by the night hours, prepares to submit again to the tyranny of the sun rising in dazzling splendour over the mountains and flashing on the surface of the sea. He hails a horse carriage, clopping gently toward the town for a day's work with the tourists. The driver stops, we climb in.

"Always I find nice transportation..."

16.

How long have I been on this island? Three days? Four? These are double days and double nights, stepping in and out of sun and shadow, moonlight and starlight. In and out of pictures Van Gogh might have painted and I wish I could…

When I join him at the café, Sunday morning, the first thing he says is, "You have a phone call from London in 20 minutes."

It turns me cold – it can only be father… How could the telephone exchange find me in a Greek café?

The minutes pass slowly but when the waiter signals me to the telephone on the cash desk, it seems too short. Why can't I pretend I am not here? But I move mechanically to the phone. His voice sounds light years away.

"Is that you?"

"Yes, it's me."

"Are you alright?"

"Of course I'm alright!" I say, trying not to sound indignant.

"Will you be staying long, do you think?" He is cautious.

"I just don't know." Casual.

"You can come back any time, you know…"

"I'm alright – I'm having a wonderful time…"

"If you need money…"

"Dad, I'm alright – thanks. Don't worry…"

The pips are sounding… he's gone…

Tasso, watching me, says, "He angry?"

"Not exactly…"

"Why you looks miserable then?"

"Oh, I don't know," I snap impatiently. "I want to be HAPPY. I don't want anyone worrying about me. I want to be FREE…"

"All right...don't shout...you make the people to pay attention..." Was I shouting? "Of course we be happy. What else except that?"

He says it as if it were easy. A week ago I thought it was.

"Anyway, your father trust me," he says, as if he is sure of it. What does he mean by that?

17.

Our life goes on but this is not ordinary life; no opening or closing hours, no proper meals. Sometimes we eat five meals in a day, or hours and hours pass without any of the customary commas and full-stops. Koniak for breakfast, retsina for tea, a perpetual state of intoxication without being drunk; the emotional extravagance of this new life burns it up in the blood. Nothing exists for Tasso save the present moment – the only valid moment of Time – of living Time. When you get up in the morning it isn't necessary to know exactly what day of the week it is. If you try to find out, it adds to the confusion. The cafés and taverns have more than one calendar on the walls, offering a selection of days, months and years. The year can vary from street to street. Presumably the banks know what year it is after the birth of Christ – for everybody else there is only the past and the present – never the future because the future holds the threat of death, the end of the living moment.

Jukeboxes spray the air with Greek melodies under the blazing sky by day and the star-rich, cricket shrilling night; worn records, worn needle, full of sand and grit. Fruit cake emotions, vibrant deep voices sticky as raisins dried in the sun and Arabic semitones wriggling like worms in the blood. "Why must they have it so loud…?" is the querulous complaint of the middle-aged, middle-class English couple trying to enjoy some 'peace and quiet' at a café table on the edge of the sea. I don't want it turned down. The fat melodramatic melodies written in the air lance the boil of my emotions and make them bearable. There is a desperate sweet sadness in their music that opens the soul; feelings as yet unidentified and anonymous ripen in an instant and burst like seed pods in the heart, identifying deep and fundamental truths – about life in some unknown part of oneself.

"What do the words say?" I am always making him translate because he often succeeds in writing a poem of his own, like a child painting with the limited but bright colours of his vocabulary.

"How many songs have I written for you?

76

How many wines have I drunk to you?

With all your poorness – with all your richness

I love you, Sweet Life!"

Is Life the only thing he will ever love because he is alive? Is that a good enough reason? The Greeks think so, but Life has given them the sun, wine, song and dance. It has given us grey skies, beer and boring jobs.

*

Then came an evening when, expecting to meet him as usual at the Bar Greco, the waiter handed me a note, written in Tasso's English: *"Darrling – pardone me pliss bat mai sister arrive of Athens with his husband. I mast be round with them tonite. Don't be angry – your love Tassos"*.

When I had made out the message – having read it more than once – I accepted it without question. I ordered a beer and a cheese pie, pondering on the significance, if any, of "your love Tassos". All it stated was the fact that I loved him – which I already knew.

I felt lost without him to lead the way in and out of experience, that hall of distorting mirrors; alone, my appetite for adventure dwindled to nothing. I felt vulnerable to the brown eyes which tried to encounter mine; they no longer seemed friendly, but flat and demanding, like the eyes of the icons.

I was glad to walk back to Evangelia's, though I couldn't imagine how to pass the time there, all evening.

Evangelia, sitting for coolth on the veranda fanning herself, was surprised to see me back so early. Her hand asked, "What happens?"

I shrugged. "Nothing."

Was I ill? I shook my head. "Tassos – where is?" the hand asked. I made a vague gesture. She made me sit down beside her, stroking and patting me affectionately.

After that first evening Tasso had not come to the house again, always leaving me at the gate. What was her attitude to morality? She was so kind and friendly, but now her hands began to ask questions I did not want to understand, or want to answer with words... She pointed to her wedding ring, then rubbed both index fingers alongside each other, suggesting some sort of togetherness. She indicated her children, staring at me with eyes of toffee. Then came the inevitable twist of the hand – the question mark? What? I feigned stupidity, as if unable to fathom what she was on about. How do you answer in hand mime that you don't give a fig for anything except to be with him night and day forever? She sighed, stroked me again and called Marianthi to take me for a walk.

The child took me by the hand and led me off. We climbed a bit of hill at the back of the house which overlooked the cemetery, bristling with marble, and gigantic cypress trees like great green flames. In case I was incapable of understanding even a cemetery, Marianthi mimed the dead by crossing her hands on her breast and closing her eyes, then dusting her palms together with a graphic finality.

I pointed to a neglected bit outside the cemetery wall, where there were only two iron crosses – one with a heart shape transfixed by an arrow. She ran her thumb vertically up her throat as they would kill a goat – romantic suicides. She stuck her nose in the air and rubbed her fingers together and shook her head. I understood – dispossessed, unblessed. Then she knocked down some almonds from a tree, cracked them efficiently between two stones and gave them to me to eat. She stroked me too; so much older and wiser than poor mad me.

18

A couple of nights later, he told me I would have to go. We had been at the taverns on the beach, we had been happy – now in the darkness by Evangelia's gate, he told me gently but without sentiment, "You must to go. Not tomorrow…not after tomorrow…you will know the time…" He did not explain. He waited patiently while his message sank into me, then he drove away.

My veins filled with a dark poison almost paralysing me, a bitter taste filled my mouth as I dragged myself into the house and lay down on the bed without undressing. I did not sleep. A soft, intolerable weight lay on my chest like the Cheshire cat grinning. They say death is the loneliest thing – how can it be when there is Love? Love is much lonelier, an arrow shot into the blue which comes to rest in your own heart, impaling no-one but you.

My limbs felt cold and heavy as lead; like being dead, but more brutal because I knew I was alive and would go on being alive with no option but to crawl back into the sloughed off skin it had cost so much madness to reject. That was the hell of it. I had gambled and lost.

What had he said? The words were like one of their songs on the jukebox. "*Not tomorrow…not after tomorrow…you will know the time…*"

From his hand I had to accept the sentence: I had failed the 'seven-days-on-approval' test. Each one of those days had been significant, like being promoted to a higher class, having to learn fast, once and for all. But I had failed. I saw that the gift of my Total Self I was so determined to bestow on him was about as valuable as a rice pudding. Well, I would take my pound of flesh nearest my own heart. *I would stay to the end of the month.*

Next day, Sunday, I knew I would find him drawing out his pictures at the café table under the acacia trees. He didn't look up when I sat down near him; our silence lay between us like a drawn sword.

Finally, he put down his pen and looked at me. He did not find in my face what he expected. I had done my homework during the night. Painful it had been, but I had learned this latest lesson and had it by heart. We took each other in, eye for eye. It was a good moment. The moment of loving dedication between combatants who know they mean to kill each other if they can. So this was Love! Not a super friendship with sex thrown in, but a fight to the death.

He laughed gently and knowingly, as if he knew me very well but was seeing me for the first time. Then he called to the waiter to bring me a koniak and two fried eggs. It often seems that the only obligation a Greek takes seriously is to feed a guest.

"I know you *hangry*," he said.

"I'm not hungry."

"Yes, you are!"

"Do you mean *hungry* or *angry*?"

"Yes! That's what I mean. I know you hungry *and* angry." Damn it! He had made me laugh! The obligation to depart was never mentioned between us, but it did not go away.

19

In the evening, we circulate the taverns in the town, while he waits for the night to declare itself. The night has to open like a flower and then be plucked. Sometimes it is like waiting for the Glastonbury thorn.

Preoccupied solely by emotional currency, I find him puzzling and morose at this hour, quite forgetting that his preoccupation is with real currency and how to get up enough to Be Enjoy.

Tonight he is jubilant. "We are ready for action. The night belong to us! And I have a wonderful surprise!"

We tear along the dark road on a scooter with a very dim headlight, no moon, only stars. Looking up at the stars from an island in Greece gives you vertigo. Stars above stars, stars behind stars. You know they go on forever...beyond, above and under you. You don't question it, tearing along an island road on a twirling planet.

"Tonight we happy for sure!" he shouts, pulling my hand from its place on his chest and kissing it.

Silly thing to do. The next minute – a bang, a shout. I fly through the air and clap hands with the asphalt. Tasso, running to me, says "You okay?"

"I think so..." I'm getting used to surprises. I try my legs; they work. I get up, asking him if he's okay. The answer is no, but he is not concerned with his own physical hurt; he turns his attention to castigating the driver of the cart we have run into, which had been ambling along in the middle of the road without a light.

The driver listens politely to Tasso's tirade until he tires of it and, urging his sleepy horse forward, disappears into the darkness. The disappearance of the cart does nothing to stop the flow of Tasso's vituperation. The noise brings an old woman out of a roadside cottage, bearing a paraffin lamp aloft and keening like something in Greek tragedy without knowing what situation requires her grief. In the light of her lamp I see Tasso's trouser leg is torn and soaked in blood. I point this out to him. "I know," he says, and continues his diatribe with the old woman joining in as an operatic duet. Then he picks up the bike, tries to start it. I point out the pedal is bent backwards, at which he shakes it like a rat and starts pushing it back along the road we have come, shouting to me to collect the pictures and our pullovers, which are scattered all over the road.

He pushes the scooter toward some lights which turn out to be a small roadside tavern where a man and woman are sitting over their evening meal under the canopy of an extended roof supported on sturdy pillars in the traditional way. Tasso pushes the bike right up to their table where the paraffin lamp illuminates the amber wine, pink water melon and the bright plastic table cloth. He is a dramatic sight with his bloody trouser leg. They regard him without pausing in the probing of their teeth with toothpicks. The woman eventually murmurs "*Pó-pó-pó*", the meaningless sound with which they greet anything extraordinary, joy or sorrow.

Tasso launches into a dramatic account of the accident. They listen, chewing on their toothpicks. He tells the woman to boil some water to wash his wound and follows her inside, where he takes off his trousers and shouts when she pours ouzo over his wound as an antiseptic.

I sink onto a wooden bench against the pink stucco wall, beginning to feel a bit peculiar. The old man brings me a thimbleful of koniak. As I look up to thank him, I see myself reflected in his gaze as one of those foreign girls who appear in the summer months like swallows…youthful as children, with light eyes and who like quite simple things and laugh and smile over nothing at all …all crazy and coming from another planet called "Ev-rop-ee", or a planet remoter still – "Americkee" – where many of their own children have disappeared to and from where they send back money.

I feel worse after the koniak, but Tasso appears looking fresh, even *chic*, in a pair of their son's trousers, as if he were just setting out for the evening. Anything that pumps the adrenaline through his body gives him an even keener sense of being than he has naturally – which is a lot. He stokes my neck affectionately. *Oh, that we might have an accident every night.* I think to ask,

"By the way, what was the *vunderfool surprise* you had in store for us tonight?"

"Oh, I don't remember – but happens anyway." Thus confirming his magic powers.

Only one car passes along the road. Tasso flags it down, exclaiming, "Ah! we very lucky." It contains 'a-good-friend-of-him'. The driver, listening to the second account of the accident, hardly looks at the road; it doesn't really matter as there is no traffic; the only danger on the road tonight was the horse cart we ran into.

The car drops us at the edge of the town, and we limp through the back streets on stiffening limbs but in a high state of intoxication with each other. We have had an accident, we have bruises and wounds. We might have been killed or maimed, but we have survived. Clasping the pullovers and the portfolio and each other, we limp along. He starts singing softly and intensely: "*It's a long way to Tipperary -it's a long way to go...*"

"How do you know that song!"

"Of course I know it. They put me in jail for singing that song."

"In jail!"

"In the wartime. I singing that in a tavern one night, the Italian patrol pass and they arrest me. They take me to the Big Prison. Nobody escape from there – but I did…"

"How?"

"A girl help me."

"What girl? How?"

"Ah, that is a story…she live above the tavern where I was and see them take me away. A pretty girl, 18…she like me very much, like schoolgirl…you know. I don't do anything with her. She come to the prison every day to bring me food. They don't feed us… the Captain of the Guard want to have her… She flirting him much, and say she go with him if he let me out. He an honest Italian one, he do it. One night I hear footsteps come to my cell. They take prisoners out to shoot them at night. I ready to make fight but she have tell the Captain that, he whispers: 'Be quiet, just follow me.' He take me down to the side door in the small tower and push me out. She wait for me in the trees. When I see her – I know what she have do for me. Believe me, I carry that on my back forever – what she do for me. I am not worth so much..." He bows his head, then suddenly cries "*Now* I feel to dance!" and hails a taxi to take us to the Cottage Night Club.

The tables set in the garden now under the orange trees, jukebox manhandled onto the veranda under the sagging vine giving its sandpaper roar to the night, moths dazzled by its light fluttering hopelessly about its glass bosom.

The waiters gather round as Tasso hauls up his trouser leg to show the bloody bandage, listening to the second version of the accident. It was quite a short accident – now it seems much more dramatic. He limps over to the jukebox, seeking the right sound to express his emotions; and choosing a *Zembekiko*, aromatic as garlic:

"Farewell beautiful life...farewell women, midnights and torturing griefs!"

He dances – cigarette stuck between his lips, his face sad but glowing. Was he remembering the girl and the gift of freedom? I envied her the gift he would never forget...

Snapping his fingers, moving in the mystery and impulse of the dance, he might be a witch doctor dancing over a sick child. His eyes pin me like a butterfly to a board but I am feeling trivial. Could I have done what she did? No. I could not be that generous. I want *all* of him – forever, not in a moment of gratitude.

He raises his arm against the star-filled sky as if to pluck one and toss it sizzling into my lap. This man could make a woman love him more than was absolutely necessary...

He limps back to the table. "My leg hurt me much," he says with surprise.

My mind is on that girl... "What happened to her?"

"Katina?" He has already forgotten her. "Oh, she marry, she make her childrens. She live here in town."

"Do you see her sometimes?"

"Of course – in the street we good friends. What else?"

"I suppose what you have is animal magnetism," I say thoughtfully.

"*Magnetismos*! Yes, is very Greek word."

20.

I don't remember getting back to Evangelia's, but I was standing in the room when there was a knock on the door. Evangelia stood there in her nightdress, very agitated, pointing to the front door, pointing at me. Was she complaining at the hours I kept? Did she mean me to leave?

I stand there like a guilty schoolgirl. But, twisting her fists back and forwards and making *brumm-brumm* noises, she makes me understand she knows about our accident. How could she?

She starts tugging at my clothes. I try to assure her that I am not hurt, but she insists I take off my dress, and I am surprised to see my thighs are black and blue, and a piece of skin has been gouged off my hip. Evangelia *pó-pó-pó*s very fast and rushes away. I climb onto the hard bed and would have fallen asleep, but Evengelia's husband comes in to the room, carrying a stone pestle and mortar which he sets on the floor. Evangelia bustles in carrying fresh green herbs, onions and garlic which he pounds together in the mortar while Evangelia massages my bruises with olive oil. When the mixture in the mortar had become a paste, she slaps it onto my legs, binding it in place with strips of cotton, and makes the sign of the cross over me with an Easter palm cross, then tucks it under my pillow and kisses me goodnight.

Next morning, I find Tasso at the café as usual. He has been to the doctor with a deep gash in his shin, and is very pleased.

"The dog-tor give me ten days free of my job! The world belong to us!"

"You might have broken your leg."

"Bah! My mother make me of iron."

Vassili, the waiter, brings the coffees to the table. He looks severe. He too knows about our accident; rumour has been at work in several versions in which we were either in hospital, maimed, or dead; the moral being that running about with foreign girls is not good for the health. Vassili wags a finger in my face. "No goot you to follow Tassos. No goot Tassos to follow you!"

He repeats the message in Greek at Tasso, who makes a gesture of swatting a fly.

When I tell Tasso about Evangelia's midnight poultices, he says, "I hope to find another room."

"Why? She's so kind!"

"She talk too much," he says darkly, "we must to find some place to rest up where noborry bother us…"

As we get up from the table, we are caught by the three Greek women who were at the taverna where I lost my ring. *How long ago was that?*

"You still here!" cries the one with the English, her almond eyes bulging and glittering. "*When* are you leaving?" she demands. Am I obliged to tell her?

"Not yet," Tasso answers for me, which surprises me.

"Ah…no yet…" she ponders, looking searchingly at us both. "How long you steying?"

"She has time," says Tasso.

Changing her tack, she starts enthusing over me and stroking my face. "Ah, she is so preety…!" Insufferable woman, why doesn't someone cut her head off! Before we can be rid of them we have to shake hands with them three times.

"Who are they?"

"Ah, poor things, they government secretaries, they have one month holiday now but they ugly and find no company…" So that's why she wants to know how long I am staying.

Two days later, he says, "I have find a place more better for us", and puts me in a taxi to collect my things from Evangelia. I am embarrassed by her puzzled signals when I pay her. I flap my arms up and down, hoping she will think I am leaving by plane. Unable to express my gratitude for her loving care and friendship, I am sullen and confused and glad to escape in the taxi which takes me away.

It stops around the corner, Tasso gets in. We take the road we walked that first night – aeons ago – and stop by a simple two-storey house standing in its own garden with no neighbours. A woman bent over a wooden washtub raises her head, wipes her hands on her apron and comes to the gate.

"Spirithoula good-friend – she don't mind...you know..." So Spirithoula doesn't mind...Evangelia did. What is their attitude to morality?

She leads the way up the stone stairway to the front door – the ground floor being reserved for the animals in these old houses; the upper floor being divided into two bedrooms, a kitchen and a front room, all with deep-silled windows and shutters opening outwards.

The room I am to have contains an iron bedstead, a rag mat, a chair and a peg on the wall to hang clothes. No bathroom; I am given to understand that the lavatory is the shed in the corner of the garden with the door hanging by one hinge. No wonder Evangelia had fingered the chain with pride. The only water is from the well beside the washtub under the vine pergola, and roses and bougainvillea cascade over the porch. This will be yet another experience. This is what I came for, to have experience... Isn't it?

There seems no end to experience on this island. Each day seems to offer a new lesson, a new challenge. I learn fast. He teaches me the dance – the *Hasapiko,* danced by two men, even three. Side by side, with arms across each other's shoulders, we move step for step, not so much dancing to the music as submerged in it, swimming in the current like fish in a stream.

"Why is it called a Hasapiko? What does it mean?"

"The Butchers' dance," is the surprising answer. Where else but here would the butchers dance? It isn't a dance you learn as any other dance – I must intuit his movements as he improvises the patterns the music dictates to him. It is like freshly baked bread, the same, yet never the same. Each man makes his own dance of it. Yannis follows him well, though another man, a good dancer, will not – this dance belongs to twins or triplets of dancers; it requires sympathy and brotherhood, one leading, the others following, yet moving spontaneously as one. I draw nearer to him in this dance than in the sexual embrace. The real bonding has begun.

We dance it wherever we are, day and night, in taverns to the jukebox – at the Beach Night Club to the basouki. His leg hurts but it never stops him dancing. "You follow me well – better than any other one."

We siesta in one of Michaeli's cell-like rooms, the strong light insinuating itself through the closed shutters, feeding on the whiteness of the wall. Sweet to lie beside him in the creaking bed, though it breeds its own despair. I am happy with him, but the nature of this kind of happiness seems to be tension, not tenderness, and tension has to be maintained to be effective. I have given myself over to the adventure of him and the poetry of the flesh while it lasts.

"But you don't *love* me!"

"Who knows what Love is?" he says. "All that matters is that we are here *now*."

It will never be enough for me. Soon I will have to go and buy a ticket.

"Come – we must to find transport back to town…"

Sitting in the road waiting for a car to pass, a white sports car appears with Italian number plates.

"Ah! I find bee-ooutiful transportation!" he says, stepping into the road to flag it down. The driver stops willingly. Tasso speaks to him in Italian; the man, tall, bronzed, Roman-looking, in white towelling vest of the latest style, peaked cap, and string driving mittens, glancing in my direction, is happy to give us a lift. Italian chivalry presumes that Tasso will sit in the cramped back seat, and I beside the driver. Greek chivalry presumes no such thing; with equal suavity, Tasso negotiates me into the small back seat while he sits beside the driver, who annoyed now, drives rather fast. I close my eyes. Tasso is saying to him, "More gently please – we have not so nice roads as you in Italy."

It makes no difference. The driver, ignoring Tasso, speaks to me over his shoulder. "You are English?" His English is excellent. "Ah, London! I was a student there. Lyons Corner House – the best place on earth!"

Visions of Russian salad, chicken mayonnaise, bacon and egg superimpose themselves on the whizzing landscape of olive and cypress, making me feel sick.

"Your English is not very good," the driver says to Tasso, and suddenly they come together in Italian, talking man to man. Without being able to understand, I know they are discussing me. When Tasso directs him towards Spirithoula's, I am deeply suspicious. Is Tasso just a beastly foreigner after all?

"So this is where you stay," the Italian says with interest, as he helps me out of the back seat with unnecessary zeal, holding my wrists and trying to engage my eyes. I shoot a furious look at Tasso and, dismissing them both with a cold "Thank you", enter the garden. Tasso goes back to town with the Italian.

I wash in a bucket, change and take the bus back to town. The day may be over, but the night is about to begin.

I find him at the Bar Greco. "Why you have your face like a shoe? Someone bother you? Tell me who is him and I give him lesson he never forget."

"No one bothers me except YOU! You were talking about me with that Italian."

He knows I do not understand Italian and looks at me with something like respect. "You *Morgen* for sure…" he says, invoking that British Sergeant Major again, as if I were displaying just the qualities he has always admired in the British – they look such fools but you don't fool them so easily. "You are right!" He has become serious, "And I will tell you the *clean thru* (the clean truth), then you can see who is the *Baster* – him or me."

I wait coldly for the 'clean thru'.

"He say to me in Italian language: 'Why don't you go to my hotel and take my wife?' You understand what that mean?"

No, I do not. I don't want to know, but he spells it out: "He ready to give his wife to me – to have you."

Life has not prepared me for this sort of thing. I am only British. (*What is the use of being British?)* When my panic subsides, it occurs to me to ask, "What did *you* say?"

"I say I need to see his wife first." He is laughing. "I know the way to pay the *Basters* – don't fret!" Seeing I am still confused and frightened, he says, "For *God-ni-say!* I do many things in my life – but I never sell the *womans*..." He crosses himself. "*Panayia Mou!* Even the dirty business I make in wartime was clean stuff. Come on – we get out of here..."

21.

We take to the alleyways by our usual route. Glancing into the wine shop on the corner, he suddenly stops. "Oh, come in here a minute – I see a very good friend of me." He goes straight to the man sitting at a table in the corner. "Hullo, Hamiss!"

The man focuses on him with difficulty, but then rises unsteadily to his feet, revealing not trousers but a kilt suspended on lean loins.

"Tassos! SWEET FELLOW… I'm afraid I'm awfully drunk…"

"Hamiss come here with the British when we finish with the Germans. He verry good friend of Greece…"

"I ADORE the GREEKS!" Hamish enunciates passionately in an Oxford rather than Scottish accent. "The Most Super People in the World!" Glancing at me, he adds: "Oh, Sweet People! I can see you both adore each other! I LUV Love!" And he clasps his hands together, raising them toward the ceiling. "And you do believe in the immortality of the soul, that we don't just go *phut*! like that!" – attempting to snap his fingers unsuccessfully.

"Of course, I believe in the God…" says Tasso.

"Oh, I *am* so glad! That is good news! What a splendid person you are!"

"But what I know is one thing – we are here now – for the rest, don't thinking much."

"Oh, dear – what a pity! Hamish gives out an anguished cry. "Oh, I SUPPOSE I'll have to APOLOGIZE to those two BLOODY WOMEN back there! I can't remember where I left them… Oh, sweet people – come with me.!" and he plunges into the street.

As we follow his thin legs in long socks, Tasso says, "Don't think him a stupid one. Him a Professor, and knows many things!"

At a restaurant in an alley with its tables in the street, Hamish stops and peers: "I think this is the place…perhaps they've gone…"

A woman sitting at one of the tables looks up and exclaims, "Hamish! Where *have* you been!" in the tone of a nursery governess, her teeth coming horizontally out of her mouth. There are two women; the other, a washed-out, well-bred type, says nothing.

"Who are your friends?" the toothy woman asks, not very politely.

"This SWEET FELLOW is Tassos, – an artist," says Hamish, at which the toothy one immediately pulls out the chair beside her, saying, "Oh, *do* sit down!"

Tasso does so, and Hamish drops into the chair he had vacated, while I am left standing. There is no chair for me. The other woman urges me in a feeble way to take a chair from the next table.

Tasso starts entertaining them with the story of our accident, hauling up his trouser leg to show the bloody bandage. The women exclaim, "Have you been to a doctor?"

"Of course. He give me ten days off my job." The value of the wound to him. Nobody asks if I have a wound.

"I thought you said you were an artist?" says Toothy, as if short-changed.

"I am – but I have to be electrician to eat. I am not Picasso."

"Have you a studio? Can we see your pictures?" Toothy asks eagerly.

I offer the information that his studio is a café table; nobody hears me.

Where three women are gathered about an attractive male, the one who is 'with him' will be elected not to exist.

Hamish seems to have sunk into a coma. "He ought to eat something," says the kind, feeble one, whose name is Lavinia.

"I'll order," says Toothy, tackling the waiter with "*Parakaló!*" This is not her first holiday in Greece. She orders stuffed tomatoes in her Greek; the waiter brings tomato salad. "That's too

93

acid," says the kinder woman… Toothy sends it back and orders meatballs.

Toothy resumes her interrogation of Tasso, "Do you live here all the year – or just in summer?"

Tasso, baffled, replies, "I born here, I live here and I going to die here", crossing himself against the eventuality.

"It is a LUV-ly island!" Toothy rattles on, "But *such* a lot of *poverty!*"

Poverty? It is their richness that makes the deepest impression on me. They are rich on so little and ready, on the instant, to give you their all. I feel poor beside them, as if the more you have in material assets, the less you enjoy. Above all, I envy their capacity to enjoy this element into which we are born, and which bedevils us from cradle to grave. She calls it Poverty.

"POVERTY?" Hamish, suddenly snapping out of his coma, expresses my sentiments exactly. "You call the sun, the moon and the stars…the grapes over your head and in your glass….the scented air…to be able to sing their songs, and dance their dances…POVERTY!"

Even Tasso is offended. "Excuse me, please, but we don't die of hungry here – in the wartime, yes…but no now."

Hamish, thoroughly roused, is not to be stopped. "You bloody woman, you want them to have televisions and washing machines, instead of the richness of the soul!"

"Oh, SHUT UP, HAMISH! You shouldn't drink so much duty-free gin!" Toothy snarls, betraying the fact they have been to a party on board a yacht, but Hamish is unstoppable now. Picking up a hunk of bread from the bread basket, "THIS is still the STAFF OF LIFE to them, Old Girl!" It flies out of his hand and lands on the ground. Tasso picks it up, automatically kissing it before placing it back on the table, a conditioned reaction to avert the Evil Eye.

"You see!" says Hamish, understanding Greek ways, "They *revere* the things we have forgotten the meaning of! Bread is still *the body of Christ* to them. What is it to us?"

"Fattening…" murmurs Lavinia.

"In your country," Tasso suggests diplomatically, "I think, you don't need bread anymore."

"That's it!" cries Hamish. "Let us Eat Cake! May it choke us. It will! It will!"

"Hamish! You are terribly drunk," the Teeth says viciously.

"I don't give a damn! I'll drink as much as I bloody-well like. I HATE YOU ALL! You always think I'm talking balls..." At which moment the waiter places in front of him a plate of meatballs in a tomato sauce. He looks at it with surprise and horror. "Oh, God! Must I eat this?"

"Yes – you MUST!" says the nursery governess.

"It will make you feel better," Lavinia says gently.

"I don't believe it." He is staring at the plate, like a Penguin at the egg between its toes. Tasso takes over, cutting up the meatballs and offering Hamish pieces on the end of his fork. Offered the Greek way, he cannot refuse.

"You're *so good* with him..." Toothy murmurs intimately. He accepts her admiration with an exchange of looks. If she wasn't so ugly I would suspect him of flirting. Noticing my expression, he laughs. He can read me without words, but I want words to use as stones or cannon balls. His look mocks me: *Don't you know the game I'm playing?*

"Are you two married?" the one called Lavinia asks.

"Not yet," Tasso replies. *What does he mean by that!* Turning to me, he says, "It is time to leave our good friends, darr-ling..." They are not friends of mine!

"Oh but we must see you again...we must see your pictures!" they protest.

"For sure you see me again..."

"Where shall we find you?"

"Don't worry at all, I will find you..." he says blithely.

When we are around the corner, I pounce: "You were flirting with that woman!"

95

"No – *she* flirting with *me.* Ah, the poor thing, what she going to do with those terrible tooths. Anyway she going to buy, that's for sure."

So that's the game called 'Mediterranean Chivalry'.

22

He never asks when I will leave, but I don't doubt I have to go. Watching the great ferryboats slide across the horizon, I know that one day I will have to buy that ticket to set him free and, like walking the plank, fall into the fathomless ocean and leave not one small scratch on the enamel surface of his ego. I shall make the buying of the ticket into a balloon of monstrous size, so its shadow falls across us both. No, I dare not. I have learned from him that the present moment is the only moment, neither the past nor the future must be allowed to spoil it.

The three Athenian Civil Service typists we met when I lost my gold ring seem to lurk behind every Acacia tree on the Platiea, and every olive tree near the beach. I call them the Three Gorgons. "You are very right..." he says, as their voices hail him over any distance, always using the polite form of address. "*Kyrie* Tassoo! *Kyrie Tass-ooo!*" they wallow toward us through the heat like barges in a heavy sea, waving their beach towels over their heads. *"You are still here?"* gasps Bulging Eyes, sweating through her heavy sallow skin. *"WHEN are you LEAVING?"* – as if my only aim in life is to thwart her. On parting we pump hands all round, as they wish me *"Bon Voyage... Bon Voyage...Bon voyage"* three times.

"For sure I don't like those womans..." he mutters as we escape yet again – the slate of his gallantry is wiped clean as far as they are concerned.

In the vaulted tavern in a side street we eat the dish of the day, bean soup. His head against the bright plastic tacked on the wall behind him turns him into a Van Gogh portrait. He is looking at me with a soft gentle expression. I am wondering what is wrong with it, when he says, "I am a *Traditore.*" *Tra-di-tore!* rings through my head. Which opera? Could it be The Forces of Destiny?

"Why are you traitor?"

"I have tell you a lie."

"Which one?" His laughter ricochets off the thick tavern walls like machine gun fire. It is such a good joke, he shares it with the old man behind the counter, who smiles benignly at me, nodding his head.

"Well? Which one?" I want to know now.

"The time I leave a message for you at the bar to say I be around with my sister – I was not – I was with Ursula, the Dutch one."

"The girl with the sad face and the nice legs?"

"Exactly."

It had never occurred to me that when he was not with me he might be with somebody else. How incredibly foolish; it made my blind magnificent elopement look sillier and sillier. An act of pure egoism.

"What am I to do, *darrling!*" he is saying. "She look around all over town for me." Being 'in love' with this man is like joining a queue for fish – which isn't even fresh.

"I meet her before you come back – you understand? So what I going to do? She stay for one month at the Club. She a good girl…" (*Aren't we all*). "So what am I to do, darrling?"

What is he to do? What is she to do? What am I to do…?

I look up to the vaulted ceiling of the tavern which is like a barrel; suddenly, I know what I must do – the only thing to do: *Laugh*. Like a bubble bursting deep inside me, a piece of me is given up and blows away. I feel it go with some alarm for the space is instantly filled with new incomprehensible knowledge. This is happening all the time I am with him. It is like being blown up by a mine every day. Will anything be left by the end of the month?

"Come, he said, getting up, "I show you something."

He leads the way back across the Platiea to his work shed. He is on duty that afternoon to answer the telephone, but he will sleep on the chairs, then prepare his pictures for the evening. He opens his locker; on the inside of the wooden door is pasted a faded photograph of his mother and father, along with a list of female names: Manette, Colette, Ursula, written in biro onto the wood. While wondering how one earns this special ranking, I have no wish to be added to it. He pulls out a cardboard box stuffed with airmail envelopes, and tiny black and white snapshots with serrated edges.

"Are they all from women?" I am awestruck. "Why do you keep them?"

"Is no kind to throw away." *Was this vanity or Mediterranean chivalry?*

"Do you write back...?" I ask, having experienced his limited but graphic style.

"Sometimes. They need to have that stuff, poor things, in the grey places where they live..."

"Can I take them?"

"To do what?"

"Read them..." Not out of vulgar curiosity. Hasn't he brought me to this bran-tub to show me I am not the only female fool in the world, that I belong to a sisterhood? I want to know the landscape in which I stand.

"Don't broke them!" he says anxiously.

"I *promise* on the honour of *a British Sergeant Major*!" This most binding of oaths satisfies him; he lets me take up the box to carry back to Spirithoula's on the bus.

23.

I sit cross legged on the bed with the box in front of me and pull out the first letter addressed to *Monsieur Tassos,* with the name of the island; recognition can go no further.

"*Je pense à toi sans arrête…*" My school French is sufficient for this. I pull out a postcard of Monmartre. "*Toujours je pense à toi… (I think of you all the time.) Ce que nous avons fait sous les oliviers…près de la mer…*" (*What we did under the olive trees beside the sea…*)

In German, all I can make out is "*Lieber Tassos…*" No reason to think the sentiment any different from another in English: "*How much I miss you. I want so much to come back*", which makes me glance quickly at the signature – not mine – thank God! As I pull the letters out of the box it becomes unnecessary to try to read them. In any language they are the same, only in French they sound better…

"*Gentil Raquin…*" Gentle Shark? "*Ne crois pas que la peur du danger a empeché mon élan d'amour envers toi…*" (*Don't think the fear of danger has inhibited my ardour for you…*) '*Elan d'amour…*' that's good…you can't say it like that in English. "*I feared that you wanted from me only 'the physical instant', and I didn't want to be for you a woman like all the others…*" Exactly! "*parce que un sentiment inoubliable m'attache à toi, Tassos…*" (*An unforgettable sentiment binds me to you, Tassos…*) She has said it perfectly. I look for the signature: Ursula – the girl in the Platiea. I look at the postmark: August last year. Last year?

I push the box away, enough is enough; but suddenly grab it back. Are any of mine in there? Yes – here's one. Was that girl me? I tear it up and fling it on the floor.

It is the middle of the afternoon, Spirithoula is away somewhere. I am alone; this is a chance to have a real wash. I go down into the garden to get the water from the well. I have seen her sink the bucket enough times to carry the water up to fill the tank above the kitchen sink, which lasts about a day if she has filled it sufficiently. I drop the bucket into the well – it doesn't sink but stays buoyant as a cork on the mocking eyeball of water at the bottom of the shaft. I bring it up and dash it down again…and again. I thought anybody could do this!

Suddenly, it sinks like a stone so quickly I just catch the rope as it wriggles like a snake over the coping. My God, if I had lost the bucket down the well…an inept foreigner, all education and no knowledge.

I get the bucket up full of water this time, and carry it upstairs. Is water so heavy? One drinks it easily enough. Spiritoula carries up buckets all day long. Just as I am putting my bucket on the table, the gate squeaks. Spiritoula back already? But it is Tasso who appears in the sunlight of the door, hot and sweaty from his work. Seeing the bucket, he sticks his face into it, sucking up the water like a horse. "Aa-aach!" The sound of his exhalation echoes through Time.

What is he doing here in the middle of the afternoon? "Were you worried about your letters?"

He comes at me like a flame to scorch me up. *Oh, no, Monsieur Tassos – peintre, danseur, electrician d'Installations Elleniques….* We struggle through the small rooms. I am crushed against the window sill. I cling to the doorframe, resisting him with all my strength. I have no *'élan'* for an *'instant physique'*. He is angry – and hurting me –but I will not be 'a woman like all the others'. His anger breeds a joy in me – a burgeoning sense of power as we fall on the bed, glaring at each other, puffing in the heat.

Suddenly, he strokes my cheek – oh, so gently… "I am sorry you not a man… We could have a *real* fight…a be-ootiful one…"

He notices the pieces of paper on the floor. "I know you going to broke them!"

"It's only *my* letter…" I watch him gather the pieces as he gathered up the petals of the flower on the beach that day I lost my ring. Perhaps this is Love? Anyway, whatever it is: tomorrow…or after tomorrow…I must buy the ticket that will take me away.

Next day, Mr 'Alfa Romeo' stopped by the house. Spirithoula was in the garden at her washtub. He asked for *'la mademoiselle de Tasso'*. She understood only Tasso's name, shook her head and pointed towards the town. He drove away. When I met up with Tasso half an hour later, I told him.

"He stop by the house? He talk with you? He bring you to the town?"

"NO!" I had to explain *three* times before he would believe I hadn't had anything to do with the man. "It's *your* fault for showing him the house!"

We are standing by the Arcades when I spot Alfa Romeo only yards away lounging at a café table. He sees us, and the next minute is shaking my hand, looking at me with eyes trained to smoulder, and complimenting me on my dress.

"I have the car here, why don't we go somewhere to dance," he says, as if Tasso doesn't exist. The expression on Tasso's face makes me want to whinny like a horse. He responds instantly. "Good idea!" as if really enthusiastic, before adding, "but where is your wife?"

"She has a headache. She stayed at the hotel."

"Oh, I am so sorry for that!" All sincerity.

"Where is the best place for dancing here?" says Alfa Romeo, still gazing ardently at me, leaving Tasso to be concerned for his wife.

"I know the best place, of course," says Tasso, "but the problem is one – *who will you dance with?*"

Alfa Romeo reads the message, shakes hands with exquisite courtesy and walks away.

"Poor Alfa Romeo," Tasso murmurs, watching him go. "He is looking to get himself and his beautiful car all broke. Come on! Let's get out of here."

24

Taking the usual way of the back streets, we come upon Hamish, Toothy and Lavinia eating at the same restaurant in the alley. Has he come this way on purpose? The old blind guitarist is sitting with them, singing through his nose. Hamish, head bowed reverently, mutters, "Oh, this is simply heaven…" as if he is at a concert in the Albert Hall.

The women's faces light up at the sight of Tasso. "Oh, do join us. How's your leg? Do sit down. You're limping a lot."

"Never mind! Tonight you see me to dance!"

"The Greek dance?"

"Of course."

"Oh, we've never seen it. Where do you do it?"

"Anywhere! But I must to have the music."

"MUSIC!" Hamish comes to. "What we need is a Bach Fugue or 'My Blue Heaven'. Shall I fetch my harmonica? It's no trouble…it's in the car." Getting up, he knocks a glass of red wine over Tasso's trousers.

"Now LOOK what you've done! You've ruined his trousers!" Toothy rages.

"OH, SHUT UP! All of you! I didn't do it on purpose… I can't stand *anymore*!" And he lurches off up the street.

"He'll sleep it off in the car, like last night," Lavinia murmurs in conciliatory mode. Tasso, looking at his trousers, says to me, "How I going anywhere now…"

"Oh, God!" says Toothy viciously. "I don't care about Hamish! Now we can't go anywhere to see Tasso dance."

"Wait here," Tasso says, "I'll be back." And disappears.

"Where's he gone?" says Toothy, looking accusingly at me.

Hamish is not 'sleeping it off'; he suddenly reappears with his harmonica. "Now what shall I play?" he asks, sitting down at the table. "I could do *Jesu joy of man's desiring* if I wasn't so bloody pissed…"

"I had that at my wedding,' says Lavinia, without enthusiasm.

Tasso is soon back too, in freshly laundered trousers.

"Have you been home?"

"No, home is not a place for me. I remember I have clean pants in the laundry – just here. So where is your car? The night belong to us!" He can say it with such conviction.

It is another sports car. Tasso puts himself between Hamish and me in the back. Lavinia drives it.

Island nights are cool. I have his pullover draped over my shoulders, but not because I feel cold; I enjoy the embrace of its empty sleeves. Suddenly Tasso asks Toothy if she is cold. She isn't the type to feel the cold, but impulsively he pulls the jersey from my shoulders and puts it round hers. As my body registers my reaction, he digs his elbow into my ribs, signalling, "It's a game…." I *know* it's a 'game', but does he really expect me to play it too? Yet to remonstrate in front of the others would be vulgar and degrading. I seethe in silence as he directs them to the Cottage Night Club. It is empty, the waiters are standing around; even the jukebox is silent.

"It's very quiet," says Toothy, surprised.

"The night no begin yet," Tasso says, confident that nights only begin with him.

Hamish in the back of the car is still trying to blow into his harmonica. "I don't seem to have enough blow, damn it…" Then, falling into a dream, he murmurs "…the trouble is I only feel at home in the arms of a woman… Have we arrived anywhere? Oh, this is a splendid place," he adds, recognising the Cottage Night Club. "I can bring my guitar in and sing you a few ditties…"

"For God's sake, Hamish – we've come to see Tasso dance!"

"I'll bring it in anyway. I've got a divine engraving of a pregnant woman in my guitar case – I must show it to you…" A look of hopelessness passes between the women, as if all three of them are married to each other.

At the table, Hamish produces the nude engraving, and another 18th century etching so explicit, even I understand it. We pass them between us in silence as Hamish gets his guitar out. "Any requests?" None. "Then I'll start with The Hole in the Elephant's Bottom…it has 99 verses…I don't know them all…" And he lumbers into a song which he can neither sing nor play. The waiters gather round, asking Tasso what sort of music it is. "Chinese," he says in Greek. They turn away to smile.

What has happened to the Greek night? How has it slipped through his fingers? Why don't they start the jukebox and blast Hamish out of existence? I am seething with hatred for the race to which I belong, with its inhibitions it can't liberate until Nanny can't see – and then they pull down their knickers and show their bums.

I catch sight of Panayoti on the terrace peering into the garden to see what the night offers him. I nudge Tasso, who calls him over. As he approaches the table, carrying his guitar in its tatty plastic case, his eyes fix on Hamish's guitar, then on Hamish singing his laborious ditty. "Forte! Forte!" Panayoti cries by way of encouragement. Hamish immediately begins to falter, losing confidence. He gives up. "I can't…I wish I could…it's not my style, you see. I'm a dreamy sort of chap…"

Panayoti's hand reaches automatically toward the guitar. "*Voos permettez?*"

"Oh, of course, dear chap…" Panayoti puts down his own guitar and, cradling this instrument, strikes chord after chord, another and another until sounds are pouring out of it – sounds it has never heard itself make.

"Oh God!" Hamish groans. "He's *so* good. Where did he learn to play like that?"

Panayoti, son of peasants. God had breathed on Panayoti and he played.

The night takes off now with Tasso and Panayoti singing brazenly in harmony, or whistling duets until the juke box interposes its aromatic melodies and Tasso gets up to dance. Limping onto the cemented disc, smooth for dancing with a silly little illuminated lily pond in the middle, with two plastic lilies floating on it. The light from it illumines Tasso's features as he dances his unique *Zembekiko;* no sign of a limp now.

105

"He's one of the best-looking men I've even seen…" murmurs Lavinia. Toothy, leaning forward devours him with her eyes. As the music finishes, and he limps back to the table, she stands up and flings her arms round him, murmuring into his ear, "But you don't look happy when you dance…"

"When I dance *Zembekiko*…" he detaches himself gently, looking at me, "…I am reading the book of my life." Following his eyes, Toothy looks at me as if I were the traitor. I have never had such a look, but then I've never before had anything another woman might covet.

Hamish, groaning in ecstasy, is saying, "One of these days I shall kill myself – I know it – but if I could dance like that I wouldn't have to… The Elizabethans could dance…we've lost everything! What have we got – bloody ballroom dancing! Tasso, Sweet Fellow! Have you ever thought of killing yourself?"

"Me to put Me out of the Life?" he questions, "*For God-ni-say!*" He crosses himself against the Evil Eye. "I going to kill everybody in the University before to kill myself!" Turning to me, he says, "My leg bad for sure…"

Why look at me for sympathy? You are teaching me the rules in this game. You've already taught me the futility of tenderness…

"Have you been to the doctor? Have you changed the bandage?" Toothy drags his attention back to her.

"No."

"But you could get septicemia! You could lose your leg!"

"For God-ni-say! I never going to lose my leg!" But she has frightened him. In Greece, predictions bring the Evil Eye.

The evening is over. They wake up Hamish, who had fallen asleep like the Dormouse, and stuff him and his guitar into the car. They drop me at Spirithoula's; Tasso follows me into the garden.

"Don't go off somewhere with them," I whisper furiously.

"No, my leg very bad, I must to sleep in a bed tonight…in a minute it will be too late." They are tooting the horn discreetly.

106

"Darr-ling, I must to go to my house...*She* close the door at midnight."

"She?" I force him to say it.

"My wife!"

"You'd better go then."

Nothing more to be extracted from this evening, we have had its quota of joy, disillusion and pain. He limps back to the car; I stand in the darkness of the scented garden, listening to it drive away.

*

Five minutes walking through the rabbit warren of the old town brings him to the house. The door is still unlocked, the house dark and quiet. He goes to the salon filled with Victorian furniture, throws himself onto the cheap metal frame bed in one corner. The town clock strikes midnight. He doesn't hear the footsteps that pause outside his door, or the turning of the key in the lock.

25.

I go down to the harbour and buy my ticket for the ferry. Returning to the Bar Greco, intending to slap it under his nose without a word, I am foiled by the Three Gorgons who catch me at the corner of the arcade, shaking me by the hand the ritual three times. "When are you LEAVING?" the one with the bulging eyes demands.

"After tomorrow," I say with a sullen truthfulness, using their definition of Time.

"Ah! *TOMORROW*!" Her eyes bulge even more at this piece of information.

"*After* tomorrow," I repeat, as her eyes swivel to fix on Tasso, who has emerged from inside the bar.

"But why you look so sad?" she goes on indefatigably. "Is not Englandt nice place?"

"Of course it is," I pout, forced into defending it.

"Ah, bat it has no SUN, and not the face of Mr Tassos. Mr Tassos verry beeootiful man."

"We have other things…" I say, trying to think of them.

"Ah, yess…Marxx-an-Spenzaar, verry naice shoppings."

"Yes, it is a great consolation." *Why doesn't somebody cut her head off?*

"So you leaving *after tomorrow*?" She is suspicious that I might not be telling the truth.

"Yes." The British have to tell the truth, but really I am giving the message to him.

"Then we will say again *Bon Voyage*…" And the performance is gone through all over again like some cult ritual.

"I don't like these womans at all," he says, plunging back into the bar to finish his retsina at the counter. "Honest to God. These womans bother me much."

We leave the bar, cross the street as he takes the route we followed that first evening. By taverna stages we reach the edge of the town, where he flags down a passing taxi. We end up somewhere by the sea in a shabby taverna where the counter supports a hundred siestering flies while another battalion circulate the central air. The tavern-keeper, hairy and brawny in his vest, makes coffee, stirring the little aluminium pot over the gas flame; then takes down a key and leads the way by an outside staircase to the upper floor where cell-like rooms open onto a veranda, the canopy supported on sturdy pillars. On each pillar hangs a tin tank for water with a little tap at the bottom; an aluminium basin on a Van Gogh chair under it.

Tasso sleeps hard, deep, shut off; wakes, gets up, goes out, turns the tap on the little tin tank – no water – curses, and goes down into the sun-dappled garden, calling to the tavern-keeper to bring him a coffee and koniak. I follow.

The tavern keeper sits down at the table with us, uninvited; Tasso does not talk with him, and presently gets up and walks away. He hasn't indicated for me to follow; I presume he has gone to the gents.

The tavern-keeper, looking at me, brings out his cigarette packet, writes the number 19 on it, points to it and then to me. I understand this semaphore game from Evangelia; he is asking if I am 19. I shake my head and write 30. He looks surprised, and indicates with a wave of the hand that I am 'very fresh'.

Where is Tasso? He hasn't come back. Suddenly I see him sitting in the taverna across the street. Why has he left me here? Anxious and confused, I leave the table to go to him.

"You want koniak?" the man calls after me.

Tasso is making a sketch of the village street. He says nothing as I take a seat on a chair. An old man sits on a bench against the apricot wall. He wears a Panama hat, a thick wool vest, a waistcoat and jacket; his hands rest on the knob of his stick as he watches blankly the empty street. It is hot and quiet, no traffic except a scooter ripping through like an angry wasp. A blowy wind fans us; chickens scratch about, a sheep scouts about some garbage like a dog. The old man sighs from the depths of eternity within him. "Aa-ach! *Panayiá mou!*"

A thin-chested little girl with gold rings in her ears, large liquorice eyes in her head, comes to watch Tasso making magic marks on the paper. A woman comes from inside the tavern, to go to the well built into the wall outside the doorway. She hauls on a rope to bring up a basket from the cool depths containing a huge green water melon like a bomb. She carries it inside, and reappears carrying a tray loaded with the pink slices, urging us graciously to eat, as if we are her guests.

Tasso, concentrating on his drawing, suddenly says, "He flirting you much, the Baster! I come away or I going to kill him, and he not worth so much."

To get back to town, he stops another taxi.

"Why are we taking taxis when you have no money?" He has given his last drachmes to the woman at the taverna.

"Never mind! I pay next day – next month – next year!"

"Where you want to go, Tasso?" the taxi driver asks.

"To the Noufara!" The Cottage Night Club.

No sooner are we seated under the orange trees when a waiter comes over to whisper something with a nod in the direction of a woman alone and pensive at another table. I recognise her too. Ursula. He looks at me in desperation.

"She come to find me…she looking all over for me – the waiter tell me. Oh, darling, what I do now? I cannot leave her alone."

"Okay – I'll wait." *I'm not a rotter either.* I recognise now that it is not easy to draw the line between one woman and another.

"No! I cannot leave you alone here…we must to go together." We are all the same woman with whom he has an eternal relationship. He cannot make us all happy without making us miserable as well. Reluctantly I follow him.

Her face, sullen in its sadness, comes alive with gratitude as she looks at him. I take a seat at the table; she knows I am there but she does not see me. They talk in French, which puts me outside their intimacy. I can relax into my one-dimensional Britishness. He is apologizing for having let her down so badly…

"*C'est la vie,*" she shrugs in the French way. "*Je dépars demain…*" He tells her he will come to the harbour to see her off. She looks happy at that. *What is the happiness of Love? How many legs does it have?*

Suddenly the lights go out, the jukebox is struck dumb and the garden bathed in the steely light of a full moon turning the trees and tablecloths to silver, and our faces to marble masks of frozen emotion. The lights come on again – a laugh of relief at joy and pain returning. While we have pain we know we are alive.

26.

It is my turn now; he comes to the harbour with me. It is all over. I put out my hand to shake his. "Not like that!" he protests, leaning forward to kiss me. I walk into the mouth of the ferryboat as into the mythical underworld, aware only of the stubble on his chin and the dryness of our lips. Percolating to the upper deck, I come face to face with Alfa Romeo, followed by a woman who looks as if she has a perpetual headache. He shakes hands with an empty formality; that, too, is over.

From the upper deck, I look down on Tasso. He hasn't gone away.

"Write me a letter when you arrive at England!" he shouts up to me. I shake my head, thinking of 'the box'. He understands. "*You* again!"

He stays on the quay as the boat moves slowly out of the harbour.

At Brindisi, the clocks tell Italian time. I must live a whole hour again without him. At Milan, I have eight hours till the night train to Calais. I find a compartment with a flustered Englishwoman in a panic over an international crisis of which I am unaware.

"I couldn't bear to be out of England should anything really dreadful happen – could you?" For me the only really dreadful thing is returning to England.

The other occupants of the carriage are an Italian couple who refuse to have the window open, an Italian typewriter mechanic bound for Manchester, and a furnace man from Sheffield, who has been riding a bicycle around Umbria. He has a bottle of Chianti on the floor by his feet which he keeps kicking over, saying "Oops – sorry" and mopping up the mess with tissues provided by the English lady.

We huddle down for the night in the blue-lit dark, my every bone and muscle longing for the dawn. When it comes, the compartment looks like a battlefield and smells like a tavern; bottles roll about the floor together with paper cups and screws of tissues. The furnace man suddenly says, "Lil", the name of the station, not his girlfriend.

The English woman dribbles her experiences into my ear. She has been spending the summer as governess to the children of a very rich Italian family – a perfect nightmare! "The children so rude and uncontrollable! The boy threw a knife at me. The Contessa drank, and the Count didn't pay my wages. I wonder what time we'll get to London? ...Oh, do we? Then I could get the train to King's Lynn."

I am wondering what taverna he is entering or leaving – what record is playing on the jukebox. ....

"I could ring my friend from the station if it isn't too late...I don't want to be a bother...she'd have to air the bed...she's over seventy, you know – a wonderful woman, very highly strung and musical ..."

So is mine.

Victoria Station.

27.

Father hoped the 'Greek Experience' had played itself out, but then the letters with the stamps depicting Classical struggles between gods and beasts began to flop onto the mat again:

"My leg very bad. The Dogtor make me operation. Write to me!

I can stop to like you! I can stop to love you! But I cannot stop to thinking you!

Love from your Monster."

"Dear Monster! Your English has improved since your operation. I did not know you kept it in your leg."

My letters were not the only ones he was receiving.

"Cher Satyr,

Tu me parles souvent de ton voyage à Paris pour venir me voir! (You often speak of coming to Paris to see me.) Ça me ferait grand plaisir... (That would give me great pleasure.) Colette."

"Dear Monster!

I have the infernal British cold tonight. It is almost a cure for love, but Greek music is very good for a cold in the head. I will come back in April, as you say, for the Greek Easter."

"Tassos chéri – Il fait nuit depuis longtemps et je ne puis pas dormir (It is night and I cannot sleep...) Je joue mes disques grecques, et je danse toute seule. (I play my Greek records and dance alone) Ils semblent loin, maintenant, le clair de la lune et le bruit doux de la mer...(It seems far now the light of the moon, and the sweet sound of the sea.) Ursule."

114

"Dear Tramp! I have bought a second-hand Lambretta scooter for our 'nice transportation'. I had to pass my driving test in the snow! The effort of getting back to Greece seems almost too much – three days and nights! Yes, I will bring you a red shirt and nice walking stick for your bad leg."

"Cher Satyr,

Quant à ton voyage à Paris…? Ecris-moi vite!" (What about your trip to Paris…? Write to me quickly!)"

"Affreux brigand,

Pourquoi ton silence? Qu'est-ce qui se passe?" (Dreadful cad, why your silence? What's going on?)"

*

"I forbid you to drive that damn machine across Europe!" Dad had insisted.

"Don't worry! I can take it on the train."

28.

If I was returning to Greece like a moth to a candle, it would have been easier to be a moth.

Stranded at Bari at three o'clock in the morning, the waiters in the buffet watch the English girl getting sleepier and sleepier. They have to shut the buffet. "*Dove va, signorina?*"

"Greece." I am still proud of my destination.

"*Grecia?*" They indicate a train standing in a siding. "Go Brindisi sei ora…Brindisi-Grecia…"

They help me into a first-class carriage and sit with me in the darkness. "*Prima bella…*" one murmurs.

"M*olto sympatica…*" murmurs the other.

I understand enough Italian now to say quite firmly "*Non molto sympàtico.*" At which they remember they are tired and need to sleep, stand up, shake my hand courteously and depart.

At Brindisi there is no sign of my Lambretta scooter. The Capo di Stazione is very helpful, the chestnut eyes beneath the shiny black peak of his scarlet cap regard me warmly. I have reached the South again, region of warm reaction to the female of the species, especially agitated English girls who have lost their scooters. He tells me there are five more trains by which it might arrive, and that he was a prisoner of war in "*Bella Scotlandia*", and offers me coffee.

I spend the day hanging about the one main street between the railway station and the harbour, paying visits to the Capo di Stazione every second hour. The scooter arrives by the last train, giving me just time to catch the ferryboat. Eagerly I sign the papers, and prepare to dash off, but the Capo detains me. *What now?*

"One kiss, *signorina,* per souvenir?" He takes my emphatic 'NO!' philosophically, shrugging his shoulders, shakes hands courteously instead. It is I who have no manners.

To the night on the ferryboat there seems no end, curled up in an uncomfortable aeroplane seat surrounded by the smell of garlic and strong cheese, and snores. I go out on deck as the island reveals herself slowly in the dawn. It takes another two hours to dock in the harbour, the great car door descending to reveal the stage set with stucco houses, the fortress and the officials standing on the ramp in shirt sleeves. No sign of *him.* I am a day early…

My only idea is to get to the Bar Greco, and drive round the harbour wall dodging the potholes, so unlike the smooth surfaces of my country of origin. People stare at me; I feel like the whore of Babylon sitting on her ass. Girls do not drive scooters in this country, where it is indecorous to sit astride.

To my surprise, Tasso is standing in the middle of the road outside his workplace.

"How did you know?"

"I have five telephone calls already."

"Who from?" Puzzled.

"Who knows?"

"You mean anonymous calls?"

"Exactly," he says, leading the way into the shabby little taverna under the fortress wall, making me sit at a wobbly table between the beer crates and the back door, as if I were something to hide. He has not said he is pleased to see me. A thought bothers me now.

"Will I be the only girl driving a scooter?"

"Oh, that's for sure!" He says it without enthusiasm. It seemed such a good idea in England, to have our own transportation.

"You'll have to drive then."

He shakes his head. "Is not allowed me to drive. It have British numbers – the police will make me troubles." I should have known that in Greece a problem is always complicated by its solution. "We must wait till to be dark be around."

The tavern-keeper, tiny as a vole, brings a plate of small fried fishes to the table and tea with hot milk. He beams at me and shakes my hand. "Welcoming," he says.

"We don't have hot milk with tea!" I protest irritably, venting the distress I am beginning to feel.

"Yes. Yes. Is very British," Tasso insists.

"It isn't! We *never* have hot milk with tea!"

"What you want then?" he shouts.

"I don't know!" I shout back, wanting to weep; everything feels wrong, and the blood-thump of the jukebox from the other room fills me with foreboding.

The 'Peanuts' boy suddenly appears looking for Tasso; one of a herd of small boys who hawk peanuts and postcards around the town and do errands. Tasso uses him to take the shopping to his wife's house. The boy is gesticulating and pointing into the town. Tasso's face darkens with rage, and he sends the boy away with instructions to do something and come back and report to him.

"What's the matter?"

"I am not ready to say." He is standing by the wooden counter biting his knuckles and steaming like a steam engine in a siding. This is not the joyous reunion I was anticipating.

"This is the finis!" He spits out the words. "I never going back to that house in the rest of my life!" He is not talking to me, but I sense in my bones it is to do with me.

"What's happened?"

"*She*..." (he never refers to her by name) "...know you are here already and have throw all my things in the street!"

For years, 'She' had been the dark area he simply ignored as the only way to deal with it; now it had exploded, spewing the meagre contents of his personal life all over the street in the eyes of the neighbourhood, as in an air-raid or an earthquake. The anonymous callers had been very busy.

"I wonder she didn't do it years ago," I say flippantly, wondering how it is that she appears to be the only woman with which he does not have a *rapport*; how, out of all the women who have been infatuated with him, he managed to choose the wrong one. Or would it have happened anyway? It is something to think about.

"Why did you marry?"

"That's not a question!" he shouts. "Every man marries! The woman have her hour to take the man – she crazy for me, she make me troubles to marry her. Her family don't want me. That make me angry. In the end I marry her to fuck them. That is the story." With his hands he mimes the rope put around his neck which ritual pulled tight; describing it more graphically than words. "The True is One: A Man Must to Thinking Much before he Marry."

"I think *she* should have *thinking much* before wanting to marry you."

"Oh, that's for sure," he concedes, as if this was the chief service she might have rendered him.

29.

We arrive at Spirithoula's after midnight, tired and rather drunk, to find the door locked. He curses, "I tell her we coming…"

"Shall I knock?"

"No!" The sound would travel miles.

He goes down the steps to force the door of the ground floor storeroom; a match reveals a damp unkempt place with an iron bedstead and a straw palliasse on it. His face in the light of the match is grim, even a little frightening. "We sleep here tonight," he says, dragging the straw palliasse onto the floor, muttering.

"I think it's rather funny!" I am ready for any experience as long as it is with him.

"Funny!" He's angry with me now.

"I mean it doesn't bother *me*!" I say with cheerful resignation, forgetting that is an entirely British festival, like Afternoon Tea.

"Always my Black Destiny follow me. I have make everything in life – I have sleep on chairs, tables, rocks! Prisons… No woman can follow me."

"I can!" Convinced of it. He gives an irritating laugh, not his good laugh.

"You read too many books, I think."

"What's wrong with books?"

"They destroy the mind."

"You never read a book!" It's my turn to be scornful.

"I *am* a book." Unanswerable.

"Woomans…woomans…woomans." And he pulls me down onto the prickly straw mattress. I struggle to defend Romance but he crushes me without mercy, and sleeps like a dog. In books, lovers sleep in each other's arms. My arm has gone dead; when I pull it away he grunts and turns his back on me. Perhaps he's right about books…damn him!

At first light through the dingy window, he gets up like a sleepwalker, pulls on his trousers, goes into the garden, draws a bucket of water from the well and splashes his face in it. His muscled back is beautiful like an animal's; I want to stroke it, but dare not. He puts on his shirt, lights a cigarette and walks out of the garden without even a word or a glance. I don't exist. If I don't exist for him, I don't exist for myself. He can't do this to me. I want to run after him, and kick him. Instead I sit on the chair by Spirithoula's washtub, watching the garden fill with the brilliant light of the sun, flashing on dewdrops fat as tears.

*

For him, walking to town in the early light, the moods and emotions of the previous night evaporate in glorious steam, as the sun rises over the mainland mountains to blaze on the surface of the sea. He is new-minted daily, ready to use each day to the utmost as a gift to enjoy or spoil, according to whim or fortune.

*

Spirithoula, discovering me in the garden, throws up her hands, embracing and patting me. She drags a bucket of water out of the well and carries it to the room for me to wash. I wonder what to do next. The only thing is to drive to the town, to sit at the café and wait. Will he appear?

The waiting is like a cold death creeping over me. Yannis comes in, gives me a nod and goes out. Is he spying for Tasso? Later on, the telephone rings. The waiter answers, glances at me, and says "Nai", which sounds like no and means yes. He is checking up on me. What game is he playing? To think I have lived a whole winter in anticipation of this. Well, I am not sitting here waiting for him; it's un-British.

I pay for my coffee. The moment I get up from the table, he comes in, looking like an assassin in search of a job. I walk straight past him. "Where you going?" He is surprised.

"I'm going to find something to eat. I'm hungry!" – having had nothing to eat for nearly 24 hours.

121

"Wait! We go together." He takes me to a dim dark milk shop in a back street where no one will see us. I make the best of very sweet *baklava*; the silence between us is oppressive. For something to say, I ask, "What does *'kookla moo'* mean?" A man called it out as I passed on the scooter. (It translates as 'my doll'.)

"Who say that to you?" It's as if I have stuck a pin in him. "My God! I don't know what I going to do! Basters right and left. I cannot kill all!"

"Why are you so angry?"

"We are the Biggest Scandal in the *University!*" he says – meaning the town. "Don't you know that? People right and left talking about me and you."

"What business is it of theirs?" I am indignant at this intrusion into my emotional life.

"Of course is their business." For him there is no doubting it. "In this place everything is everybody's business, from the moment they be born to the moment they be die. Is very normal." In England it is normal to know nothing of your neighbours.

"Are you the first man in this place to leave his wife?"

"Of course no!"

"You haven't exactly been an exemplary husband, have you? What about Colette, Manette, Ursula…"

"Shut up. They were not like you are with me. People know that." Silence.

"Do you want me to go?"

"Go where?"

"Back to England."

"You only just arrive. Why you want to go?" His voice is full of suspicion.

"I *don't!*"

"Well, then. *Sit down where you sitting,*" *he says* – their version of 'stay where you are'. It doesn't clarify the situation, but makes me feel better.

30

Spring in the Mediterranean – wild irises the blue of a summer twilight, asphodels like pink feathers floating under the olive trees. Hot sun, cold shadow, rain falling in stair rods; houses impregnated with an invincible dampness. When the sun shines, clothes festoon the trees, shoes decorate sunny walls, mattresses propped on chairs stand outside every cottage door, blankets and sheets are draped over the branches of trees, windowsills and balconies, and the huge black umbrellas are hung out to dry.

At Spirithoula's, I sleep in my clothes to keep them dry, and to be warm alone in the bed. He dare not come here. I drive to the town every morning, conspicuous on the Lambretta, prim as Queen Victoria, with my nose in the air, trying not to come a cropper in the pot holes. The Lambretta has become a millstone round my neck. I wish I had never thought it a good idea.

"My sisters bother me much!" he says. He has always been the Black Sheep, the most likely to bring the family into disrepute. Fortunately they live in Athens. They telephone him at the café, and a shouting match ensues; he slams down the phone, only to pick it up, dial the number and start shouting again. It is an opera, the music loud and emotional, the libretto in a foreign language, and he gives only hints as to the plot.

"They say I must to go back in my house – for the h'onnor of the family." He makes it sound like the gravy boat of a once distinguished dinner service. "I say I *never* going back in my house. Of course, I caring for my childrens – I look after them, but I never going back in that house! I have *my* h'onnor!" His own gravy boat?

When I suggest that if she threw him out, it must mean that she doesn't want him back, he explodes. "Of course she want! The woman never let go of the man…and divorce is not possible in Greece."

All of a sudden, it has got so complicated. Where I do stand in this drama? Have I a leading role, or a bit part, and how long is the performance likely to last? All I came for is 'to Be Enjoy'.

In back street taverns he has emphatic conversations with friends who make that circular movement with the hand that has so many nuances. They worry that he is angry, and drinking too much. They look at me not unkindly, but since I am without their language, they presume I am deaf as well as mute, and because I am 'in love', mad as well. They don't condemn him for not being able to live with a wife – they are realists. They don't condemn him for going with foreign women when he attracts them so easily and knows their languages. He provides their entertainment, expanding their dreams and fantasies. *What's the French for fiddle-di-dee?* The poetical aspect of Love, which we make so much of, means nothing to them, which makes me indignant, for it is the sincerity of my emotions that makes them alright.

All these conversations end with the reiterated phrase, "*Ma ta pethiá,* Tasso...*ta pethiá...*" The children. As he doesn't keep domestic hours, he hardly ever saw them at home, but they come to the café in the afternoons where they are sure to find him making his pictures. They haven't appeared since the day she threw his stuff into the street. They are the only weapon she has, but it has a sharp point, and he is on the end of it.

No question now of 'to Be Enjoy'. At the Bar Greco I sit at a table in the corner; he stands at the bar looking down the street. He doesn't make his pictures – has nothing to sell, no money.

Suddenly he sees the two young children walking up the empty afternoon street. He does not rush out to them. They enter the café; a very self-possessed girl of ten holding her little brother by the hand. He indicates a table with a nod of the head; they sit down. The waiter brings cream cakes and glasses of water; they eat with quiet dignity, asking no questions, while he stands at the counter watching them. He orders the waiter to give them some pocket money as he has none, and after asking them if they are okay, he sends them off home with another box of cream cakes for which he cannot pay. As she gets up from the table, the girl looks towards me. I am sitting in the farthest corner from him, nothing to connect me with him; she has seen him with foreign women many times but the look she gives me tells me she understands everything. Taking her little brother by the hand, she leaves with the same composure with which she entered.

His fears evaporated, he raises his arms exuberantly, "And so – No Problem!"

"What is that supposed to mean?" I almost hate him for that child's look.

"Nothing! No Problem! But we must to keep a little bit out of 'the Eye of the People', that's all."

The Eye of the People? I visualize a large optician's sign with him and me stuck like flies in the middle of it. As the only girl driving a scooter on this parochial, pesty little island, how do I stay out of the Eye of the People?

*

The days are hot, the nights cool and damp. It rains often. The taverns on the beach are not open yet so every night we go to the Cottage Night Club to dance to the roar of the jukebox and eat the eternal *plat de nuit*, bicycle tubes in tomato sauce. We dance with furious abandon in the tiny space between the tables where the small audience, who know about us, watch like cows as we whirl about in improvised dances to the squiggly semi-tones with passionate lyrics:

You are my LIFE/ my DAWN/my RUIN!

You have opened a FIRE in my HEART!

Don't TYRANNIZE me BECAUSE you LOVE me!

AAaa-ach! THE PAIN!

That last scream – AAaa-ch! The pain! – says it all.

Then down the dark road between the olive trees to Spirithoula's and love. But what makes him leave to walk back to the town to finish the night sleeping outside the tavern near his work shed?

"That way I be in my job before the others!"

"But why go?"

"I must. If the police find me with you, they send me to the jail."

31.

There is a change in our relationship; it has blossomed but what it amounts to, I am not sure. Either I am supposed to know without asking, or what he feels is his own business and none of mine. A physical exchange is not enough for me, I want words, but all he will say is, "To stay with one wooman and no be tired is a miracle." I want more than that, but he puts his finger to his lips: "Sssh... don't say anything. The important thing is one: we are here now."

I lean out of the window as he goes through the gate, and drop my shoe on his head. He picks it up and throws it into the hedge opposite. I watch the red glow of his cigarette moving away from me in the darkness. Next morning, under Spirithoula's puzzled eyes, I search for my shoe in the grass by the side of the road.

The grass gets greener and greener, the sun gets hotter. I sit in it with the lizards and cats, taking hope and strength from it. In the mornings, the smell of orange blossom; at night the bittersweet scent of wisteria. The tourist season is beginning; the waiters are rewinding the metal chairs with plastic ribbon.

When the 'Tourists' appear, white flesh bared to the sun, the people of my country of origin, I see them with different eyes now from the no-man's land of my situation. What can they know of this place in a couple of weeks? Blue sea, flowers, the toothless smile of a peasant woman, the instant brotherhood of a waiter plying them with ouzo and cold chips? But what is the advantage of seeing the face behind the mask of this beautiful island?

The tourists arouse him to opportunism again. After he finishes his job, he sits at the café drawing out the sketches first in pencil, then in ink, putting in the washes. He finishes them off, mounts them on card in the bookshop, pressing them under a load of books. After an hour he says, "We are ready for action!" We drive to a hotel, where he makes his exhibition, and gets up the money to Be Enjoy.

Life is just getting back to normal, whatever that is, when Fate throws another spanner in the works.

126

"You must to go to the Police Station," he says as I approach the café table where he is working.

"Why?"

"I don't know."

"Who said I must?"

"*They.*"

"*Who?*"

"The Police!"

"How do you know?"

"Because they tell me."

"Why do they tell you?"

"Because you are with me." It doesn't seem very official "Anyway, if they ask you about me – *make the party of the stupid.*"

Bureau d'Etrangers had a sinister sound; I couldn't see what I had to fear as a British subject, citizen of the United Kingdom, but my heart was pounding as I climbed the flight of steps to the door of the Police Station, guarded by a policeman with the physique of a Greek Statue. I had begun to notice the discrepancy between the Ideal and the Real.

I stood holding my passport in my hand; nobody knew what I had come for, neither did I. I was about to go away again when a man coming out of an office noticed me and called me by name. I had never seen him before. How did he know my name? He was not in uniform, but his intensely virile appearance gave an unpleasant idea of force rather than authority. His manner was courteous enough as he ushered me into the room from which he had just emerged; a high bare room unadorned except for a calendar showing the wrong date, and two large photographic portraits of the King and Queen of Greece, smiling resolutely as monarchs have to do. Sitting at a desk with nothing on it except an old pen rack supporting a biro and a chewed pencil was an individual with a pallid face, boot button eyes and thin dark moustache: the Chief of Police.

"Your passport, pliss," said the interrogator, taking charge of the situation as the man behind the desk had no English. *Her Britannic Majesty's Secretary of State requests and requires in the Name of Her Majesty…This Passport contains 32 pages.* He looked at them all, handed it to the Chief of Police, who did the same.

"Why you come in Greeze?" It seemed an odd question.

"Because I like it." I couldn't think of a better reason.

"You have money?"

This vulgar enquiry shocked me. "Of course."

"How much moneys?"

With proper hauteur I replied, "A hundred and fifty pounds in travellers' cheques."

"Let me see, pliss"

I dug them out of my bag. He counted them. The Chief counted them. They were handed back to me. "Thank you."

"Pliss," said the brutal young man, maintaining a scrupulous courtesy that did not look natural to him and might suddenly stop. The two men discussed me in Greek. I recognised Tasso's name, and watched attentively as my interrogator mentally arranged his next question in English. The Chief dived under his desk to blow his nose loudly. My interrogator, placing his hand on the breast of his leather jacket, began with: "I am a friend of Mr Tassos…" It seems everybody is a friend of Tassos, even his enemies "…and I am a gentleman. I not like to have to ask this question of a woman." He would say 'lady' if he were a gentleman. "Why is Mr Tassos away of his house these many days?"

Making *the party of the stupid* as instructed, I looked at him blankly. "Why don't you ask him?" I said, adding, with an arrogance that only blooms once in a Greek police station, "It is not my business to give you information about *Mr* Tassos"

Confused by my logic, he said, "You mean you don't know?"

My passport was returned to me. I was told to go. Relieved, and rather pleased with myself, feeling I had behaved as a British person should, I hurried off to find Tasso.

Listening to my account, Tasso is more concerned to know who is 'him who claims to be a friend of his'.

"Is that him?" he asks, indicating a man in a leather jacket buying cigarettes at the kiosk near where we are sitting.

"Yes!"

"He follow you."

"Don't be silly…why should he follow me?"

"To see if you come to me."

"We're not criminals!" I am frightened now, and struggling to keep a British sense of proportion.

"In a way, yes…" he says. He is Greek, and this is Greece.

"Surely, the police can't force you to return to your house, if you don't want to?"

"No! I never going back in my house. My No is No!" He is emphatic. "They don't put me in the jail, because of my sister's husband – him a Big Shot. But we must to be careful…" In other words *to stay out of the Eye of the People.* "I know what we going to do. We take the scooter and we go."

"Go where?"

"Athens!"

"Athens – on the scooter? That's miles and miles. Isn't it all mountains?"

"A few – but they make the roads new now. We go straight…straight…like an h'errow."

"Hero?" It sounded heroic.

"Hero!" He is irritated by my obtuseness.

"Arrow?"

"Yes – that's what I say!"

I collapse into the relief of laughter.

32.

We take the afternoon ferry to the mainland and set off into a landscape cleaved asunder, boiled and put back together at the creation of the world, crawling through it on a scooter, as relative to it as an insect. There is no traffic other than a few sheep and goats, one old woman in black by the side of the road like a musical crotchet escaped from a vast oratorio. The scooter climbs the twisting mountain road like a goat, and descends like a bird. Tasso starts to sing a strange wild song "*Aetos! Megali Mou Aetos!* The song of the Eagle!" he says, pointing to a great bird circling in the sky above us.

We drive for hours in the blazing sun, Tasso with his head wrapped in a towel, me with a sun hat tied on with a scarf. At sundown we arrive at the only town in the area, driving into the main square at the hour of the evening *voltá* with the townsfolk promenading up and down. As we climb stiffly off the scooter under the Memorial Clock, the sunset gun goes off, and the band starts playing the National Anthem. As we stand to attention, I am taken by a giggling fit. Tasso frowns sideways at me for making a spectacle of myself. "I can't help it!" I gasp. Raising my head to the sky to stop the flow of giggles in my throat, I see three storks standing on the roof of the building opposite. The surprise cures me.

Cursing his 'Black Destiny' again, we stay the night in a dilapidated Turkish-style doss-house in the market area. "I have no money for better..." Watched by the speculative eyes of the man who gives him a key, I follow Tasso up the creaking wooden stairway, past a poster on the wall of a plump lady in décolletage and button boots reclining on a chaise longue, cherubs swirling around her head, with the legend '*Perfumes for the Handkerchief*' in French. The room at the end of the wide corridor is just big enough for the bed which we crawl onto from the door, and sleep like the dead until four in the morning, when the sound of cartwheels on the cobbles outside wakes us as the market begins to set up.

During the night the corridor has filled with improvised beds like a hospital in the Crimea. Horny hands support piratical heads, as snores ricochet off the walls, and coughs and spittings come from the direction of the facilities, one tap and a lavatory with two places to put your feet. I quickly follow Tasso down the stairs, past the lady serene in her button boots attended by her cherubs. "We must to drive as much as possible in the cool," he says.

Mountains give way to orange and lemon groves, followed by tobacco fields, the road twists like a snake along the shoreline, and is filled with donkeys, carts, wide-hipped women with bundles on their heads; buses lurch out of blind bends. Bridges spanning the watercourses are decorated with black tyre marks, the railings twisted into grotesque shapes; and the latest wrecks lie like dead tortoises in the ravine below.

Darkness comes down. Lorries now covered with coloured lights hurl toward us like rabid Christmas trees. "How much further!" I ask in desperation as the promontory pushing out from the land, alive with twinkling lights, is never the one he is looking for.

"Five minutes more,' he keeps saying. "We must to get to Roula – she will give us a bed."

At a Tourist Pavillion set in a garden of pine trees at the edge of the sea, we enter by the kitchen where the large woman at the stove screams at the sight of us. "*Pethiá mou*! My Children!" hugging us in a hippopotamus embrace. She used to keep the café near Spirithoula's where I took my coffee in the mornings of the summer before this one.

Plying us with food, she listens avidly as Tasso explains our story. She cannot give us a room, the guest house is full, but she gives us blankets to make ourselves cots out of the canvass chairs in the garden. We sleep to the gentle swishing of the sea, waking in the early morning to a sky suffused with apricot, and a cat curled up on my feet. As the sun threatens the backs of the mountains, we get on the move again, joining the new main highway into Athens, still under construction and without shade; the nearer we get to the city, the hotter it gets, like a furnace door opening in our faces.

At the flap of taverna tablecloth in a pool of shade, we throw ourselves off the scooter and drink two bottles of beer each. He looks at me critically. "You cannot be in Athens like that."

"Like what?"

"In pants."

I change into a frock in the smelly lavatory, but a girl driving a scooter in a dress is not right either; faces peer at us in astonishment from passing cars, with guffaws and obvious comment on a man riding pillion to a girl. Tasso, getting more and more furious, starts fooling about playing an imaginary banjo, anything to entertain the audience, and 'save his face'.

When I stop at the first traffic lights, he says, "Why you stop! Go on!"

"It's the traffic lights!"

"Never mind. Go on!" he orders, wanting to escape the grinning faces.

At the next junction, he shouts, "Turn left here."

"I can't – it's no entry!"

"Never mind – go there!" He has no idea of the rules. *When did he ever live by the rules?*

We drive around in the mad circus of Omonia Square, looking for the lead off to the hotel of a 'good friend of him', where we will get 'a special price'; an old place with a birdcage lift, and smelling of mortadella from the shop next door.

We sleep till the evening, then he starts phoning around the family. After a shouting match with his sister, Antigone, he slams the phone down. "She angry much. We must go to the theatre to find Marina." If Antigone is against him, that should make Marina for him, exploiting the rivalry between them.

At an open air theatre in the main park, the stage door is between two bushes. "Wait here, I better to go alone." Through the trees I see the bright lights and can hear singing. He is soon back, looking less confident. "For sure I am in troubles with my sisters. You know something – Marina have sent tickets for my wife and kids to come in Athens. They here with her."

132

With no doors open to him, and little cash, we wander round the great market halls near the hotel where the stalls are heaped with bloody bulls' heads and piles of dismembered animal parts, tubs full of entrails, blood everywhere. The Fish Hall presents a more aesthetic picture of octopus, with their tentacles neatly folded back like pearly pink flowers; crabs in tubs with orange bodies and emerald claws clamber over each other; men stagger past, bearing the gleaming grey-black body of a swordfish on their backs.

At the hotel he discusses our problem with the two elderly brothers who own the place and spend their waking lives at the ancient wooden reception desk. They gaze at me over their spectacles in a kindly way, full of wonder and perplexity, even fantasizing a little, perhaps.

After two days in this hot, unattractive, legendary city, he says, "We go home. Can you cash one traveller cheque?" To ask for money of a woman is another humiliation.

At four o'clock in the morning, we drive away from the city. We sleep again in the garden at Roula's – a wild night filled with flying pine needles – and set off at first light to cover as much ground before sun-up and the buffeting hot wind sandpapering the skin and cracking my lips. In the mountains, a small boy minding goats doubles up with laughing.

"Why is he laughing?"

"He never see a woman to drive a scooter. He going to tell the village tonight."

And on the teeming main road a man suddenly shouts, "Christine Keeler!" I am outraged at being identified with the latest British sex scandal.

"What do you expect?" he says.

At a petrol station, the man at the pump raises one finger. "Ein? Won? Una?" to show his familiarity with foreign tourists.

"Fill it up," says Tasso in Greek.

The man opens his eyes wide. "You Greek?"

"More Greek than you!" shouts Tasso, urging me to get out of here before "I kill him and we have trouble for sure!"

In a wild stretch of pure scenery with the sun getting low in the sky, and nothing on the horizon but a nomad shepherd's wattle hut and a billboard pronouncing MISKO MACARONI IS BEST, the scooter konks out. We are far from the next town with no garage for miles.

Four small boys and an old man materialize out of the emptiness as if grown there in some vegetable way; they gather to stare at us as if we had dropped from Mars. Tasso makes the boys push the scooter to get it to start, but nothing happens. The old man is offering us the hospitality of his hut, when the only Patrol Car in a 100 kilometres stops by us. The chap gets out, cleans the sparking plug, and tells us to buy a new one in the next town where we end up spending the night in another Turkish-style doss house.

As the ferry noses in toward the island, Tasso, crosses himself with relief. "Honestly, darr-ling – I cannot be anywhere but here..."

33

High season now – jukeboxes blaring, waiters pounding to and fro with loaded trays; the perpetual sunlight by day, the emotional fireworks by night, the fizzing, stinging, banging shower of coloured sparks. If being with him creates its own excruciating tension, the strain of the tautened string, it has its own relaxation – while spinning through the air, I have come to roost. All I want is to be with him. Each day is a new minted coin. Will it come up heads or tails? I know the dangers of happiness now.

At the taverns on the beach every night, we dance the *Hasapiko*. I follow him step for step, like Siamese twins. Sweet to wake up beside him in the rickety bed, in one of Michaeli's cell-like rooms with the sun forcing its fingers under the door and round the closed shutters. The sea so near is irresistible, I extract myself carefully, half wishing the tentacles to close around me again. No – he sleeps. The door scrapes on the cement floor, the air is warm and dry; the sea blazes like a shield under the sun. The empty tables flap their cloths idly, the waiters sleep on their camp beds under the trees.

I slide into the fresh chilling water to be suspended in it; below me the fish parade in dignified silence, and rainbow shadows lilt over the sandy floor. An almost compulsive desire to dissolve in this airy fusion of sea and sky invades me. Is it the answer? What is the answer?

Egoism draws me back to the room to see if he has missed me. No, he still sleeps. I stand by the bed lonely, disappointed, until an arm reaches out, pulling me down, down, down to struggle in the poetry of the flesh while it lasts. He tastes my skin, puzzled at its saltiness, but it is behind the walls of flesh I seek him. *Let me in! Don't just take, and go your way.*

"I know what you want," he murmurs, without my having said a word.

"What do I want?"

"You want to be loved for sure."

Yes, that's what I want. That's all I want.

135

*

Walking towards the wine shop, carrying his Blackthorn stick which he told me to bring to town, I suddenly feel it grabbed from behind. Turning, I find a strange woman hanging onto it. We tug the stick back and forwards between us for what seems a very long time – time enough to notice her pale skin, her conventional hennaed hair, and that she is a little shorter than I am. When people stop to watch, she rises on tip-toe and, summoning the saliva into her mouth like a snake, spits at me. The droplets fall between, us glinting in the sunlight. She lets go of the stick so suddenly I almost fall over, and walks quickly away – a thin, taut figure, disappearing by the edge of the Arcade. I walk on as if ploughing through deep sand, my body almost unmanageable; my mind clear as crystal.

In the wine shop he is leaning against the counter. As I pass him, making my way carefully toward the table in the corner, I say in a dazzling sort of way, as you would deliver a line on the stage, "I think I have just met your wife."

His face registers nothing, but I have his whole attention. "What happen? Tell me."

I tell him. "I thought you said she never went anywhere."

"She go to the cinema sometime or to baptize her hair."

"Baptize her hair?"

"Colouring! To the hairdresser!" he says irritably. "Anyway, she don't know which is you – she have recognise the *bastouni*." The Blackthorn stick I bought for him in Harrods; it has become part of his persona.

At that moment, the brutal young interrogator from the police station walks into the shop. "*Yia sou*, Tasso!" he says, greeting him in a friendly way. He buys a packet of cigarettes at the counter and goes out. Tasso looks after him with his *thinking much* expression, the tip of his thumb held lightly between his teeth

"They will send you away," he murmurs thoughtfully.

"Who?"

136

"The police!"

"What have they got to do with it? It's none of their business!"

"In Greece everything is their business. Come on, let's get out of here."

Taking the scooter, we drive out of town. "If he want to follow – let him!"

Halfway up a steep road twisting through terraced olive groves, we run out of petrol. He flings the scooter in the ditch in disgust. I had told him it needed petrol, he thinks it runs on nothing. "Never mind! We take the way of the donkeys."

A path of carefully laid cobbles leads up between the terraced olive trees; we come to the spring, where women are filling plastic demijohns with water. They stare at us, but give back the traditional greeting, "*Xerété!*" *Be Happy.* If only we could!

The path brings us right into the middle of the village and a full-blown wedding celebration. "For crazy!" he curses, diving into the nearest empty *cafenion.* "I forget this is the day for the weddings."

Through the open doorway, I watch the village women in their best costumes of multiple skirts, velvet bodices and kerchiefs on their heads, swaying gracefully in the ring dance to the energetic noise of a fiddle, guitar and drum.

"Did you go through all this?"

"I was drunk. I don't remember anything. They looking for me around the tavernas on that day."

"You mean you forgot you were getting married?"

"No, I remembered. I thinking to jump a ship an' get the hell out of it. Better that! But... in the end I don't want to make her sorry in front of the people. Now the God pay me – and her."

Outside in the little square, the wedding couple circulate among their guests, the bridegroom wearing an ill-fitting black suit, loud tie and red socks, while the bride, in a voluminous lace crinoline, maintains the unsmiling pride of Queen of the Day – or is she marrying the wrong man?

The line of dancing figures passes the open door, led by a burly fisherman leaping indefatigably like a salmon, hopping and twisting, throwing back his head, drawing the women after him with a red cotton scarf. Where else does a man live so freely and expressively within such a limited context?

I thought of Tasso's wife. *She* had existed in my mind as an invisible, unpredictable poltergeist. She had the bit labelled 'husband' as you might possess the pelt of a ferocious beast. I could not know the peculiar bitterness of being wife to such a man, but I could see that, though neither of us possessed him, if she sat tight on the nest, she had less to fear than I did.

The next day, a man walked up to me in the street. "I am of the police. You must go to the Aliens' Bureau." He spoke in a gentle way; he was not in uniform but I didn't doubt the authenticity of the message, which cleaved me like an axe. I did not say anything, but my eyes must have told him the wound had been received.

Tasso found me in the wine shop, he knew something had happened. When I told him, he was thoughtful. "This time we go together," he said. Locked in my own despair, I missed the significance of this.

I trail behind him up the steps to the police station. We are immediately shown into the office of the Chief, who stands up to shake hands with Tasso.

"The Chief is very good friend of me. He buy many of my pictures." *He hasn't mentioned this before.* The Interrogator is also present. The three men discuss my situation while I sit on a chair, understanding nothing and resenting everything; all men, all Greeks, all in collusion in disposing of me and my emotions as if they were of no value. I know Tasso is angry – why doesn't he shout now? He is all sweetness with them, turning to me, saying, "Honestly! The Chief is very kind to us!" as the Chief holds up a paper stamped with the purple indelible ink they mark the carcasses with in an abattoir.

"This paper say you must to leave tomorrow, but the Chief – because he is very kind to us – give you three days more." I remain unresponsive. "Smile a bit – say him thank you."

I can't. The bottom has dropped out of my world; I know I will not be allowed back. Can't they see I *won't* survive it? No, they know I *will* survive it. The Chief mumbles something, and dives beneath the desk to blow his nose.

"The Chief say you will thank him one day."

"I won't!" I believe in my emotions. What else have I to believe in? They are treating me like a parcel wrongly addressed, to be returned to sender, but I posted myself. This has to be the right address – there is no other.

Tasso shakes hands with the Chief and the Interrogator as if the matter has been settled to everybody's satisfaction. No oriental subtlety is available to me. I walk away expressing British indignation without saying a word. I hate them all.

34.

Michaeli has a room free. "We stay here till to you go – to hell with my job...with everything!"

Three days. I sit in the sun like an invalid for whom there is no hope of recovery. "Will you finish with me in three days?"

"I never finish with you in the rest of my life." It is a statement of fact, not sentiment. "I find the way to bring you back, don't fret. I am more angry that you – believe me!"

I do not believe him, and ask cynically if he is going to be St George, and kill the dragon to rescue the maiden. The idea appeals to him. "That's it exactly!" But this dragon has dull brown eyes, a little moustache, and all over its body are purple rubber stamps. What weapon can penetrate the armour of Authority?

I thread flowers through the thongs of my sandals, indulging in suicidal fantasies impossible to execute while there are a few hours, minutes, seconds, left to be with him at a table by the sea with a pink moon rising...

The afternoon drops off like a rock sliding into the sea, Time crumbling into the mummified dust of memories. Tomorrow I won't be in this place. Twilight whispers into darkness, the lights come on among the vine leaves. Yannis restlessly awaits a French girl from The Club. Panayoti cradles his guitar, singing softly. England won't be like this...

"I thinking much what you do there," he says, as if reading my thoughts. "You would be happy with me..." I would be happy being *un*happy with him. "Oh, that's for sure," he says, though I haven't said a word. "That is the Absolutely Thing you can't buy with money," he adds. "Didn't I tell you Love is pains the neck!"

Responding to the heavy music from the jukebox, he murmurs, "Oh, I like this on*e: Addio women, midnights and torturing griefs...*" He dances alone, a cigarette stuck between his lips. Some English tourists stop to watch. He takes no notice of them, this dance is for me. I know what is expected of me. Like a magician's assistant, I take the wine glass from the table and place it on the cement floor in front of him. He dances around it like a shaman, making the ritual movements of a forgotten mystery, going down on his knees; picks up the glass in his teeth, raising it until the wine runs into his mouth and down his vest and, jumping up, lets it smash on the floor; then, turning to his audience, of whom he has till now seemed unaware, says "To dance like that you must to be IN LOVE!"

"Oh, yes," murmurs one of the English women, her arms clamped tightly across her breast, "I *do* understand."

*

The journey back to England was easier than I anticipated; travelling anaesthetizes pain, and I was no longer in a fever of anticipation and hope. I had no hope.

"Will you tell me, said Alice, which way I should go from here?"

141

35.

Tasso was not given to conscious thought; his way was to act out his crisis in dramatic gestures which signalled to friends, foes and family the seriousness of it. He went to the barber to shave his head.

"All?" protested the barber.

"All!" shouted Tasso. Hadn't Achilles shaved his head when they wouldn't let him have the slave girl, the daughter of Briseis?

He emerged from the barber's shop looking like a criminal Buddhist monk. This startling effect did not repel '*the woomans*' – they came to him like flies and he sat with them outside the Bar Greco right in 'the Eye of the People' For years he had been subscribing (in his own way) to the moral code by not leaving his wife or deserting his children; he knew he could walk back into that house, but *she* had broken the last thread holding him to the marriage by throwing all his stuff into the street, making him *lose face* in his community.

The only way to by-pass the moral code was to establish a higher one – no less than 'the Absolutely Thing: True Love, a human right, surely, if you can win it? The problem was how to bring the English girl back. It was a hard nut to crack. The key to the situation lay with his sister, Antigone, and her husband, the Big Shot: the King and Queen of Spades. It wouldn't be easy convincing them of the value of one woman over another; he had to make them afraid.

He knew his sisters, and they knew him. A fierce tribal energy united them all, making them extract every last drop of blood and juice from every situation. They had inherited from the mother the fear that, with his temperament, he would come to a bad end; he must make them afraid *for him,* so that they would rush to save him – *from himself.* He must wait for the moment when emotion and incident combined to bring the blood up into his head.

Meanwhile, he dedicated his ego to 'the Absolutely Thing' by burning the contents of the Love Box – though some letters unaccountably survived. He sent a cryptic letter to England:

"An Angry man does not stay with his hands in his pockets. The time coming when you see what my Love mean."

36.

Saturday Night at the taverna on the beach, he was alone at a table with two glasses of wine – one for him, and one for *her* – and drank both. The season over, the nymphs departing gave a desperate melancholy to the voice of the jukebox. Three Greeks came by with a couple of French girls. He knew the men – one was an old enemy. He knew the girls too. They recognised him even without his hair and ran over to his table excitedly – "*Vous avez rasez la tête! C'est formidable! Comme un sauvage…*" – and, leaving the men, sat down with him. He knew the moment had come.

The Greeks demanded the return of the girls. Tasso said gently he wasn't keeping them…they were free. The girls, feeling the tension, became alarmed; he told them that they could stay with him or go to the others. It was obvious they preferred to stay with him. They trusted him.

"You see," said Tasso, "they prefer to stay with me…" at which one of the Greeks hit him across the face. The girls squealed. "*Mon dieu! Qu'est ce qui se passe!*"

"Do it again," said Tasso quietly. The man hit him again. Tasso did nothing. The Greeks, surprised, swaggered away to sit at another table. Tasso called the taxi that hung around waiting for business, put the girls into it, paid the driver and told him to take them back to The Club. Afraid and excited, they didn't want to leave him, hanging out of the window of the taxi as it drove away.

Tasso went back to his room at Michaeli's, changed into his work clothes, laid the blackthorn stick reverently on the bed. He would never use a weapon – too dangerous in his hands. He returned to the gap in the fence just in line with the table where the three Greeks were sitting quite off-guard, thinking he had gone and that his reputation was unfounded. He projected himself through the fence like a cannon ball, striking the table with his shoulder; men, chairs, tables, bottles, glasses crashed over with the impact.

The men recovered themselves with agility and sprang at him; hitting, kicking, punching they fell in a mass over the low wall onto the beach, going for each other like dogs. The waiter ran off to find the solitary policeman on duty at night. He was drinking ouzo in one of the taverna kitchens and, buttoning his tunic, he hurried slowly towards the action.

The fight had reached the pause before the kill. Tasso had a cut over one eye; the others in the same state. By instinct, all sensed the approach of the Law. The important thing now was to disappear. By the time the policeman reached the scene, he was relieved to see nothing but the overturned tables, chairs, broken bottles and glasses, and to listen to the waiters telling different versions of the event. All it amounted to was that a Spiro, a Costa and a Tasso had been fighting on the beach – but which Spiro, which Costa, which Tasso? These names abounded on the island. Every other man is a Costa, Spiro or Tasso…

Back in his room, Tasso examined his face in the little mirror. It was satisfactory, sufficiently cut about, lips swollen, the brows bloody. He changed his clothes, took up the blackthorn stick reverently and, entering the Beach Restaurant, danced a triumphant Zembekiko.

Next morning, he stayed around the town out of sight, receiving from Yanni the various versions of the fight – a fight with knives, two wounded, one in hospital not expected to live…the police looking round for him… Good. Just what he needed. He took the next ferry to the mainland, hitched a lift with a German in a Mercedes, and arrived in Athens in style.

Knowing Antigone would have heard of the fight over the police grapevine, and would be waiting for him to show up on her doorstep as he always did when in trouble, he purposely let her stew in her own juice for 24 hours. He knew she would be going around her kitchen swabbing the marble surfaces, keening "*Where* is my brother…*where* is my brother? *O Pónos Mou!* My Pain!"

The next evening she was still muttering over her knitting. The General told her to shut up. Then the dog barked in the garden, the doorbell rang; she leapt to it, flung it open. There he was, head shaved, chin unshaved, the cuts on his face now three times their original size. He had come – the battle could begin.

"You dare to come to my house like an assassin to disgrace my husband!" she cried, sweeping back into the saloni, alerting the General with her eyes that it was time to take a stand with her relative – she gave him full powers, but first she wanted to know if he had been to see his other sister, Marina. No, he wasn't that stupid when he wanted something from Antigone. Satisfied that he had come to her first when he was in need, she returned to the settee and took up her knitting.

The General, looking like an effigy of Stalin, enthroned on his armchair (even with his shoes off, he had the air of authority), reached for his worry beads; flicking them through his fingers, he said nothing. Antigone, the epitome of an enraged domestic goddess, continued to hurl abuse at her brother.

"You have disgraced our family, and the name of my husband!"

Tasso dismissed her rage. "I have come to speak eye to eye with Pericles." With him lay the power.

"Well?" said the General, acknowledging that the real business was between men.

Tasso began with all the sweetness of an oriental courtship. "The story with my house is finished. Whatever happen, I am never going back in my house."

"You leave your children for a *nereida*?" screamed Antigone, as if English and American girls had assumed the role of those nymphs of ancient times who stole away men's senses and left them idiots.

"Leave him to speak!" commanded the General, refusing to have his authority flouted; a man must seem to have command over a wife. They all knew they were performing a family ritual; the aggression they showed towards each other confirmed the bonds that united them must never be severed entirely.

"To stay in the Life, I need the English Girl. If she doesn't come back, my children will be without a father..." This was shorthand for his disappearing from the island; they would never see him again.

146

"The Ingleza!" Antigone threw her knitting aside, "She will leave you! They are all *putanas!*"

"I know the British. I don't make a mistake. This is the Absolutely Thing."

"So?" said the General, having told his wife to shut up again.

"Pericles, if you let her come back, I promise to you my children will have a father. Otherwise you never see me again." He held out a piece of paper with the telephone number of the island's Chief of Police.

The General, continuing to play with his worry beads, said, "Tomorrow."

"Pericles…please…tonight….I promise to you I will be honest."

Greek regarded Greek; a face had to be saved, *two* faces had to be saved. The General, taking the piece of paper, rose to his feet and padded to the telephone in the hall, with no loss of dignity even in his socks. The order given and received, he returned to his chair, reaching again for the worry beads,

"So tell me about the fight." A Greek loves a good fight

Returning to the island, Tasso had one more important call to make. For this occasion, he wore his black corduroy jacket and bought a trilby to cover the bristling nakedness of his head, and went to the police station. With his blackthorn stick, he tapped gently and reverently on the Chief's door, and was bidden to enter.

The Chief knew why Tasso had come, and shuffled a few papers about importantly. Tasso knew that he knew why he had come; most interviews between Greek and Greek are carried on with full knowledge of what the other is after.

The Chief sent the boy out for coffees. As they sipped at the tiny cups, they talked of many things: modern trends in society…divorce, for instance. Tasso expressed undying faith in the moral role of the police, admitting he had seen the inside of too many police stations in his life, but from now on intended to be a model citizen.

The Chief expressed the opinion that there was no need to interfere with a tourist so long as that person went out of the country every three months – even if they came back the next day. Finally, Tasso presented him with two of his best pictures. The Chief, though he had no opinion of art as an occupation, accepted them as a suitable gift

On his way out, Tasso paused at the top of the steps to light a cigarette and survey his kingdom, conscious of having risked it all for the sake of this new ideal, 'the Absolutely Thing'.

"For sure," he said to himself, "I am the King of the Good Basters!"

37

'Alice had got so much into the way of expecting nothing but out of the way things to happen, that it seemed quite dull and stupid for life to go on in the common way.'

*

At 10.30 every night, Dad says, "Well, I'm ready to turn in – I expect you are too."

I'm not – I wouldn't be. The night is only beginning there; which taverna is he entering or leaving? What record playing on the jukebox? With him, Life was lived with the freedom of birds, eating when hungry, sleeping when tired. Here, every day is the same, an eternal preoccupation with domestic things. "Have we got enough potatoes?" Dad says at breakfast. I shut myself up with my Greek records.

"I wonder what the neighbours make of that music?" he speculates with amusement.

At night in my room, I hear Dad going about his routine: a glass of milk for the tot of whisky, see the fire's alright, put the guard round it; open the front door, see if it's raining, take a deep breath of night air, close door, turn key, try the handle twice; ascending the stairs, the pause outside my door to say "Goodnight. Sleep well."

O Tassos – ils sont loin, maintenant, le clair de la lune et le bruit doux de la mer…un sentiment inoubliable m'attache à toi, Tasso.

Are you going to kill the bloody dragon?

We are having tea by the fire when Anthea, a neighbour, one of the 38 widows in this village, pops in "just to see if you need anything. But, of course, you have your daughter now. Will you be going back to Greece, do you think?"

Dad answers for me too readily and with too much satisfaction. "Oh, no, that's all over and done with!" – just managing not to add "Thank God!" *I hate him for it.*

Two minutes after she has gone, a telegraph boy passes down the lane on his bike, looking at the gates. He comes back to ours and stops…

"Hullo!" Dad says, "a telegram?" But I am already at the door.

"A telegram for Miss…" I have already taken it from him. "They're querying the text, Miss…"

"No need, I understand perfectly," as I read:

COM BAK DARLING THE DRAKON IS DED.

*

Father insists on coming up to London to see me off at the same station from which we departed for that holiday that was to do us both good, and consoles himself at his favourite Soho restaurant – situated, ironically, in Greek Street.

*

The ferry is full of Greeks returning from Germany, young Americans with backpacks, and a group of nuns in denim robes, leather belts and rosaries. On the deck at sunrise, one of the denim nuns stands at the rail, prayer book in hand, her eyes closed. As the sun rises above the mountains of the mainland, she throws up her head, the light glancing off her polished black skin. Is she a Christian or a pagan votary? What's the difference? Does it matter?

The ship seems to pass through an invisible barrier – impossible not to feel the thrilling certainty…at last, Real Life lies straight ahead.

PART II
'THE ABSOLUTELY THING'

"The 'Absolutely Thing' you don't buy with nothing..." Tassos

1.

"What a life you are living! It sounds like a dream – quite beyond my imagining. Still, it is a marvellous liberation of spirit for you, and I am delighted...and that, reading between the lines, you are enjoying exuberance without intoxication. Dancing in public, and swimming at seven in the morning!

Write frequently for I like to hear particulars of your dream life. Your letters seem to take about a fortnight. I was getting rather anxious I must admit...what with all the news of earthquakes in that part of the world...

Enjoy yourselves!

Love Dad.

After the first month of our conjugal existence, he looked at the place and said, "I will get Maria to come and clean up. She will like the money."

I don't shake the mats, sheets and blankets every morning, as they do. But I have one virtue: I make the pictures, and he signs them when he comes home.

The first time Maria came in to clean up, she was as shy of me as I was of her. But she didn't treat me as a simpleton, or patronise me with instant Greek affection. She makes our inhabited space look like a dentist's waiting room in a country where you would never wish to have a toothache.

I have come to recognise the delicate way she has of asking to be paid. The front door is always open, so I have more light when

151

working at the table in the hall. I shut it when it rains and the water comes in just the same.

Suddenly I am aware that I am not alone; turning my head, I see Maria's two children framed in the doorway, a girl of six and a boy of four, regarding me and my occupation with large toffee eyes. When they see that I have noticed them they advance with the vast solemnity of an infant priest and priestess performing a ritual with which they have been charged, carrying a fresh egg in each hand.

A demoralising fact is that I have got nowhere with the language. If I ask him what a word means, he says, "Something."

"I know it means *something,* I'm asking *what!*"

He counters with, "Who say that to you anyway?"

It doesn't seem worth pursuing a language into a minefield. I give up. The truth is, he doesn't want me to be able to speak to anyone, or for anyone, especially men, to speak to me. His friends ignore me politely and, saying "She doesn't understand, does she?" speak freely in front of me, man to man. It stimulates my intuitive faculties like a blind person seeing colours with her fingers. I surprise him with how much I *have* understood. "You like me," he says, "one word give you the whole idea." I have heard him telling his cronies that I am *exipnos*, literally 'awake', meaning 'clever', so that he does not 'lose face', having chosen to defy the rules of his society, by living with an idiot. He is breaking new ground by living with me, when he has a wife and two children in the town, for whom he is still doing the shopping. The truth is I can only be received in his world through him. He knows the territory, while I am on a voyage of discovery.

Even after five years, the peasants around the house perceive me, a foreign girl, as a superficial creature, born on another planet where all women do is play; never grow up or grow old on the realities which coarsen their skins and hands. They stroke me indulgently as if I were a child, call me *koukla,* meaning doll, and ask him if I can cook. Of course I can cook! Dad, at this moment, is missing my cooking. But it is no use cooking the British way; it has to be redolent of garlic, swimming in olive oil, and the colour of blood from the tomato paste. When I ask him how much oil to use, how much garlic, he simply says, "Enough." *What the hell is enough?*

He does the shopping and leaves it in the wine shop. I have to drive to town to collect it. I spend a lot of time at the corner table, reading and writing letters, waiting for Tasso to reclaim me like a piece of left luggage.

2.

This morning, looking down on the peaceful scene from our balcony, I watched a man trying to get on his donkey. He had tied it to one of the cypress trees. A loop of rope formed the stirrup, but the moment he got his foot into it, the donkey started teetering round the trunk of the tree with the man hopping on one leg, shouting and cursing. It was so comic I had to move inside and watch through the window. When he got his foot out of the loop, he tied the donkey's face right up against the tree so it couldn't move. When the man finally got up onto the high wooden saddle, he had to lean so far forward to untie the rope from the tree that he could barely reach it; the moment the donkey was released, it took off up the path at a gallop, with the man clinging on for dear life. I had witnessed a donkey's revenge.

Tasso comes home saying he too has had a "very comic morning. All day comedy…they give me the job of cutting off the electricity to the houses where the bills no paid. But today it was the Bank Manager, he a very-good-friend of me, even if he know I never going to put money in his bank. He buy my pictures so is no kind of me to take away the electricity. He lose face if peoples understand that, and if some *baster* tell him that I do that to him, maybe he no buy anymore my paintings. So I going to the bank. He very happy to see me, he call for coffee, we talk a bit – but in the end I must to say I am obliged to cut off the electricity to his house. Of course, he send the boy 'right quicko' to pay the bill. And now he like me more than ever…" he adds with satisfaction. To have a person of importance under obligation to you is one of the first principles of Greek Life.

"The next was my *Bootcher,*" he explains, crossing himself for emphasis. "I owe him too much money – you know that." Without credit he couldn't juggle his obligations. "So is Big Problem, because is Saturday, and if I take out the fuse he going to be without electricity for his fridgerators till to Monday. I take out the fuse, put it in my pocket and go into the shop. He greet me very happy, no thinking anything until he don't hear anymore the sound of the fridgerators. Then he look at me and see my uniform and understand everything. He come at me like a bull with the big knife in his hand."

"What did you do?"

"You think I going to be afraid of my *bootcher*? I put up my hand like a traffics policeman. 'Don't try that with me, Spiro. You lucky is me and not some other one. I know your pocket full of money. Go to pay now before the office close – I wait you in the taverna opposite. Bring me the paper and I put the fuse back – otherwise you lose everything.' He go like a sheep. That's why they give me that job, because I make the basters to pay their bill right quicko."

"But the best was the last," he goes on. "You going to smile for the rest of your life! One crazy old woman – she bother the company much. She say the meter go too fast. They send someone to check – there is nothing wrong. Still she bother them – so they send me. I look at the meter – nothing wrong, but I don't say that. I say, 'Yes – you *very right* – is something wrong, but is no use to bother the Company. They *never going to fix*, because *they don't want to fix it*. But *I* show you what you going to do.' I tell her to bring me a glass of water, and a piece of paper. I put the glass of water on the meter and the paper on top of the glass. I tell her, 'Keep like that and you won't have any more trouble.' She so happy she ready to kiss me! She give me a koniak and a 100 drachs, the poor thing…she won't bother the Company no more. You see how much I worth to that job – never mind if I take time to sit down with the Tourists!"

3.

Philippa, my old school chum, sends me the books she thinks I need in a foreign country: Shakespeare, the Bible, Keats' poems. You cannot buy English books here. I collected another from the post office this morning, a book on Greek cookery in English. "I saw this in a bookshop and wondered if it might be useful…"

When he appears in the wine shop I say, "I want to make *dolmades* today!"

He picks up the book. "Greek Cooking by an English one – I don't think if is any good."

"Bring me the stuff. I want to try."

He goes away and comes back with the ingredients, plonks them on the table, crosses himself – "The God know what we going to eat today" – and departs.

I drive home in a rage, open a bottle of retsina, prop open the book – already regretting my choice of a recipe for cabbage leaves stuffed with rice and mincemeat in a lemon sauce.

When he comes home, I am exhausted, rather tight and ready to be aggressive if he says anything. He doesn't. Going into the kitchen, whistling through his teeth, he lifts the lid of the casserole. "Oh, looks *vunderful*! Let's eat. I ready to die of hungry."

He pronounces them the best dolmades he has ever tasted, and he doesn't make compliments to me anymore. Did he ever?

In my letters to Dad, I tell him as much as I dare about our Greek life. I must have made too much of this domestic triumph, as it evokes a curious response: "*I don't like to think of you as an oriental slave! Any more of that attitude and you may have to make a firm decision – to leave him! You can always come home. Don't hesitate. Let him do his own cooking and see how he likes it.*"

What has got in to him? Well, I know – he has to do *his* own cooking.

During the siesta, I dream of him standing by the garden gate holding out a steaming platter of the Roast Beef of Olde England. He has been very patient. He's over 70 now, I'm over 30; Time is running out and Love a terrible thing.

4.

Christmas Eve and raining so hard, the water rushing down the street came straight into the wine shop, reaching the legs of my table in the corner. *Kyria* Roula swept it out with a broom, *pó-pó-pó-ing* all the time. This meaningless ejaculation covers the full chromatic scale between comedy and tragedy.

As the evening wore on, with customers coming in, struggling to close their big black umbrellas, *Kyria* Roula's *pó-pó-pós* extended to päa-paa-paa! and finally to paaw! paaw! paaw!

Tasso, often without money at this time of night, eyes my umbrella, the new one I bought in Italy. "No!" I say, putting my hand protectively on it. "It's mine!"

"Why don't you want to sell before you lose?"

"It's *my umbrella!*"

He shrugs, mystified at my attitude, and calls up a glass of wine.

A friend comes in. "*Yia sou,* Tasso." Coming over to our table, he too eyes my umbrella. "That's a very nice umbrella," he says.

Tasso immediately says, "You want to buy?"

"How much?" the man asks.

"NO! It is MY umbrella."

They both look at me as if I were being excessively possessive.

The door flies open to admit three men with a violin, an accordion and an umbrella. They take up a Breughalesque stance and bray like donkeys the carol *Ai Vassilis echété* – St. Basil is coming – their version of a Christmas carol. Mr Sotiris gives them money, they go.

Next to enter are the loony boy who sells lottery tickets and the simpleton with dreamy eyes and the round nose of a clown who helps in the cemetery, both wearing trappers' hats with the flaps down. The tall one strums tunelessly on the guitar. The simpleton has a toy instrument played by turning a handle; the handle comes off and someone has to put it back on for him. They count their money at a table before leaving. There is only the one carol, it fills the town on this night. It isn't like Christmas at home, no puddings or presents. New Year is their festival.

New Year's Eve, around ten o'clock. Tasso comes into the wine shop carrying a large round baking tray – a funny thing to be carrying at this time of night.

"What's that for?"

"For the Turkey," he says, pronouncing it 'Torquay' like the English seaside resort.

"A turkey? For us? How are we going to eat a whole turkey?"

"Never mind, it is the custom. Come – we must to hurry. I don't want to lose the torquay!"

"Where is it?"

"At my butcher's."

We walk smartly down the dark alley to where the butcher's shop is firmly closed.

"Stakti kai barooti!" (Ashes and gunpowder!)

"You expect him to open at this time of night?" I say, laughing at the sight of him standing outside the shuttered shop holding the empty baking tray.

Greeks have the foresight of newts; like children they grasp the present, never wasting it as we do by relating it to the past and the future, so that the present moment isn't grasped at all.

Next morning he gets up early and disappears on the scooter to dig the butcher out of bed to open the shop and give him the turkey. "I have pay for it, for crazy!" He brings it back, peels a mountain of potatoes, puts them in the dish with the bird, and what he calls 'sheep's butter'.

We have only a small gas ring. "How are we going to cook it?"

"We take to the baker's." He ties the whole thing in a cloth and carries it out to the car.

During the night the car has developed a flat tyre. "*Stakti kai barooti!*" He opens the back to get out the spare. The spare tyre is flat too. "You didn't take it to the garage last time," I remind him.

"We must to take the scooter!" He drives. I'm on the pillion, struggling to hold the turkey in the dish.

It is a day of champagne sunlight with a peacock blue sea; the mountains of the mainland crested with snow; the town festive with people strolling in their best clothes – men mostly. The brass band thumps about the streets, snorting like wild horses. The bus has two balloons tied to its nose. Groups of men on street corners are playing the coin game, throwing up three coins and betting on the fall-out, a ritual for this day. A pile of presents grows visibly around the white tub where the policeman, in white gloves, directs the minimal traffic. This is the day the public honours its police force.

Tasso buys a bottle of ouzo and adds it to the pile. At my raised eyebrow, he says piously, "For sure we need the police...especially you and me" – a reminder that our mutual existence is at the courtesy of the Aliens' Bureau.

Tasso carries the dish to the first bakery. All the town's dinners are cooking in the baker's ovens, there is no place for it. He tries another without success. *Ashes and gunpowder!*

Back in the wine shop, he calls the boy who now waits on the tables, a bright kid of 12. "Oresti!"

"Mr Tasso?" He is ready for anything.

"Take this to a bakers." And he gives him five drachmes.

The boy puts the dish on his head and disappears. He is soon back, still with the dish. Lowering it carefully onto the table beside Tasso, he whispers confidentially in his ear. Tasso bursts out laughing. "You know what he say? Why don't you sell the whole thing and go to eat in a restaurant! Honest to God, I thinking the same thing."

Eventually he finds a place for it, After four hours, when we have drunk too much and eaten too little, "I hope is ready," he says, leading the way into the baker's flour-dredged interior, where the great oven swells out of the corner like a brooding fertility goddess. The old baker is probing its womb with a long wooden paddle. He has bristles on his head and bristles on his chin, but at the sight of me, a foreign female, he stops paddling the oven and bursts into a love song through toothless gums. Tasso, furious, says, "Get out of here quick before I break his head and we lose the torquay for sure!"

I exit quickly, the baker shouting, "The man who marries you is the luckiest man in the world!"

This sort of thing inflames Tasso's anger and limits my freedom, coming between me and anything I take a harmless interest in.

We clamber back onto the scooter, the dish now swimming in gravy. At the final hill, he stalls the engine; I manage to hop off the back, still holding the baking dish. "Don't lose the *saltza*, that's the best!"

At home he has a plate of macaroni with the saltza. I pick at drumstick and throw pieces to the cats peering in at the door.

"For crazy! All that troubles for a plate of macaroni!" And he falls into his siesta. That's him all over.

I feed the cats for a week on the bits. It never occurs to me to ask what a New Year might bring…

5.

'How are you finding it now in this second phase of your Greek Adventure? You certainly have chosen a rough road, but you appear to thrive on it. Here the weather has taken a most welcome turn for the better – I think I'll have a jaunt to Brighton to eat a few oysters.

Love Dad '

It has become a regular thing for The Hon. to sit with me in the wine shop; Pooter often joins us. She ignored me for a long time, until one day, to my horror, she tottered towards my table and sat down.

"I've been on my own all weekend! This morning I said to myself, I *will* speak to that gel – at least she smiles with her eyes." Waving a gloved hand at Mr Sotiris, she ordered a glass of wine in atrocious French: "*Donnay moy ewn verre de van blank, s'ee voo play...*' and to me, "He speaks French you know...and makes a very good French omelette" – achievements that obviously elevated him above other Greeks.

Then Tasso suddenly appeared and plonked a newspaper package of shopping on the table in front of her; and, taking her hand, bowed over it, saying "Ah, *Madame* – what an Honour!"

I was horrified but, to my surprise, she simpered, (and she is not a simpering woman): "Oh, you make me feel young again!" *What he can get away with*!

When he had disappeared again, she remarked, "He's very good looking, your man", as if he were my butler, and when I got up to leave, she said, "I DO wish you and YOUR MAN would come to tea. I have some excellent Earl Grey." This indicated the extent of her loneliness. Tea-time doesn't exist for him and me.

This morning, when Pooter appears dressed in his best suit and carrying gloves, she exclaims, "How *smart* you are today, M'sieur!", her sarcasm grating visibly on Pooter's nerves.

He is, as usual, full of local information. "Have you heard...?" he loves to impart the gossip so long as he is the first to do so ("I dislike imparting stale news...") "Count X is here for the opening of the new Casino."

When she says, "Oh, I knew the Count in the South of France!" it is Pooter's turn to raise his eyebrows. "He's quite a sweetie...we went to the casino every night in Cannes...I *luv* gambling !" says the Hon. "Anything to do with losing money..."

"Well, it's going to be quite a big affair," Pooter goes on importantly. "I must say, making a casino of that white elephant of a place is a splendid idea – it's been empty for years. It was last used as a hospital during the war. It's bound to bring people to the island. Just what it needs..." He looks at his watch, like the White Rabbit. "I'm afraid I must leave you ladies, as I am calling on the Chief of Police this morning." The Hon. raises her eyebrows. "He's quite a cultured individual, if you stretch culture to include ethnic dancing. He's a superb ethnic dancer, and tells me it makes him sad now that he's attained the rank of Chief, he mustn't be seen dancing in public places anymore." This touch of local colour is completely wasted on the Hon., who cannot conceive of a dancing policeman. "Good day to you, ladies!"

And taking up his gloves, he goes.

He keeps his back resolutely turned; once he has given you quittance, it is against his principles to re-engage.

"That suit must be 20 years old!" She notices clothes.

I suspect he is going to kowtow for his residents' permit. It will be my turn soon; it's worse than going to the dentist. One has to go through this ceremony every six months. Tasso always comes with me; for him, it is like redeeming a personal article from the pawnbrokers. As long as he continues to do so, I know I retain my value.

We mount the steps to the police station, cross the bare boards of the hall to a pale grey door. Tasso knocks discreetly and is bidden to enter. A pugilistic man with a small black moustache sits behind the big desk. This is the Chief whom Pooter visits in gloves; he rises to greet Tasso as an old friend, and gives me an uneasy nod. They sit down; I am left standing until a chair by the window is indicated. I sit on it; the scars left by my first encounters with this 'Body' throb like old wounds. That was when I learned that being in love is no excuse for trying to live in this country.

They talk together in their semi-oriental way of many things; the purpose of this visit isn't even mentioned, the Chief knows anyway. At the proper moment, Tasso indicates me in the dunce's corner. They both look at me as if I were a piece of furniture which should not have been brought in to the parlour. The Chief orders a secretary to take my passport. A white paper is typed out, my photograph, like a victim of rape, attached to it. The Chief bangs a purple stamp on it, and even pays the stamp-duty because Tasso has no change. This is privileged treatment, because Tasso's brother-in-law is a General in Athens.

Regaining the outside world with this piece of paper is a mini-resurrection. Everything that might have been getting a little dull, slack or exasperating is tight and bright again

*

6

In the evening, preparing to go to town, I am surprised when Tasso puts on a tie. He never wears a tie.

"Why are you wearing a tie?"

"My sister and his husband are here from Athens for the opening of the Casino. They call us to go there."

"Why didn't you tell me! I've got nothing to wear to the Casino." He is what I put on to confront the world.

"You look alright. Anyway, you are with me," he adds, expecting me to follow him barefoot over the Himalayas. That's what it feels like most of the time.

We drive up the steep twisting hill and through the narrow street of the village to the main gates where floodlights illumine the trees and the neo-classical facade of what looks like a newly iced wedding cake.

Last time we came to this place we entered through a hole in the fence and climbed up the steep overgrown garden to emerge on the terrace among the posturing statues of the nine muses. Memories take you by surprise. Love was different then. Is it more now, or less? Anyway, it's different. The caretaker, recognising Tasso, let us see inside the place. I remember the porcelain cherubs crawling up the lavatory cistern in one of the grand bathrooms.

We park the car and approach the grand entrance; a bewigged flunky pulls open the heavy bronze door. In the reception, where the guests have to present their passports, the receptionist gives him the wink; we are free to ascend the red carpeted staircase, where giant *putti* gallop out of the walls like baby elephants, holding bronze lamps aloft; saccharin marble philosophers meditate on the landings; goddesses with pink nipples float on the cloud-covered ceiling, where Hellenic heroes, with flesh like margarine, drive chariots around the cornice.

"For sure they make it a High Life place now," he says, while I am wondering what happened to the porcelain cherubs on the lavatory cistern.

A large man is plodding up the stairs close on our heels. "Him a policeman, for sure," says Tasso. "Always they follow me."

"When you wear a tie, you look like Al Capone!"

The man follows on our heels, into the restaurant, right up to the table where Antigone and the General are finishing their meal, at which point he melts away like butter. "Didn't I tell you..." Tasso says.

Antigone and the General present the implacable image of the King and Queen of Spades: fierce and benign. Antigone turns her brown eyes on me to fire them like cannon – still suspicious of my commitment to her brother.

"You want to stey in Greeze for-ever? Why you no want to stay in England? You no like England? England verry nice...very good shopping." She is looking at me as if I were a spoilt child who has thrown her plate of cabbage on the floor. At least she attempts to tolerate my relationship with her brother now, without believing it can last.

The waiter brings a *mézé* for us. "You getting fat!" Antigone says. I have put on a little weight from having to live mostly on macaroni, when he forgets to do the shopping.

They rise from the table to go to the roulette. "They going to make themselves more rich," Tasso says, watching them go.

I suggest they are not bound to win.

"They always win," he insists, expressing a family pride in them. "We lose because they make me the troubles to come here, and I don't sell no picture tonight and I have no money to pay the bar."

I am watching the bandleader in a white tuxedo, a huge man like a whale standing on its tail, breathing the distorted lyrics into the microphone held to his mouth.

"You like him?"

"Who?"

"The bandleader."

Here we go! I must keep my eyes on a dish like a female martyr, but really it is because he hasn't got money for the bar. "Give me your two English pounds," he demands, knowing I always carry two English banknotes as a sort of talisman, or security, though what two English pounds could secure me from, I don't know.

"I want them back!"

"Don't worry! I get from the first English tourists we meet."

I fish them out of my bag. We approach the bar, and Tasso confidently orders a gin and tonic for me, a brandy for him.

A small man sitting on the tall stool at the other end of the bar is constantly being approached by the Teutonic personnel who plod up to him on reverential feet in highly polished shoes. Tasso looks inquiringly at the barman, who mouths behind a napkin, "The Count."

Suddenly, Tasso goes over to the bandleader. *Surely he's not going to do the Butcher's Dance here?* The bandleader, mouth to microphone, bends his ear to Tasso, and nods. Immediately the music switches to a *Hasapiko*. Tasso signals to me; I am forced to join him on the dance floor.

We dance as one, seamlessly; then, as the rhythm accelerates into a *Hassapi-serviko*, he flings out his left arm, I grasp it like a handlebar, and we career around the floor, my feet giving out little kicks like a rabbit.

Before the music ends, he runs back through the tables to the bar, the audience of diners applauding rapturously. As I reach the bar, breathless and exhilarated, the Count slips off his stool, grabs my hand and, squeezing the fingers in a painful grasp, plants a kiss on the back of it, at the same time leering up at me with the eyes of a squid. Released, I put myself firmly on the other side of Tasso, who is speaking in German to him, while the Count continues to stare at me. The audience want us to dance again, but Tasso has achieved all he set out to do; he can leave with 'H'onnor'.

Outside he gives me back my two pounds. The Count had signalled to the barmen, there was nothing to pay.

"Him flirting you much, the baster!"

"*Droit de seigneur!*" A favourite epithet of Dad's.

"Not with me!" he says vehemently.

We drive home in thunder and lightning. All night the bucket by the well is trundled about by the wind, the front door blows open, the alarm clock goes off. He throws it on the floor, where it is thoughtful for a moment before persisting in its duty. *Brrrrrrrr!* At the same moment the bed collapses at one end, the metal legs giving way. It settles like a camel. Tasso sits up and says it's my fault.

Next morning, he borrows two beer crates from the taverna. When the taverna wants them back, he finds two White Horse whisky boxes. They are the wrong height for the other two legs, so he twists them off and finds two more boxes. As we lift the legless bed frame onto the boxes, the metal ribbons forming the springs leap off their hooks and fall in a tangle on the floor.

"Why don't you just buy a new bed?" No. This one is defying him and must be subjugated. Anyway, he has no money for a new bed – the Season is over, the harvest done and he hasn't saved a penny. Money isn't for saving. Getting and spending is the name of the game, and he has a superstitious fear that if it stays in his pocket it might destroy him. He wouldn't have an outlet for his energies.

Fortunately the conventional life has no appeal for me. The agony of living with him has become a sort of drug; I'm addicted now. What if he hadn't found the way to bring me back?

7

It is hot enough when the sun shines, but when it rains for days the damp gets into everything. We have a paraffin heater, but he forgets to bring the paraffin. He got soaked to the skin coming home on the scooter, and is coughing. He coughs so much, he coughs blood. Must he do everything to excess?

"I feel very bad," he says. "I must go to my dog-tor."

The doctor sends him to the hospital. I drive him there, exasperated and frightened by the frailty of this strong man.

The hospital, built by the British circa Florence Nightingale, is opposite the prison, also built by my efficient countrymen. "I've been in there too," he says, holding the bloody handkerchief to his mouth.

He is allocated a bed in the men's ward; the large window has bars on it, and a policeman sits by the door with a stengun across his knees. No sign of a nurse or a doctor.

"Have we come to the right place?" I query.

"Of course, yes!" As if I am being stupid.

"Why is a policeman sitting by the door?"

"It means we have a prisoner in here. That's what it means. The only way to be escape of that prison is to be sick so they bring him here. If he try to make the escape – never mind for me to have bronchitis! Always the *malediction* follow me!" His past is full of narrow escapes.

"Oh, well…I'll leave you then," I say, presuming I should get out of the way, as one is obliged to do in an English hospital.

"What you mean? Where you go?"

"Home."

"To do what?" He is full of suspicion.

"Well, I can't stay here."

"Of course you stay. Where else you going to be?"

Then I notice the room is crowded with people, peasants in village costume sitting round every bed. A village woman wanders into the room carrying a bedpan. Still no sign of a nurse, or a doctor. It is not like an English hospital.

He changes his mind, "No – I have a better idea. Go to my butcher, get meat to make soup, and bring me here. I pay later – he knows." When I look surprised, "You think they feed you in these places!"

Driving into town, I wonder how I can carry soup to him. On the way to the butcher, I spot a little shop with dinner pails hanging on from hooks outside. I buy a bright blue enamel dinner pail with bucket handle and tight fitting lid. Perfect! I feel really pleased with it. Then I see The Hon., conspicuous by her height. At the sight of me, she breaks into a wail. "Look what I've found!" she cries, pointing a gloved hand to a grating where a tiny kitten is mewing. "It's TOO AWFUL! Nobody cares about the animals."

Having just come from the hospital, it seems to me humans and animals have much the same chance in this country.

"How can I bring it some milk?"

I suggest a yoghurt pot, mumble about Tasso being in hospital, but she is too concerned about the cat, and takes no notice. I leave her to it.

In the evening I return to the hospital with the soup in the blue enamel bucket. Indicating the next bed, he says, "Him is…"

"Who?"

"The prisoner."

It is safe to speak in English as nobody understands. Out of the corner of my eye, I see a lad of about nineteen, with dark curls looping over his forehead.

"What did he do?"

"He kill his father with the help of his mother." He presses his head back into the pillow wearily. "I don't want to know such people" – sounding just like The Hon.

I stay by him till ten o'clock, when he says, "Okay – go home now…" and I drive home to the cheerless, cold damp house which seems almost to reject me – without him.

A pattern is established – bringing food, and sitting by the bed where I am an object of curiosity to everybody else in the room. They ask him the ritual of questions: what am I? What is my age? Have I children? Am I married? In that order. He counters their curiosity with half-truths, myths and frank lies. The doctor on his rounds flicks his eyes over me briefly as he speaks with Tasso, and moves on to the next bed. I ask what he said. "He say not to drink too much, not to smoking...to make the quiet life...not too much... you know..."

So that is what I saw in his eyes. I resent the implication, not knowing if I am a riotous luxury or just another bad habit.

8.

He and the boy murderer have become the best of friends, sharing a cigarette cadged from the policeman on the door. Neither are supposed to smoke. When the doctor comes round, they are expert at passing the stub between them under the level of the beds, probably a skill learned in prison.

Every night when I get up to leave him, he says, "Go straight home."

"What else would I do?"

"That's what I say, don't do anything…" he says with that quizzical look that so exasperates me. I know he is thinking that because he is tied to a hospital bed, I am free. It makes me so angry, on my way home I stop at the local taverna which has a jukebox and a telephone. It is empty except for the proprietor, a kindly old man who knows us well. I go straight to the jukebox, choose a *Hasapiko*, and ring the hospital. There is a phone in the corridor; an orderly calls him to it. "Mr Tasso, telefonó!" He comes.

"Is this what you mean?" I say, holding the receiver to the sound of the music. "Where are you? Who is there? Go home before we be sorry both! Or I come in a taxi!"

"Oh, don't be silly. It's only a joke…"

"Give me the boss there." I hand the phone to the kindly old man.

"There's nobody here, Tasso – In the name of God… She's gone."

I drive home, climb between the clammy comfortless sheets and cry. The time for little love victories has been and gone.

When he is allowed to get up, he wanders the Crimean corridors in his pyjamas with a coat over his shoulders, looking like a wounded soldier from the First World War. There are always women around him. He entertains them with preposterous stories which make them screech, holding coarse hands over their missing teeth. Youth leaves them early. When I enter, their eyes level on me like cannon loaded with incredulity; even he looks as if he wonders how he acquired me. Our relationship doesn't seem very plausible even to me.

One evening, there was a kestrel perched on the head of the boy-murderer's bed. I thought it was stuffed until it turned a yellow eye on me.

"How did that get in here?"

"It fly in through the bars." Nobody did anything about it, and in the morning it had gone. "It fly away at the first of the light…"

The boy- murderer's bed was empty too. "They take him back in there, the poor fella...." Having bonded with the boy, he was really distressed. "What him going to do now…20 years in that place! Perhaps he have a reason to do what he do…if the father was a *baster*…we no be inside that story! They let me out of here today too. I wait to have my papers, then I free. Then I will go in Athens to see the dog-tors there. Is more better…" *Does he mean to go alone?*

"What about me?"

"You stay here."

He has never left me anywhere before. "What am I going to do alone here?"

"Do as you like…" he says with a cynical look. This comes as a shock. He has never given me this much licence before. I feel cold all over. In adapting to the ways of his country, my freedom has been eroded to the size of a doormat. I cannot do anything on my own. I cannot even walk through the town, without him receiving the information.

"When will you go?"

"Why you want to know so specially?"

His senseless jealousy again! Once it had been a piquant ingredient in our relationship – slightly intoxicating, even an attractively dangerous weapon. How did I fail to notice he has control of it – not me?

I get up and walk out of the ward. "Don't be far – I be ready in a minute," he calls after me, putting a laugh into it, but this is not a joke. *What does he mean by this?*

Outside in the yard, my impulse is simply to drive away, but it fizzles out in the limbo peculiar to myself. Where can I go on this limited island without having to come back to him? I have nowhere to go. I have only him.

I am still sitting in the car parked behind the tree; it embarrasses me to have a car when the doctors have to walk.

He appears on the steps dressed for the world. It is a nice moment when he fails to see the car and thinks I have driven off; at least I have taken him by surprise. Then he sees the car with me sulking in it; opening the door and getting in, he says with satisfaction, "Now we are free! The world belong to us. Drive to the town...can you?" to humour me.

In the wine shop, when he orders a wine, the temptation is too great, I can't resist it. "The doctor told you not to drink..." He makes Mr Sotiris pour away half the glass. He lights a cigarette. "The doctor told you not to smoke..."

"For crazy!" He chucks the cigarette into the street.

And in bed: "The doctor said..."

"Can you shut up about what the dog-tor say!"

Later, he says, "If I go in Athens – we go together. I know what bother you, but you don't know what bother me! Every night some *baster* phone to say he see you around the town!" Mr Anonymous again?

"And you believed it!"

"I don't believe anything. I hope you honest, but it nervous me much."

What am I looking for on this incestuous little island with him? Life in the sun is nastier than I could ever have imagined it to be.

Next day, Tasso came back from town in great distress. "You know what happen to that boy in the hospital?"

"The one who killed his father?"

"He hanging himself in his cell. Pó-pó-pó! They bury him today. One of the police who watch the door in the hospital tell me. So I buy flowers and go there and ask for him. They take me to the room where he lying in his coffin and he have one eye open! Imagine that! How that eye speak to me! It say, 'Tasso? You here...' I put the flowers on him and kiss him above that eye. My God, I be his age when they put me in there. How many wild things I do when I his age... I kill people too – but that was war time. Poor fella. He had no luck! Luck mean everything in the life!"

And he kept repeating: "He have no luck!" before falling into a deep siesta in which he still muttered his distress like a dog.

I think I know why I love this man...

9

"What kind of idea is that!" he fumes at the new regulation for 'Early Closing Wednesdays & Saturdays', which means the wine shop is closed, and he must find another 'safe' place to put me while he does his evening circuit of the town. He chooses the Cake Parlour, a long-established family business, where the old mother of ninety-two sits at the cash desk taking the money, while her daughter Persephone, who has the bulk and features of Dr Johnson, serves behind the counter; and Stavros, the old flat-footed waiter, is straight out of Chekhov. Customers come in to buy the over-sweet traditional pastries, *baklavas* and *kataifi* dripping with honey, or to order the cream cake confections which have to be eaten with a spoon.

Pooter, passing down the street, sees me through the window and comes in, managing his umbrella expertly, wearing a Burberry and a trilby, just like an English Civil Servant.

"I didn't know you patronized this place?"

"Only grudgingly." I am still regretting the wine shop.

"I can't stay long…" he says as usual, calling for a coffee in impeccable Greek. I can see he has news to impart.

"Have you heard about The Hon.? She's had another fall in the bank and hurt her knee."

I visualise her loping along like a praying mantis in her old Dior suit, hat and gloves, with the dachshund on the lead. Only the other day she remarked, "I'm told nobody wears gloves in Bond Street anymore."

"Her money isn't coming through from Africa – too much trouble there. She owes money all over town and lives on omelettes and Nescafe."

"But only the other day she ordered Sotiris to cook a steak."

"Ah, but that was for the dog. She's a vegetarian…"

I remember now she had the steak wrapped up to take away.

"I've offered to try to find her a small flat here in town – it would be much better for her, and cheaper. Where she is now, the neighbours' children throw stones at her…and call her *skylosparo* (dogfish). Her attitude doesn't help her. She has lived in China and in the South of France, but she's quite impossible with the Greeks. She doesn't understand them. The other day she complained because the baker had invited her to his daughter's wedding. *'As if I would go to a tradesman's wedding!'* She doesn't realise it's a great compliment here to be asked!

"Another time she said the laundry man was 'making up to her' in a vulgar way. I had to go and explain to him that she couldn't pay her bill this week. I must say he's one of those charming lively Greeks of about forty-five who are redolent of sex…but it doesn't mean anything."

I suppose Tasso comes into that category.

"Well, I must leave you," he says, getting up as if he has urgent business to attend to. He pays for his coffee at the counter, reclaims his umbrella and goes.

At nine o'clock a taxi slinks to the door of the shop. The old lady brings out her black straw hat from under the cash desk, and claps it on her head. Stavros helps to extricate her from the cash desk and offers his arm in gentlemanly support as they make the slow progress to the door and into the taxi. The daughter takes her place in the cash desk, filling it like one of those Staffordshire pottery figures of a Calvinist preacher in a pulpit. Glancing over her specs towards me, I hear her say to Stavros, "She has a lot of patience, that girl…"

10.

This morning, from my corner table in the wine shop, I watched the Hon. accost a respectable looking man in her atrocious French, asking if he knew anyone who could pack and remove her furniture to the new flat. Removal people don't exist here; the best she can hope for is someone with a handcart. Pooter, having found the flat, has withdrawn from the situation. "I can only do so much…"

The man replies, but she can't understand him. "Do you perhaps speak English?"

The exasperated man says, "I AM speakin' Engliss!"

"Oh, I AM so sorry, I didn't realise…" she says, as he bows, turns his back on her and walks away.

Entering the wine shop, she stands at the counter trying to engage Mr Sotiris in her problem when the lemon seller comes in, jostling her with his basket. Looking down on his greasy cap, she says, *"VOUS ATE TRAY IMPOLI!"* He takes no notice until she shouts, "GO A-WAY!"

Suddenly, looking up at her from his 4ft 5, he mutters, "*Skylosparo!*" (Dogfish!) and goes.

"Oh, thank goodness you are here!" She has noticed me in the corner. "I am having an *awful* time, trying to find somebody to move my *things*…" She is not so thrilled with her new flat as Pooter is. "It's like a third-class railway carriage… but it doesn't really matter," she shrugs with a new resignation, "so long as I have my *things* around me. At least I won't have men's trousers decorating the fence. My d*e-are,* the women drape their washing over my fence…it was so *infra dig,* I poked them off with a stick!" No wonder the children threw stones at her.

Tasso comes in. She accosts him. "Do you think you could possibly dismantle my electric lights for me?" He agrees immediately. I only hope he remembers…but after his siesta he says, "Come on – we must to go to fix the old woman's lights – I promise her."

I knock on the door of the ground floor maisonette in the jerry-built flats where she lives. "Come in," her voice calls out, "I'm not dressed, but it doesn't matter…" Entering cautiously I see a long gaunt skeleton in bra and pants like an insect with its wings pulled off, tottering into the bedroom. Her *things* are piled in cardboard boxes everywhere on the floor.

"What she got here – a museum?" says Tasso, staring at two Elizabethan portraits, a Chinese porcelain horse, and a crystal bird. "What she doing with all this stuff?"

The Hon. appears dressed in an elaborate chiffon peignoir, and coughing sepulchrally; she does not look well. Seeing me gazing at the exquisite crystal bird, she coos, "Don't you love it? And my horse – he came from a Chinese Temple… they've been all round the world with me."

"Those look as if they should be in the National Gallery." I point to the two portraits.

"Oh, they want them – my ancestors, the Pagets – but they can't have them yet."

A peasant woman appears in the doorway. "Oh, it's the little woman who is going to help me move, her husband has a handcart."

The woman enters smiling intensely, her sharp eyes excited by what she sees, especially the crystal bird on the table. She takes it up in her rough hands, saying *"Poly Oréa!" (very fine)*

"Oh, *PRENEZ GARDE*!" cries the Hon., speaking loudly as if to a deaf person. "I'm so afraid she will break it with those hands."

Tasso speaks sharply to the woman; she responds in mime, placing her hand on her breast to indicate how much she cares for the Madame and Madame's Things. Tasso does not seem impressed. He continues dismantling the fittings, and then we leave.

"Don't mix in that situation," he warns me – as if I were a free agent. I am only at liberty to meet the Hon. in the wine shop.

"I know that woman," he says darkly, "She a *kleftés* – a stealer. Too many things never going to arrive at the new place."

A few days later, the Hon's things having been transferred to the new place on the handcart, "So *infra dig!* Worse than being in China!" she exclaims. "And I am having *such trouble* with that woman! She has taken *so* many of my *things*!'

So Tasso was right.

"My crystal bird that you admired so much…my cut glass salad bowl…my silver fox fur… I *gave* her two couturier dresses…though how she could get into them I can't imagine…and when I ask her where are my things, she runs around like a hen looking for them. We look for them *together* but I know she *must* have taken them."

"But she doesn't understand English," I suggest.

"Oh, she *understands,* the cunning little thing! *And* I made the mistake of giving her a key. Now she comes and goes when I am out and helps herself to anything – and leaves a bowl of boiled potatoes on the table. She knows I'm vegetarian…and do you know…" Suddenly she looks guilty. "I was so hungry, *I ate them.* I MUST get Pooter to speak to her…"

11

"You will see I have changed my address but judging by what the doctor says there is no cause for alarm. An attack of jaundice. I have to remain in this bed for four weeks with no milk, fat, soup or flavour of any kind. I didn't think there was a man who could take the taste out of baked beans but we've got him here…and no alcohol for six months! I had just laid a case of Champagne too! Write often. Your pagan letters are a joy in this place…"

A chasm opens up under my feet. Dad's never been ill in his life – he will bounce back…won't he?

"You look as if you have had bad news," says the Hon., approaching my table in the wine shop. I mumble something about my father and hospital. "Oh, I am sorry! Will you have to go back?" she asks, putting the finger on my fear.

Pooter joins us. Parents become the topic of conversation.

"I ADORED my Pa!" the Hon. says. "He knew how to spend money… gambling, race-horses…and wimmin…he left three surviving wives. He gave each of us children a Daimler when we were 18 – but we had to learn how to take the engine to bits and put it back together again. When I did mine, it would only go in reverse… He had a diamond mine in Africa and a 30,000 acre estate…"

Pooter's expression is easy to read.

"I always wanted to go there," she continues, "but Ma said I wouldn't like it. Later I found out he sent his cast-off mistresses there – they had a grand piano…" She does not want us to think he left them without consolation in the African bush.

This triggered Pooter into confessing, "My father was an excellent man, but he was a tradesman, whereas my mother came from a middle-class background."

The Hon. winces.

"I loved my mother very much, but I have never really forgiven her for marrying beneath her."

The Hon. winces again.

12.

Cold windy Carnival Time – Time of Misrule before the austerity of Lent. In more sophisticated places the beast is dead, but here he has his hour. At night the town is invaded by extra-terrestrial beings in masks and dominoes, gathering in mischievous knots before sallying into the bars and cafés to tease people with the impertinence of anonymity. Impish figures dance round us in the street, chanting his name – and mine – wicked little eyes glinting behind the masks. I have enough devils in my head without these manifestations.

"Who are they?"

"Schoolgirls," he says as a dominoed figure rushes up to thrust a little package at him and, giggling, runs away. It contains a cheap china ornament. "Someone be in love with me again..." he says philosophically. He's old enough to be their father.

Fathers...I dread the post.

Letter from Dick: "*He's not getting better. You ought to come home.*"

Letter from Dad: "*Remember I am not asking you to come home. What would you do alone at the cottage, while I am in here? But when I am better you might fly home, and we could go on a holiday TOGETHER...not with a doddering old man but one restored to confidence. It would give you time to take a fresh look at your destiny...*"

Why the capitals underlined? What does he mean by that? I don't need to take a fresh look at my destiny. I am very happy with it. I'm very glad I achieved a destiny at all. I don't want to be anywhere but here, and I never will want to be anywhere but here. How many times can one escape? If I go back I'm lost. We've hit a turgid patch...

I don't discuss the situation with Tasso. Greeks revere their parents as the 'givers of life', and swear their most binding oaths (which they don't keep) on the 'souls of my father and my mother'. His parents were killed together when the bomb fell on the family house. When, much later, the houses were cleared, the bones were put in little piles outside the cemetery wall, with anything that might identify them. He recognised his father's belt buckle. He goes every November to the cemetery to light a candle on the grave.

As I enter the wine shop Mr Sotiris says, "You have a telephone call from London in ten minutes..." How do they know where to find me? They have rung the Bar Greco across the street where Tasso is, he tells them to put the call through to the wine shop in ten minutes. There is no escape.

Dick's voice on a crackly line is saying, "He's not going to get better. You must get a plane..." At my silence: "Can you hear me? Are you there?"

Pause. Then I hear myself slowly say: "I'm not coming back..." Are the noises on the line or in my head?

"You're afraid to see him die!"

It's not as simple as that...the truth is far worse – I am afraid to see him live.

"You always did funk everything!" Anger toward the younger sister, Dad's little girl.

The line goes dead; he's gone. I replace the phone on its stand, and wade through guilt to my table in the corner. What has made me into this monster? Love? The love one runs after, or the love one runs away from?

Tasso comes in. "You take the call from London?" I nod. He looks at me carefully, asks no questions, but tells Sotiris to bring me a koniak. He goes again.

13.

The days pass slowly, heavily. No more news? I've put myself outside the circle.

Then Tasso comes into the wine shop, with a telegram in his hand. "You have the telegram." Of course he has read it, he knows what it contains.

"NO HOPE NOW - COME QUICKLY."

I remain dumb. Tasso watches me with the sagacity of a dog "You don't go?" He shakes his head at the mystery and goes away again.

No sign of the Hon. or Pooter. Thank goodness. Alone with this patricide, I sit at the table, numb; I can't share this with anyone. I am like a climber on a rock face unable to move hand or foot.

Tasso returns and sits down with me. Speaking quietly as to a child who has not been properly taught, he says, "He waiting for you. You must to go to close his eyes. He cannot go till you come." He has understood much more than I. "You must to go. That way we be clean." He has accepted his part in it, and the need to turn me round, and point me in the right direction.

Suddenly I can see that while I have been hanging on with all my strength waiting for Dad to release me, he has been hanging on with all his strength waiting for me to release him. It unlocks my catalepsy. I must go now – and quickly...

But the Devil is in it. I can't leave the country without the car being sealed in customs. In the large drab room with wooden counter separating the petitioners from the assortment of individuals sitting at desks piled high with folders, the atmosphere is heavy with cigarette smoke. The coffee lady crochets baby socks beside her table with the gas-ring and the tiny pots for making individual coffees. A mature typist sits stroking her belly meditatively with blood-red fingernails while waiting to be given something to type.

While we wait, being systematically ignored, an old man sitting by the window, hands folded on the knob of his stick, calls to one of the clerks, who leaves his desk immediately to help him into the lavatory. I look at Tasso questioningly. "Ah, poor fella – he have a stroke six months before him ready to retire, they let him sit here – that way he don't lose his pension." So the system has a human side, though it is not applied to the general public.

The Chief of Customs sits in an inner sanctum under a paper icon of Christ in his crown of thorns. Businessmen enter with bowed heads as if going into church, and come out with their prayers unanswered. The procedure must be gone through again and again…tomorrow…and tomorrow…

Just when we seem to be nearing the completion of our business, they run out of the special taxation stamps. Tasso is told to get them from a pavement kiosk a quarter of a mile away. He accosts the businessmen coming in for the stamps; they search their wallets obligingly and produce enough for us. The typist slowly sticks them onto the form, using her blood-red nail to tear off the tiny perforated triangle on each one. It takes time. Even Tasso dares not show impatience here "or we lose the battle for sure…"

At the airport, the official flicks through my passport, black and blue with 'In' and 'Out' stamps; both the car and I are 'foreign vehicles'. Raising his head, he clicks his tongue against his teeth – the oriental negative. He picks out one detail, missed by the Customs because it was not their department: a small circulation tax on the car has not been paid. Until this has been paid, I may not leave the country.

I am in despair now, my plane leaves at 9am for Athens – I will miss the connection to London. Tasso rushes me to the municipal building in a taxi. The man on the door won't let us in because the office does not open until 10.30am.

Tasso disappears to phone a friend who works inside the building, to come down and get us past the Cerberus on the door. It works. We dash from office to office, trying to find the right one in which to offer the money. We find it, but the man behind the shabby desk ignores us while he sips his gritty Greek coffee; no appeal rouses these dedicated civil servants. With only minutes left, the money is taken, but we must wait for the receipt to be written out by hand.

I catch the plane with seconds to spare and the island drops away from under me...

14

The journey takes over, offering palliatives of caviar and chicken supreme between Athens and Rome; smoked salmon and cold beef between Rome and Paris, orangeade between Paris and London; warm lager at Victoria Station, where I phone the nursing home. "Should I come tonight?"

"Oh, yes," the nurse says.

The "Brighton Belle" speeds through the darkness with pink shaded lamps reflected in the glass of the window; a delicious smell of hot buttered toast from the galley; waiters passing up and down the corridor slide back the doors: "Anything to drink, sir/madam?" and bring gin and tonics…so familiar, yet so strange…

At the barrier, the ticket to witness a death is taken from my fingers. As I walk toward the exit thinking "I'll have to take a taxi to find the place", a stocky figure looms up beside me and Dick says, "I calculated you would be on this train."

Having bounced like a ping-pong ball across Europe and told no-one I was coming, I am amazed when my brother says, "I *calculated* you would be on this train." This is supernatural.

"But how could you!"

"The nursing home rang me…"

Oh. British Efficiency, not the Supernatural.

The nursing home turns out to be a row of terrace houses knocked into one, close to the blustery sea front. We follow the nurse along narrow passages papered in powerful red roses. It is like a theatre; I half expect a bell to signal the beginning of this last act.

But what play is it?

The nurse pushes open a door leading into a small room where the bedside light sheds a soft glow on a gaunt head with gummy eyes and a beaky nose, lying on the pillow, two bony hands resting on the turned back sheet like an effigy on a tomb. Have we come to the right room? *That's not Dad. That can't be Dad.*

"He's been waiting for you," she says, shaking the effigy quite roughly. "Your *DAUGHTER'S HERE FROM GREECE!*" She rouses him to keep this last appointment.

"She's here, Dad!" says Dick.

"You'll have to speak louder," says the nurse. Only she knows what part to play. We stand at the foot of the bed shouting. "I'm here! Dad?"

Suddenly the head jerks, a gurgle comes from the gaping mouth, and a solitary tear slides from under the gummy eyelid, traversing the side of the beaky nose, skirts the dark hole of the mouth to fall from the precipice of the chin. Literature prepares us for the death rattle, but never mentions the last tear. The nurse feels the bony wrist, lays it down and immediately stoops to turn out the gas fire – an action more final than death itself.

"I'll make him look nice," she murmurs like a mother tending her child, tying up the gaping jaw. "He was waiting for you," she says again as she leaves the room to us.

Is that really Dad on the bed? The spectacles on the side table are him, and the old pigskin suitcase on the top of the wardrobe. But where is *he*?

We hang about in this mystery until the sour smell drives us from the room, but *he* comes with us – the business of dying done, we can all go and have a drink. In a nearby pub, we are in hysterics, remembering only the funny, endearing, unforgettable things, the laughing things of love…of love…

"Do you remember how *you* had to teach *him* to ride a bicycle – and when Mum sent you both shopping for something special, and you came back without it. He said, '*I* remembered, Dick forgot!'"

We talk of him till closing time; No acrimony now; Dick only wanted me to participate, not to have to go through it alone.

At the cremation service, the ritual words are broken like an egg over the dead whether they want them or not, and can no longer reject them. He would have preferred a bottle of Champagne broken over his bows as the conveyor belt rumbles like the digestive system of an elephant, trundling him like a piece of airport baggage toward a hole in the wall while the vile blue satin curtains shuffle hesitatingly toward each other as at the end of some amateur performance.

Is that it, then?

15.

The relief at touching down on Greek soil at Athens with the sun shining – to be told the flight to the island is cancelled due to bad weather. There will be no plane till tomorrow. I am adrift between the Living and the Dead like a ghost in Hades, needing to drink blood to regain my reality; only Tasso's vitality can give me back to myself.

In despair, I lurk in my carcass like a thing of jelly, glued to a plastic seat, while the cleaners sweep round and under me. What do I do now? I must *do* something, but...*what*? Take a taxi. Where? You have to tell a taxi to go somewhere.

I manage to direct the taxi to the hotel in the market area, where we always stay, where the proprietors are the 'very good friends of him'.

"Iss no goot place!" the driver insists, wanting to take me to Sintagma; but I *must* to go there, clutching at this tenuous thread connecting me to Tasso and swinging on it like a spider to be saved. It gives me the force needed to prevail over the will of an Athenian taxi-driver.

He dumps me at the edge of the market. I find the hotel by the smell of the mortadella sausage shop next to it.

I enter the foyer, feeling conspicuously alone. The two brothers, the proprietors of this hotel, look at me over their spectacles like Tweedledum and Tweedledee.

"Where iss Tassos?" they demand, as if I have no business to appear without him.

I try to explain that I have arrived from London, that he is on the island, and I am here because the plane does not go there.

They shake their heads. *"Oxi! Oxi!"* The Greek negative. "Iss heer!" they say unanimously, bringing up the visitors' ledger to show me his inimitable signature, with yesterday's date beside it.

I am taken up in the creaking birdcage lift and shown to a room with unmistakable evidence of Tasso in it – his socks drying on the radiator, the transistor radio by the bed, things as redolent of him as father's spectacles and the pigskin case were of him.

But where is he? A piece of paper with his writing on it gives the time of the London/Athens flight as 5pm. He's at the airport expecting me to come off that flight, and I am not on it.

Exhausted and hungry, trapped in this room until he comes back to it, I lie down on the bed and fall asleep.

He storms in three hours later, angry with disappointment that his wonderful surprise has failed. "Where you have be?"

"I arrived at 5 o'clock this morning…"

"And where you have be all this time?"

"I waited at the airport till they cancelled the plane and then I came here."

"No! No! You be around Athens. You have some secret rendezvous."

"Oh, don't be ridiculous!" I point out that if the domestic flight had not been cancelled – I would be *there* and he would be *here* or I might have gone to any other hotel in Athens.

"Why you want to go to another hotel?"

"I don't. I didn't!"

What's happened? Our meetings used to be the best part almost. Has father's death altered things, making *him* responsible for me now in a way he wasn't before?

"Look – if you don't want me here, I will GO."

"Why you want to go?"

"I DON'T!" Two weeks in England has unfitted me for this lunacy – playing Desdemona to his Othello?

"You think to go away of my hands. I KILL you first!"

Is this Love? Do I know what Love is now? No, it's more of a mystery than ever. It has been a long night and a long day of hope and frustration; I feel weak and bemused.

"I'm hungry…I haven't eaten all day."

"I'm hungry too – you think I eat till I find you!"

We descend in the birdcage lift, angry and disappointed in each other. The brothers smile to see us reunited, experiencing the romantic relief we have failed to achieve.

In the street, Tasso draws my arm through his, clamping it to his side like Adam taking back his rib. "I never let you go," he says, speaking seriously now, making a mystic ceremony of his commitment (and my obligation to do the same). In this grubby Athenian street near the Fish Market, he says solemnly, "You will close my eyes", evoking the gummy lashes and the last tear… If it is some sort of triumph to bring him to this declaration, it seems to contain the price that may have to be paid for it.

"I'm awfully hungry…" I murmur.

"I am terrible hungry too – now we go to eat for sure."

The restaurant is a gaunt emporium, the high ceiling coated in grease from the cooking range where the casseroles are set out for customer inspection. The cook stirs each pot to demonstrate what lurks beneath the heavy oil: hunks of meat, fish or beans rise despondently to the surface and sink down again. *"Poly oréa! Verry goot!"* says the cook, as if to pronounce a thing *poly oréa* changes its molecular structure nearer the ideal.

On the menu, in large letters, I read:

KALI OREXI – BON APPETIT – *HAVE A GOOD DESIRE.*
Laughter reduces me to hysteria.

"What happens with you? You crazy?" he says, looking at me with disapproval. I point feebly to the words, where he sees nothing funny. "Can you stop to laughing – the people look at you. We going to eat something nice now. I have order language."

"How do you eat language?" I am baffled.

"*Language!*" he insists. "This! *Glossa!*" He points to his tongue.

"Oh," I say weakly, "you mean tongue". The pitfalls of translation dissolve me again.

"That's what I say!" He is exasperated. *"Ellá, yia sou!"* – another of their meaningless exclamations which spit on your hopes and dreams.

I'm back! This is what I wanted. Nothing else will do. *"Have a good desire!"*

16

Spring has started; Judas trees beginning, the bay tree in flower, wisteria, violets, anemones... In the tiny house I recognise as home, I inhale the flowers Maria has put on the table using a luncheon meat tin as a vase.

"See how nice Maria clean up."

Going into the bedroom, I notice the shelves where I keep my clothes are empty. "Where are my clothes?" Surely he hasn't flogged them? Once I gave him a pair of shoes to take to the mender's and never saw them again. He said he left them in a taverna somewhere – or did he sell them? They were good English shoes.

"I take all to the cleaners." It must have been a moment of sentiment. "I bring tomorrow."

I hope I do get them back. I haven't any others, and you can't buy anything here.

I notice the photograph propped up on the bedside table. It is of him with his arm about a young girl, an American by the blondeness of her hair and the gushing sincerity of her smile; they are sitting together on the edge of our bed. "What's this?"

"Oh, that's Sindy – a crazy American one. I meet just after you going. Two girls was – they asking where to post their letters. I think they want *lettuce*, and I take them to the market. 'Letters,' they say. I say, 'Yes – you going to buy nice lettuce here.' When they make me to understand, we laughing much. After that, I take them everywhere. They enjoying much, and buy our pictures to take back in America."

I continue to look at the photograph without saying anything.

"Nothing happen!" he says, "You sure for that!"

Yes, I am sure for that by the trusting look on her face, and the '*I-am-the-king-of-Good-Basters*' on his.

Suddenly the idea of summer teeming with strange people irritating the surface of the island like water fleas; the girls with long hair and mini-skirts and no bras; the boys with long hair and beards and torn jeans; the middle-aged baring their flesh – the unbeautiful wearing the unsuitable; the late nights and early mornings, the dangers of company, the questions, the answers; the harvest of scandals…where will one find the energy for it all?

I express this sentiment to Pooter when we are sitting together in the wine shop. "Yes, I overheard a Greek lady saying to her friend as she watched some tourists passing by. 'They have homes – why don't they stay in them?' – a rather nice way of putting it, I thought. And it can only get worse as more and more girls stay on, bonded legally or illegally with their chosen Greek." He looks sideways at me, wondering if he has said too much.

"It never occurred to me that I was blazing a trail that others would follow," I reply, "or that Greek schoolboys, instead of doing their sums, were adding up the advantages of 'making two' with 'an English one'."

Pooter laughs outright. "I must say that is rather well put, I must remember that. Anyway, it's an inevitable process once it starts…"

17

Tasso comes home in the middle of his working morning, goes straight to the radio, turns it on, listening to it attentively as a dog as it wheezes out martial music. When I ask "What's the matter?", sensing something wrong, he presses down on the air with his hand, motioning me to silence, as the music stops to be replaced by a rasping voice reciting an endless list: *"Apogorévétai ná…"* (It is forbidden to…)

He paces up and down the room biting his knuckles and cursing, *"Kaikshooters! Kaikshooters!"* (his corruption of 'crapshooters' – I think.) I haven't seen him in a rage like this since his wife threw all his things into the street.

"What's happened?"

"We have a MILITARY DICTATORSHIP in Greece! We have sit down under the Italians…we have sit down under the Germans…and now we going to sit down under the Greeks! These *Kaikshooters!* This is for sure too much!" He is beside himself with rage.

Is he being serious? This sort of thing doesn't happen in my country. The voice continues to rasp out the endless list of *do's* and *don'ts.*

"What are they saying?"

"They say to stay in your house after six o'clock or they shoot you!'

I am still having difficulty believing in the situation when it gets to six o'clock, and we don't go to town. The evening stretches before us like a desert to be crossed without any of the usual aids or diversions; he is out of cigarettes, he hasn't a newspaper, he wants wine – so do I.

"What we do now?" He is like a caged animal, questioning the circumference of our accommodation, which has become a prison. "I have to see that situation with my own eye. I'm going out."

"I'm coming too!" I don't want to be left on my own with everything hostile around us; the darkness already seems to be pressing on the jerry-built built house, crushing it like a nut.

"No! You stay here," he orders, and disappears down the outside stair like a man going over the side of a ship, committing himself to the uncertainty of the dark heaving mass of ocean. Will I ever see him again? What do I do if I don't?

He is soon back – without cigarettes or wine. I am disappointed with relief, though I too need a drink.

On reaching the road, he tells me, he could see the houses and the little taverna tight shut, showing not a chink of light anywhere; the only light came from a patrol car cruising down the lane towards him. His body took him smartly behind a tree without waiting for instructions. They had orders to shoot that night and… "What if happen to be someone in that car no like me?" It was not the night to be putting his popularity to the test. *"The kaikshooters!"* he explodes.

But who are the *kaikshooters?* Nobody seems to know.

*

In the acid of the following days, a picture emerges of three middle-aged Army Colonels, looking like the characters in Puppet Theatre, proclaiming they have saved Greece from Communism. To endorse their integrity, they have not deposed the young King, who looks handsome and wholesome in his uniform. The country is also to be saved from European moral degeneration.

Tasso is shaving in the kitchen at the tin tank with a little mirror in which he can hardly see his chin, with the transistor propped on the sink giving out the continuous stream of propaganda which passes for The News. Suddenly it is followed by a summary in English.

"False reports have been circulated by the Foreign Press. In fact, peace and calm reign throughout the country as never before, and everybody is full of enthusiasm for the New Regime."

"*Xestiká!*" (Shit!) he swears and cuts himself. He is in a vile mood the whole time, and I tend to get the blame for everything. I get my information from Pooter, who can read the Greek newspapers and listens to the BBC.

"Only the priests are allowed to wear beards," he tells me. I can't think how this will be enforced when the tourists begin to arrive. "The Hippies won't be allowed to land but according to the BBC, people are being discouraged from taking holidays in Greece this year. Agencies are cancelling their bookings. The French Club is laying off staff and offering a free week to anyone prepared to risk it. But a rather nice touch is that in the Greek Army all ranks above that of Colonel have been abolished." Menace in Absurdity.

I am thankful Dad got off before this happened. He would be urging me yet again to take another look at my Destiny, or to simply "Come home at once". Crudely painted posters have appeared everywhere advertising The New Dawn for Greece: a straight road going toward a rising sun, and, to left and right, volcanoes belching up lumps labelled "Communism!", "Anarchy!", "Atheism!" On the road, a soldier, a sailor and an airman are following a female figure in a nightdress who is pointing to the New Dawn. The artist has had difficulty with the perspective; the figures are walking crabwise off the road, and only the lady's outstretched arm and nipples are pointing to the New Dawn. When I take the bus to town I see another pasted above the windscreen: Christ hanging on the cross and a young man walking by with something nasty coming out of his mouth. Under the picture are the words MI BLASPHEMETE (Don't Blaspheme).

"The naiveté of the artwork is astonishing!" I say later to Pooter, the only person I can discuss anything with.

He agrees. "In Athens they've arrested several people who have spoken out against the Regime…particularly the intellectuals, the artists and writers."

Suddenly I am glad Tasso is not that sort of artist.

A stunned normality returns with the shifting of the curfew to ten o'clock, but long before that the streets, cafés and restaurants are empty. The only moving thing on the roads is the patrol car like a sinister white cat.

But nothing holds back the surge of leaf and flower, or the rituals of Easter performed under police surveillance and umbrellas, as heavy slate-grey clouds boil up over the island, or march past it like the remnants of Napoleon's army on retreat from Moscow. Our candles gutter in the wind as the crowd gathers around the bandstand under the mauve blossom of the Judas trees. The priests pronounce *"Christos Anesti!"* – *Christ is Risen.* Fireworks climb the sky like tracer bullets. The people disperse without much joy, uneasy about the future, and keen to get their candle home alight to make the cross in smoke on the lintel of the door for good luck in the coming year.

The Season begins with the first charter flight. "I want to see that!" says Tasso, making me drive to the airport.

We watch a thin trickle of tourists crossing the Tarmac. "*Xestiká!*" he explodes. "But never mind, tonight we make the *exposition.*" He is a survivor after all.

The receptionist tells him there are only twelve people at the hotel, but with determination he sets the pictures out on the marble table in the foyer and, leaning on the reception desk at a discreet distance from the bait, watches until someone, usually a woman, pauses to look at them.

"Which one you prefer, Madame?" he enquires sweetly, materializing at her elbow.

She takes in his appearance; he certainly looks an artist in a fresh shirt open at the neck, and the old black corduroy jacket. With new interest in the pictures, she buys one. Behind her back, as she walks away, he flings up his blackthorn stick as if potting a bird – *bang*! one for the bag.

He sells another couple after supper, making the bag up to three – not bad with only twelve people. It's a good start and confirms his faith in his ability "*to milk a flea!*"

"Where to go now," he ponders as we leave. With the arrival of the tourists the curfew has been lifted altogether. "Anyway, drive *that* way…"

On the main road, we are stopped by the Military Police who flash a torch over us and ask where we are going. His manner is disarmingly affable as he tells them what he hasn't told me: "The casino." They wave us on.

He spends the next mile swearing "*Kaikshooters! Kaikshooters!*", wishing they were the Gestapo again, the foreign enemy, to be tricked and bamboozled in dangerous games of audacity – he has done plenty of that.

"When I be twenty, I don't care half-a-cigarette for my life!" The memory takes him by surprise, as if the years have robbed him of something vital.

To get my own back, I point out with satisfying pessimism: "You're not wearing a tie...they won't let you into the Casino."

The advantage is short-lived; at the Casino they are glad to see anyone, he is welcomed with open arms. This is going to be a bad year for this new venture.

"Give them your passport," he says to me.

"Why?"

"So you can play."

"I don't want to play. Why don't *you* play?"

The receptionist shakes his head sadly. "Mr Tassos no permit to play. Only people from outside the island. It is rule of the Casino."

"I haven't got my passport." He knows I don't carry it with me.

"You don't have your passport!" This is a charade – what game is he playing? Whatever it is, it works. One of the amiable Storm Troopers comes into reception and, recognising Tasso, waives the need for identification and escorts us upstairs to the bar, where Tasso suddenly hands me a 100-drachma note. "Go to play something."

"I don't know how to play!" I am exasperated.

The amiable Storm Trooper, who looks like Parsifal, offers to escort me into the salon and initiate me into the game. I look dumbly at Tasso. "Yes, go with the gentleman," he says.

Herr 'Parsifal', assuming the air of a Knight of the Holy Grail, holds open the door for me. At the guichet on the landing, where the cashier sits like a heavenly bank manager, I give up my pink banknote and receive five bilious yellow pieces of plastic, which doesn't seem much of an exchange. 'Parsifal' escorts me into the salon where the green baize tables float like islands under the low hanging lamps; perched on a high stool, the croupier's white face hangs like a moon above the bowl with the spinning wheel in it.

"Faites vos jeux, mesdames et messieurs." There are only five *messieurs*, Greeks from Athens, and one *madame*.

Pulling out the gilt chair, 'Parsifal' places me next to her and, bending solicitously over me, whispers the mysteries o*f rouge et noir, passe, impasse, carrés, and transversals.*

I wish he wouldn't – being with Tasso has made the proximity of other men intolerable; my skin prickles, I may even come out in spots.

Suddenly the woman sitting next to me asks sharply, "Is this your first time?" and, when I admit it, violently pushes back her chair and removes herself to the other side of the table, as if I had B.O. 'Parsifal' explains this mystery too. "The lady is afraid you will have Beginners' Luck."

The croupier spins the wheel, the ivory ball shoots from his fingers, skipping and twirling like a little ballerina up the sides of the deep mahogany bowl, skidding over the whirling numbers. As the wheel slows, the little ball seems beset with a tantalizing indecision before finally settling in one numbered slot, which it rides triumphantly to a standstill. The croupier extends a long wand with a T-bar to scrape away all the plastic pieces except those on the winning number. With a flick of the wrist he sends an arch of coloured pieces in a parabola to land in front of the gentleman with the long face at the end of the table. The gentleman carefully adds them to the little towers of plastic on the green baize in front him, like a child with building bricks.

I watch with interest, but it doesn't make me want to risk my pieces. 'Parsifal' tactfully suggests I try something, so I shove a piece on *rouge;* it comes up *noir.* I try a number; that piece is ruthlessly clawed away. Wherever I put it, the claw takes it away. It wasn't much money, but there were other things we might have done with it – such as eat it. I feel guilty at having lost it, and angry because he is going to be angry with me for having lost it.

My pieces gone, 'Parsifal' with inexhaustible punctilio escorts me back to the bar; bending over me from his great height, trying to look into my face. (I haven't looked at him once.) "Perhaps…" he delicately suggests "…you are lucky in Love…?" *What a stupid remark! Who makes up these clichés?*

"You lost all?" Tasso is genuinely surprised.

"It was *your* idea, remember?"

I knew that when he handed me this ball, he expected me to score some sort of goal with it. In front of 'Parsifal', he dismisses it blandly. "Never mind…"

But on the way home, after being stopped again by the police, he reverts to the subject. "So quickly you lose all?"

"It was only 100 dracs, for God's sake!"

"Never mind the God. I mind my pocket. You don't win *anything*? And what that SS one doing with you all that time?"

"Just now you say 'you lost the money *so quickly*' – now you say' '*all that time…*'"

"Him flirting you much, anyhow…" *Here we go*! Cue for a bloody row, but I am too tired, or haven't had enough to drink.

At home he goes into the kitchen to make soup out of one onion and a tin of tomato paste – all there is. I go to bed. I'm just sliding into anaesthetizing sleep when he calls, "Come to eat. I have make wonderful soup!"

When I don't stir, he comes to drag me out of bed. I scramble up and start hitting him as hard as I can. "LEAVE ME ALONE! I don't want your bloody soup! I want to sleep!"

"But we don't have eat anything."

"It's your fault we don't eat," I cry, kneeling on the bed wailing and gasping.

He looks at me as if Greeks never behave like this. "You have be to drama school?" he says with calm distaste. Damn him! Take a leaf out of his book, he changes the rules.

He goes back to his soup. I try to get back to sleep, feeling hungry – but for what, I don't know.

19

The town is a quiver this morning with last night's drama. Pooter is full of it.

"You know the police are wearing guns now – even off duty. Consequently, one has shot his fiancée, then shot himself... and you've heard the Colonels' latest edict – plate-smashing is to be banned in tavernas from now on, as a barbarian custom giving tourists a bad example of Greek Culture."

The Hon. raises her eyebrows; she has never been to a Greek taverna. "Plate-smashing?"

"It's a traditional thing to throw the plates from the tables at the feet of a *Zembekiko* dancer, or the *Hasapiko* dancers. It's quintessentially Greek – a sign of approval, just as we clap."

Envisaging a dinner party where all the guests throw their plates on the floor, the Hon's eyebrows rise even higher, causing the monocle she sometimes wears to fall out. "I've never been to a Greek taverna," she murmurs without enthusiasm.

"Then, Madame, 99 per cent of Greek life is a closed book to you," says Pooter.

It is obvious she has no desire to open it though we try to explain how a Greek evening takes off when a man spontaneously gets up to dance alone a kind of 'space flight' of the soul, or when two or even three men dance 'the Butcher's Dance' – and how the waiters put down their trays to take over the empty floor space and fill it with bird-like postures.

"The tourists love it! Especially the British. They throw everything, even the salt and pepper. We've had a plate of sardines thrown at our feet."

"When I take my foreign friends to a tavern evening," Pooter pooterishly, continues, "I make it quite clear they are *not* to throw the plates from the table. You ask the waiter to bring the cheap plates provided for this custom. It saves a great deal of misunderstanding when it comes to the bill."

The Hon. listens with a reaction that could be described as *emphatic*: a closing of the pores. She cares nothing for the customs of the country whose shores have become "*the butt and seamark of her utmost sail...*"

"Well, I must leave you, ladies," declares Pooter, getting up in his decisive way when you have exhausted your allotted time in his schedule. "I shall not be able to join you in the wine shop in the mornings or evenings for the next few weeks," he announces, keeping the best information to the last, "as I am to be acting Dutch Consul while that gentleman is on holiday. So I shall be obliged to keep the Consul hours." He is secretly thrilled with the idea. "My bedside reading for the next few weeks has to be the Consul's handbook: 1,400 pages of instructions as to what to do with distressed seamen and pregnant girls." Then he adds, "I suppose my private life will have to be impeccable..."*pity about the distressed seamen* "...though I shall be diplomatically immune, of course..." As he goes, he says to me, "You know they've arrested Theodorakis?"

"Why?" I am shocked, his music is the sound of Greece, just as ouzo and retsina are the taste of it; it's on all the jukeboxes. "He's a Communist."

When Tasso collects me from the wine shop, he is in a fury about Theodorakis. "I want to see what happens!"

We go from taverna to taverna, looking on the jukeboxes for his music. He doesn't find any. "Where's the records of Theodorakis?" he shouts at the tavern-keepers, who shrug and turn away. He calls them "*An-andreï*", non-men – a terrible insult.

"Ellá! Tasso...it is a new time now."

When he won't shut up, he is told to get out.

20

We go to the Salamander, it doesn't have a jukebox. The young American is sitting at the bar. He turned up three months ago, supposed to be writing a novel, but all he seems to do is sit about in bars drinking and provoking anybody with enough English to talk politics. He doesn't speak Greek.

He greets Tasso loudly. Tasso acknowledges him briefly, but doesn't engage as he usually does with foreigners. I ignore him, as I have learned to ignore all men.

He leans over toward me and says, "You're English, aren't you?"

"For sure," Tasso acknowledges for me.

"Then why doesn't she open her mouth?"

"The British *buy*, they don't sell," Tasso smoothly replies. *I couldn't have thought of that! No wonder I love this man!*

Jason tries another tack, bawling out to the whole company, "I never thought to see the day when the Greeks would stop talking politics – as if they've had their tongues cut out, and now they're afraid to listen to Theodorakis."

"I don't lose my tongue, Jason," Tasso says ominously. "What you doing here anyway? From far you smell to me of C.I.A. and I say this – it is the fault of the Americans what happens here. "A ripple runs through the other Greeks at the bar.

Jason gasps with laughter as if it's the biggest joke in the world, but Madame Ellie shrieks out like a night heron, "*Se parakáló*, Tasso! *Taisez vous voyons*, in the name of God!", using three languages. She wants no subversive talk in her cocktail bar, and looks indignantly at me. "*Mon Dieu!* Can't you control him!" – the inference being that British women, though no good in bed, have the virtue of the British Nanny – discipline. Why doesn't she go for Jason? He started it, but he is a good-looking young man. Madame Ellie likes young men.

As Tasso is about to open his mouth again, she comes flying out from behind the bar, furious with beak and claw. "Get out!

Get out!" she screams, pushing him towards the door. He allows himself to be pushed: "Never try to fight a furious woman."

As she closes the door on us, her shrill voice exclaims, "*MON DIEU! We want to die in our beds!*"

The bed has always been an important arena for her.

21

He lurches up the street towards the Old Tavern, more drunk than I supposed. At the entrance he bumps into a man coming out. They recognise each other.

"*Costa!*"

"*Tasso!*" Wrapping their arms about each other in instant brotherhood.

Turning to me, he oozes, "Oh, darling..." (always a danger signal) "...him one of the best actors in Greece!"

The man smiles professionally at me; I recognise the face that has been grinning rather fatuously at us from posters all over the town.

Nothing will satisfy Tasso but "to show our good friend the studio..." Is he mad? We don't have a studio. The friend indicates his pregnant wife, a girl much younger than he is, but Tasso is not to be deflected in this mood, thumbing the buttons of brotherhood no Greek may ignore, though the pregnant girl-wife, tinselled and bleached, whines peevishly, "I'm *tired*...Costa...." A Greek may not seem to give way to a wife; she loses the battle, Tasso wins.

We squeeze them into the tiny Fiat. "*O, Máná-mou,*" groans the girl, having to squeeze her belly into the back seat.

She quavers again at the sight of the track down to the house. "Where *are we going*?" she wails, tottering on high heels, clinging to her husband, who is wondering too.

Inside the house, they are dumbfounded at being brought here; a peasant house would be clean and tidy. The girl rakes me with eyes that say, *"Is this how foreigners live?"*

"Make some coffee," Tasso says. Can my humiliation go any further – I never make the gritty stuff and we don't have enough cups.

"No-no – don't bother," the actor says in English, "we can't stay ..."

Tasso is rootling around the 'studio' looking for one of his pictures to sell him; the night has not yielded, and he left the 'ammunitions' at the Salamander when Madame Ellie kicked us out. Here, he has only the crazy pictures even he has never been able to sell. My face, reflecting a growing disillusion, makes Costa, a good-hearted man, fling his arm about Tasso.

"Tasso good! Very good boy! He *bohème.*"

"Pamé na figoumé," (Let's go) the girl whines.

We are obliged to drive them back to town. On the way up the track to the car, I suddenly realise Tasso is not with us. Costa says, "He's not coming…he drink much…"

Tasso never lets me go anywhere alone. Where the hell is he? They are anxious to get back to town; the girl is whining. Where the hell is Tasso? But I am forced to take a chance – to drive them quickly back to town and be rid of them will take no more than ten minutes.

When I get back to the house, the door is open, the lights on, but no sign of him. I am standing by the table when he comes crashing up the steps, grabs me by the throat and flings me through the door. I hit the banister and clutch it to stop falling down the steps.

"Where you be, you *putana*!" He kicks me in the thigh.

In a daze, I get down the steps, wondering what to do. I have locked the car, the keys are on the table.

"Let me have the keys…they're on the table."

This sets him off again, he comes down the steps like a Rottweiler. I run into the darkness of the orange trees, and stop, mesmerized, as he comes at me, hitting me round the head. I hear rather than feel the blows…then hot syrup on my hands…from my nose. *I hope it isn't broken…why is this happening…when will it stop?*

I let myself fall. He kicks me. I get up again.

"Please stop hitting me, I'll go…" I am wishing above all to be reasonable.

"You no going anywhere," he says, dragging me back into the house, where he lets go of me.

I wander into the studio. I want to lie down…in the dark…alone. *This experience hasn't become reality yet. It is travelling towards me from infinite space like a beam of light. It can't become reality till I reflect it...*

He is standing over me again, shouting, "Tell me! Where you be?"

"I had to take them back to town...didn't I?"

He doesn't know what I am talking about. He has forgotten them. He goes back to the other room, the bed creaks; he will sleep now. No...he's back dragging me up from the floor.

"I cannot leave you here...you will be cold!" he says. *How considerate...*

Putting me into our bed, he lies down beside me and falls instantly asleep.

I am trying to wake up from this one.

22.

Next morning, Sunday, he wakes at his usual time, goes into the kitchen to make his coffee, drinks it at the open door, smoking a cigarette.

"Can you see my gold chain anywhere – on the stairs?" I mumble through lips like rubber tyres. It must have been lying at his feet; he comes into the room with it. "Why you chuck it out?" It was his gift.

"Not me…You…" I say it without emphasis. He looks straight at me, gets back into bed, falls instantly asleep as a deliberate act.

When he wakes, he turns to look at me, hoping the pumpkin head on the pillow painted with congealed blood is not true. I now have his complete attention, and enjoy his horror.

"How happen that?" he asks slowly.

"You…"

He crosses himself in awe. "I dreaming you go off with a man…in the car…I try to follow…to kill you and him. Pó-pó-pó…" He is crumbling before the evidence that it wasn't a dream. "But why you go off like that?"

"I had to drive them back to town…didn't I?"

"Who?"

"The actor and his wife." Talking through this face is tiring.

"*Panayia mou*…!." He is bending over me in anguish. "I don't remember *anything*…" Now he leans forward with the intention of kissing me.

"No sentiment, please…" I am unable to bear the weight of sentiment on the extended surface of my face, tender even to his breath, which stinks of wine.

"You very right." he says, withdrawing. He is sorry, very sorry, but he will not say he is sorry, because in his terms, *"when the damage is be done, is too late to be sorry. Not to make the mistake in the first place is the point."* I accepted the logic of this a long time ago, and expect no formal apology.

He gets dressed to go to town. I don't want him to stay; I want to be alone with the experience he has given me. As he goes through the door, he says, "Don't make anything...I be back early..."

I am granted a holiday!

I lie in bed happily enough, my body stiff but almost proud to have sustained this battering. Inside my head, the demolition done, the work of reconstruction begins.

If father were still alive, I would have to take up an attitude toward this experience as his daughter, but as myself, I can make what I like of it; I can lie back and enjoy it.

Curiosity drags me out of bed to the small mirror; my face is too big for it, but in it, I see 'Buddy' again, the large, flat-faced cotton doll I had as a child. The swollen lips, two deep scratches on my neck as if clawed by a tiger; the eyes with red and blue aureoles are quite impressive. *"Two Lovely Black Eyes – Oh, what a surprise..."* I wonder egotistically if they might be the biggest black eyes in Eastern Europe at this moment...two Balkan Black eyes...

In the evening, he says I can't go to town with him, "for people to see you like that! *Ó Theos na filaxi!*" God forbid! He crosses himself piously; because I have gained a face, he will lose one. They know how these things happen, even if it is all new to me.

He goes alone, but comes back early with wine and nice things to eat, and even cooks it "like my mother make it". We sit on the balcony in the moonlight. The transistor obliges with *classiki musiki*. We are lovers and friends again.

"Did you ever do that to your wife?"

"For *God-ni-say*, no!" The answer is simple: "I was never there..."

He comes home next day to find me tending a small bonfire of his letters and mine. He pauses to watch the bright airmail envelopes curl up in the flames. I think I am taking a subtle revenge until he murmurs, "Pity to broke such sweet stuff..." and goes up into the house, leaving me as the vandal.

23.

When he starts coming home after midnight, I rebel. "I'm coming to town tonight!" I vow, finally bored with watching the sunset round my eyes. "I can cover the marks with make-up and wear sunglasses. You can say we had an accident in the car. I had to brake suddenly and hit my face on the steering wheel." (Just possible.)

Seeing I am determined, he grudgingly consents.

"Why are you wearing sunglasses at night?" Pooter asks.

"We had a bit of an accident with the car, I had to brake suddenly and hit my face against the driving wheel..." I take off the sunglasses.

"Oh," he says, understanding all, but with his usual discretion he goes on to talk of other things. "You know that woman who helped The Hon. with her move...and so many things went missing? Her silver fox fur and the crystal bird? I'd spoken to her, saying that Madame would have to go to the police if her things didn't reappear. Well, when the Hon. was passing the furrier in the main street the other day; he called her into the shop, and gave her the silver fox fur. He knew it was her fox fur because she'd given it to him to clean when she first came here. And now suddenly the crystal bird has come back, stuffed behind a cushion on the settee. She's a very cunning little woman, that. We haven't managed to get rid of her even yet, she still has a key. But The Hon. is delighted to have her fur and her crystal bird back."

Tasso comes to collect me early, hoping I will consent to go home. I have no intention of going home; I have spent enough evenings on my own in that dog kennel.

"Okay, we go a little to the Paradeisos," he says, hoping it will be empty at this early hour. For the moment I have the upper hand; it is so intoxicating I abandon my sunglasses. "I can't see to drive!"

When we get to the Paradeisos, he tries to make me put them on again.

212

"Don't be silly. It looks ridiculous at night – people will wonder more why I am wearing them." I win.

As we enter, a woman sitting at a table opposite the door looks up and screams, "Tasso! *AGAPÉ MOU!*", shoves back her chair and flings herself into his arms.

He pretends to know who she is, until real recognition sweeps his face. "Oh, *darr-ling...*" He turns to me. "You don't imagine what I find tonight! My First Fiancée!"

It is my turn to have the expression wiped off my face. What does he mean by his 'First Fiancée'? But more than that – *she has a black eye too.* We stare at each other with lively curiosity.

Still holding this woman with hennaed hair and haggard eyes in his arms, he is saying, "When she sixteen years old, she want to be marry with me..."

As I have two black eyes and she only one, I remark, "How glad she must be that she isn't." With a burst of laughter, he translates this for her. Abandoning her clasp on him, she flings her arms round me in womanly fellowship.

We sit down at her table, where her companion, an elderly peasant woman, turns out to be her mother. She explains to Tasso that she is back on the island to escape her lover who gave her the black eye, but she is so bored at home, she dragged her mother with her tonight. She eagerly continues to tell him the things a woman can tell a man who is no longer her lover. *(I can't tell him anything – he doesn't listen.)* How she misses the boyfriend who gave her the black eye so much, and is longing to get back to him.

As the jukebox vibrates with yet another love song, she lifts her hennaed head like a doe and begins to sing in a dark, bruised voice, conveying all the agony and confusion of desire, and the eternal hope of love. "She a night club singer," he says.

She signals him to translate the words for me.

"You are my love, my pain, my mistake/ Nothing heals the pain of Love/ But should I see you again/ I'd make the mistake again / of loving you!"

Putting his wire-wool head against her hennaed one, he adds his kippered voice in harmony, both pairs of glossy eyes looking not at each other, but at me.

"Tassos LUV YOU," she manages in English and, raising her glass, clinks it against mine. "You lucky much! *Ipomoni!*"

I wonder what that word means, and look it up in my dictionary next morning. "Patience and Endurance," it says.

So Love must be endured...

24

The orange trees hum with bees in the noon-tide, and the scent of the blossom is overpowering at night. The mountains are crystal clear with snow on the highest peaks; the sea under the sun and the wind, a deep ultramarine.

Pooter, in his element discreetly promulgating illicit information, says, "Four bus-loads of political prisoners were brought to the prison here yesterday...and rumour has it that five hundred have been shipped to detention centres on other islands." Nobody talks about these things. Life goes on.

The hotels are half-empty; the tourists are chiefly British or Dutch and know little or nothing of the political situation. They have come for the sea and the sun. Tasso displays his pictures on the marble table in the foyer. Nothing deflects him either.

A Dutch couple take an interest in me. "You have been long in Greece? You like it better than England? The climate is better?"

I answer "Yes" not very responsively.

"And the men..." The wife involuntarily glances towards Tasso. "...are more...?"

"Yes, very full of life," I say quickly. They go.

The next to invade my privacy is a small man with a North Country accent who says, "I don't know what relationship you have with the gentleman selling the pictures...I saw you both dancing the Greek dance last year...are you his daughter?" I am too stunned to reply. "You *are* English, aren't you?" I can only nod. "Will you be dancing tonight, do you think? I want him to teach me. You see, in Stockton, where I come from, we have Greek evenings in our 'modest way'. Oh I'm thrilled he's here tonight. It *makes* my holiday..." Turning his head to where Tasso is selling a picture to a middle-aged woman, he carries on impetuously: "I've quite fallen in love with him... in a *nice* sort of way, of course. You see – he *symbolizes Greece* for me..." he gushes, in a desperate attempt to convey his emotion.

He symbolizes Greece for me too, but my silence is full of wonder at the power of symbols, particularly that of the chimera, with the lion's head, goat's body and serpent's tail, *"or any incongruous conception of fancy",* as my dictionary says.

But we don't go down to the pool-side bar, to liven it with impromptu dancing of the Butcher's Dance. As we drive away from the hotel, the figure of the little man from Stockton gazes through the glass doors, like a deserted child.

I had forgotten about him.

25

"Go *there*," Tasso says. I know where 'there' is now.

Driving through the sweet-smelling darkness, a peculiar gas pervades my veins until it reaches my head, filling it with an insane desire to gamble. The idea 'Parsifal' put into my head about being '*Lucky at cards, unlucky in love*'... Which is it? I want to know, and anyway, after two black eyes, 'the gods' owe me something.

The flunkey in breeches and wig, who pulled open the bronze doors the first time, has gone; business has failed to justify him. We must use our own strength to push it open, but we have the *entré* now – no passports needed.

We ascend in the red plush lift this time. It has a mirror; we regard each other in it.

"I want to play," I say.

"How? I have only enough for the bar."

"I'll play my two pound notes." It must be my own money or it won't be a proper test.

"Okay – try," he says, looking at me through the mirror...seeing what...seeing whom?

We emerge from the lift beside the cashier's guichet. I hand over my two pounds; the Heavenly Bank Manager crisps them between his fingers. When he turns his back for a moment, I expect to see little wings sprouting from his dinner jacket. He smiles in a paternal way over half-specs as he gives me the plastic pieces, reminding me a bit of Dad.

I know the way to the salon now. It is empty; I surprise the croupiers demonstrating the mysteries of the game to the plainclothes policeman on duty. They look up guiltily at my approach.

"You wish to play, Madame?" the head croupier enquires from his elevated perch.

"Yes, please." I am still possessed of a confidence I rarely feel even in ordinary circumstances.

The croupier spins the wheel and shoots the ball. I place one piece on red – all I know how to do. Red comes up. I leave the pieces on. It comes up again and again and again, multiplying my winnings, which I have not removed. I take them off just before it changes to *noir*. I shove a piece on a box marked 1-23. It trebles my stake. I perceive the charm of this game – it's *poly-oréa-ness....* I choose a number, 26, my birthday number – it comes up! Even the cynical croupiers are surprised now, and the policeman is thoroughly excited. I make little piles of my pieces, I have two blue pieces worth 200 drachmes each.

Suddenly I lose a hundred dracs. That's it, the gas is turned off at the mains. Gathering up the pieces with difficulty, I make for the exit, but the croupier calls me back, making me understand that the winner owes something to 'the table'. I have no idea how to behave, but throw back a few pieces, at which they bleat in unison: *"Merci pour les employees..."* in a funny voice – like sheep.

I pour the pieces onto the bar in front of Tasso. He crosses himself solemnly. "I never hope," he says, really astonished, never having thought of it seriously as a way of making money. His conversion is instantaneous. "Go! Put all on...25!", thrusting some pieces back at me. I run back to the salon, my heels clacking on the marble floor.

"You wish to play, Madame?"

"Yes!" I am irritated by the supercilious ritual.

The croupier smirks as he bends forward to shoot the ball. They see this happen all the time. I bang the pieces onto 25.

"Vingt-cinq!" Twenty-five comes up! The croupiers look blank with amazement, the policeman does a pirouette, letting his breath out in a hiss. The head croupier displays his skill sending the arch of coloured plastic parabolling onto the green baize in front of me.

I scoop it up, not forgetting the *pourboire* this time. *"Merci pour les employees..."* they bleat like orphan boys. *I've won... I've won!* The strange thing is I *knew* I would win. *I knew I would win!*

218

Colliding with 'Parsifal' as I come back into the bar, I am steadied by a firm hand on my elbow. As I unload the heap of plastic onto the bar in front of Tasso, it hits me; the encounter with Parsifal triggers it. I am not lucky in Love...

Tasso tosses a generous amount to the barman to pay for his drinks. Turning to me, he notices my expression. "What's the matter with you?"

"I'm not *lucky in Love*..."

"Don't be stupid," he says, "you have Me."

But on the way home, after being stopped by the Military Police, he says, "That Gauleiter touch you!"

"What *are* you talking about?"

"Him – he touch you!"

"Don't be ridiculous! I banged into him!"

"Is not ridiculous. Is enough for me to kill him!"

Thus I perceive that the winner is the loser. He has pocketed the money. I have lost my two English pounds and may receive in exchange another pair of black eyes.

26.

He has put me into one of the cafés on the arcade tonight. It is the hour of the *voltá,* with people promenading up and down, or sitting at the café tables under the arcades and under the trees which are full of the noise of the sparrows settling to roost as the iris blue twilight deepens into darkness. The electric lights are on. Waiters shout their orders for *"Dio froota...dio zokalatina...tessera spezial!"* carrying the loaded tray shoulder high, breasting the mainstream like ferryboats crossing the Bosphorus to reach the tables under the acacia trees. A basket on a string dangles in the door of the café, lowered from the mezzanine under the vaulted arcade. A waiter takes out an empty ice-cream glass and some money. The basket waits, rising obligingly to let people in and out, but does not go away; it is waiting for the change, before disappearing upwards like a *deus ex machina.*

The American Navy is in the harbour – the only navy that visits now, being 'supportive' of the New Regime. Five sailors, looking like newly hatched chicks, place themselves at a table next to me, and order a bottle of local brandy. They pour it out in tumblerfuls, and settle down to drink it owlishly to obliterate another night in a place which isn't home.

Pooter, passing along the arcade, looks in and, seeing them, not me, enters, approaches their table and starts talking to them in his habitually informative way. They focus on him with difficulty. He is dressed differently tonight, a jacket without lapels, and a flamboyant tie. I've never seen him like this.

Then he sees me, and looks shocked. "What are you doing here?" – as if it were most irregular.

"It's Wednesday," I remind him. The wine shop is closed.

He sits down "just for a second" to explain to me why he approaches sailors. "I always tell them the facts of life in Greece," he says, as if performing an inestimable service, "i.e. not to approach women." Does this directive come from the Consular Handbook's chapter on distressed seamen? "I tell them to go to the White Cat, a dive in the harbour. It's the only place – they can get everything they need there." Wiping behind his ears with his handkerchief, he licks his lips like a lizard. "It's very warm tonight…Well, I must leave you… Goodnight to you."

As he is going out he bumps into Tasso. He has come from the café next door. Taking in the sailors, he says, "Anyone bother you?" though it is obvious they have no interest in anything but brandy.

"I have find two very ugly Dutch women – so nice, they are – really! And if you hear the lies I am saying, you going to kill me for sure! They are excellent!"

The Greek lie is not an un-truth, but the lie as entertainment, or the truth with a little salt and pepper. The Greek's intuition guides him in the choice of the lies or truths he serves up, so that it becomes what the listener wants to hear; it could be classified as an art form, or even a public service, not meant to deceive, but rather to add zest to life. Foreign tourists need that stuff, that is why they come abroad. It is a Greek's duty to share his zest for life with them.

Bored with inaction, I plead, "Can't I come there?"

"I want you for sure, but if you come now you will *exployed* all my work. They ready to buy our pictures… and we need that to be around tonight…"

But instead of going, he stands thoughtfully scratching his head. "But…we have another problem…"

Something in his expression tells me it must be to do with women, and automatically I recite the list: "Odette… Manette… Collete…Ursula…"

"Exactly!" he says, showing relief at my *clairvoyance*.

"All?" I am startled.

"For God-ni-say, no!" The idea makes even him sweat.

"Who? Which?"

"Manette and Ursula…both at the club. Panayoti tell me. Don't be worry – Panayoti tell them about you "

"Do they know about each other?"

"That's the problem," he confesses.

221

"What are you going to do?" I'm awed by the situation.

"Bah! is no so great problem! We take them round with us."

"Together?"

"No! One night one, and one night the other…"

"Who's first?"

"Ursula. She wait for us at the Beach Restaurant tonight."

27

At the Beach Restaurant, he puts me at a table and goes off to look for her. They return together. "I remember you," she says. I remember her too, but pretend not to from a certain delicacy – I have read her letters to him. *"Un sentiment inoubliable m'attache a toi, Tasso..."* It always sounded better in French. I ruined her holiday when I came back that first summer.

She looks older, harder, with close-cropped hair, and large dangling pink plastic earrings which make her look like an embittered cabaret dancer in an Impressionist painting. She asks for a whisky and drags deeply on a cigarette; she doesn't attempt to talk, and he doesn't know what to do, afraid of us both.

"Don't be angry, *darr-ling...*" *Which of us is he talking to?* "Ursula is our sister now...everything alright..." *If I had a gun I would shoot him for her sake and mine...*

I am glad when he takes her off to dance, with an anxious order to me: "Don't *do* anything!" Like what? Get into the car and drive off? I'm glad he's a little bit afraid...that's something. On the dance floor she is transformed into a living being, tasting the salt-sweet savour of a lost time – *I envy her that.*

Back at the table, she lights another cigarette and asks for another whisky. *This is an expensive night for him...* Soon she decides to return to the club and says goodnight. He promises her we will meet again; she nods, ice-pink earrings swinging, tanned slender legs gleaming under the flowing skimpy dress. She strides back along the beach, her hopes for this holiday dashed again.

We stay the night at Michaelaki's and next morning, Sunday, we wait for Manette at a table under the trees by the pebble beach. He tells me the Manette story.

"Was one night here – long ago now – must be ten years now, some French people from the club call me to sit down with them. They make a party for the birthday – her birthday. I don't know her at all... Never see her before in my life. Someone ask her what is the best present for her birthday, she look straight at me and say 'Him!' I take her to dance, but she don't dance well. I thinking she be a little bit drunk.

"Anyway, I give her a rendezvous for next day in town, and wait for her at the Bar Greco. But when I see her coming up the street, my God! I am ready to get the hell out of there before she see me...she have a broke leg for sure!"

"You mean a lame leg."

"Yes, exactly...my friends going to joking much to see me around with her, but then I thinking 'Poor Thing – how much she need to have something...' So I take her around with me and she enjoying so much with me, *Pó-pó*! She stay a whole month with me – she lose her job in Paris. And when she go – she crying so much at the harbour I want to kill her. I hate the *woomans* to crying...you know that. But as the ship going, I climb up on some boxes to waving, the boxes be down, the God pay me! And all my friends laughing much! But it was a nice thing that I do..." *Mediterranean Chivalry.* "Ah, she coming..." he says, getting up to greet the woman limping along the beach, wearing a very full skirt.

She greets him the French way with three formal kisses. He draws her arm through his to bring her to the table. She knew of my existence that first summer. He was writing to her; her replies were full of warnings: *Mefie-toi des Anglaises! (Don't trust English girls!).*

"*Bonjour*," she now says civilly, in that lilting way of a Parisienne, apologizing for not speaking English well enough for conversation. I have to admit my French is the same, which makes her think I don't understand it either.

I leave them together, taking myself off for a long swim, thrusting lazily through the water or hanging under the jetty watching the fish grazing the sandy bottom. I can hear him saying laughingly, "What dictionary did you find to read my terrible French?"

"*Mon coeur,*" she replies with humourless sincerity. *How funny, so did I...*

When I return to the table, he goes into the taverna to order something and doesn't come back. I know he is having a koniak at the counter. *I could do with a koniak too.*

In the extended interval, she turns on me a hard, puzzled scrutiny. "Can you cook?" So she can speak English. "*I* am a verry good cook", dreaming of the meals she might have set before him. I have a vision of him in blue overalls, with the baguettes tied to his bicycle...

Silence falls between us. This is straining me to the utmost. *Why doesn't he come back, the coward! He set this up...*

Suddenly, Manette's voice, rich with emotion, is saying, "Do you *lo-ove* him?"

Startled, I reply rather sharply, "Would I be here if I didn't?" I have spoken too quickly, she hasn't understood. I repeat flatly, "Yes, I do as a matter of fact" in a very English sort of way. It convinces her I am incapable of loving him as deeply or sincerely as she does. *Mefie-toi des Anglaises!*

I decide to go for another long swim, perceiving that there are advantages in sharing him; we wouldn't have stayed at the beach this long, except for her. *Perhaps I could rent him out by the hour...*

They both stay the three weeks. We take them out alternately. What does this do for the Eternal Triangle? I call it the *Elastic Triangle,* and get bored holding up my end of it, but if I let my end go slack, his eyes accuse me instantly. So long as I don't let go, he need not hurt them, wanting to show them – using the same technique with both – that there is warmth still, if no flame. They speak with him in French, presuming I don't understand. I don't need to understand – women in love with an idea speak the same language, without even understanding it themselves. I may not have learned Greek being with him, but I have learned the language of women.

Yet *he* can still take me by surprise. I watch in wonder his gentleness with them (*he's not gentle with me),* his sensibility to their feelings. When does he show sensibility to my feelings? Certainly not lately. It irritates me that they presume to know the man so much better than I do, but the Tasso they know is only half the man; the real confrontation is with the other half...

A week of this and he is heartily sick of his harem. "For crazy – what I have understand of all these *woomans* is one: never mind to be rich, never mind to have good job in Paris or London, anywhere…if the *woomans* no have the company she need for the life – it is an empty barrel!"

He dare not go near the Bar Greco for fear of finding both waiting for him. The idea makes even him sweat. "*For God-ni-say!*" he mutters, crossing himself.

28

Summer ends. A thrashing storm scatters the party like an angry parent: *"Now you will behave yourselves!"* Even the sun reappears in a kinder form, the sweet friend to mankind. The tired olive groves are refreshed and almost immediately the green begins again, pushing aside the burnt out stalks of grasses and thistles. Spring in autumn, the cyclamen unfurl their necks, and the pink trumpets of the amaryllis sound with silence.

Driving out to the hotels he murmurs, "Something smell to me tonight", meaning he senses something. "You notice no police around. Nobody stop us…I hear rumours…something happen in Athens."

There is a winding down in the hotels – a growing darkness, the pool-side bars are empty, the lone barmen lurk in the shadow of the bar polishing glasses that will not be used. The lights on the tables illuminate the faces of the middle-aged, served by a waiter who treats them as reverently as a son. The nymphs have departed.

At two o'clock in the morning, driving home with Panayoti and Tomá in the back, Tasso says again, "You see…no police…nobody stop us… Something happen for sure…"

Even in the town there is no sign of the Military Police. Tasso flings back the sunroof and, standing up, starts bawling *La Marseillaise*. The others in the back beg him to shut up. "Tasso…Tasso!" He calls them 'Butter boys' and goes on singing at the top of his voice.

Infected with his insane jubilation, we drive around the town twice. No sign of the police. Panayoti and Tomá beg to be let out of the car; we drop them off in the old harbour. Panayoti slinks off like a cat down a dark alley, but Tomá pauses to mumble in English, "Nothing love me like my stomack…" words from the hungry belly of a wartime child. It sobers me up. Scared now, I put my foot on the accelerator, terrified we might be stopped before we get safely home. Tasso, biting his knuckles in impotent rage, does not stop me. "I am no more me!" When a man feels that, a woman can do nothing.

Next morning, Pooter tells me the King made a counter coup with some elements of the armed forces. It failed. "He has left the country – gone to Rome. I'm afraid we'll have the Colonels for a long time yet."

29

Winter. The hotels closed, no nightly harvest to be reaped.

"We must go to see the *Pappás* on Sunday," he says. Not for spiritual comfort; the *Pappás* buys the pictures for the monastery's souvenir shop.

We drive the narrow road, twisting like a snake between the olive groves, offering vignettes of paradise at every turn.

"NATO going to make new road," he says. "They make secret place in the rocks on the bay to put their ammunitions, the basters…. This road too narrow for them."

The monastery perches on the promontory over the rockbound bay where the viridian green water kisses the small shingle beach, undefiled now by girls in bikinis or the middle-aged with reddening white flesh.

I park the car outside the white-walled monastery with the icon of the Virgin and child in a niche above the door. A notice says "NO BIKINIS. NO SHORTS" in several languages; in summer, a row of skirts hangs on the gate for the tourists to cover themselves before entering.

We climb the well-trodden white-washed steps to the courtyard with a well in the middle. Funny that there should be a ladder going down into it.

He goes into the church where he lights a beeswax candle on the brass stand, kisses the icon and crosses himself.

A peasant woman in costume appears in the bright white space of the open door. "Ah, *Kyrie* Tasso!" She greets him with affectionate recognition and, going to the brazier, automatically snuffs the candles we have just lighted, and throws them into a box for re melting. It always irritates me. At least the Catholics let your hopes burn out.

He asks if the Pappás is around. *"Nai! Nai…stó spiti einai"* (*No. He is at the cottage*). We pass through the arch in the belfry following the path beside the cottage-like cells where three old men with white beards, dressed in drab monkish robes and smoking cigarettes, watch me avidly. The tourist season over, the dull winter without distraction looms.

The path leads to a simple cottage tucked in the corner of the terrace, a vine straggles over a trellis in front of the door. The woman bustles in with all the authority of a housekeeper, going straight into the little kitchen to make us coffee.

A narrow room is filled with a rustic table, the walls covered in fading photographs of old men in tall stove-pipe hats, and grey beards straggling over their chests; their eyes challenge our presence. What are we doing here?

The peasant women calls loudly, "Pappà! *Kyrie Tassos einai ethó!*" (Mr. Tassos is here!") A sleepy voice replies. It is about six o'clock in the evening. We sit at the long narrow table; the woman brings the tiny cups of coffee, placing them before us in a sacred ritual of hospitality.

The Abbot appears from the inner room, scratching away the traces of a good sleep: a man with an ample stomach, the curly dark hair and beard make him look like the advertisement for Captain Morgan's Rum.

"*Kalos ta pethia!*" (Welcome children) The brown eyes flicker over me. He knows why Tasso has come, and eagerly shovels the ten pictures together like playing cards, handing them to the old woman to take to the souvenir shop they have made in one of the several unoccupied cells of this religious wasp's nest.

He and Tasso settle to the business of what he will pay for them, like two men playing a board. The *Pappás* knows Tasso brings the pictures only when he needs the money. His eyes stray in my direction, "English goot. Verry goot! Buono! Buono!"

I decide to go outside on to the terrace where a young village girl is vigorously shaking a blanket over the wall above the turquoise waters of the bay, the hem of her full skirt revealing the softly rounded backs of young knees. This is a monastery.

Tasso comes out with his pockets bulging. The corporeal ghosts of the two old monks drift with us towards the car, and wistfully watch us depart.

At the ramshackle taverna at the end of the beach, he calls for wine and brings out of his pockets envelopes filled with coins and counts them into small piles on the table. "I want to be sure he don't *sharrack* me."

"Why are they a funny colour?" I ask.

"He have the profit of the *pigathi*" – the well in the courtyard. So that's why the ladder was there. "Tourists throw money into the well for luck, you know…imagine how much money that make in a summer…"

On the way back, we drive over an enormous "OXI!" (NO!) freshly painted on the centre of the road, opposing the Military Regime's own graffiti, "TRUST IN THE 21ST APRIL" and "TRUST IN THE NEW DAWN", which is displayed everywhere.

Further on we pass a posse of scratch militia walking the road to catch the brave ones making these signs. It puts Tasso into a fury again.

"For God-ni-say – I am no more Me!" He smashes his fist at the dashboard. 'Because of YOU happens that!"

I get the blame for everything now.

30.

A session in the wine shop with Pooter.

"Have you met the newest addition to our ranks?"

By "our ranks" he means eccentrics like himself, The Hon. and me, as well as the growing number of English girls – more every year, but we are not a British Colony, not a gin and tonic brigade: too wary of each other's Englishness and the baggage that entails.

"A Countess no less…admittedly a *third* Countess," he concedes, "her husband was married three times. She's writing a book about her religion, an unusual brand of mysticism, I gather. As a lapsed Catholic convert I steer clear of that sort of thing myself…she's already causing quite a stir. She should liven us up a bit…" Satisfied with having promulgated the latest nugget of gossip, he goes.

Then Bobbie, one of the English girls, comes in, surprising me by making straight for my table in the corner. We see each other around but don't "know" each other; our shared Englishness inhibits rather than encourages intimacy. She has been with her Greek for some time now. Pooter says they plan to get married.

"I'm glad to find you here,' she says. "Can I talk to you a minute?"

"You're getting married soon?" I feel I ought to ask.

"That's what I want to talk to you about. Have you heard anything?"

"Like what?" I'm mystified.

"About me. I'm pregnant, you see…I'm going to be sticking out quite a bit at the wedding."

"I haven't heard anything…" Obviously Pooter hasn't twigged. "Anyway, Greek brides are often sticking out on their wedding day – don't worry about it, to them it's normal. They don't want their sons marrying a dud." It consoles her a bit, but she is not happy.

"I hope so," she says sadly, not convinced. "Well, thanks…I'll see you around…"

Bobbie's young figure is replaced in the doorway by The Hon's elongated skeleton, tottering on shoes that seem to have become loose on her feet. I am not surprised she is always falling down.

"How Luv-ly to see you – it's been so long!" she wails, waving a gloved hand at Mr Sotiris. "*Donnay moi oon verre to vin, s'il vous plaît…*"

She is bursting with the Countess.

"My *de-are* – she was at Madam Tomatoes" (her corruption of a Greek name) "soirée the other evening, in full swing – telling them how she spent the night in a cave full of snakes in Borneo… She dresses entirely in primrose yellow – her 'Astral' colour – whatever that is – and covered all over with topazes and pearls. I told her the pearls weren't real. She didn't like that. 'You know a lot,' she said. 'I know pearls, those are either Japanese or Teckler.' And I was right! *And she wears sandals…*I ask you – a *white* woman! I thought we had some weird people in Shanghai! Of course, Pooter runs around after her like a flunkey. He's such a snob. He's been avoiding me lately…someone told him I had referred to him as a 'funny *chap*'. '*Chap*' is a word I *never* use…"

I ask Tasso if he knows of the Canary Countess.

"Ah, yes," he says, recognising the reference instantly. "The Canary Contessa! I meet her in the grocery shop. She making a noise like a sheep. Spiro don't know what she wanting, so I say, 'Madame, What do you looking for, please?' She pointing to the yoghurts and say, 'Is the yoghurt of *you*?' I say, 'Madame, is not yoghurt of *me*, is yoghurt of sheep.' 'That's what I want!' she say. She so happy she ready to kizz me. She another crazy British one, for sure."

Then he tells me he has had a letter from Elsa, the Valkyrie.

31.

He acquired Elsa about the same time he acquired me. Elsa, the tall blonde Rhine maiden, and her elderly mother, came into the wine shop wanting to buy soda water and could not make Mr Sotiris understand. Tasso came to rescue as usual. Since then they have been coming every summer and stay two months in the best hotel. And every summer Elsa wishes she would not find me sitting at the corner table. "Ach! The lady from Lon-don!" She speaks little English, and I have less German, which saves me having to take any part in the conversations they have with him in which she constantly exclaims, "Ach! Mein Lieberman!"

"Why are they are coming in winter?"

"They coming for Weinacht – the first of the year, you know…? They wanting to buy land here to make a small house for their holidays. I tell her foreigners no allowed to buy land here, she must to find a Greek one to buy for her with her money. For that you need an honest Greek. She want me." She has been longing to tie him into some form of relationship.

"To be her honest Greek?"

"Of course, I be honest to her, but I say, 'Elsa, is not my business. My business to sell my paintings, nothing else. I try to find you somebody."

She must have been disappointed. I am relieved.

"Now we must to find Harry, to tell him they coming…"

"Who's Harry?"

"He is one who help the foreigners to buy land here, and take money of them. He call himself Land Agent now. I know him. He no so great *baster*, him a stupid, that's all. He buy a new suit and have a car now. What else you wait for? Now is winter he go back to his village to make his wine."

Looking for Harry takes us down to a taverna on a beach on one of those Mediterranean winter days that rival summer, a crystal clear synthesis of warmth, colour and light. The track down to the beach is too steep and rough for the little car.

"We'll never get it back up! Why are we looking for Harry down here?"

"He have a piece of land down here where he grows his grapes."

We abandon the car and take the cobbled donkey stairway down through the olive terraces to the peacock-blue sea. On the beach, I kick off my shoes to let the waves lick my toes; an outing like this is a flight over the abyss. Lord! – have I forgotten what happiness is?

At the small white taverna at the edge of the beach he asks for Harry. "He's not here. We must to go back to the village." We have a couple of retsinas and depart.

Going up is not so easy as coming down. He coughs and curses the Valkyries for their power to make him do their bidding. I am surprised too. With difficulty I turn the car on the narrow track, the wheels spinning on the loose stones; he has to push until the wheels grip and I can get to a flat bit. He follows, coughing and cursing. *My Hero.*

In the village, it being Sunday, the *cafenions* are full of men playing cards, slapping them onto the table with unnecessary force. Old men sit outside in the sun, hands quietly folded on the knob of a stick in perpetual patience, waiting for something to happen with a deep resignation that nothing ever will; yet they are open to surprise. Women in traditional costume carry tins of water balanced on their heads past the cafés full of idle men. They have been doing this from girlhood.

He asks for Harry and is directed along an alley of low stucco cottages where the old women sitting on their doorsteps eagerly confirm to the stranger that the large arched doorway with the decorated keystone is where Harry can be found.

Tasso knocks hard on the heavy oak door painted viridian green. It is opened furtively; a parrot-nosed face peers out and spreads with relief at the sight Tasso; this is Harry.

"Tasso!" He opens the heavy door wide enough for us to enter. We step into a large dark room with exposed beams, and wooden vats, barrels, wine measures, wicker demijohns and a large black umbrella hanging from a nail along with a rat trap and an old sword in a scabbard. He leads the way through to the stone-flagged kitchen with a huge cooking range with the great hood bulging out of the wall above it.

Looking at me, he unctuously apologizes in a mixture of languages: *"Ma maison…très pauvre…maison paysage* – not like nice England haus…"

The kitchen door opens onto a yard full of flowers in painted petrol tins, and a lemon tree. *How can he apologise for this?*

A middle-aged woman standing in the kitchen does not react to our presence at all. Is she his mother or his wife? He does not introduce her, just tells her to get some glasses; she does so automatically, like a robot. She has the look of someone who has touched the bottom of life and does not aspire to rise again.

He takes down a bottle of wine from a shelf, the cork tied down with string. "Me…make… Is my wine…" he says proudly, pouring it out. The first sip is always the worst; after the second it begins to taste of…what?

Tasso gives Harry the warning about the Valkyries' imminent arrival, and urges him to do right by them. Where do his loyalties lie? Has he come to save Harry, or the Valkyries? The answer is both.

32

Wednesday night, wine shop closed, he puts me in the new "Cake Parlour" furbished with modern chrome tables and chairs, a mirror on one wall and a refrigerated counter full of cream cakes. Petros, the owner, a plumpish person like a dormouse, with brown eyes and a moustache, sits at the cash desk opposite the door, looking dreamily into the street.

The place is empty, except for myself, and a husband and wife sitting at a table, eating two cream gateaux each, followed by ice-cream covered in nuts and cherry syrup. The husband, with the inevitable moustache, is dressed in a dapper black suit. I think he is a chemist. The wife is large, and genteel in a vulgar way. They sit firmly side by side, drawing their plates up to their chests to dig into the contents with careful, neat movements. Her tongue comes out to meet the spoon, and at the same time her eyes roll upwards, their eyes rolling upwards in unison at each mouthful. Having consumed the cake and the ice-cream, she sits with hands clasped under her ample bosom, sucking her teeth audibly.

Tasso is across the street at the ouzerie; a great deal of laughter has been coming from there, but when he comes to retrieve me he is in a different mood, cigarette stuck belligerently in the corner of his mouth. He doesn't know where he will find money to Be Enjoy tonight.

"Like that, is it?" I say.

"You send me record from England one time called that."

I remember it was a pop song called '*This is it, you're the one for me!*' It had seemed so right at the time. I am surprised he remembers it.

"So horrible music I never hear in my life before. I sold to the record shop."

Love: a journey on a scenic railway with naively painted scenery, no perspective, no proportion, figures one-dimensional, sometimes two, where the eye and heart have taken turns in achieving surrealism.

"Come on, let's get out of here," he says.

Back at the car, it is too early to go home. "Go *there*," he says, "to see something…"

No need to say where *there* is…

At the Casino – instead of going upstairs, he says, "Wait a minute – I want to see something. I hear they have 'froot' machines now – I want to see what is that." He has never seen a fruit machine.

I follow him through the connecting ante-rooms to a final salon where these robots are lined up against the walls, watched over by an attendant in a green uniform. He is pleased to show Tasso what these brand new machines can do.

"*Poly Oréa*, Tasso – in the name of God!"

He shows him how to insert a coin, pull the handle, and watch the drums with the innocent symbols of lemons, oranges and strawberries revolve. When three lemons come up, a cascade of coins is released into the metal pocket. He shovels the coins into his pocket and starts feeding them back into the next machine, and another fall of coin. "*In the name of God,* this is wonderful! A machine to give you money!" With him happily jingling the coins in his pocket, we go up to the bar.

At the Heavenly Bank Manager, he exchanges some coins for plastic. "Go to play – play 17 and 27, and do exactly as I say."

I pad off to the salon. It is empty – the croupiers are perched around the green island, illuminated by the hanging lamp. The toad-like figure alone at the table, is Mrs Dexter, her fur cuffs resting on the green baize like sleeping white cats; her shoulders hunched, she scribbles each number into a notebook. Her American husband floats like a pale freckled gecko in the surrounding darkness, occasionally approaching to place a small bet just to pass the time until Mrs Dexter rises from the table, a triumphant winner or a ferocious loser. They frequent the Salamander and are very thick with Madame Ellie.

I am so busy watching Mrs Dexter's pendulous Levantine jowls in profile, 17 comes up and I'm not on it… *Panic*. What should I do now – go for 17 again, or for 27? I put a piece on 27 – 17 comes up again. Three times? In desperation I shove the rest of the pieces on 17 and 27. It comes up zero. The plastic pieces are ruthlessly scraped away by the croupier's claw.

The bar is empty, he is chatting happily with the barman, Greek to Greek. I open my empty hands. "You lost all?" He is astonished but turns back to the barman asking when the 'Boss', meaning the Count, will be coming again.

"New Year…for sure, he will be here."

He is silent in the car. We pass the militia men again, walking along the side of the road. Later we are stopped by the police; they recognise us as we are so often on the road at night. They wave us on.

At home he explodes. "What you doing in there to lose the money! You play exactly the numbers I give you?" I am hurled from one side of the room, in a pitch and toss I seem to watch rather than experience. This macabre ballet which ends in the other thing – until he sleeps.

I dream I am getting married to him in a fish shop in the market street, one of those primitive booths with a marble slab. Pooter comes past, immediately offering his 'felicitations' in a very Pooterish way. I reply very forcefully, *"I am only getting married to him so I can DIVORCE him, because you can't divorce a man you're not married to!"*

I awake, stunned by the significance of this. There is no authority that can release me from my commitment to him – except myself. I chose him, he didn't choose me. I jumped onto his hide and buried myself in him like a tick – one calls it 'Love'. I still don't know what Love is – unless it is a sort of cannibalism. Love? What the hell is it? There is something quite wrong about Love. I am all wrong with love – an exquisite meal that congeals on the plate.

In the morning he gets up – makes his coffee, goes to his job. I do not go to town. He returns at three o'clock.

"Why you no come to the wine shop this morning. I leave nice shoppings there," he says as I fling a plate of spaghetti on the table and leave him to it, going into the studio to fiddle out another picture.

239

"You don't eat? So nice is... Why you don't you come to eat?"

"I've eaten."

"Take some more – it break the appetite to eat alone."

He has such a way of putting things...and of being totally reasonable when not being totally unreasonable. "What's the matter with you?" he innocently asks, choosing not to understand, so that the crisis is only in me. Resentment pours out of me – I trashed Dad for this man. That's my problem. His problem is the Junta, and being no longer the young delinquent who didn't care half a cigarette for his life – now he does, and smokes 60 a day. We are two cymbals clashing against each other.

He looks at me with genuine surprise.

"Put out of your mind that bad things you *thing-king*. All that belong to yesterday. Today is another thing." Conjuring the Eternal Now out of Greek opportunism.

33

The Valkyries arrive in the Mercedes Sports, resplendent in Prussian tweed, fur hats and boots, having driven swiftly down from Austria. Elsa's 'winter Princess' image makes more impact on him than her summer one. Her "Aach! Mein Liebermann!" is triumphantly conscious of it.

They have never seen the island in winter and exclaim at the greenness never experienced in the dry hot summer months. The weather is perfect. We spend an afternoon driving about in the white Mercedes with the hood down, Tasso and I in the back, while Elsa swings the car round the tight bends, exclaiming "*Herrlich*!" and "*Wunderbar*!" The low winter sun dazzles the eyes, and draws out grotesque shadows from the posturing olive trees. We stop at a particular vantage point looking out over an empty beach, blue sea. To record it on her instamatic, Elsa sits up on the back of the driving seat, asking Tasso to hold her as she leans backwards as far as possible to get just the right shot. *Snap*! A donkey under an olive tree extends his nostrils wide to pump the air through them in a series of derisive sobs which completely express my feelings. *Herrlich*! *Wunderbar*!

At a taverna for lunch, it is warm enough to sit under the vine where a few shrivelled grapes hang among the rusty leaves. An enormous fish is grilled and brought to the table stone-cold, accompanied by mayonnaise tasting of motor oil. Long live Greece! Elsa commemorates it with the instamatic flash. The Valkyries do not drink. I help Tasso with the retsina. I don't want him drunk.

The best moment of the day comes when a drowsy fly zooming in settles on Tasso's face. I take a tremendous slosh at it and kill the fly! His lips draw back over his teeth as I hold up my hand with the fly sticking to it. His eyes say, "You happy now…you pay me…" and laughs the laugh he would give to a beloved enemy he could kill, yet grieve to destroy. Masculine and Feminine, Male and Female – mutually attracted, irreconcilable elements. With other women strapped about us as padding, the battle could still be fun.

"You know," said Tweedledum very gravely, "it's one of the most serious things that can possibly happen to one in battle – to get one's head cut off…"

34

New Year's Eve, the Valkyries have arrived before us at the casino, absorbed into their own milieu with the Count and Parsifal at the bar; Elsa in a dress of peach chiffon embroidered with rhinestones, a totally different image, but less successful than the Prussian tweeds as it reveals her thick wrists.

Tasso bows over her mother's hand, Parsifal bows over mine, Tasso kisses Elsa's hand, the Count kisses mine. Tasso turns the ritual into comedy by kissing the Count's hand and I could kiss him for that.

But he hasn't come here to perform social rituals. It is the one night in the year the locals are permitted to play. He dumps me in front of a gin and tonic at the furthest end of the bar, away from the Count and Parsifal, and disappears into the inner sanctum for his rendezvous with Lady Luck, convinced he will come back a millionaire. Elsa looks crestfallen at the swiftness of his disappearance.

I am dreading any attention either from Parsifal or the Count. I would rather be losing money at the tables. Staring at the bottles on the shelves behind the bar, I see a world-weary face regarding me from between the Tzonnie Valker and the Gorton's Tzin – my own. The eyes make me think of a line of poetry: "*I suffocate and give birth to a stone*".

In the same mirror, the Count glances towards me from time to time, but he doesn't approach. I hear him ask the barman if *all Greek men are jealous*. So he has been warned. The barman shrugs.

Tasso returns in a very short time – not having won, and not having lost, but outraged nevertheless. "For crazy! The whole town be in there! Is like football. Is no possible to be near the table. I going to fighting if I stay there! Come on – let's get out of here." He chucks some money to the barman. I sense Elsa's chagrin as we leave. It is the only night we go home early and without having a bloody row. *Ach! Mein Liebermann!*

Before they leave the island, the Valkyries have to go to the court for the signing of the contract for the land.

"For crazy! She want me to be there."

"Why do you have to be there? "

"She don't want to be alone in that situation. But I be in trouble with my job - the new Director don't like me. He don't give me time off for anything...the *kaikshooter*!" he fumes, lumping him with the Regime. "I have to pay Costa to finish my shift. Is too much troubles. I don't want these obligations."

"Why do it, then?"

"Because 'no' never arrive in my mouth!"

It does when he's with me. This power that Elsa has over him doesn't threaten me, just fills me with wonder and a tinge of envy. What is she looking for with him? She couldn't live 24 hours with him, or he with her.

The court is not in town, but in the centre of the island. I have to drive him there. "Where are we going?" I ask as he directs me down a dirt track between olive groves.

"To the court of the district where she have buy the land."

"I thought her land is near the sea?"

"It is – but the court is this way."

We come to a crumbling Venetian gateway leading into the courtyard of a ruined monastery. This crumbling wasps' nest is a county court? All that indicates Greek officialdom is a pole painted blue and white – above a doorway where a young policeman stands, nonchalantly holding a carnation between his teeth.

"Are you sure this is the place?"

"Of course, I'm sure!" – as if I were stupid.

An old man's head pops out of an upstairs casement; recognising Tasso, he calls him to come up.

"Him a very old painter..."

No sign of the white Mercedes, so we mount the worn wooden stair to the old man's room. A card pinned to the door reads 'DORIAN – Peintre/Zografos'. The old man shuffles to greet us dressed in bright blue pyjamas like a wounded veteran of the

Great War; horny toes protrude through his sandals. The floor is covered with newspaper.

"Watch where you put your foots," Tasso says, "I don't trust the floor at all..."

The old man fixes his eyes on me, which activates some remnants of English. "Here make Real Art!" he declares with a provocative sideways glance at Tasso. "ME STooDENT...PAR-RISS..." And he waves a hand towards a murky canvass on the easel with a messy palette of paints beside on which a skin had formed, and dust. Shuffling over a table on which stands an old Vitrola gramophone, a plate of spaghetti and two human skulls, he rummages in a drawer and pulls out an old sepia photograph of the romantic pure young man who was himself. "I...Me...." he says, pointing to the photographer's stamp, *"Rue de Gallette"*.

A boisterous shouting below indicates that the lawyers have come.

The white Mercedes too pulls into the yard. We must go down.

The old man shambles over to his desk, and sits down to eat the congealed spaghetti that was either his supper from the night before or his breakfast; resigned to the fact that nothing comes of these encounters anymore.

"For sure he know to painting," Tasso says, "but I know how to sell..."

To get to the courtroom we pass through a small tavern which seems to be part of the complex, and squeeze into the little room adjoining the courtroom which looks like a Baptist chapel. There are nine of us now with the lawyers, the clerk of the court and Harry the land agent.

In a burst of chivalry from the men, the Valkyries are allowed to sit on the only available chairs. More have to be fetched from the courtroom. A struggle begins to get the chair through one half of a double door. I point out to Tasso that they could unbolt the other door; he gets the credit for solving the problem. "Bravo, Tasso!"

Elsa sits like the Rhine maiden, the dachshund on her lap, looking seriously attentive, understanding nothing as the clerk reads the contract aloud, all ten pages in the official bureaucratic language. In an aside to me, Tasso says, "She want me for interpreter, and I don't understand the Greek." He gets up and walks around his chair like a caged tiger. "Didn't I tell you I don't want these troubles?"

The reading drones on; corrections have to be made. One of the lawyers fiddles with a pocket transistor, letting little bursts of music leak into the proceedings. He stares at Elsa with eyes mad with speculation.

Harry, looking more like a parrot than ever with his bulging nose and goggly eyes, leans toward Elsa to pat her knee reassuringly. The little dog goes berserk, barking hysterically. Harry quickly withdraws his hand to place it on the breast of his pin-striped business suit, which looks as if he has slept in it; and assures her in fractured German that he is the most "honest Greek on the island" and her "liddel haus" will be *fertig* with all speed and efficiency.

Even when the contracts have been signed, it is not the end. Harry has laid on a feast of stewed cockerel, salad and wine in the little taverna. The Valkyries are dismayed but have to submit as Harry places his hand firmly against Elsa's lumber region, and propels her to the tavern. The clerk and the lawyers follow as eagerly as dogs. The mad-eyed lawyer with the transistor grabs up the wicker demijohn to pour out tumblers of blue-black village wine.

"Ligó…ligó" (a little…a little), Elsa demurely protests in her minimal Greek. "LIGÓ…LIGÓ! BRAVO! BRAVO!" roars the lawyer, filling her glass to the brim. It is the same with the stewed chicken. "Ligó…ligó" from the Valkyries; "LIGÓ! LIGÓ! BRAVO! BRAVO!" bawls the lawyer, doling out the largest portions.

Elsa gazes sadly at her little dog. The lawyer, to prove he isn't afraid of dogs (which he is), grabs it savagely by the back of the neck and shakes it hard, leaping back and laughing loudly as the dog goes berserk again.

"Him a stupid one," says Tasso, "never mind to be a lawyer."

When Harry and the lawyers are on the second demijohn, we leave. They don't notice because their attention is fixed on the clerk of the court who is demonstrating how to smoke a cigarette through the hollow stem of an old courgette plant.

The Valkyries depart next day; he has to see them off at the harbour. As I was not there, he tells me, she kissed him on the mouth. He was shocked. "I do not like these obligations…"

35.

Since then we have been to the Casino six nights in succession. Entering the salon night after night is like entering the same dream. The faces of the croupiers float white as moons in the gloom beyond the light that concentrates everything upon the table where Mrs Dexter's toad-like bulk broods, her white fur cuffs like cats on either side of her. At regular intervals, the attendant approaches to brush the white hairs from the green baize with a special brush.

I recognise now the Athenian gamblers who fly in every weekend. The sea captain is back, with his floozy in her tight black skirt, tight pink blouse and pungent scent of B.O. conjured into her skin by her excitement. I have to move round the table to get away from it. He strides up and down in the dark space beyond the light of the table, playing his worry beads and barking out his bets to the croupiers at the last moment.

I trot between the salon and the bar, carrying the plastic pieces. When I return empty-handed, he demands, "Where you put the money? You put like a blind one? Do you see where you put it? Do you watch?" fantasizing that I am leaving a fortune on the table, that I have broken the bank on 50 drachmes, or that the croupiers are *sharracking* (cheating) me. He says this is an English word. I don't know it. It's rather good.

The thoughts I have trotting to and from the gaming tables: *Not love lost – love surviving…the hardened edges, sharper angles. The first magic shapeless, and plastic becomes two sold forms united and separate. I do not remember anything of the beginning of love. It is too far away or too near, like looking through the wrong end of a telescope…*

The money gone, we drive home to get the drachmes he left under a jug in the kitchen. When that's gone, we return home again but not to sleep. His fury breaks out within four walls.

We wake in the morning as if nothing happened the night before. To carry forward anything is to wake the monster before its appointed hour. I don't smile anymore…

When he comes into the wine shop where I am sitting with Pooter and the Hon., he is the epitome of mature masculine health and muscle, the charm of a horse or dog and the same co-ordination of the faculties. The blood circulating under that tanned hide gives a lively colour, contrasting well with the crisp greying hair. It is not obvious how much he drinks, he has such powers of resurrection. Even I can hardly trace the outline of the beast where it sleeps in his chest like a curled cat.

These morning meetings seem to take place outside the stockade where we fight our nightly battles. At this ante-meridian hour, the violence of which he is capable is mythological; its abstract quality makes it almost possible to bear. It has little to do with what we are to each other, too much to do with what he is to himself.

Watching him from the safety of my position between Pooter and The Hon. in the passivity of this hour, I speculate on my relationship to them and to him. On the surface I relate to them; in my depths, I relate to him, or I wouldn't be here. Nothing that has been, or will be, can happen if that were not so.

36.

Pooter is not amused. "After six years of co-operating with the police – teaching them English for a very small fee – my resident's permit has been reduced to six months."

Any change in the regulations fills me with dread; I am hoping they will put the telescope to their blind eye as usual for me…but you never know…

"At the same time," he continues, "the Hon., who owes money all over town and is becoming more and more of a liability, has been given a year! She continues to spend money she hasn't got…the less she has, the more she spends. She's having her couch and chair re-covered in the most expensive material, the carpenter is suing her for the shoebox he made for her… She's ordered a dozen silver teaspoons with her crest on them, when she can't pay her electricity bill! A person, who shall be nameless, has paid it for her – *without her knowing, of course* – she couldn't abide charity- it's so *infra dig.* I wish *you* could persuade her not to be so extravagant…" *Me?*

He goes. I am surprised he didn't mention the Canary Countess. I am continuing writing my letter, when I look up I see what can only be the Canary Countess herself, making straight for my table. There is no mistaking her – a shapeless body in a lemon yellow duster coat, baggy yellow trousers, and bare feet in sandals; beige hair dragged onto the top of her head and fixed with combs, pins and a piece of yellow ribbon; her throat draped in pearls and a huge pendant topaz.

She plonks herself down at my table, looks at me critically, and says, "I can tell you what to do with your grey hairs." I have one or two grey hairs coming, but I didn't think it was that noticeable. "A friend of mine went grey after her lover hit her on the head with a bottle. Do you think *he* will love you as much when you're grey?"

She knows about me and him? What have Pooter and the Hon. been saying?

"You don't see a grey hair on me, do you?" *She is in her seventies, if she's a day!* "Olive oil is the answer." She calls to Mr

Sotiris to make her a cocoa. "I never drink alcohol," she adds, eyeing my glass of wine, "and I don't eat meat or fish – the animals are our brothers…and it interferes with one's vital forces. Don't you know that?" – as if I had missed a primary lesson. "You must learn to sublimate…to work from inside yourself, without dropping off to sleep. It's much easier if you have a man with you…"

Looking at me critically again, she asks, "Don't you know that?" as if I were a child who has failed to learn her lesson. "But *he* must learn to sublimate too…mustn't let it all go away…down there…you understand?"

I am dumb. *Tasso – where are you?* I can't get up and go – if he doesn't find me exactly where he left me, there is hell to pay! *For God's sake, come and get me!*

Almost immediately he appears – like a genie out of a bottle, carrying a newspaper package under one arm. "Ah, what nice company you have…" He kisses her hand, saying to me, "I find some beautiful fresh sardines to cooking for supper…"

The Countess perks up like a cat. "Oh, why don't you come and cook them in my place? I'm quite alone." *I thought the fishes were her brothers.*

"Oh, so nice idea…but we have to meet friends…they wait for us …at the Casino. We are late already…" *The Greeks think fast.*

"You go to the Casino?" This with a keenness she immediately modifies. "Ah, but as I have taken Holy Orders…I may not gamble…"

We leave her drinking her cocoa.

In the car, he says, "We go home to cooking the sardines." Then, immediately changing his mind: "No! No! I feel *something*…go there."

We go there. He scribbles numbers on the back of his cigarette packet and sends me in to play them. We lose all the money he made in the day – no, *I* lose it. It is *my* fault.

Tooth and claw session when we get home. At three in the morning, having had nothing to eat. It's a relief when he sleeps.

Does every love fail? Persevere with love – you find yourself tied hand and foot to a monster. If I can endure the grotesque experience of Love – what is left…will be…Me.

In the morning, I chuck the sardines to the cats.

37

Pooter is sitting with me in the Cake Parlour. I remark on the fact that there seem to be an awful lot of priests about, observing a young priest in black robes and stove-pipe hat, sitting with his wife and two children, who stare at us while filling their faces with cream cakes.

"It is one of the Colonels' objectives to promote Christian Values. They're subsidized to take their families out for treats to put themselves in the public eye. You are aware, I'm sure, that we have the 'elections' tomorrow. There's a ban on alcohol as from this evening…"

The idea of having to get through a night without alcohol…

"It will be interesting to see how it goes… It's simply a matter of voting Yes or No to the New Regime. The voting is compulsory, but as you can imagine, the outcome is not in doubt."

The ban on drinking proves not to be a problem. We are served retsina in teacups, or koniak in the tiny coffee cups. They don't do it for everybody, but they do it for him.

Next day he comes home in a foul mood. "You voted?"

"Yes – of course I voted, but you know what? They have a policeman at the door handing out 'Yes' papers to the people. The little old woomans – just take the paper and put in the box! The policeman try to give me a 'Yes' paper, I say I want the No paper. But how many going to do that? They afraid to do that!"

He is so hoping for a revolution, he has filled the car with stones and good strong sticks… "I don't go without a fight…"

The result is announced as 'All in Favour of the New Regime'. Pooter was right.

38.

In the Salamander in the evening, a curious company. Jason as usual is sprawled on a high stool propped up against the wall. Mr Dexter, without his toad-like spouse, is at the other end.

Madame Ellie's attention is focused on another foreigner – a good-looking young man. Where has he sprung from? He is formally dressed in a suit and looks as if he is more used to wearing a uniform; he also has a pronounced American accent.

"You are American?" Madame Ellie asks, eyeing him flirtatiously as she puts his drink on the bar counter. To everybody's surprise, he says with great deliberation, "I am *A KORN-ISH-MAN*."

Cosmopolitan Madame Ellie is perplexed. "A Kornishman? What is a Kornishman? I have never heard of this."

I offer the information: "It's a county in England called Cornwall. People from there are Cornish."

"But he speaks with an American accent! How can he be English?" she insists in that rather brusque European way.

"My mother was American," the young man grudgingly concedes, "but I am *A Kornishman*." He makes it sound like 'Kazakstahn'.

At the other end of the bar, Jason is killing himself with laughter and doesn't attempt to come to the aid of his countryman. "Don't believe anything!" he bawls. "Not even me." *As if anybody did.*

"If is in England this place, why you don't say you English?" says Tasso, aggressively. "You an American one for sure! You have a mission here!"

"*Taisez-vous*, Tasso!" warns Madame Ellie, ready to throw him out again.

The young man looks strained; obviously he had no idea that in being sent to Greece he would find himself pitched into a nest of English speakers.

"My mother was American," he repeats, looking like someone threatened with drowning. "But I am a KORNISH-MAN," he insists. Doggedly.

Mr Dexter, the pale freckled gecko of the casino, takes no part in the situation the American Kornishman finds himself in. Where is Mrs Dexter? She can't be at the casino alone.

"Give me another whisky…Ellie."

Mr Dexter drinks up his whisky and goes bleakly into the night.

"That man is a Saint!" Madame Ellie exclaims as the door closes behind him. "His wife goes mad every seven years and he does all the housework. Mon dieu! Of course – it's *her* money…" And, turning her attention back to the interesting stranger, she says, "You have beautiful hands...." The young man immediately tries to hide them in his pockets, and then can't pick up his drink. "Silly boy…." she murmurs indulgently.

Little does he know he is more in danger from Madame Ellie than the political situation he has been sent into. She will have him between her sheets in the blink of an eye. Everybody suspects Jason for spending so much time on her bar stool.

39.

"We going to move from this house," he says – just like that, with no warning. "The landlord want more money. I have find another place for same price – much better."

It is only 200 yards away on the path up to the main road. It has neither more nor less mod cons. A room big enough to take a bed and a room too small to be anything except a passage between the bedroom and the kitchen, which has been built on as an afterthought; the loo boxed into the corner of the kitchen, with only a curtain. The Greeks have no idea of space. How the hell did they build the Parthenon? A vine straggles over the back door leading to a small garden where the landlord grows his tomatoes and aubergines.

We carry our things there – the broken bed, the whisky boxes, our clothes, my books. It is soon done but I've lost the view, I've lost Maria; instead we are surrounded by audible and visible neighbours, doing their chores outside, bent over wooden washboards or cooking in pots blackened by the wood fires.

A granny dandles a young baby for hours, cawing a monotonous chant: *"Pa-POO! Pa-POOO! Pou einai o Pa-Pooooo?"* I find myself repeating this endless question which translates as "Where is your grandaddy?".

Immediately above us on the steep path is a tiny taverna kept by our neighbour, *Kyria* Rosa, for the minimal trade of passing workmen, or a couple of tourists in summer who sit under the vine for a simple meal of bread, cheese, olives and wine. Tasso goes in there now when he returns from work. It is an hour before he walks into the house, drunk. He is drunk twice a day now, before noon and before midnight. It is not just the Regime that angers him now. His dear old boss at the Electric Company, who loved him as a wayward son, has retired. Of the new man, he says, "I don't think I am going to eat sweet bread with him."

I wonder how I shall get through the arid winter months with no tourists, and without Maria – and these new neighbours who know him but nothing about me, except that I am a *xeni*, in pronunciation so like our word zany. They know our story but it

256

is an old *skandaló* now; they are not hostile. They think all foreign women are mad. Even I know I am mad trying to live with him.

40.

At the wine shop Pooter says, "Have you heard the good news?"

"I haven't heard anything good lately."

"Bobbie has had her baby. A boy. You know how important that is to the Greeks. It will mean a lot to Bobbie too. At least she's got that right."

"Yes, it must be good to get something right…"

Pooter looks at me obliquely. "You seem…" He hesitates before he decides to say more. "I understand Tasso is gambling heavily." He knows the croupiers. "Can't you stop him?"

"Nobody can stop the ultimately Greek boy-child…" I say dully. Pooter smirks, but tactfully does not pursue the matter further.

He goes. I have just resumed writing my letter, when the Hon.'s figure appears in the sunlight of the door with the little dachshund on a lead. As she totters over to sit with me, her shoes seem to be loose on her feet; no wonder she is always falling down. I notice a hole in the sleeve of her jacket.

"I had to go to the doctor…my leg was so painful after that fall. My de-are…the waiting room was full of peasants! Pooter said he was the best doctor in town! I told the doctor his clientele was very *déclassé* – I don't think he understood…"

She is full of the Canary Countess. "I was at Mrs Tomatoes' *soirée* last night. *She* was there – holding forth…and would you believe it, just as I was leaving, she said, 'I'm coming to supper with you.' 'But I've only two eggs in the house!' You know how I luv cooking…" she purrs, making a face. "But *she* wasn't to be put off. 'Then we'll make an omelette,' she said.

"So there I was at nine o'clock at night scrambling eggs, while she was jumping up and down in my kitchen saying, 'Don't you want to stay young like me – and have a man to bed with you!' I gave her such a look! I never let my husband into my bed unless I wanted him to pay my bills, and then I raped him…"

She had just gone, when Parsifal walked into the wine shop. He didn't see me at my corner table, and was standing at the counter buying a bottle of whisky when Tasso walked in. His eyes went straight from Parsifal's lofty Teutonic back to me, but he greeted him with customary Greek fellowship.

Parsifal left. Tasso came over to me. "Why he come in here? He know where you are!"

"He didn't even notice me."

"Pay attention. I don't like that story…it stink to me…" He plays Iago to his own Othello.

When he has gone, I realise he hasn't brought any shopping. I drive home and make a sauce for spaghetti again. Why am I not having a nervous breakdown? *Perhaps you can't have a nervous breakdown on spaghetti…*

In the evening – the Casino. "*Faites vos jeux, messieurs et mesdames!*" He tells me to play zero. I put the whole lot on it. "*Rien n'va plus!*" ZERO! In a moment of utter abandon, I leave it on. "*Rien n'va plus!*" ZERO!

With difficulty I get my plastic pieces onto the counter in front of the Heavenly Bank Manager, who smiles paternally as he changes it into real money; his leonine head reminds me of Dad.

At the bar, I hold out both clenched fists. "Choose."

Looking like a dog at the prospect of biscuit, he chooses the right hand. It must contain the equivalent of £50. "Pó-pó-pó…" He crosses himself. I open the other fist – another £50. "Pää-pää-pää….' The Greek croupiers, having finished their shift, march through the bar in military style, reflecting the Teutonic influence. They wink at us. "Good, eh, Tasso!"

"Thank you, *pethiá*! he calls out to them, as it if has been in their gift. With the amazing naiveté which exists in him alongside everything else, he says, "Oh, darr-ling – you see – the God worry if I go home empty tonight. I owe too much money in town…"

"God *and* I were worried… In fact…*I was more worried than God…*"

41.

In the morning, at the bang of the door closing behind him, my nerves jump slack as if slashed with a knife. I lie there like an unstrung instrument, unable to crawl off the bed, thinking: why have I woken up? For what? I am no longer enjoying the life. That's a crime I can't handle after sacrificing Dad to it. If Tasso was the solution to being Me, are all relationships just an excuse to be for somebody else what you fail to be for yourself? To be somebody's mother, lover, wife, you have an identity, thus staving off the confrontation with yourself. That's what makes it so difficult to let go...to fall into the void... So if this was the answer to that – what is the answer to this? Was the dream worth dreaming now the nightmare has begun? But there was nobody like him. Did I invent him?

I am not the only one to have fallen for him... I'm just the bloody fool who tried to live with him. *La folle Anglaise!* Perhaps I could give up the man; what I can't give up is the idea. If I give up that, I am lost...

Six o'clock – time to go to town for the night shift.

"What's the matter with you – you don't move from the bed?"

"I think I'm losing my health..."

"Yes, I have one terrible dream last night, that you fall down and don't get up. *Pó-pó-pó*, was terrible dream..." He crosses himself piously, and goes to town alone.

It turns out to be flu. For seven days I lie cradled in the eye of the storm between *it* and *him*. He comes and goes. "You need anything?"

"Oranges..."

He takes them from the neighbours' trees, and leaves the bright orbs on the table. I crawl out of bed to fill my hot water bottle and squeeze a glass of orange juice. I want nothing except this weakness, the inability to feel anything but the warmth of the hot water bottle and the coolness of the juice.

He doesn't come back till after midnight. At the sound of his quick step, my heart starts pounding. He comes in holding something clutched to his chest, and leans against the door as if expecting someone to hurl themselves against it. When he was sure no one had followed him, he went to the table and poured out a cascade of coins from a small towel he was carrying them in – he has been to the Casino playing the fruit machines. He must have pinched the towel from the gents' to carry the loot.

"I get up the jackpot three times!" he says, sitting down to count the coins into little piles like a miser. "You see! – the *putana* give me in the end!" – exulting in his triumphed over Lady Luck.

Going into the kitchen to find nothing to eat – he hasn't done the shopping for days – he charges back to the front door and throws the frying pan into the night. It seems the most horrifying thing he has done yet. Then he comes to bed and falls asleep instantly. I breathe again…

In the morning, I retrieve the frying pan – it's the only frying pan we have, it might take a year for him to buy another. Our neighbour, Nitza, watches me draw it out from the long grass. The neighbours are only yards away in the silence of the night; their nearness is the extent of my isolation in this so-private nightmare. She must hear… she knows, unless she sleeps like the dead.

But we smile at each other and laugh.

42.

It is almost with dismay that I feel the life-force reassert itself. My first day up is a Sunday. "You feel strong enough to drive? So beautiful day – we go to see a bit the nature," he suggests, at the same time rummaging among my clothes on the shelf where I keep them.

"What are you doing?"

"You need all these things? Give me what you don't use, because is very good quality."

"What do you want them for?"

"I know…" Guarding his secrets like a dog with a bone.

I look out some old jerseys, a pleated skirt losing its pleats, a blouse I never wear. He bundles them up and puts them in the car.

The main road away from town is still the winding meandering way built originally for horse carts – it never had the motorcar in mind. Just before the first village we come upon new road works where the olive trees are being mercilessly bulldozed.

"Stop a minute – I want to see what the Americans doing here."

"What have the Americans got to do with it?"

"The Americans have everything to do with what happens in Greece. They going to make a new road to the north of the island – to put secret things up there in the mountain."

We get out of the car to watch the brute mechanical machine butting a beautiful old tree loaded with olives, until with a splintering sound it crashes over, and the bulldozer shuffles its ugly alien body around to attack another tree. An old peasant watching with us turns to Tasso with the face of a puzzled child, to ask why they are breaking the trees.

"To make the new road, Bábá."

The old man cannot take it in – what does a new road mean to him? He mumbles something and turns away, shaking his head.

"You know what him say? He says 'to see that tree to be down, is like to see a man die'. Him very right!" He is biting his knuckles, which he does only when he is very angry. "So help tree you don't imagine...is like a cow to give you milk, meat, leather, butter...and live for a thousand year! Him working all his life with that tree...and now the *kaikshooters* destroy so the Americans can make a secret place to put their ammunitions."

We get back into the car, but I need to know where we are going.

"Go to the monastery..." I wonder why as he has no paintings to sell.

The winding road is beautiful. The low sun slanting through the olives trees illumines great patches of emerald grasses between the posturing trees, their silver-green leaves like shoals of minnows overhead. To think of the bulldozers like grazing dinosaurs trashing this paradise of wild marigolds, asphodels, orchids...the thousand million natural things waiting in the soil to come to birth in the spring.

At the rock-bound bay under the monastery, the sea heaves gently in jade green waves on to the beach now littered with flotsam rather than tourists. Driving up to the brow of the hill, I have to stop for a hoopoe picking insects from the road. It flutters fearlessly in front of the car, not recognising the threat to its existence.

"So beautiful stuff..." Tasso murmurs. Finally it flies off and we drive on up to park by the white wall of the monastery. He takes the bundle of my old clothes out of the car and with it under his arm, we enter. A fine solo baritone voice sounds from within the church.

As we cross the courtyard, the Pappás comes out of the church, still singing liturgically. Ox-eyed, brown-bearded, full-stomached, the thick sheep's wool vest peeping from the décolletage of his cassock, he greets us still singing: "*Ka-los ta péth-i-á.* ... (welcome children)...*Kalos, O Tassos.......* Ka- los, O *katrigáros!*" (O gangster!) Unabashed, Tasso sings the response: "*Kyrie Eleison...Kyrie Eleison. ...Kyrie Eleison...*"

Inside the cottage, the Pappás eagerly accepts the bundle of my old clothes; quickly stuffing the blouse under his arm, he disappears into his room with it before the old woman comes. She throws up her hands at the sight of the clothes, especially the pleated skirt. I leave him to haggle and go outside to stand on the terrace looking down on the heaving mass of the sea. What a setting for the spiritual life.

Suddenly a young monk (we've never seen a young one here before) comes out of a door near me, at the same moment as Tasso comes out of the Pappás' cottage. The wind is strong and I put my hand up to my hair. Tasso's eye opens and shuts like a camera. *Snap*! He says nothing till we are driving down the hill.

"What you doing with him?"

"Who?"

"You know." *That's the trouble, I do know.* I know how his mind works.

As he raises his hand, I say, "If you go on like this," quietly and without emphasis, "you will end up in the Crazy House."

As if even he is aware of this possibility, it freezes him.

We drive on in silence.

It is still Sunday, and still early afternoon. He indicates the road that leads to the casino. It's only three o'clock, it won't be open. But when we get there, the gates are open. He indicates with one finger to drive in.

He makes straight for the fruit machines salon. It is full of peasants from the village, dressed in their wedding-funeral best, yanking the handles as hard as they can. Playing the fruit machines has become the locals' Sunday occupation. They too have discovered 'the machine to give you money'.

"*Stakti kai barooti*" He hasn't anticipated this, but grabs a machine as it is vacated by a fat girl, whose husband is holding their baby. She takes the next machine but keeps peering at Tasso's the moment the drums stop revolving. It irritates him; he moves to another machine across the room. Immediately she puts a coin in the one he has quit and gets the jackpot.

I retreat to the Louis Quinze *escritoire* in the ante-room where I have a view into the salon, and watch a sturdy man, legs set well apart, pulling the handle of a machine as if it were a test of strength. His wife stands at his elbow goggling owlishly at the revolving lemons, oranges and strawberries, then at the metal pocket where the coins will fall. When they do, she raises her eyes to heaven, crosses herself reverently, whispering the name of the local saint with gratitude. If nothing happens, her attention deflects to her best shoes, which are killing her. She comes out into the room where I am, sits on a chair, takes off her shoes, pressing her coarse jointed toes to the cool marble floor, while examining the offending shoes inside and out. A sudden fall of coin in the next room brings her onto her bare feet; waddling to the door, shoes in hand, she peers in hopefully.

Tasso emerges black as thunder. "Come on – we get out of here. So many stupids I never have see in my life before..." He says this without equating himself among them.

We slide down the hill toward the fishing village at the bottom, and stop off at a simple taverna on the sea front, where old men sit at the tin tables flicking worry beads between their fingers with a clicking sound, which is 'essence of Greece'. The big pan of charcoal is already alight to roast the *souvlakia*. It is the magic hour of the evening; a graceful red *caique* is just setting out for a night's sardine fishing, towing the boat with the nets heaped in it, and the four little boats with the big lamps mounted in the stern. When it is dark, their lamps will form their own galaxy on the dark surface of the sea.

I am enjoying this though I have no doubt we are going back up there... We are waiting for nine o'clock when the tables open.

The view darkens over the sea, the mountains disappear, the lights of the sardine boats are now bright jewels in the distance. The jukebox moos one of those songs: *"The door is closed and locked...rain in the street...Where are the years...those years...when I had a sweet love...to keep me warm..."*

The boys from the village come in, take a table next to the jukebox, dragging out the chairs and straddling them with a masculine emphasis. One of them thumbs the buttons of the jukebox, and the heavy beat of the Zembekiko fills the place like an animal seeking blood. A boy with heavy black brows over almond eyes – like the bronze of the "Charioteer" at Delphi – drags his Van Gogh chair to the centre of the floor, lays it on its back and begins to dance around it. With shocking suddenness and grace, he springs onto the supine chair and, balancing there slowly, tips it upright with a skilfulness that is almost cruel. Leaping down, he takes the back between his teeth, tosses it in the air like a dog killing a cat, catches it deftly in one hand, replaces it at the table and sits on it as the music ends.

Two others immediately take the floor, circling round each other like classical wrestlers. One boy leaps at the other, clamping his legs round the other boy's waist, arching his body backwards till his dark curls almost touch the floor. They sway to the music like mating snakes, snapping their fingers to the beat. Is this how they danced in Plato's day? They detach as lightly as thistledown from the stem.

They have not glanced at us. They are not looking for attention; to applaud would be an intrusion into their very private adolescent rites of manhood. They leave the tavern as they came, without a glance right or left and silent amongst themselves.

"You looking much at them." Tasso's voice intrudes into my thoughts…the night is about to begin.

"I engage with the Snark every night after dark in dreamy delirious fight:

I serve it with greens in those shadowy scenes and I use it for striking a light…"

The Salon is crowded, hot and stifling, the weekend gamblers are here from Athens. I have to fight my way to one of the tables. I bet heavily. It's no use winning a little, it has to be a lot or nothing. It makes no difference, the money has no meaning; it can't solve anything for me when the other woman is that fabulous creature – Lady Luck.

I come and go like a gloomy swan, praying not to encounter Parsifal on the stairs. The bar is dimly lit – nobody there except for Tasso perched on a high stool, chatting to the barman who is glad of company.

266

Suddenly the Count enters. Quickly I put my hand behind my back – a gauche reaction. In high spirits, not a little drunk, he reaches round to grab my hand and kisses the tips of my fingers. *Are there degrees in this? If so, where does it end?* Impelling me towards him, he clamps me to his side and places his lips to my cheek. "Ziss is permitted?" he asks, looking provocatively at Tasso. I feel as helpless as a sheep with its legs tied together waiting for the knife. But Tasso smiles – one of his many smiles – and gently wags his finger as if cautioning a naughty child.

"*Nein, mein Herr, das ist verboten…*" He means it. The Count takes a sharp breath through his nostrils, and tightens his grip on my waist.

"I am a JENTEL-MANN!" Crunching out the words like a boiled sweet. "A KRISTIAN JENTELMANN…but I am alzo A MANN!" he adds, taking another quick peck at my cheek before releasing me. I quickly put myself on the other side of Tasso.

"And I," Tasso says sweetly, "am the King…" (the Count's eyes snap at the assumption of a higher rank) "…of *the Good Basters…*"

A silence, as distinctive as the cracking of ice in a cocktail glass, until the Count's metallic laugh rings out. "AH-ha! Zat iss GOOT! I LIKE ZAT! Zee King of zee Goot Basters! Very goot…Ah-haaaa…." (*Game, set and match to Tasso. Pride in him returns…*)

Feeling in the inner pocket of his dinner jacket, the Count produces a small coin and presses it into Tasso's hand. "Zat iss for you!" He turns on his heel and marches out of the bar. Tasso examines the coin hopefully.

"Bah!" Disappointed, he puts it in his pocket. "Never mind, I find the way to sell…" It is the Count's personal currency with his head in profile on it. He shoves some of the plastic pieces at me. "Go – put all on…27!"

Twenty-seven comes up! A good win. The croupier taps the pieces with his wand to identify the winner, but before I get my hand up, a woman sitting at the table claims it as hers. I know it is mine – there was nothing on that number when I shoved my pieces on. The Athenian Virago starts shouting and screaming, saying she has been playing that number all night. It has the nightmare quality of a road accident as she exhorts the people round her to bear witness that it is hers. They remain dumb as cows; the vulgarity of squabbling over a piece of plastic – but it isn't plastic, it's money.

I make a desperate appeal to the croupier. He is on my side, but must have confirmation from somebody at the table. A man nods in my direction, and the croupier pays out to me. I grab the pieces and run – not forgetting a generous *pourboire pour les employee...* The woman's voice pursues me, screaming that she has been robbed.

On the landing I almost collide with Parsifal, who steadies me with a hand on my elbow. "How many kilometres do you walk in a night?" *Oh, very funny.* I pull my arm away, but I don't smile. I don't smile at anything anymore.

I pour the pieces on to the bar in front of him. It's a lot. He brings winning to its ultimate absurdity by refusing to change the plastic into money "in case someone see and put the Evil Eye on it!"

On the stairs we manoeuvre around Mr and Mrs Dexter. She, an infuriated toad, rouged cheeks aflame, has one of her fur cuffs raised to strike her patient husband, accusing him of having lost all her money. "Now come on, honey...time to get home...mother's waiting..." So the mother has been shut in the car all night. Are we all mad? Either that, or we are trying to appease the madness of our other half.

43

In the wine shop, waiting for him to bring the shopping. When he appears, he has no shopping. He stands in front of the table, scratching his head and looking thoughtful. "Can you go to the bank to cash one travellers' cheque? We need for the rent."

"We won a lot last night."

"It going. I owe too much money. For crazy! We must to stay away from that *MALEDICTION PLACE!*" And he turns away to the counter to order a wine.

I leave the wine shop, go to the bank; it is the first time he has had to ask me to do this – he who would '*milk the trees*' rather than ask for money of a woman.

In the evening, the car has a flat tyre, and as usual the spare tyre is flat too. It's his fault, but I am to blame. We take the scooter into town. Being Wednesday, he puts me in the Cake Parlour.

When Pooter comes in to join me and orders koniak, Tasso drifts in from the ouzerie across the street with a bottle of beer in his pocket which he hides in Pierrot's pulpit. There is some joking going on. He goes again. There is much laughter across the street. Tasso comes in again, with another bottle of beer. Because Pooter is with me, he comes over to explain, "My friends joking with me – they take my wallet and put in the fridge, so I steal the bottles..." He goes again.

Pooter smiles. "He really is a delightful man..."

"I can't remember." I don't remember anything about the beginnings of my feelings for him. It is too far away – or too near, like looking through the wrong end of a telescope. He looks at me sharply and, changing the subject, asks, "What are you reading?"

"The Bible – I haven't got anything else except a dictionary."

"As an ex-Catholic convert I can say I have read the Bible from cover to cover, which is more than most people can say. Magnificent language...Where have you got to?"

"*Deliver my soul from the sword...my life from the power of the dog.*"

He looks shocked; either he understands everything, or nothing at all. The British are like that. He calls the boy over to pay for his koniak. "Well, I leave you… Goodnight." He goes.

Tasso returns, saying emphatically, "Tonight we go home early for sure." But it is too early. Now the Casino has become the drug, what do we put in its place?

"Go to the airport…"

"What for?"

"To take a coffee and see the plane come in…to see who arrive from Athens."

The few people waiting for the plane are peasants with sad faces on their way to hospitals in Athens, sighing that deepest of all sighs, "Aach! *Panayia mou*!", to the Virgin Mary.

Tasso talks to the barman he knows. The policeman on duty, carrying a stengun, puts it down on a table and is going toward the gents' when a child of five rushes up to grab it. The policeman swerves back just in time.

"Is it such a good idea to come to the airport?" I say, feeling it would be safer at the Casino.

"You are right. We get out of here."

But it's still too early. Where to go now? He scratches his head, before indicating a B-class hotel belonging to a 'friend of him'.

The place is dark with only one light over the reception; the bar where the new television set flickers is empty except for the barman, and a man with his shoulders hunched up to his ears, pacing up and down the empty space like an emaciated heron. "Ah! I find one very-good-friend-of-me!" Tasso says with joy. "We was in the navy together!" They embrace like brothers. "On the same ship…"

"She is English?" the man enquires of Tasso, before addressing me in excellent vintage English. "We were on the same ship," the friend concedes, "but I was an officer, he was…what is your word for it…? A rating, as I think you say… I will tell you a story about this man." He is pedantic as a schoolmaster. "We were anchored off Mykonos…you know where that is? The Aegean Sea… I was in charge of the Shore Patrol, and unfortunately, because we came from the same island, I chose *this* man."

"I remember very well…" Tasso laughs.

"We go ashore – everything went very well. No problems. We get all our men back on board by midnight. Then it was that *this* man," still with his arm around Tasso's shoulder, "says, 'We have done a good job. Now we can go to a taverna and have something to eat.' I should have known…but I agreed.

"Of course the tavern keeper doubled the price for strangers. Tassos gets angry – a fight broke out…everybody in the taverna is fighting everybody else. And what is the result?" He pauses dramatically. "*He is the Only Man we have to carry on board that night!*", beating out the rhythm of his words on Tasso's shoulder. "But – *listen to this.* When Tassos, with a black eye and cuts to his face, was brought before the Captain, the Captain was very angry, but he says, 'I don't want *him!* I want the bloody fool who chose him for shore patrol!' And I got the reprimand. How do you live with this man?" he demands, eyeing me sharply.

"I am the other bloody fool."

He looks at me with renewed interest almost amounting to admiration.

After more reminiscences and several drinks, we leave him – and go home.

It is the beginning of a weird week of staying away from the Casino. Going home early to the comfortless place that serves us in much the same way as a dog kennel; we don't live in it.

In bed, he reads the newspaper, cursing at photographs of the *kaikshooters,* their uniforms decorated with gold braid and tassels, opening new factories, or roads – always accompanied by a posse of priests in their black robes and stove-pipe hats, swinging censors, bringing the grace of God to everything. *Stakti kai barooti!* His elbow lying heavy against my ribs forms the bridge between us.

A week of this is enough for both of us. The next night he says, "We go a little bit to the Salamander…to see what happens there."

Jason is at the end of the bar as usual; Mr Dexter at the other. Madame Ellie is there too, her ageing features carefully made up, her double chins discreetly screened with a soft scarf, and her hair hennaed in the manner of ladies of her age in the Middle East. Her tiny feet scuffle about rat-like in smart little boudoir slippers.

A surprise element is the two English girls – not very young, one is already going grey. Madame Ellie is demanding of them in guttural English, "But why do you come to Greeze in the winter time when it is co-eld and raining?" as if it were proof-positive of the congenital idiocy always suspected of the British, who, when they are not being very clever and dominating, are very, very stupid. Her glance in my direction proves it in her mind.

"Well, we saw this ad-vertise-ment in the paper to go Greece for only £15," said the girl called Marg (with a hard 'g'). "We didn't know what we were letting ourselves in for - did we, Noleen?"

"It took 15 days… we got stuck in Yugoslavia in the snow," said Noleen.

"It was just an old van filled up with spare engine parts this guy was bringing into Greece. There was another girl from South Africa – we slept three in a bed…didn't we, Noleen?"

"The South African didn't wash the whole trip," said Noleen, "and the driver had nothing to talk about except his past sex-u-al ex-peer-iences."

"And those of his dog…" said Marg. "He joost couldn't get his sex life into pro-porshion, could he, Noleen?"

"And now we've got here – it isn't even hot! I brought my bikini – heck! We might as well have stayed in Scunthorpe."

Madame Ellie is not amused by their candid naivety, and turns to comforting Mr Dexter. "How is Clio?"

"Oh, not so bad…she has her ups and downs…the psychiatrist said she'd have her ups and downs… I'd better be getting back."

When he has gone I hear Madame Ellie telling Jason, "As if it not enough to have mad wife – he has her mother as well. If I invite them to supper they have to bring her, but she stays in the car."

It does not surprise me when Tasso says, "We take the girls to be enjoy a bit at the Paradeisos."

"We haven't got the car." Flat tyre again.

"Never mind, I call a taxi." He puts us into the taxi and follows with the scooter.

The Paradeisos is empty. Marg and Noleen are unimpressed.

"It's got a jukebox though." Going straight to it like a homing pigeon, Marg shrieks with delight. "Look what it's got! Rock and roll – God, this is archaic!" She thumbs the buttons expertly, and they take to the floor by themselves, gyrating about in the new way that requires no male partner. Tasso tries to join in, looking silly trying to wag his hips. They don't even notice him. Baffled, he gives up in a coughing fit. *"Mysterio pragma…"* he says, watching the girls gyrating in a world of their own. It is a shock to find how far behind the time we are on this island.

Panayoti lopes in carrying his guitar, proving the efficiency of the bush telegraph. He has heard there are foreign girls about, that Tasso has got them and, putting two and two together, hits the bull's eye. Dragging his guitar from its case, he begins to play and sing. Noleen seems instantly transfixed – she can't take her eyes off him, though he is no oil painting, with that wide tartar mouth and low brow. Marg whispers, "Look at Noleen…she was married to a rock guitarist. He was rotten to her…they broke up. That's why we're here reee-lly. She had to get away." Only to be mesmerized by the same image at journey's end? Is there is any point in trying to escape?

The door opens again, Jason lopes in. We have never seen him here before though he lives somewhere nearby. He and Tasso are drinking whisky, deliberately provoking each other to talk politics which is *Apogorévétai* (forbidden).

At two o'clock in the morning, Tasso decides it is time to go home. Noleen has disappeared with Panayoti, which leaves Marg to be taken back to town. The three of us squeeze onto the Lambretta. He drops me off at the bottom of the path and drives on with Marg to the town.

At home I climb into bed with the Bible again – which will surely put me to sleep. Twenty minutes later, I hear footsteps on the path, then Tasso shouting. The door flies open, he charges in, coming straight at me. My body curls up like a hedgehog, my arm flings itself over my head as the blow falls like a sledge-hammer. He dashes outside and drags somebody into the house. It is Jason, presuming this is Tasso's way of inviting him in for a drink – until he sees me sitting up on the bed, regarding my smashed wristwatch.

Taking in the situation quickly and astutely, he starts talking as only an American can. Tasso is shouting incoherently, but Jason talks and talks and talks until Tasso begins to feel uncertain. So when Jason says, "Well, brother, there's one way to prove this sort of thing" and starts to unbuckle his trousers, Tasso is appalled.

"No...no...Jason...please...come on...I am only joking. We're friends..."

"Then where's the drink you offered me, you son of a bitch?"

Hospitality being the essence of Greek life, this puts Tasso on the wrong foot. He has nothing to offer. "I never drink in my home, Jason...honest to God..."

"That's because you drink too bloody much out of it!"

Tasso goes into the kitchen to make coffee. Jason turns to me. "Are you safe with this guy? Do you want to come away? Shall I wake up the neighbours? Call the police?" I shake my head in alarm. God forbid, that would only make him harder to live with.

Tasso comes back with two tiny coffees – nothing for me. There being no chairs, Jason sits on the floor, sipping the tiny coffee slowly to delay as long as possible the moment when he must leave me to my fate.

Suddenly he says, "If I see a mark on that girl tomorrow, I'm going to tell this story all over town. I'll make you look the biggest bloody fool on this island...you'll never live it down!" He has majored in Greek psychology after all...

"Come on, Jason...nothing happen. We are good friends. For God-ni-say..."

What does that make him and me? I do believe that if I should fail to wake up tomorrow, done to death by him, he would be the only one to be surprised and probably stand over my corpse

274

begging me to get up. He's got me so well-trained, I probably would...

Jason cannot make one tiny Greek coffee last till dawn. He has to go. The door closes behind him. Tasso takes the cups to the kitchen. This is the moment when all his insane suspicions will come surging back.

I scramble off the bed – better to be standing up, holding the Bible in my hands as my only weapon, ready to hit him with it. *"Deliver my soul from the sword – my life from the power of dog!"*

He comes back into the room, ignoring me; gets into bed. But just before settling into instant sleep, he says, "Anyway – tomorrow pack your things and go."

When he snores, I crawl onto the bed beside him – no danger now. He even turns towards me; cradling his body to mine and flinging an arm over me, he mutters. *"Theos na filaxi!"* – God forbid! – holding me in an even tighter grip.

I fall instantly into a vivid dream.

In my dream, a fire has broken out, the kitchen is ablaze. I run to tell Tasso. He takes no notice till the flames have reached gigantic proportions. The fire brigade arrives; a number of people have gathered, among them a female tourist. She asks me to explain the significance of the two flowers she is holding – a yellow pansy and a purple one. I tell her that if she wants sex, she should wear the yellow pansy; if she doesn't, she should wear the purple. "Oh, thank you! I'll wear the yellow."

A large company now, we go into the taverna at the top of the path, sitting at a long table under the vine. Suddenly I see a man strangle the person next to him. I jump up. The strangler's eyes fix on me. I know I am the next victim. I try to tell Tasso, but he doesn't listen. Terribly frightened, I run off down the road to another café, which is full of men who leer at me. Madame Ellie is among them, flirting with a young man. I tell her what has happened. *"Mon Dieu!* What did you expect?" she says, and goes back to flirting with the young man.

I go back into the road, which has now become a London street. I wait by a bus stop but no buses come. I want a taxi, but have no money. Then I see an enormous British policeman and run up to him like a little girl. He bends his ear to hear my story. "Alright, little missie," he smiles, and comes back to the taverna with me.

Tasso is shouting in deadly anger, "Where is she?" He comes out wearing the face I have come to fear. I try to explain to him why I ran off. The policeman tries to explain too. *"Don't try to tell me anything! I will hear it only from her."* The people around us try to convince him my story is true. Then we are all sitting at the table again, including the strangler. The people ask me, *"Do you feel better now?"*, stroking me as if I were a child. *"No,"* I say, *"I would like to be as I was before it all happened..."* – and wake up exhausted. It is five o'clock.

I get up. Opening the kitchen door, the scent of the garden encompasses me like an embrace – or rather what one used to imagine an embrace might be. The cat and her kittens are curled up together on the canvass chair outside the back door; the six eyes look out at me, and stretch any number of legs. Love – all warm and furry and forever kind... I don't want to know anymore how many legs it has, or teeth, or claws. It has as many as you stupidly allow it to have.

I pull out my suitcase from the cupboard, and start putting things into it. At six o'clock, he calls from the bedroom, "Can you bring me two aspirin?"

I take him the aspirins and a glass of water. He falls asleep again. He wakes the second time, saying, "I'm late for my job..." As he gets up, I move into the garden where a snail crawls slowly up the coiling vine stem, leaving a glistening trail like bleached blood. Every blade of grass spears a bead of dew. I observe this phenomenon intensely, translating it into yet another analogy for Love. How long can it stay there before evaporating? Longer than you would think, even under the intense eye of the sun.

The door bangs after him. With him gone, I put some water on the gas to wash. I look at the damage now; my upper arm has a bruise the size of a large saucer, quite black. Another under my broken wristwatch, another on my brow, and my ear. That blow could have broken my neck if my body had not saved me by curling up like a spring. Feeling wobbly, I sit down.

Why sit down now? For God's sake, girl, give up! He told you to go.

He won't remember saying that...

But he did say it.

To be kicked out like a dog after all I've put up with from him! If I go, people will think *I* am guilty. That's how they think. That's how *I* think now. I *am* guilty – but not in the way they will interpret it. Guilty that, having chosen him out of all the world, I am not able to take the consequences...a romantic little fool. That's a crime you pay for. It is my fault in a way; putting that stupid maxim about 'cards and love' to the test pitched us into the maelstrom of the casino. I deserve a lot of what I'm getting, but not from him.

Returning to my suitcase, I stare into it. It is empty – the things I put into it have disappeared. I find them stuffed back into the shelves . *So he does remember he said it.* I experience an absurd flicker of hope. Hope of what? I have to give up, I must give up...but how? It's not easy. I am on an island. I have to drive across Europe...I need tickets, insurance for the car. An icon of St Nicholas, a blue bead, a bit of fishing net and a clove of garlic won't insure me from the toe of Italy to the White Cliffs. *Think, girl... you've got to think!* What must I do? *Send for money.* That can take weeks... *Then get on with it!* Must I give up? *Yes, of course, you must – you're British.* A British Sergeant Major wouldn't give up – they never give up... *You are not a British Sergeant Major – just a stupid woman.* But I shouldn't give up too soon... *You mustn't give up too late!* But it was YOU who urged me to fling myself on Destiny and ride it to the end. *It was the right advice at the time, and it's the right advice now.*

Okay – I will write to the bank...

The car is in the garage being fixed, so I have to take the bus. Even that is not without incident. At a junction, a horse and cart wambles across in front of the bus, the carter's head sunk on his chest asleep. The horse panics, the carter wakes up and struggles to regain control. We all laugh. On the whole there is less danger on the road than in the bedroom.

I post my letter to the bank, and walk toward the wine shop. At the corner of the arcade I see Jason – and he sees me. To be caught at this point – the worst possible place for losing one's reputation – my instinct is to cut him dead, but he calls out, "Are you okay?" I nod and keep walking. He follows. Hell! I feel all eyes on us.

"You know what…" he says, walking beside me. I keep eyes front. "I was waiting for the bus this morning, he came by on the scooter – and offered me a lift! I said, 'Man, you owe me an apology!' You know what he said? '*What for?*'"

It is so typical I can't help laughing, but keep walking toward the wine shop, followed only by Jason's American amazement. "He said, '*WHAT FOR?*'"

The Hon. is in the wine whop. "My dear gel, you look beaten to death in a barn!"

Looking at the little dog sitting on her lap, I say slowly, "To call a man an animal is to insult the animal. Men are much worse than animals!"

"Have you just found that out?" she says, raising one eyebrow.

The little dachshund is gazing up into her face. "Yes, darling…the man is cooking your steak now. He will wrap it up, and we will take it home for you to eat, my poppet… I 'm afraid we'll have to go now, I must give Poody his breakfast."

When Tasso comes in he is whistling cheerfully as if nothing in the world has happened. "The car is ready – can you go to the garage to pick up? And I have find so nice fresh fish – make soup, can you? It will be fantastic."

I drive home, pack my suitcase again and put it onto the back seat of the car. *I must keep the advantage.*

At three o'clock, returning from his job, he shouts from taverna window above us, "I have meet nice people – come up here, will you?"

I find him sitting with an elderly gentleman whose silky white beard fans out over the astrakhan lapels of a very Balkan overcoat; the lady with him, younger by some years, has the deportment and style of an opera singer. They are having a simple lunch. The lady levels her eyes on me with a bright, discreet curiosity. Taking the social initiative and speaking English with a foreign accent, she asks, "How long have you lived..." she nearly says, "with him", but corrects herself "...here?"

I make no bones about it, counting it out deliberately in the ratio of a dog's life at 7-1. She laughs richly. The Balkan gentleman takes no interest in the conversation, and Tasso has disappeared; I suspect to get some pictures to sell them.

The lady suddenly asks. "Are you married to him?"

"No!" I say, rather too forcefully, having drunk my glass of wine too quickly on an empty stomach. "But you *can't divorce* a man you're not married to!" quoting from my own dream.

"Aah!" she breathes, "I think I understand you very well. But I think you are rather brave to think to live with him," she says.

Finding relief talking to this benign goddess who understands everything, I grandly reply, "The British are the only romantic race in the Universe..."

She laughs her rich operatic laugh again. "I see you are *very* British. *You can laugh at yourself...* I shan't worry about you anymore."

Tasso returns with the portfolio of pictures, setting them out on the chairs in his usual style. They look at them without enthusiasm.

"Do you paint too?" she asks me. For the first time I say 'Yes', wanting her to know.

"That's good," she says.

The old gentlemen signals silently for the bill, and pays it. We rise to leave. She links her arm through mine as we go towards the door. "Don't despair!" she whispers. *Am I in despair? Rather it hurts me that they cannot see in him the man he used to be...* "And anyway..." lowering her voice "...men either make you suffer...or they bore you death!"

She did understand everything.

44.

Returning to the house, he is angry at not selling them anything. I don't trust his mood and go straight out of the back door into the garden, perceiving the usefulness of neighbours, but they have all disappeared to their siestas.

"Why don't you come to eat?" he calls from the kitchen.

"I'm not hungry."

"Come to sleep then…"

I don't want that either. I give him time to fall into sleep, eat some of the cold spaghetti, and shovel the rest to the cats. They won't let you touch them; they just want the food – to survive. *Is that all one has to do with life – survive it? How do you survive love?*

He wakes; we go to town. *Does he really not notice my suitcase on the back seat?*

As we drive round the bay, a pink moon is rising in a lilac sky, the sea stretches away, iridescent as taffeta. Enchantment and disillusion go hand-in-hand in this country. Only a few hours separate us from the emotional abattoir of last night, and probably the night to come.

We park in the square. Now he glances over his shoulder at the things on the back seat. "What the hell you got there!"

"You told me to pack my things and go…" The words I have been waiting to say all day.

"You crazy for sure!" he mutters, crossing himself piously. "And anyway – I know nothing happen… there was not time." Jason walking from the Paradeisos via our path would take as long as for him to drive to town and return. It's not that we were innocent but that we didn't have time to be guilty.

Getting out of the car, he walks away.

"Why don't you scream now?" Alice asked, holding her hands ready to put over her ears again. "But I've done all the screaming already…" said the Queen.

When he collects me later from the Cake Parlour, "Where we go now," he ponders, before taking the way leading into the rabbit warren of the Old Town. We haven't done this for a long time.

He pauses by a small door that might be the entrance to a badger's set in a children's story, and peers through the greasy pane before pushing it open. It has one of those organic interiors with niches in the thick irregular walls, filled with crudely contrived wooden shelves. A wooden counter painted cerulean blue, crude tables and Van Gogh chairs. The place is empty except for the family who run it, and whose livelihood it represents. A man and two women look at us with bovine surprise. They are just setting out their own meal on one of the tables. Tasso calls for two wines. They return to setting out their own meal of boiled greens, cheese, olives and bread. Tasso wishes them *kali orexi*. "These people have no profit except what they have on the table," he says.

We drink up and go. They give us the traditional leave-taking: *"Na parte sto kalo…"* *May you go toward the good… One feels blessed.*

We make our way through the narrow alleys. Suddenly pausing to light a cigarette, he nods towards an ornamental gateway. "That is it."

"What"

"The house of my kids…" – meaning his wife's. "That house never like me…"

In the car we are silent. Are we really going home? Where the road divides, he indicates the way which leads *there*.

"NO! You said we must stay away from *THAT PLACE*!"

"I know…I know…" All sweet reasonableness. "You are very right, we must to stop…but just this time, one more time – I promise to you, then finish."

"NO!" As I swing the car toward home, his hand locks on the wheel.

"Just this one time…please to do me this favour…just one more time… I am *sure we win. Oh, darr-ling…*" A sure sign he is flirting with another woman. *Luck be a Lady tonight…*

In the battle of wills, mine shrinks to the size of a seed, a seed containing us both. *To think I had power over this man once…*

At the casino, the fruit machine salon is empty and we surprise the attendant taking a pull at them himself. He looks sheepish, as if caught in an act of masturbation. Tasso, free to choose any of the machines, keeps bringing me the coins "to save for later". This is new.

When he leads the way out of the casino, for a moment I think we are going home, but because he owes money to the bar and needs the money he has won on the fruit machines for the tables, he proposes to sit in the car.

"I am not walking to and from the car park all night!"

As we re-enter the Casino, a taxi draws up; out of it step two young men. Their arrival seems to put the casino staff into a buzz. It is visible in Parsifal's face. "They clean up a fortune last night. The story all over town this morning…"

Tasso chooses to sit on the white and gold chair on the landing, looking like his Satanic Majesty, and sends me in to play from there.

The salon is full, two tables working. My attention is hooked by two young men who are sitting right up near the wheel: one has a baby face, pink skin and fair hair, must be British or Colonial; the other, an Oriental student type in dark suit, tie and horn-rimmed spectacles, quite passive and relaxed, until just before the croupier calls *"Rien n' va plus"*, when he snaps into action, striking like a cobra, dropping the pink pieces, the highest value, all over the board. He wins every time. Soon they have a mountain of pink pieces in front of them. The croupiers exchange nervous glances.

Throughout the evening, the Oriental student conducts himself with the same passivity until the moment for action. His pal sits beside him, knuckling his eyes like a small child kept late from bed. The croupiers watch them. Parsifal stands beside the head croupier. Tension is high.

Suddenly an outburst from the other table shocks the already tense atmosphere like an exploding bomb. A huge man, claiming a winning number is his, screams out "I WANT MY MONEY! I WANT MY MONEY!", flinging his arms about like a windmill. Staff rush in from everywhere, homing in on the giant; Parsifal lends his Gauleiter bulk. The man is hustled from the salon, arms still flailing, bellowing for his money like a cow in labour.

It is very tense now at the table, all eyes fixed on the student. The system he has evolved is working just as it did the night before. The croupiers look almost frightened; I keep forgetting to put my piffling bets on. I want to stay and watch but I had better go back – he'll start wondering what I am doing so long. I get up a small win and drag myself away.

The chair on the landing is empty. He is not in the bar…where the hell is he? I need the loo – always dangerous when I have lost contact with him. I risk it. When I emerge, Parsifal is talking earnestly with the Heavenly Bank Manger at the cash desk.

Suddenly Tasso is there and, seeing me coming, not from the direction of the salon but from a dark doorway, he puts two and two together and makes five.

"Where you have be?" – glancing over towards Parsifal

"I went to the loo…here you are," I say, holding out the plastic pieces. He hits me across the face right in front of Parsifal and the Heavenly Bank Manager. There is much one will bear in private that is not to be tolerated in public. I fling the pieces at him, and run down the stairs.

As I reach the bottom and am dragging open the heavy bronze door, Parsifal emerges from the lift, signalling to the staff to close the place. The student has broken the bank. *Rien n'va plus!*

45.

I am halfway to town before I ask myself: where am I going? I can't go home – not this time. Where can I go where I will be safe from him, and have an alibi? The Hon.! But it's two o'clock in the morning…. *Never mind, she doesn't sleep much… and she is a woman of experience.*

Her flat, on the ground floor of an old building, has a door on the left of the stone-flagged entrance. "Who's there?" she calls, more out of curiosity than alarm. She is not asleep. Recognising my voice, I hear her struggling to get herself together. "I'm coming… I'm coming…" She flings wide the door, revealing herself in a peignoir.

"MY DEAR GEL! Come in!" she cries, responding at once at the sight of me. My teeth are chattering now and I am trying to apologise for waking her. "Of course you were right to come here. My dear gel – let me get you a brandy…" And she pours me a stiff one.

"This is really quite like old times!" It's as if she is enjoying my intrusion. "I had a friend in Cannes who was always hiding in my flat from her jealous husband. She ended up in a mental home…poor soul…" *You mean this way really leads right round the bend? That you can get there?*

"I have nothing to give you to eat!" she wails at the inadequacy of her hospitality. "*HOW I WISH I HAD KNOWN YOU IN CHINA!* But…" A sudden thought, "I *can* offer you a hot bath!" She goes off immediately to prepare it.

A hot bath…how long since I had one? I lie in it soaking *him* out of my neck and shoulders. The little dachshund runs in and drops his ball on the floor. It must be a game he plays with his mistress. The brandy, the hot bath, the borrowed satin nightdress, like something from the 1920s, induce a sense of euphoria in which it would be pleasant to die.

"I *do hope* you will be able to sleep," she agonises, having made up the couch in the sitting room with clean sheets. It seems the most comfortable bed I ever lay upon. Is it because I am alone? My body has not belonged to me for a long time…yet once it was actually important to lie beside him.

"How I wish you'd get away from here," she tells me, talking from her own bed in the other room, "and meet someone nice!"

I don't want anyone nice, not a new man or a new love…just the old one back again… *"For I have thought thee bright and sworn thee fair who art as black as hell and dark as night."*

Just as my eyes droop, I hear her say, "You must stop him knocking you about. It's so *INFRA DIG.*"

Oh – that's what it is…

46.

In the morning I go to the bank. Money...money...money... It is lying all over the large shabby room where bank clerks chuck it from desk to desk among the cigarettes burning in the ashtrays; it could all go up in smoke. The English money is located somewhere on the floor under a chair.

Standing in front of the manager's desk in the corner of the room is the Oriental Student; his *sang-froid* seems to have deserted him as he tries to understand the Bank Manager's Esperanto of French, German and Greek. "You must to have one *papier* – stempen zo!" the man says, banging his fist on the desk to demonstrate. "You must go other bank – no here..."

"But I have just come from there. They sent me here." Poor fellow, they will have him cleaning the Augean stables and killing the Hydra before he gets his Golden Apples out of here...

I buy my tickets for the ferryboat. At the wine shop I order coffee and aspirins. He comes...*the love of my life*...and places a packet of meat wrapped in newspaper on the table. Before he can say "Make a soup", I say, "I'm going to England. I've got to take the car out of the country anyway", throwing this string bridge across the chasm between us. It is important he doesn't try to stop me going.

With the lightning duplicity of a Greek, he says, "Very Good Idea... I thinking exactly the same thing!", as if he has been waiting for me to make the move that must save us both. "When you think to go."

"Tomorrow."

I will enjoy England. Freedom, friendship, hot water coming out of taps... sausages...kippers... But I cannot bear to see the island disappear.

Only when all trace of it has gone do I go to the rail. A tear from the corner of my eye travels my cheek and – driven by the breeze – slides sideways across my neck, cutting my throat.

I don't know what to ask for anymore...

PART III
THE CHIMERA

'A fabulous fire-eating monster with a lion's head,
goat's body and serpent's tail –
or any incongruous conception of fancy.'

1.

The little car broke down at Foggia. I left it at a garage there, saying I would pick it up in three months. Would I?

I took the train. I phoned Verena from the middle of the channel. Verena is one of the friends I gained from being with Tasso.

"I need a bed…"

"Come straight here – stay as long as you like. I've broken my leg, I *need* company." She puts me into the flat on the top floor of her house in Belgravia, which used to be the nursery. We spend our time discussing Life and Love, marriage and partnership. She insists I *must* go back to Tasso, while insisting that *she must* divorce Robin, her amiable Etonian husband.

"Why? Has he ever given you a black eye?"

"No, of course not!" she says, adding thoughtfully, "I rather wish he would…"

"He waits on you hand and foot!"

"I know…that's part of the problem. It's like being married to the butler."

"Well, Tasso *isn't* like that and *that* is part of the problem."

"Oh, Tasso is a child of Nature…you'll destroy him if you don't go back."

"He'll destroy me if I do!"

"The point is – what can you do *without* Tasso?"

She was right. In spite of the luxury of the nursery in Belgravia, it took only fifteen days for England to defeat me, clutching at me from advertisements in tube trains: THINKING OF CHANGING YOUR JOB? WE HAVE JUST THE JOB FOR YOU. COME TO US. GOOD HOURS, GOOD SALARY, PENSION OPPORTUNITIES.

What job had I ever done as well or as conscientiously as being with him?

"The fact is, England bores me. It always did – except when I was a child, of course… Its higher standards only serve to lower the value of life and experience. It offers security but not Joy in life!" I am getting carried away. "In England you must edit yourself, say things you don't mean and watch others doing the same like fish under water mouthing bubbles." Now I'm thoroughly worked up. "It robs you of the courage to be yourself!"

She agrees but says, "I was brought up in America, and England was the escape route for me."

I soak in the luxury of the bath, singing the yearning Greek songs: *You were the dance…you were the song…you were the laughter…you were the fight…after the laughter…the pain in the head after the wine…the death after the dance. Silence after the song….another song rising at the death of the song…*

You were… Who knows what you were, except me…? If I tell, who will they believe? They will believe that you were charming, amusing and kind! You, the Chimera, will defeat me with your lion's head, goat's body, serpent's tail – or *any incongruous conception of fancy*. No! You are real! As a conception of fancy *I* would have made you charming, amusing and kind…

I am already counting the 100 days I must stay away…as his letters start to flop through the letterbox:

"I am no sure if you have the letters of me. I send many! Also your last letter very cold and angry. Why?" He still doesn't know why? *"Tell me exagly the day you to coming back. I meet you in Rome. So nice idea. Oh, yes…darrling…"* (How is he to find his

way to Rome?) *"and don't forget the after-save.."* That is what we are going to need – the 'after-save'…

"I think you and Robin are rather alike," Verena muses.

Yes, I can see that – we have both enrolled ourselves in the service of Juggernauts.

There is no way I can thank Verena for such high-class sanctuary. "It's been super! It needed all of three months for my nerve ends to re-grow!" We embrace under the Belgravia portico as she sees me into the taxi for the station.

"Give my love to darling Tasso! I'll visit you in the summer – without Robin! Bye!"

From Calais I share a couchette compartment with a lovely Swedish girl going to take up a job as an au pair in Rome. Does she know what she's in for? I wonder, remembering the au pair job I took in Athens that second year when it was the only way of getting back to Greece and him.

2.

The Greek family seemed nice. Both husband and wife spoke fluent English; Aliki, the wife, was heavily pregnant with her second child. The little girl of eight, Christina, was to be my charge. I was told to take her to the Museum the moment I arrived. "You won't find it difficult," she told me, though I had nothing of the language and no notion of the city. "You take the number three trolley – ask for the museum. It's the same word."

Down in the street it was like being crushed between two millstones, the heat from the pavement and the heat from the sky. The traffic came from the wrong direction, the child pulled me back just in time.

Squashed onto the crowded trolley, I asked for the "Mew-seum". The conductor shrugged. "Moo-say-um!" shouted my charge. I didn't understand the money either; she had to help again, contempt visible in her eyes. She could see I was not like any other grown-up, and must have come from the land of deaf mutes and idiots. Forced further and further into the car, I hung by the greasy straps, Christina hanging onto me. How would we get out of this? And when? I didn't know where we are going. Christina did, and at the right moment began to push like a billy goat. Forcing your way out of a trolley in Athens takes as much effort as being born, and there are no midwives. If you are polite about it, you don't succeed.

The tranquillity of the museum…the silence of stone speaking for the flesh and the spirit without the muddle we make of it with emotion and words. That's *his* back…sudden recognition…

The bored child pulls me on. She and I dislike each other already, but I have to rely on her precociousness to get us back to the flat.

"I want you to give Christina an English lesson every day," the mother decides.

Christina, an apt pupil, says, "You speeky mummy – me no have Engliss lesson today."

My duties are not confined to English usage. "Give Christina her bath" or "See that she uses the bidet." "Has Christina done her 'big job' today? I don't want her constipated like the Anglo-Saxons." I sit on the edge of the bath while Christina squirms around on the loo...

At night the Greek music drifts in the open windows, conjuring images in large impressionistic blobs, accompanied by an unbearable nostalgia. His letters flop through the letterbox, promising he will come to Athens.

"You have a Greek friend?" Quizzing the envelope she hands to me. "What does he do?" To say he is an electrician is too little, to say he is an artist, too much. "Why don't you talk about him?"

She gets nothing out of me.

The house is in the suburbs on the side of a mountain with a classical name. The baby is due any minute. When nature begins to take its course, Aliki sweeps into my bedroom like a ship in full sail. "The waters have broken. Read this and see how long I've got!" she commands, holding out a childbirth manual written in English. Skimming through False Labour, Early Labour, True Labour, Cramps and Contractions, I venture an opinion: "I think you've got 15 minutes or 24 hours..."

Aliki decides she has got time to get to the clinic if her husband will finish his breakfast. He refuses to be hurried and comes into the hall eating apricots to prove he is being hurried. As I watch them drive away, relief sweeps through me, and joy – I am FREE. Christina has been sent to her granny. But where is *he*...? Why isn't he here?

They return too soon for me, bringing the new baby with them; a peasant woman is hired as a nurse. I have little to do with it until Black Thursday, the peasant woman's day off. Aliki is having a bath when it starts crying in the middle of a long hot afternoon. "Pick it up," she calls from the bathroom. Reluctantly I put down my book. I pick it up gingerly, but it goes on crying.

"Sing to it!" The only song that comes to mind is the hymn 'Darkness is over me' It astonishes the baby into silence for a couple of seconds, then it bawls louder than ever.

"Really, you must have no maternal instinct at all…" Aliki says, coming in damp from her bath. When it refuses to stop crying in her arms, she panics. "It must be in pain! Read the book!"

I read aloud from *The Authoritative Common Sense Guide* under the sub-heading 'The Crying Baby': "*The parent must accept that the crying baby is a very common phenomenon.*"

"What do you do about it?"

"*Be calm,*" I continue, "*the mother should go and visit friends…*"

"How ridiculous! I shall ring the doctor!" she snaps, handing the creature to me. I am wondering why the Greeks have given up the practice of exposing their infants on the mountainside, when she returns. She is silent.

"What did he say?"

"He said I should calm down and go for a walk."

Wind in the baby's belly, wind in the pine trees. Long hot hours filled with impotent longings and potent irritations. This Chekhovian existence is not what I came to Greece for. The peasant is sacked for suggesting the baby should be made to eat its own excrement as an infallible remedy for crying. The maid gives notice – this place is too far out of Athens for her social life. Neither are replaced. Aliki does the cooking, I wash up, make beds, chop vegetables. There was to be 'plenty of free time' with this job.

In desperation I post my letter to him, care of the Bar Greco: "*When will you come to Athens? If I send you a boat – will you come? If I send you a plane – will you come? If I send you a pair of boots – will you come?*"

The telephone rings early one evening. "It's for you…" Aliki hands me the receiver with a quizzical look. His kippered voice bursts on my ear. "I am here in Athens…I wait you at my sister's." He gives the address. "Don't be long!"

I claim my free time – running down the hill to catch the bus into Athens, repeating to myself the place where I must get off: UMBELOKIPI. It sounds like umbilical – I have had enough of them.

I find the apartment block, the front door is open, Beethoven on the record player. We rush towards each other, clinging like people in a gale force wind.

"How long are you staying?" I breathe.

"Till tomorrow," he says.

"What!"

"Honestly, when I read your letter, I smile so much, I leave my job without permission and take the plane and come. I going to be in trouble with my job, but you happy now?" *Yes, in a desperate sort of way.*

We plunge into the roaring Attic night. He walks fast; it is a job to keep up with him until he stops to have his shoes cleaned by a shoe-shine boy squatting on the curb. All manner of things are being sold in the street. Kiosks obstruct the pavements, selling everything from chocolates to socks, ties, sunglasses, toothpaste, postcards, and the use of a telephone on which people shout above the roar of the traffic. Lottery ticket sellers shout "AV-RIO PLEE-RON-EE!!" (Paying tomorrow!) Flower-sellers thrust gardenias under your nose, the scent for an instant overcoming the smell of roasting meat. Have I ever seen so much food? Cheese pies, bread rings, nuts, meat on sticks, pastries dripping in honey, ice-cream and everybody shouting.

Alone, I have gone about these streets blind and defensive, but with him, my eyes open, everything becomes new and exciting... The streets become steeper and narrower, vibrating with the jangle of the *bouzouki* music from cellars, walled gardens. Above us, the Parthenon sits like a duck on its nest.

"Where are we?"

"Plaka..." We dive in and out of bars, down cellar steps and up on rooftops. These people work, live and play hard.

In the heat of the next afternoon we rattle in an ancient train with mahogany seats to Piraeas – where the oldest ships in the world are gathered, rusty flank to rusty flank, at a quayside full of quaint cafes with lopsided iron canopies, and melancholy waiters with pencil-thin moustaches, who bang down the glasses of ouzo and retsina on the wobbly ironwork tables.

"Why are you going by boat?"

"I have no more money for the plane."

The small rusty ship, its decks filled with passengers like refugees, will take 16 hours to reach the island. As I watch it draw away, my heart is ready to burst. If I jump into the gap between us, will he jump too?

I do not put it to the test.

I return to the Chekhovian existence on the side of the mountain. Aliki and her husband are quarrelling in English.

"You see what he's like! What would I do without you!" she cries, flinging herself into my arms. "Stay with us forever!"

How much more can I take? The situation resolves itself quite suddenly. Aliki is visiting her mother, Christina playing with her friends in the house. I am sitting under the cobwebby pine tree in the garden reading when I hear satyric whoopings coming from my bedroom.

Running up onto the terrace, I find the children rummaging through my things, throwing them all about the floor. Christina, capering about in the middle, sticks her tongue out at me. A Greek prison is hardly enough to deter me. She sees it in my eyes and runs away screaming, and the others disappear like magic. I pack my things, lock my case – my mind made up.

Aliki returns; Christina throws herself into her mother's arms and has hysterics. "Christina says you hit her – tell me the truth." Not scrupulous about the Truth themselves, it is expected of the British.

I tell her the truth. "I am leaving tonight."

"But why?" Her manner changes instantly. "I will make the children apologise..." I shake my head. "Will you go back to England?" I shake my head.

We are standing under the pine tree in the twilight, the sky the luminous blue of a wild iris. "Ah, you will go to your... Will you marry him?" I shake my head. "You English girls are..." She searches for the right word in English, and finds it in French: "...*bizarre*", and stalks back into the house.

I coast down into Athens on the bus, full of the joy of liberation and with only one idea – to take the plane to the island…

These memories surprise me. Looking at the Swedish girl, I feel almost maternal toward her. Perhaps I should warn her that life in the Mediterranean is not all fun and sun, and can be more restrictive than liberating…if you try it for more than a fortnight.

3.

The train rolls into Rome station. No sign of him – where is he? Then he comes down the platform waving a rose over his head, which he presents to my young travelling companion. It is so typical I don't resent it, though it embarrasses her. He insists on helping her claim her baggage, we give her coffee at the buffet; he tells her she must be careful because Italy is full of *basters*... As we see her into a taxi, he neatly extracts the rose from her fingers. "You see," he explains, "it is for my Love here", and after that I have to carry it.

He has found a small hotel near the Spanish Steps and is already accepted as a long lost relative by the family who run it. We go to examine the Spanish Steps.

"Many artists selling their pictures...did you make some?"

"Yes."

"Good. That way we pay the hotel...wait and you see..."

After a siesta, he dresses carefully in his old black corduroy jacket, applies the 'after-save'. "Stay here, can you? I go to see the *Principessa*. She live in the next street and will be so happy to see me..." He takes up the rose, now in perfect bloom since I put it in water.

"I thought that rose was for me?"

"It is – but now I need again..."

"How to make one rose do three women..."

"How well you know me!" he says. "I don't be long..."

I sit in the sunshine on the tiny balcony overlooking the rooftops of the ancient city. The Principessa...she came on a yacht, the guest of a rich shipping mogul who often called on Tasso to provide local colour for his guests. A sad woman in her late thirties, sitting on the deck in a bathing wrap, examining her toes with concentrated attention...but she must have noticed him His gallantry to sad women is expert – though he never lays a finger on them – that's what attracts them. He knows how to behave very well, as well as very badly.

He is soon back, satisfied with the brief visit. One of his maxims is *'never try to stay inside of the nose of the Big Shots...'* "The Principessa is so glad I come to see her in Rome."

"I thought you came to meet me?"

"That, of course! But she very kind to me and make me sign the visitors' book. Do you imagine, I put my name right under that of my King!" (The King who is now in exile in suburban England.)

"You never liked the King," I point out, "you never had a good word to say for him."

"For sure that is true, but now I like him better than the *kaikshooters* we got now who kick him out!" Politics. *Plus ça change, plus c'est la même chose... "*

Next morning, we take the train to Foggia to retrieve the car from the garage where I left it three months ago. It has been thoroughly overhauled. The mechanic asks where it was repaired before. *"Grecia? Non enginare in Grecia."* Instead of taking offence, Tasso agrees with him.

On the ferry, the Greek police welcome him like a long lost brother. The customs give him a different reception. He is Greek, and Greeks know Greeks; everything has to be taken out of the car, all the things he has bought in Standa Supermarket. He is insulted that his countrymen don't trust him.

Finally we get everything back into the car and drive home.

4.

The tiny house contrasts oddly with Belgravia.

"We going to make different life now," he says confidently. "I *finis* forever with that Malediction Place, the Casino! You know how much I give to those basters?" I clap my hands over my ears. "You right – better not to know. I give the money to the bank now. The Bank Manager so happy – he never wait for me to put money in his bank… *"How long will this last?*

"You don't have to worry at all." He reads my thoughts. "I give the bank book to my daughter. I give the money to her – she take to the bank. She 18 now… you can't imagine what kind of character she is," he says proudly. "She wait for me to give her the money like a cat wait for fish, and even if I cut her throat, she never going to give me back the bank book!"

So there is one woman who has power over him. For him to be putting money into the bank is a miracle of no small proportion. Perhaps one should never despair of anything. My three-month absence seems to have paid off. *Why the hell didn't you do it earlier, you fool!* But I could not give up the sun rising over the mainland mountains, the mystery of the moon entering the night – the natural Greek things. I would rather be here than there, so where do we go from here?

"We going to move from this house," he is saying. "Georgos and Rosa going to rent to us the bottom flat in the new place they have make."

It is only yards away across the little bit of green where a row of original croft-like cottages stands. Georgos and Rosa's cottage has been pulled out like a tooth, a mini-skyscraper of two floors built in its place, with a little penthouse on the roof.

Next morning, Rosa proudly shows me over it. The ground floor, where we will be, is long, narrow and very dark; the flat above is much better, with a parquet floor in the main room with a balcony. She opens the shutters to let in the light, exclaiming ecstatically: *"Oneiro, den einai!"* (A dream, isn't it!)

It is easy enough to carry our stuff across the bit of grass to the new place, not so easy to fit ourselves in. The front door opens straight into the main room; a long narrow corridor connects it with the tiny bedroom, and the kitchen, with a tiny bathroom tucked in under the stairway leading up to the flat above, but it has a shower, a flush loo and an electric water heater.

I exclaim to him, "A shower! A flush loo and a water heater! It's as good as Belgravia!"

"What do you expect?" he says. "Now we going to live like other people."

"If I'd wanted to live like other people, I wouldn't have chosen *you*!"

"Oh, that's for sure," he concedes, turning the tables on me yet again.

The bedroom proves too small to take a double bed; we would have to crawl onto it from the door. He buys two single beds to put against the walls in the front room. It is goodbye to the White Horse whisky boxes

And yet…why do I feel bereft?

5.

"Oh, how lovely to see you back!" cries the Hon. "How was England? You know Pooter is leaving? Yes – quite made up his mind."

The little dachshund sits on her lap, dressed in a tube of coloured wools, making him look more like a sausage dog than ever. "That's new, isn't it?"

"My oldest English friend sent it for Sooty – didn't she, poppet! You cannot imagine the furore it caused at the Post Office when I went to collect it. You know how they open everything that comes from abroad... They held it up in the air, wondering what on earth it was. I told them it was a jacket for the dog! They couldn't understand at all. So I put it on him – *my deare*! It caused a sensation! Everybody came to look at you, Sooty darling, didn't they?"

Pooter confirms that all his plans are finalized.

"My friend...he was my house-boy in Cyprus before the war when I was teaching there. I got him into the English Army, the only Turk in his regiment at the time... Now he's a successful businessman in the South of England, a Purveyor of Entertainment machines...got his fingers in a lot of pies. He has bought a tiny semi-detached pseudo Tudor Cottage, for which I'll pay a minimal rent. His wife is dealing with the furnishings. I've written to her saying, *'In case you are unaware, my favourite colours are white, yellow and blue.'* I can only hope!" How well he arranges things – or other people.

He leaves me with a copy of the Times. "I don't want it back." Glancing through it, my eye catches – in the 'Marriages and Engagements' column: *"Sparkes and Love: a marriage has been arranged..."* and *"Fragrant Memories of..."* in the 'In Memoriam' column, and I realise that I am trying to erase what I know about sparks and love, and have some stinking memories...but I am putting the stinking memories behind me, aren't I? Yet a pocket of puss lies at the heart of our relationship; a tiny incident could lift the manhole.

But now there are no slugs in the loo or ant-holes in the floor. I miss the little cats in the garden. I am getting used to sounds made by my next-door neighbour, a little peasant woman "not from here – from over there", in the mountains. Her husband died and she has no family. She sings heart-wrenching melodies with thought-provoking words.

"The herb of love doesn't grow everywhere,
It isn't every place that grows it
Nor every land that makes it thrive…"

Their music is full of the pain and the sweetness of life – addiction to Life good or bad, as if to suck the sweetness and bear the pain is to know you are not dead.

The flat above us – Rosa's 'dream flat', is empty, too fine to rent to anybody or to live in themselves. They camp out in the tiny penthouse on the roof.

He keeps buying new things for our place. A boy turns up on the doorstep delivering a chandelier with bronze feathers on it. Have I got to live with this? He has a wardrobe made to "take all our things". It takes only his. When I point this out, Tasso says, "Always you bring the malediction."

But spring is beginning; the pigeons coo at night, the almond trees are in bloom, and there is that damp sweet smell of the earth.

Driving out of town in the twilight there is just a crest of snow on the mountains like a long, irregular fin floating in the air, between sea and sky. They are the same tone, the water without a ripple, heavy as oil with a dark line across the distance where the ferryboat slides along.

"They don't make winters anymore," he says. "Stop here – I want to see something." We stop in the village. "I want to see what Stamati have make of his new place…"

The old taverna has gone, which used to have the butcher's shop in one side and a café in the other. The roof extended to rest on pillars gave shade in summer and protection in winter. The old men of the village use to sit at the tin tables playing with their worry beads and watching the growing traffic; the tourists from the nearby hotel came in the evenings for Stamati's steaks and chicken cooked on the big charcoal grill in the corner. Now - in its place - is a cement and glass box. Stamati, the butcher, a thin wiry man with a face like a skull who looks like an assassin in his blood-stained apron, and his butchering knives dangling at his waist, rushes out to greet us. "Ellá – Tasso!" He is eager to show us his new place, which is bare, a characterless interior with a refrigerated counter, chrome chairs and tables – and for decoration an oil painting of ballet dancers. His grotesque visage burns with zeal as he points to the strip lighting, the walls plastered in textured whirls. "*Poly luxe! den einai?*" *(very luxurious, isn't it?)* He points to an appalling oil painting of ballet dancers in an over-ornate frame... "*Poly spania, eh?*" *(Very rare.)* he says, looking at me with his burning eyes to confirm it.

"It's hideous!" I say, "And it isn't even Greek!"

He doesn't understand and looks to Tasso. "What she say?"

"Nothing!"

The assassin hasn't finished. Eagerly he drags us over to two white doors with aluminium handles; one with the symbol of a high-heeled shoe, the other with a bowler hat. "Twalettas!" he exclaims, flinging wide the door to reveal a brand new proper toilet.

"*Bravo, Stamati!*" Tasso enthuses. To me he says, "In a minute we lose everything for the tourist to have a place to pissing."

From the village street a man on a scooter calls to the assassin, who immediately hurries off and climbs onto the pillion, shouting to a girl who is fiddling about behind the counter to keep the shop well while he is gone. He disappears to kill a sheep.

"You want retsina, Tasso?" the girl says, already reaching into the fridge to bring out a bottle. We have never seen this robust young girl before, but she knows us. Opening a bottle, she pours out three glasses – for him, for me, and one for herself.

"She is his daughter... Where's your brother?" he asks her. It would be the boy's job to keep the shop.

"Gone to the Army," she says, and knocks back her glass of retsina in one gulp and pours herself another.

"*Thá fass xyló!*"(You will eat wood!) Tasso warns her. Her father's going to beat her. "He don't joke." The assassin would not hesitate to take a stick to her.

"*Den birazi!*" (It doesn't matter!) she says, dismissing the threat, and filling our glasses again. She goes to the jukebox, reaches round the back to release the glass hood, plunges an arm into its mechanism and brings out a packet of cigarettes, offers him one and lights up herself. "Ssh... Don't tell my father..." Tasso asks her name and how old she is. Frossoulá is her name, she is a very muscular 16.

She thumbs the buttons of the jukebox to bring up 'Franco Syriani'. "Come, Tasso – teach me to dance like the Inglezá. Babbá won't be back for an hour..." And, throwing her arm across Tasso's shoulder, she forces him to initiate her into the *Hasapiko* that we dance. Where has she come from, fully fledged like Athena from the thigh of Zeus?

A woman in black drifts across the street from the cottage opposite. Frossoulá shoos her away like a chicken. "Go home, Mama..." The woman drifts back across the road. So that's it. Frossoulá has been watching the taverna from across the road since she was baby.

"Come on, Tasso – show me again," she demands, sticking her cigarette in the corner of her mouth in the traditional way of the men when they dance.

Suddenly sensing the hour is up, she becomes anxious. "*Tasso mou...*" using the intimate form,"...tell my father you had the two bottles of retsina – okay? I make it up to you another time – yes?"

Later he muses, "She not a girl, she is a horse!"

6.

The spring here is like a flowered leopard leaping out of the ground. Orange blossom scenting the night, fireflies flashing in galaxies under the trees, roses; but spring melancholia gets me every year. Is it jealousy of the earth renewing itself while we stay the same?

But on April 21st, the anniversary of the coup, the weather always turns foul yet the brass bands fart round the town and the firework display exceeds the Easter festival. People accept it just as any other yearly festival, but driving to town in the evening, the air is filled with a roaring sound like the noise of a vast football crowd.

"What is that noise? I've been hearing it all day."

"Is from the prison. The politic prisoners – you know. They bring here from all over Greece."

The roaring from human throats continues for 36 hours.

Pooter confirms this when I meet him in the wine shop for our last drink together before he leaves the island forever. He talks of The Hon. "At least I've been instrumental in helping her. Someone – I won't specify who – has paid off the Hon's debts of £125. When I told her, she said, 'How Perfectly Sweet of him – do I know him?' I thought she should be told. 'Oh, yes…I think I met his wife at Mrs Tomatoes'…what exactly is her accent?' I said, 'Middle-class, of course'. 'Oh – *middle*-class.... I did wonder…' Really, she is incorrigible."

I hardly see her now – unless she can crawl to the wine shop. "Well…this is our last drink together," he says, "but you must write to me – I shall be hungry for news of the island. I doubt if a small seaside town in England will be able to compete with a Greek island."

Taking up his brief case and umbrella, he passes through the wine shop door for the last time. I shall miss Pooter.

A peasant comes into the wine shop with two baskets heaped with the tiny wild strawberries, the scent fills the shop. Tasso asks the price and crosses himself. "When I was a kid they cost two drachmes." The sudden entry of a middle-aged Englishwoman in raincoat, sensible shoes and headscarf is a startling apparition. She stops in her tracks at the sight of the strawberries, takes a deep breath and murmurs ecstatically "How divine!" Then, looking round questioningly: "Telephone? *Telefon*? *Telefono*?"

Tasso points to it on the top of the sweet cabinet. She dials a number, puts the receiver to her ear. "Oh, *Mon Dieu*!" Quickly returning it to the cradle, she looks round for help.

"Can I help you, *madame?*" Tasso says. *Here we go…*

"Umm – do you speak French?" she asks in English.

"Mais oui, madame…" At which she drags a map from her raincoat pocket and continues impetuously in English. "I'm terribly interested in the island. I was here last year – it's SO beautiful… I desperately want to go here…" She points to areas on the map. "And how do I get there? Where can I get a bus? And I must phone Nikos," she adds, looking anxiously toward the phone again.

Tasso dials the number for her. "Niko! *Yia soú*!", followed by a spate of Greek.

"Is Nikos there? Is his mama there?"

"Yes – what you want to say?"

"Tell him…tell him… Is his mama there? Tell them I AM COMING." She is speaking loudly, as if to a deaf person.

"Yes, he knows." He has already told Niko that a crazy English woman is trying to contact him.

"Oh, *thank you*!" She is swamped with British relief. "Now, where can I find a taxi. A TAXI? TAXI?", repeating everything twice in her excitement. Tasso indicates the taxi rank a few yards away.

With a brisk "F. HARRY`S-TOE!" (for *efharisto*, 'thank you' in Greek), she whirls out of the shop, forgetting to pay for the phone call. Watching her departure, Tasso says, "To see that stuff is like to see the first swallow."

Mediterranean! Mediterranean! *"Screw a sea view in a room for two." "What country is this?" "Don't know – give us a kiss." The viledom of villas, the dementia of discos, the spawning of awnings, pollution of plastics. The sun can't fade it, the rain can't stain it, Nature can't maim it. The only bio-degradable thing in all this is the Dream. The Nightmare perpetuates itself.*

He pulls a letter out of his pocket addressed simply to *"Tassos – peintre, The Bar Greco."* French stamps.

"What's it say?" He speaks French, but can't be bothered to read it. I can't speak it, but read it well enough to make out: *"Tassos Chéri! J'ai bien reçu ta photo…"*

"You sent her a photograph?"

He shrugs. "Perhaps I send her something Christmas time…I don't remember…"

"She says you haven't changed. You are the same as she remembers…that Paris is grey…she is very depressed…that her thoughts of you are sweet, and no one can take them away… *Ecris moi! Je t'embrasse bien de fois, tendrement comme tu sais* …. She embraces you tenderly, as you will remember…"

He is unembarrassed. "Who is it?"

"Manette."

A thoughtful pause, smoking his cigarette. "I afraid she going to bother us this summer."

7

The next day, he comes home saying "I have meet a woman…"
Surprise me. "I was in Alecko's – this woman tourist come in,
come to me like I am boss and ask 'What can I eat here?'

"And you said 'Me'."

"How you know that! For sure you the hell half of me…" He
crosses himself.

"And?"

"She wait for us tonight at her hotel."

"Us?"

"You think I go without you?"

"She may not be expecting *me*…" I offer, with British
foresight.

"Oh, you crazy for sure!" he says, dismissing the idea.

We drive toward the rendezvous in the early evening, tourists
visible on the ground like mushrooms walking the road between
the hotels and the village. Seeing a tortoise in the middle of the
road, I cry, "Oh I must save the tortoise!" and stop, getting out to
pick it up and put it in a hedge.

Turning back to the car, I see he is chatting to two British
tourists walking along the road. I slam the door, put the car in
gear. "I see you at the hotel tonight," he calls to them as I drive
away. "Why you be angry? You say you stop for the tourists."

"I said the tortoise!"

"Anyway, stop a bit at Frosso's – is early yet."

Frosso, the butcher's daughter, is in full command of the café
now, standing outside accosting the tourists walking through the
village. "Come here, pleez – is nice place – I teach you Greek
dance…you like wine-beer-ouzo…?" She is picking up English
quickly. At the sight of us, she charges over like a young heifer.
"Kizz me pleeze!" she demands. She is wearing her frizzy hair
combed forward in a fringe and tied behind with a flowing pink
chiffon scarf, a short skirt with knee socks and sandals; her

chiffon blouse keeps coming undone; the effect is of an ancient Greek vase painting.

At the same moment, a hotel mini-bus ferrying tourists stops suddenly – a woman jumps out and runs towards us. Tasso, recognising the woman, opens his arms; she runs into them. "Yes – I am coming," he says. In a state of excitement she runs back to clamber into the bus. It drives away. She is small, attractive, about 45, and definitely not expecting me.

At the hotel he moves straight towards the bar, expecting the woman to be there, but it is empty except for two English women of the Hon's vintage sitting at one end of the large settee. Not to lose any opportunity, he sets up the pictures at the other end.

"Very amateur," says one.

"I like the way he takes up all the space," says the other.

The bar adjoins the dining area. The head waiter indicates that dinner is being served; they get up and go to their table. Tasso quickly fills the vacated space with more pictures, muttering under his breath, "*Skylospsaro*! Dogfishes…"

Another Englishwoman comes in, orders a gin and tonic, and without hesitation shovels the pictures aside to sits down. Now he is angry; he has come here only because of the woman.

"Where is she?" he glares at me. "She must to be here."

"Maybe she's waiting for you in her room…"

"Don't be ridiculous! Anyway, to hell with her. We get out of here." Anxious not to lose the evening trade elsewhere, he is shovelling the merchandise together when I see her enter the dining room, hands thrust deep in the pockets of her jacket, the expression on her face as if anticipating a bout of flu. I point her out to him, and he sends the waiter to her. She comes like an arrow from a bow, her face radiant now her belief in herself is restored. "*Mais je vous attendais dans ma chambre…!*" I was waiting for you in my room.

Overcome by my *clairvoyance*, I almost topple off my bar stool. They carry on an impetuous conversation in French. She hasn't noticed me. Moving up to his elbow, I say, "Could I have another koniak…please", whereupon he introduces me as his wife! My embarrassment is as great as hers, as, utterly confused

308

by the situation, she talks rapidly at cross purposes in English, until one of her eyes sheds its contact lens. "Oh, please don't move!" Gazing down at the carpet, she spots the tiny orb, licks her finger to pick it up, and puts it away in a little pouch. *Is there something symbolic in this?* I pity her for having fallen in the trap his personality creates for lonely women he has no intention of seducing; he doesn't have to seduce them, they seduce themselves.

"What we do now?" he says, looking at me. "We take 'our friend' down the taverna on the beach...?" He defies me to challenge his decision. We are so entangled, we have to stay together to find the way of unravelling ourselves.

She accepts the invitation and is stuffed into the back seat of the Fiat. When I get into the driving seat, she is surprised. "You drive?"

"Yes... In the car, I *am* in the driving seat...the trouble is one never knows where one is going..."

She laughs nervously. "Ah, yes! I am understanding he is very charming unusual character of man..." Or *any incongruous conception of fancy...*

At the taverna on the beach, he quickly gets involved with some people at the bar, leaving us together at a table. She stares at me in a disconcerting way, as if trying to see what I have that keeps him from taking up the opportunity offered by her.

"You must have just such an open heart to live this life," she says suddenly, looking at me curiously.

I think about it, wondering why I am obliged to offer myself up to inspection by this humourless woman to save her face. It isn't worth wasting emotion on this kind of thing anymore, it's undignified, and I don't want to spoil the slowly hardening varnish on my soul. "Well, mine was opened with a tin-opener, and left a jagged edge."

She stares down at the plastic tablecloth, tracing the pattern on it with a finger decorated with a large diamond and sapphire ring. "I think I understand... Oh, yes I think I understand," she says, "but...it is also difficult...to live...with a man..." now she is tracing the pattern on the cloth more urgently "…who…is not…" raising her bald eyes to mine "…a man…you understand?"

I understand. *"They either make you suffer or they bore you to death…"* It is on the tip of my tongue to say it, but I don't.

We take her back to the hotel. To me she says a formal 'goodnight', adding: "I knew I would admire you very much…" Then she flings her arms about him, pressing her lips impulsively to his face in unconsummated intimacy, and stands in the porch of the hotel waving as we drive away.

"We lost money tonight because of her," he says.

"You set it up!" I feel sorry for emotions that betray women. Having managed to bring my own under control, I am constantly confronted by other women's emotions. "If you bring me another…bring me another…" I am jabbering with rage "…cod-faced woman I have to be nice to, because you don't know what to do with her…I'll…I'll…!" I almost swerve off the road.

"Okay – watch the road now or we be in the sea."

"It isn't the women's fault!" I am shouting. "You are a cheat, making them think you mean something when you don't!" Yet I realise that if he really was a libertine, or a sensualist, I wouldn't be with him, or he with me – that is the irony of it. Sex is the chimera. Love is a chimera – *he* is a chimera. *Greece invented the chimera.*

To my surprise he agrees. "You very right…one must not to joking with the woomans over forty. Now be quiet – you have say enough."

Midnight. We are the only car on the road, when a young man in army uniform flags us down. It is automatic to stop, but instead of asking questions, he has an earnest conversation with Tasso, pointing to another man not in uniform, but with the physique of a commando, sitting astride a motorbike holding a bundle and a live duck on his lap.

"They lost something. He need us to help him look for it with the lights of the car."

So the other man can help with the search, the plastic bundle is put on the back seat, and Tasso holds the duck on his knees – "I hope he don't make a mess" – while I drive slowly up and down the road as the two men search in the verges.

"You can't imagine what kind of men is them – they trained killers. They stop at nothing. But must be something very important they lost…him in big trouble, poor fella," he adds with pragmatic sympathy.

Eventually, they give up without having found what they are looking for, take back the bag and the duck, thanking us gratefully for our help. As we drive away, Tasso is saying "And she give me so many sweet kisses…"

"Who?" I am thinking of the Swiss woman.

"The *pappiá!*" *What is he talking about?*

"How you call that bird in English?"

"You mean the duck? How do you know it was female?"

"Because she give me so many nice kisses – like that …" indicating the Duck's nibbling at his hand with its beak. "So sweet stuff is that…and nice tasting too."

Women!

8.

The days get hotter and the Summer Absurdities begin. When he notices I am wearing only bra and pants under my cotton dress, he says, "You go to town like that?" as if I were nude.

"I've got a dress on." We go through this barrier every summer.

At the hotel, to get rid of an elderly British couple who are not going to buy anything, he brings them over to me.

"She is English, you make nice company…"

"Don't you miss England?" booms the woman from her deep, resonant bust, while her husband stands meekly at her elbow holding her cardigan. When I say no, her eyebrows shoot up.

"There must be *something* you miss!" she insists, looking indignant.

I think about it. "Well, kippers…"

"You must come and have dinner with us," she offers, as if I must be starving.

I explain we spend every evening selling the pictures.

"Come to lunch, then," she insists. This too is out of the question, I explain, as we have to make the siesta. "But don't you want some *Real English Conversation*?" – as if it came in a pot from Fortnum and Mason's.

"Well, there's plenty of that really," I say, indicating the lounge full of English tourists. She gives up trying to do her duty by a young compatriot and turns on her heel, followed by the husband. As they pass Tasso, she says loudly, "Your wife doesn't like us."

9

The Valkyries return with the inevitability of painted horses on a carousel. At our ritual reunion in the wine shop, Elsa moves stiffly and painfully with a bad back, not helped by driving down from Germany. She says with more humour than I have given her credit for, "I am an *olt wive...*"

Hildegard has had bronchitis all winter and would have preferred to go to the Baltic this year. The Mercedes was bumped in the boot in Italy. Only the dachshund – always a pessimist – seems fine. Every year they arrive full of anticipation that the house they are having built will be ready to move into, only to find: *"Das liddel haus nicht fertig ist!"* The furniture has been sent from Germany, and impounded by customs; and they must pay the storage. Harry, the land agent, is in deep trouble; having taken money from the foreigners in land deals, he has spent it or lost it all.

"He go away of the island. He don't dare to put his foot back here," Tasso says. Harry is the legal owner of the property.

"Mein lieber Gott!" Elsa exclaims, and makes the *faux pas* of suggesting that the Junta is a good thing, as discipline is what the Greeks need. The ritual presents are produced – a gold-plated cigarette lighter for him, with the insistence he must not give it away, or lose it. I accept gratefully the nice soap, now that we have a shower with hot water. At home he chucks the lighter on the kitchen table – he can't sell it till she goes and he doesn't forgive her for that remark about the Junta.

10.

A letter from Pooter:

"You ask how life in my seaside town is progressing? That is a large question! In most ways excellently, though of course my life here is in some – even many – ways different from life on a Greek island, partly due to the 'Englishness' on all sides and partly to my determination not to get involved with the 'wrong' people.

"I must say I was rather surprised – and amused – to read in the newspapers that 'The Colonels' have pronounced Greece 'A Democracy'!! And that you are having to vote on it to confirm the outcome as 'All in Favour'. I am glad I am not there to see this humiliation of a people I love and respect and with whom I have spent probably the happiest years of my life."

Tasso phones for me to pick him up from work. We even have a phone now. "Drive to the bus station – we have to pick up my sister."

"Which sister?" I'm curious to know which of his formidable sisters would travel by bus.

"Iphigenia."

"I thought she died when she was 18?"

"Of course she dead!" he barks, irritated by my stupidity.

"Then how can we pick her up at the bus station?"

"They send her back here to be with our father and mother!" He is so taken over by his duty to his dead sister, he is in another dimension from his normal self. *What is normal about his Self?*

I watch him disappear into the primitive bus station with some apprehension. He returns carrying a large parcel wrapped in brown paper and tied with string. "Drive to the cemetery."

I wait in the car as he disappears again carrying the parcel, and reappears after a while followed by a bearded priest in long black robes, and tall stove-pipe hat. To my surprise, Tasso opens the passenger door and, bringing the seat forward, urges the priest to get into the back. It is no simple thing for a Greek priest in a stove-pipe hat to get into the back seat of a Fiat 500. It seems to take a long time; a nervous glance over my shoulder reveals his bearded, be-hatted head and one foot are inside the car; he is trying to get the rest of his body to follow. I want to grab his beard and pull.

With another painful heave he manages to curl himself into the confined space as if in a burial urn.

"We take the *pappas* back to the town." Driving around with a priest stuck in the back of the Fiat is making me hysterical. How will we get him out? Go to a garage? Apply a tin opener? Crack the car open like a nut? "Stop here." Tasso gets out, tipping the seat forward He doesn't seem to notice the *pappas*'s difficulties. I try not to look – when I do, the *pappas* is trying to pull his foot out of the car with both hands. In the wineshop in the evening, visions returning of the *pappás* pulling his foot out of the car make me weep with laughter. Mr Sotiris and *Kyria* Katina glance at me, thinking I am in distress, understanding that I must have a difficult life with him.

11.

A telegram announces Verena's arrival. We go to meet her at the airport. She holds up her arms to show she is standing on her own two feet without crutches.

"Darlings!" she beams, handing me a Harrod's bag containing two pounds of Best English Pork Sausages. "The only thing I could think of to bring you."

"Where's Robin?"

"I'm divorced, darlings!"

Tasso is surprised, but says nothing. It poses a problem because we have a rendezvous with the Valkyries and we cannot leave Verena alone.

"We must to mix her with the Valkyries," he says. I tell Verena about the Valkyries.

"This I have to see," she says, agreeing to meet us at the wine shop at 6.30.

The Valkyries arrive first to find me alone in my corner – always a disappointment. They are heavy with *bonhomie,* but, not having enough of each other's language for intelligent conversation, we are just sitting like stuffed rabbits when Verena blows in, looking as fresh and slender as a flower, and dressed in primrose yellow *chic.* I jump up to greet her. As we embrace, she whispers in my ear, "I thought I'd look as virginal as possible…" She is carrying a peasant basket she has just bought. "I simply love it!" she whoops, swinging it around theatrically.

Elsa, surprised when Verena sits down with us, exclaims, "Ach! Anozer ladye from Lun-dun," and rather deliberately orders only three glasses of wine; I have to call up another for Verena.

Tasso appears. "What nice company we make tonight!" He kisses Verena first, before raising Elsa's hand to his lips – another shock for Elsa. When he retrieves his empty glass from behind the vase of flowers where he left it half an hour ago, Verena impetuously pours half her wine into it. "No…no, darr-ling…" His calling another woman 'darr-ling' is too much for Elsa; with an *"Aach! Mein Liebermann!"*, she pours half her wine into his glass as well.

"Okay! We ready to go – the Night Belong to Us." His old battle cry. "I go with our German friends...?" He loves riding in the white Mercedes. "You follow – yes?" he adds, escorting Elsa and Hildegard to the door. Neither Verena or I attempt to follow; seeing us in collusion, he says, "Don't be long", before being obliged to follow Elsa, who is saying impatiently "Komm!" I dissolve in laughter. "He's worried! Oh, it's great having you here! I'm sure of my ground tonight. Let's have another wine! I couldn't get away with this alone"

"You're his lynchpin."

"Yes, and if I pull out the lynchpin, I destroy him and commit suicide at the same time. I *mustn't*, even if sitting on this bloody circus cart is the hardest thing I've ever done. I've have been challenged enough times as to why am sitting on this cart at all. 'Why do you stay with him?' they say, Why does anybody stay with anybody? Because I mean more to myself doing this than if I stopped doing it. And I want to see *what happens in the end.* It's as simple as that...Oh, gosh! We 'd better go – I mustn't push my luck...!"

But I drive at a leisurely speed out of town; at the first junction the white Mercedes has been made to wait, Tasso sitting high on the open back looking out for us, wrapped in Elsa's shawl against the damp evening air. When he has sees us, he allows her to drive on. The car takes off like a racehorse, disappearing round the next bend. I stop. Verena and I count slowly to 100, then drive on at 20 mph. At the entrance to the village, he has made her wait again.

"This is a hoot!" says Verena making a rude sign to him to go on.

"To have this sense of power again is intoxicating!" I exult, though I know it will have to be paid for at an exorbitant rate of interest. But at the moment it is worth it. "I can only do it because you're here."

At the sight of Frosso's cement and glass box, Verena exclaims, "We aren't stopping here, surely?"

"It's Stamati the butcher's taverna – remember? We brought you and Robin here."

"But it wasn't like this! It was real… it was lovely…"

"This is it now. The Valkyries insist on coming here. They like good *fleisch*."

"Vampires!" says Verena, stalking into the café, demanding, "Tasso! Why aren't we going to a real taverna?" The Valkyries have never complained at the loss of the picturesque.

"Verena – darr-ling – this is nice place…"

"It's absolutely *awful*!" She stomps over to the jukebox. "Let's have some real Greek music – at any rate! I must have Theodorakis …"

"Darr-ling…Theodoraki's music is banned in Greece."

"It's too ridiculous! Theodoraki's music *is* Greece. I play his tapes all the time, in Belgravia. Anyway, I've been in plaster for months. I must try to dance again. You must teach me the Greek dance," she insists. Verena is enjoying this, and so am I.

Obliged to placate her, he selects 'Franco-Syriani' on the jukebox, and spends the next 20 minutes pacing out the dance. Verena won't let him stop. Elsa, Hildegard and I sit at the table like wall-flowers; Elsa stares in abstraction at the grubby tablecloth, holding the dachshund on her lap, his ears twitching uncomfortably at the sound of the music. She has never urged him to teach her the dance – the easiest way to be in physical contact with him. How odd. She looks sad, and I begin to feel sorry for her.

"Verena…darr-ling…we sit down now." He has been complaining about a pain in his stomach for days.

"I want to do that bit again. I must get it right," the perfectionist insists.

Through the window I see a young village girl come to take water from the well between the two tavernas; a figure of Biblical simplicity and grace, she sets her can down by the well – her eyes watching the activity in the two taverns – until a shrill cry comes from the cottages across the road. Reluctantly she draws up the water, fills her can, twists a piece of rag on top of her head, and lifts the heavy can of water on to it. Balancing it thus, and walking gracefully, she crosses the road and disappears.

Elsa, in a desperate effort to regain his attention, suddenly goes to the Mercedes to bring him a box of cigars, and I am paid for my part in the evening by having to watch him smoking a cigar. Fortunately, he will sell the box tomorrow.

At 9.30, they talk of their 'beauty sleep'; they never stay out late. He escorts them to the car, and comes back worried.

"They no enjoying, I afraid." We take Verena to Be Enjoy at the Beach Restaurant.

Next day he is exhausted. "My stomach bother me much," he complains, pressing his thumb on the place. "I must to go to the dog-tor."

The doctor tells him he has ulcers and "not to drink, not to smoke, and to make the quiet life…he say I going to be die in two years if I no pay attention."

"Did he really say that?" Alarmed.

"Don't be stupid! You think the dog-tor no have a contract with the God for when I going to be die!" He has put it into Greek perspective.

He takes the tablets prescribed when he remembers, or when he gets a pain. Life goes on…

12.

It seems a long, humourless summer. The dinner dance atmosphere in the hotels is oppressive. When the island had nothing to offer but its simplicity, people fell in love with it. Now it has flush toilets, showers, baths, swimming pools, beach umbrellas and tennis courts – even a golf course – the tourists are discontented, feeling they are not getting value for money.

The British go around armed with extra tea bags. "They can't make a good cup of tea, can they? If you pop another teabag in, it does help, doesn't it...?"

I dread the confidences of honeymooners: "All these damn twin beds! We haven't had a double bed since our wedding night." And marital relationships: "She's always making excuses. Her suntan hurts, or it's too hot, or she doesn't feel like it...it takes a bottle of Pallini to get her going. There I am – fooling about in the shower...she's making up her face. Next thing I know, I'm sent to Coventry. Last year we went to Italy and a smashing time. We weren't married then..."

Another tells me that in the two weeks they have been here, he has met the woman who lives next door to his mother, and a chap he was at school with.

In the hotel a little girl comes up to me. "Do you live here? Do you speak Spanish then?"

"This is Greece. People speak Greek here."

"I keep thinking it's Ibiza."

And there are those who say, with a glance towards Tasso, "I hope you don't mind me asking...are you married to the gentleman with the pictures...?"

Must I answer ? Truthfully? Untruthfully? And if I tell – how do I tell it? Begin with the sin or the ecstasy? It was Romance, wasn't it? Was Romance my sin or my ecstasy? Which was which? I can't remember now and don't care. Am I to spin myself into thinner and thinner thread to be woven by them into a garment that doesn't fit me – until I snap? No, he is not my husband, and has ceased to be my lover. On this paradisiacal,

320

aphrodisiacal Mediterranean island, I stayed to worship one of its local gods. Now the ribbons that adorned an ardent votary are tattered and the ship who thought she was an argosy lies dismasted in this foreign port, to be recognised by patriotic tourists with "Oh, look, there's one of ours!"

13.

In fact, there is a strange ship in the harbour like an old Scottish ferryboat with a strange mixture of people on board, mostly English. It has been here for months already. They march up and down in the harbour in homemade uniforms. In the Cake Parlour tonight, there were three of them, a woman and small child, and a man, obviously not the father, all dressed in the quasi uniforms of dark blue pullovers and trousers. He had a lanyard around his shoulder. They ordered cream cakes and, before taking up their spoons, they bowed their heads and said Grace.

Gossip abounds about these people, but then gossip is the way of life here. Tasso says it's some kind of religious navy. I must write to Pooter about it, he still knows everything that happens on the island.

He replies promptly: *"Yes it is surprising they have been allowed to remain so long, considering The Greek Orthodox Church is very intolerant; even the Pope is a heretic to the Greek Church. I fancy they have been allowed to stay because they are spending money, as my 'informants' tell me the ship's engines have broken down. That is their excuse for staying. It was an old Scottish ferry boat, I believe."*

14

"You remember which is Manette?" Because he doesn't. Why should I remember his past for him?

"You sent her a photo at Christmas," I say, recalling the ardour of her reply.

"Ah, yes. She here at the club. Panayoti tell me she looking for me. We must to take her around a bit…You know…" *Yes, I know.*

At the rendezvous he embraces a stout little woman in her forties with boot-button eyes which gaze in resentful curiosity at me, and who asks, in perfectly good English if I speak French. When I say no, she talks with him exclusively in French and doesn't speak to me all. She is accompanied by a female friend, Sylvie, a tough Parisienne lesbian.

We have to take them with us to the hotel where he makes 'L'Exposition'. Manette hovers like a parrot at his shoulder irritatingly while he is trying to sell. Sylvie wants me to show her the gardens. As we wander down the path to the beach, she tries to give me her ring, an enamel thing of no value. I don't wear rings. She insists I take it. I insist on giving it back. If this is some sort of sexual overture, it's lost on me. *This is a weird evening, and I've known a few…*

When he has got up the money 'to Be Enjoy', we go to a tavern. A live orchestra plays ballroom music now. Whatever next? Manette insists on dancing cheek to cheek with him.

"Now you!" she says, giving me permission to dance with him. I don't want to ballroom dance with him, nor he with me, but she's in charge.

"For crazy – she bother me much…" he mutters in my ear.

"And now wiz Sylvie!" He has to dance with Sylvie who would prefer to dance with me.

Suddenly, Manette fixes her glossy brown eyes on me and says – in English – "You know we woz togezzer 12 years ago!"

"Yes, I know."

She looks insulted and whispers furiously in his ear, "She does not mind?" With 'Other Women', the way I can get my own back is not to register the slightest unease…and win the battle without having to bother what the battle is. It certainly isn't *for him*… Yet the insulting bit is they always think they know him better than I do.

Tasso, looking tired, complains of stomach pains again to shorten the evening but before we can leave, Manette tells Sylvie to take a photograph, for a *bon souvenir*, and plonks her weight on his lap. He winces. He has arthritis in that knee. I have never ever sat on his lap….

As we part, I hear him say, "We come to Paris this winter for holiday. *Bien sûr*!" This is news to me.

She doesn't fail to whisper in French, *"Chéri – can't you come a-lone…?"*

·

15

I awake to my birthday (how old am I now?) with Tasso saying, "I feel very bad in my head...Something's happening." Panicking, I call the neighbours, who crowd into the room. They call the doctor on the phone. He says he will come in half an hour, so they call the police instead. The patrol car comes – the men carry him up the steep path to the road, and drive us at speed to the hospital, nearly killing two people en route.

The hospital is the new one flung up like a tourist hotel, but without the trimmings. So early in the morning, no doctors are on duty; a nurse sticks a needle in his arm. He begins to feel a bit better.

I go home to shower, cook some food, bring cushions to sleep on the floor beside his bed, joining the other families camped about the beds of their patients. I don't get much sleep – he is restless and demanding. If not him, the old man in the next bed is moaning, groaning, wanting a cigarette. I light it for him. He puffs away at it, blessing me copiously. At five o'clock in the morning a woman is beating on the hospital gates, trying to get into her husband.

At seven I go to the market. The magic morning hour – cool and fresh. I have never seen the market in the early morning, he always does the shopping.

The heaps of vegetables, fruit and fish, in bright slabs of colour; the vendors shouting. The baker's shops where the loaves of bread are birthing from the bulging ovens.

Returning to the hospital, pushing through the doors into the corridor, I step aside for a trolley with a pair of shiny new shoes sticking over the end, belonging to a body dressed in its best suit being trundled toward the lift. On another trolley lies a young girl in a comatose state, not yet dead from drinking bleach in an effort to escape the pains of love. She is trundled toward the bathroom to be pumped out. The bathroom is being painted, the painter and his ladders have to be expelled before she can be saved to love again.

Some Italians dressed only in bathing trunks are clotted together outside the door of the doctor's consulting room. An anguished cry rips the senses, the door opens, the doctor comes out, stethoscope swinging wildly on his chest, looking like a film director who has lost control of the plot. A boy, 17, is dead from drowning...

Ten minutes later all the drama has evaporated. It doesn't bother me as it once would have done. But it does when he says, "You going to sell the paintings tonight or we lose money."

"I can't sell the paintings!"

"Why not? You stupid or something? You be with me this long and don't learn anything? Do what I do!"

I go home, mount up the pictures I have ready, dress myself more critically than usual, though I haven't much to choose from. At six o'clock, I drive to the hotel, the one with the marble table in the middle of the foyer and peg out the pictures like washing. The receptionist automatically looks for Tasso, and is all concern to hear he is in the hospital.

The waiting is awful. The people seem blind. A couple walking towards the bar don't even turn their heads. Suddenly a woman swerves over to look – followed by her husband.

"You're English? You live here? How super!" They buy. Others stop, intrigued by an English girl selling pictures in a Greek hotel. I've sold seven before the people drain away to the dining room for supper. I thought it was only his sex appeal that sold the pictures. I decide not to wait for the after-dinner trade – if I stay away too long he will accuse me of using my freedom to fornicate with the waiters.

Just as I am shovelling the pictures together, a woman stops by me. "We saw these pictures last week. They're luv-ly. What's your name?" She is looking at me with beady brown eyes which have more than curiosity in them. "I thought so," she coos triumphantly. "We were at school together. Stephanie Holloway. Remember?"

Abbots Meade Boarding School... Through the mists of Time, I see the stout girl with thick black hair and brown eyes in a gym slip in the matronly young woman accosting me. "Oh…of course!" is a reflex action.

"Are you living here? How abso-lootely SOO-per!" A strong injection of middle-class enthusiasm. "Married or something?" she babbles on, while I dangle in amazement that I retain anything recognisable as *that* girl at *that* school, in *that* country who flung herself on a train called Fate, without knowing its destination.

"Something…" I say, unable to lie.

"Oh, JOLLY GOOD!" She glints with satisfied curiosity. "Funnily enough we were in Venice last year and saw Persephone King – she married a gondolier, you know."

So another girl from that school did what I did? Perceiving for the first time that I have 'married' a gondolier – a Greek gondolier – I almost forget to ask about her situation.

"And you?" She breaches a barrel of conventional ingredients: stockbroker husband, two children, Jonathan and Emily, doing FRIGHT-fully well and off to university soon, the account of their excellence unstoppable.

"Oh, that's good…"

"Come and have a drink or something – you must meet my husband."

"I'd love to," I say, falling into middle-class metre and rhyme, "but… I'm sorry, I must go…you see – my 'gondolier' is in hospital…" shuffling the pictures together like playing cards to deal another day "…and I've got to get back before they close the gates …" I almost run for the exit.

The night watchman recognises me and lets me in.

"Why you be so long?" Tasso is fretful, but pleased about the money. "Didn't I tell you…?"

"But you'll never believe this! I met a girl who was at school with me!"

"Everything happens here. Don't you understand that?" he says and sleeps instantly.

It takes me a long time to sleep on my cushions on the floor, thinking about the strangeness of things, being here, doing this – that schoolgirl who was that 'me'…and now…this 'me'… and him…and 'It' – whatever that is…

16

After a week, the doctors dismiss him with the usual mantra: not to smoke, not to drink…and lead a…

He takes back the job of selling the pictures. I am bored now sitting in the corner. Watching.

An English woman looks pensively at them, "Are they water–colours?"

"Pen and ink, madame..."

"Oh that's what it is… They'd be nice if you finished them…" And she drifts away.

He goes to the bar and orders a whisky, and chats up a group of ladies, Americans by their voices. One of them, who hasn't associated me with him, detaches herself from the group to approach me. "You look so alone," she sweetly says, sitting down beside me and placing her hand gently on my arm. For a moment I think she is going to offer to bring me to Jesus. "We ladies…" indicating the group "…are also without partners at this stage in time, and we would so love to have you join us." I point feebly toward Tasso. "Oh," she says with undaunted charm, "what an *interesting* man – and an artist. You are so fortunate." She returns to the bar.

This is not a good evening; he dumps a honeymoon couple on me to be rid of them. She is a hairdresser, chatty and confiding.

"I was married in a James Bond outfit…" Her husband says nothing.

"In church?"

"Registry office – It's my second time, you see…" The husband, looking sulky, wanders off to the bar. "He's a bit upset … we went to town shopping this evening. I wanted to buy myself a ring – Bill says I've got *him* to buy my jewellery for me now. I said 'It's *my* money – I earn it, I want to spend it'. We're not speaking now," she admits, glancing in his direction. "I'm beginning to wonder why I got married again. I had a smashing time in Rhodes last year…"

He sells one picture. "Let's get out of here..." But we don't go home; we go to the Beach Restaurant.

17

Pooter writes, *"I don't know who owes whom a letter, but I am hungry for news of the island. I have had a scrawl from the Hon. She seems very under the weather, confined to bed after her last fall. Remarkable she never breaks anything. Fortunately, the Greek lady who lives upstairs seems very kind and visits often."*

I haven't seen the Hon. in the wine shop for weeks. I feel guilty not being able to go and see her. When Tasso comes in, he says, "Why you look like that? Something happen to you?" When I explain about the Hon, he says, "We must to help her... Wait – I will be back."

He disappears from the wine shop, returning with a peasant basket filled with green beans, tomatoes, some fresh sardines, and eggs. He tells Mr. Sotiris to fill a bottle with red wine. "Take these to her – go now – you have time." It is only a short walk from the wine shop. The door of the flat is ajar, a murmur of voices within. I put my head round the door. "Can I come in?" "Oh, HOW LUV-LY!" she exclaims. "Do come in. It's been SO long since I saw you!"

She is lying in her Louis Quinze bed (*"It's been with me every-where."*) The elegant fluted bedhead padded with faded worn pink silk offers a perfect setting for her Somerset Maugham face. (*"I knew him in Shanghai – dreadful man..."*) The dachshund is playing with a ping-pong ball among the disarray of the bedclothes; the room smells strongly of dog.

"This is Mrs Pattakos who lives upstairs. She has been so kind, coming to see me every day and bringing me delicious soups. *Madame – vous ate tray tray gentil!"* She insists on speaking in French, though the Greek lady speaks a cultivated English. She looks at me sternly as if to say "*So this is one of your British friends who never come to see you*", and takes the opportunity of my presence to go away.

"She has been too, too sweet – though she makes me feel like a piece of furniture in a museum – something left behind by the British Raj."

"This is from Tasso." holding out the basket and taking a seat beside the bed, I notice a pile of dog dirt on the floor.

"Oh, *my de-are*! – how kind.... what are those lovely green things?"

"Beans"

"Oh, I used to love *mange tout!* What do I do with them…?"

"Just boil them, but you have to string them first, of course."

"String them?" She's looking puzzled. I demonstrate. I remember her saying, *"Until I came back from China I never had to cook anything – it took me ages to discover how to boil an egg."* The dachshund leaps off the bed and drops his ping-pong ball at my feet. I roll it across the room, he scampers after it. "Who takes him for a walk?" I ask, thinking of the evidence under the bed.

"Mrs Pattakos has tried to take him out, but he won't go with anybody. You don't want to leave me, do you, my Luv-kins...." as the little dog leaps on the bed again and pushes his snout in her face. "Mrs Pattakos brings him food – though not the steaks you like, my precious. He turned up his nose at it at first." Soon I have to say. "I'm sorry…I've got to go and cook the lunch."

She understands. "I DO hope I'll get back to the wine shop soon…"

18

Early evening at the Beach Restaurant. The melon man camps beside his pile of huge green watermelons, reading a newspaper. He sleeps on a bed made from a few crates, and a striped blanket. He will stay with his melons until they are sold. He has been there a week already.

We are sitting with a banker and his wife; she in a bikini, looking like a plucked swallow, reading a book under the carapace of an enormous sombrero. A speedboat chases across the surface of the sea in riotous equilibrium; the banker remarks, "I wonder if those people are happy…"

"We always hope they're not." He laughs aloud; it evokes a slight twitch from under the sombrero. Tasso indicates we must go to make the nightly 'exposition' – "But we see you later…sir…" When we return three hours later, the place has transformed into a writhing wriggling pool of frogs and tadpoles; young people from The Club, and American sailors from the visiting Aircraft carrier. He is claimed by some Greeks sitting at a table – even I can recognise '*mangas*' – spivs and pimps from Athens. Tasso orders whisky again.

"What about your ulcers?"

"They don't bother me at all…"

Three local boys, employed to dance nightly all summer, lunge about in unison dancing the *Hasapiko*, wearing fancy boleros and cummerbunds, more Spanish than Greek. I sit with arms clenched across my chest, remembering the boys in the taverna dancing for themselves, performing their own rites of passage, unheeding of an audience…The expression on my face makes Tasso remark to the Chief Pimp, "You see what the English are like!"

The man replies, with no intention to flatter, "Ah, this is a 'dry type'… a 'good' girl…" As a pimp, he is a connoisseur. Eventually they drive off in their big Mercedes.

"You know what they are… *mangas*, they bring the woomans from Athens for business…The American Navy coming here soon, I meet many like them in my life," he says, waving his hand in a circular motion. "But I never do that – to sell the woomans…

Pó-pó-pó! You know something else? I pay the bill for those bastards! For sure I am the Stupid."

No comment.

The German banker calls us to his table again. He has been drinking steadily since we left. He is carrying on a flirtation with a young French girl who, while picking at the food on the table, keeps glancing towards her boyfriend at the bar. The banker calls for Champagne. When the waiter brings it, the French girl doesn't hesitate to pull the bottle out of the bucket to see if it is really French, not Greek, and takes her glass to her boyfriend at the bar, bringing it back to be refilled. The banker's wife stares at the girl as venomously as a serpent. Suddenly, pushing back her chair, she rises unsteadily to her feet, saying in a strangled voice, "I can't stand this any longer! *I must prove myself a* WOMAN!" and totters over to Vassili's desk, where he is synthesizing his waiters. "Vassili! I INSIST you dance with me."

Experienced in obliging important customers, he shouts a few orders over his shoulder and escorts her onto the dance floor, holding her insect body discreetly aloof. With the movement of the dance, her bikini pants keep slipping, she hitches them up without embarrassment, like a little girl. The French girl drifts back to her boy at the bar. A crack of thunder comes unexpectedly. An English voice nearby says, "Hullo! Was that thunder…?" Nobody takes any notice.

Tasso calls for the bill – and insists on paying for the banker's champagne. It confuses the waiter because the German is staying at the hotel and it would automatically go on the bill. He keeps asking Tasso, "Are *you* paying for the Champagne…?" He says it once too often, it sounds offensive; Tasso ignites, jumps up and hits him. From the sky comes another crack of thunder.... The young waiter hits him back; the table crashes over, with the glasses and bottles. People move out of the way with incredible agility, even the elderly. The waiter gets in a kick, pitching Tasso at the feet of an American sailor. The sailor leans forward to assist him back into the fight. The Shore Patrol remain a motionless as statues; it is not their business when Greek meets Greek.

334

Tasso and the waiter slog at each other for that eternal moment lasting only seconds. The other waiters drag them apart like dogs, the fight evaporates like a bad dream.

The tables are quickly set to rights, people sit down again. The band hasn't stopped playing. Another crack of thunder, louder now, accompanied by a wind that shakes the coloured lights in the trees as if angry at their superficiality, and the lightning drives its trident into the sea. The fat drops begin slowly, then like a horse gathering pace, drum on the awnings which sag and belly like pregnant women. The diners run for cover as the wind plays with the chairs and the tablecloths like a big boisterous puppy, and the band struggle to cover their electric instruments. The man who sleeps beside his melons covers himself with a tarpaulin as we make a dash for the car.

Summer is over...

19.

He has received an invitation to the Principessa's wedding in Rome in October. "We must to go," he says.

"Just because she sends you an invitation, it doesn't mean you have to go – she probably just wants you to know that she's getting married at last. She must be 40 if she's a day!" And with sudden clairvoyance again, I add: "I bet you only received an invitation because you wrote your name in her visitor's book – under the King of Greece!"

"What you talking about? Of course she want me to be at her wedding! And from Rome we go to Paris to see Colette, and then to London to see our friends there."

"I am not going to that wedding."

"What you mean? I don't going without you. You know that."

"The Principessa will not thank you if you turn up with me to her High Society wedding – and anyway…" collapsing into the banal "…I haven't anything to wear!"

With his face and his iron-grey hair, he can get away with it in his old corduroy jacket. I can get away with nothing. A war of conflicting psychologies follows, which leaves us both exhausted.

I have a moaning session with The Hon. who has managed to crawl to the wine shop again, about having nothing to wear to the Roman wedding. "What a pity I've nothing to fit you…" she says The idea of her old Christian Dior clothes brings me to the very brink of the absurd.

The Hon turns the conversation back to her own problems. "I'm having terrible trouble with the bank. They say my money from Africa, it must go via America… they can't pay me anything. The British Consul has been on to them about it. He's been very good, I must say – though he wears those frightful jerseys no Englishman should wear…"

"You have the £60 from England," the woman says.

"That doesn't pay for my pills – let alone my bills!" The Hon. exclaims. "The doctor has prescribed a whole pharmacy of pills... and they make me so giddy...I dread another fall..."

"We're leaving tomorrow... think of me at that wedding...."

"I look forward to hearing ALL ABOUT IT when you come back – if I haven't had another heart attack..."

20

On the ferryboat to Italy, the plainclothes police, always suspicious, ask him "Where are *you* off to, Tasso?" They have seen me going out and in for years, but not him.

He says, "To a Princess's wedding in Rome!" They laugh and slap him on the back. It's a good joke.

We go to the same hotel near the Piazza de Spagna, where he is greeted as a family friend. He gets his hair cut for the wedding; the Roman barber does such a stylish job, he emerges looking like a middle-aged film star. People in the street look at him as if they ought to recognise him.

"How are we going to get to this wedding reception?" I ask, more and more disgruntled.

"We take a taxi, of course."

As the dreaded hour approaches I have diarrhoea, and gain control of my bowels just in time with the aid of two 'Astronaut' tablets he gets from a chemist, and two brandies.

Gritting my teeth, I clamber into the kaftan dress borrowed from one of the tourist reps who said she wouldn't be needing it till next summer. I wish I didn't need it. It swamps me. A belt made of metal links (also borrowed) ties it in, but immediately falls to bits. I fix it together with gold string from a patisserie shop. I am glad to cover all this with a long black coat. If only I didn't care, it would be funny.

He looks at me critically, "Uhm... Don't forget to bring your camera," he says.

"I'm not going to take photographs!"

"Why not?" he asks, surprised. He wants the proof for his friends.

"*Because it's Not Done!*"

"You again! Always you bring the malediction."

At the last minute I put the thing in my purse and take a photo of him standing by the taxi which then drives us at hair-raising speed across Rome, circling the Coliseum with squealing tyres before bolting like a rabbit into the Via Appia with its crumbling tombs and sarcophargii... *Quo vadis....where are we going?* Burning flares light the entrance to the driveway, already packed with smart cars and smart people drifting toward the imposing mansion. *What the hell are we doing here?*

In the hall, the Principessa stands beside the man she has married, looking larger and more historical in a Renaissance wedding dress – quite unlike the woman I remember in a sarong examining her toenails on a yacht. She doesn't look any happier. The bridegroom, a mature man of impeccable breeding, does not look at her, nor she at him, giving the impression that they have been separated by the marriage ceremony rather than joined by it. Her passive face breaks into a sweet smile of surprise as she recognises Tasso. *I knew she had no idea he was sent an invitation.* "Tasso! How kind of you to come!" she beams, and shakes my hand without looking at me.

Through the salons decorated with priceless paintings and furniture to a marquee extending the house into the garden, the guests greet each other in self-recognising groups; Roman society looks as garish as any other.

Tasso, like a chameleon, seems quite at home, while I feel vulgar and fraudulent in borrowed plumes, not knowing who I hate most: him, them or me. We wander around like things from outer space, taking a few little bits from the trays of food and drink. He is soon bored; and my spirits soar when he says, "Bah! This is no place for us. Enough is enough. We get the hell out of here." But how are we to get the hell out of it? "I make a mistake not to tell the taxi to come back in two hours."

We drift back through the connecting salons. Flashes of cameras are like minor electric storms now. "You can take picture now," he says. We are alone in the small anteroom next to the hall. I take one of him in front of a Renaissance cabinet. "Take another in front of this nice painting." I have the camera raised to my eye, when the bride's patrician father and mother, escorting an important guest to the front door, enter the chamber. Their faces transform with astonishment and outrage. The message is clear to read: *'Gatecrashers...filthy journalists!'*

The party moves on, exiting into the hall. The bride's father signals a footman, points to us. The footman pads in to the room to ask for our invitation. Tasso has it in his pocket. The footman takes it and pads away like the frog footman – like Alice, I want to eat something to shrink me.

When the invitation proves genuine, the patrician father sends for his daughter. She comes, looks at the invitation, soothes her father's disgust and, entering the room where we are, she calls the professional photographer to her. Linking arms with Tasso, she orders a photograph to be taken. She tells him it will be sent to him, and leaves the room without having looked at me at all.

The incident speeds our departure wonderfully. It has become a priority now to find us a taxi, every effort of the servants is geared towards this. The relief to fling ourselves into the anonymity of a taxicab. I would have got into any container – a capsule to the moon.

"I make a mistake to go, I'm afraid," he says after a long silence in which we simmer separately. But he concedes, "The Principessa very kind to me…" Yes, it was kind of her to save his face, my opinion of her has gone up. After a thoughtful silence he says, "But I don't think if she find 'the Absolutely Thing'."

My personal chagrin melts, recalling the politically resigned face of The Bride, rather than The Woman, and his innocence, believing an invitation means what it says: *'to have the pleasure of your company'*.

21

On arrival at the Gare de Lyon, the blow to his ego is healed by the tannoy announcing *"Monsieur Tassos ...de Grèce, s'il vous plaît..."* urging him to come to the Station Master's office, where Manette flings herself into his arms, and Sylvie shakes me by the hand. They carry us off to a nearby bistro no bigger than a railway carriage. We stay in a hotel near the station with a double bed so big we entirely miss each other.

At Calais, it is a British ferry boat.

"Oh, this is my place!" he says, at the sight of the white coated barman, like an English butler, sibilating through National Health false teeth. "What will you take, sir/madam?"

"A whisky and a gin and tonic."

"Certainly, Sir...."

"Watch out for the money! I want fish and chips for lunch." As the Cliffs of Dover appear the tannoy announces: *"Non-nationals please go to immigration."* He goes, and comes back puzzled. "They ask me too many questions... how long I staying, if I have friends in London, how much money." This is not the reception a Greek Anglophile expects; his ego is dented again.

At Dover the large sign*: WELCOME TO BRITAIN* restores his faith, but the train is hotter than Athens, crowded, chaotic, with no place to put luggage, and delayed. At Victoria, we take a taxi to the Greek hotel in the Paddington area where his sister and the General stay when they come to London. It looks like a brothel. Antigone and the General stay *here?* The Greek owner welcomes him as a long lost family member, and shows us to a dingy room off the hall with no hot water.

"Now let's go to see something." I lead him down to Marble Arch into Oxford Street where the shops are just closing. "Call our friends, can you?" That's what he needs at this moment. When I find a phone that works, I call Verena – no answer. In desperation, I try Pooter's friend Harvey, the only other person we know in London.

Harvey answers. "You're here! Wonderful! Pooter told me you were coming. Wonderful. We must make a date to meet next week…" *Next week? He needs someone now. Greeks don't take a week to welcome friends – it's instantaneous. He is the Anglophile, not me. What am I to do with him on a cold wet evening in London?* "For the moment I don't like anything," he says, marching along the pavement ahead of me.

Suddenly, a squeal of brakes, a car stops by the curb, a voice screaming "Tasso!" comes from a girl who jumps out of the car to embrace him – one of three girls we met in the summer.

"I just saw the back of his head – and screamed to Jeremy – STOP! There's Tasso!"

She directs her boyfriend to take us to a cosy pub in Camden. "When I lived in London I never met a single person who knew me; he comes to London for the first time and is recognised on the first evening in the rain! It's a miracle!" For him it is not a miracle – in Athens it happens all the time. Athens is a village – now London is his village.

"I'm living with Bethany and Jane," she says. "We've rented a flat together. You must come to supper with us… we'll make a Greek meal… Have you got our number now? Don't forget. They'll be thrilled when I tell them."

Back at the Greek hotel, the street door opens and shuts all night long, footsteps plod up the stairs by our room; a voice says, "Don't try any tricks with me. I'm not Greek." Already he has been recognised nine times in Oxford Street, by young Greeks working as waiters in Wimpy Bars who come running out, shouting "Tasso! Tasso! How is my father?" They tell him of a bar in the Edgware Road where the Greeks hang out. I hope he will forget it. After the statutory British hiatus, I manage to get Verena on the phone. "Tasso in London! Where are you staying? Paddington! You must come here – you can have the nursery flat." But he doesn't want to lose his little piece of Greece in London, happy enough sitting in the owner's office talking his own language. After being taken to posh restaurants he is bored with this High Life, "We must to find the girls…." he says. We find them in a flat in a condemned building in Warren Street, where they have cooked a Greek meal for us, and play

Theodorakis on the tape recorder. We all dance the *Hasapiko,* making the fragile building rock. "Oh, we are coming back next summer!" they sigh. "You bet!", hugging and kissing him innocently as if he were their talisman to drag them up out of the dark well of temporary jobs in London, into the bright light of Greece. After a week he has had enough of everything, pronouncing, "The lake in my pocket begin to be dry. After tomorrow we get the hell out of here." I've have certainly had enough of my country of origin.

Arriving back on the island, it is raining like hell, and the Hon. is dead. I get the details from Pooter:

"I was greatly saddened to hear of the Hon's death, though it may be for the best. I had an account of it from Mrs. Pattakos who lives upstairs, as you know. She seemed to think it reprehensible that so few of her British friends were 'apparent' at the last, but we know how she had alienated most of her 'friends' with her 'bons mots'. Mrs Pattakos found her lying half out of bed, in a comatose state – Goodness knows for how long – and called the ambulance, which came with only a driver – so they had to call two boys in from the street to carry her. But the little dog jumped onto her chest, ready to bite anybody who touched her. Mrs Pattakos managed to throw a blanket over the creature. The Hon., realising they were taking her to the hospital, started screaming 'Don't take me there...' Remember her reaction to being put in a ward with the peasant women when she spent a few days in there when she had one of her falls. They got her there, and she died in the early hours of the morning. Mrs Pattakos sat with her all night. You know how humane the Greeks can be in situations like that. One cannot help but think it was a Happy Release, though the Greeks never think of death as a Happy Release. She outlived herself and her times and to be demodé was an anathema to her. A difficult woman, but certainly a Character. We shall not see her like again. I was very amused by your account of the Principessa's wedding.

Write again soon."

22.

Christmas Eve: children come to the door braying the Christmas chant and banging a triangle. I find five drachmes he has overlooked in a saucer in the kitchen. I give them one drachma. They are followed by two boys with a trumpet and a drum. They are followed by an oboe and cymbals. Christmas makes a lethal cocktail. I never enjoy it. But it is a day brilliant with sunshine; the sea intensely blue, the mainland mountains crested with snow. "We must make an excursion, to be enjoy," he says.

We drive into the countryside, and stop off at Stamati's in the village. The place has a strange atmosphere of tension and suspense. Stamati is wearing a blue suit, tie and an overcoat, instead of his usual bloody vest and apron. He is tense and fidgety at the best of times, and now he is like an electric eel. No sign of Frosso, until suddenly she comes out of the family cottage opposite, transformed in a full length velvet skirt, lacy blouse, fawn coat with imitation fur trimmings, new suede shoes, which look uncomfortable; against her new finery her face and hands look raw and red.

She is in a dream state, showing none of her customary vigour – her little mother running after her like a black hen holding up the hem of the new velvet skirt in case it should trail in the dirt. The brother, home on leave from the army, criticizes the colour of her coat against the black velvet skirt. "It ought to be different," he says. A button is loose – the hen-witted mother rushes for needle and thread to sew it back on. The whole family is in a trance state. Frosso doesn't even notice us – she has no eyes for anything, locked into her own 'Being-ness', like a Corn Goddess. Tasso asks if they are going to a wedding and is told they are invited to the special party at the bank. "They important people now, they make money..."

A taxi draws up outside. Frosso is carefully insinuated into the back seat like a doll. Stamati throws himself into the front seat with the impetuosity of a gangster about to rob a bank. The brother seems critical again.

"Babbá!" he calls out anxiously. *"Aristocrats always sit in the back."*

The assassin of sheep, cows and goats sticks up his chin in the oriental negative. *"Den birazi!"* – Never mind! – and orders the driver to proceed.

23.

Back at the wine shop, I am happily reading my book when I am startled to hear an English voice with a North Country accent asking for seven bottles of Johnnie Walker Black Label whisky, and see a girl dressed in the quasi uniform of the 'Religious Navy' with a young Greek as her chaperone. Mr Sotiris, looking up at the bottles high on the shelf, says he has only Red Label. The girl hesitates. "They told me to get Black Label..."

"But Red Label verry goot!" says the young Greek, staring at the wad of notes she is holding in her hand.

"Oh, I don't know what to do now... they told me Black Label!" She is obviously worried.

"Red Label – same thing is. Whiz-ky!" It is clearly an important mystical drink to the boy, though he has yet to taste it.

"I'd better go back....I'm ever so sorry...." she says and goes – followed closely by the boy. She will have a job getting rid of him. When Tasso comes, I tell him about the girl and seven bottles of Black Label.

"What do you expect?" he says.

"But it's a religious cult!" I protest, imagining abstinence, sobriety.

"Yes – they very thirsty of the sex too," he says. "One blondie woman bother me much. Every time I see her, I change the road. Come on now we must to go to the Casino."

"You've given up that place!" Shocked.

"Of course! But they make a big party for the Military and the Police – we must to see that..."

"Don't you have to be invited to a thing like that?" I ask hopefully.

"Bah! The door is open to me."

The Casino is *en fête*, the foyer buzzing with excited chatter – the military and the police chiefs in splendid uniforms with more and more braid, gold for the military, silver for the police. To emphasise the Regime's moral values, the wives have been brought into the open, dumpy and shapeless in tent-like dresses bought for the occasion. They do not look comfortable. One woman keeps yanking at her dress, which is riding up into her armpit.

In the bar, he orders a gin and tonic for me, and whisky for himself. My toes are wrapped so firmly round the barstool, if he says "Go to play something", it will take a surgical operation to prise me off. The Canary Countess is on the next barstool looking like a Maharani in her canary yellow. Desmond, the American painter, is with her. Pooter, in his last letter, said, "I hear The Countess has moved in with Desmond. He'll never be rid of her. He even cooks for her...." She doesn't notice me, as they have their heads together writing down numbers on a piece of paper. She pulls an embroidered purse out of her ethnic satchel and gives Desmond some money. He shoves it in his pocket and makes for the door.

"Oh, you here!" she says, suddenly seeing me.

"Are you having a flutter...?" I suggest tactlessly.

"Oh dear me, no! I don't gamble. I have taken Holy Orders. Desmond is just doing it for a lark. I gave him a little something to help the poor fellow...." Suddenly she seems to go into a trance, sublimating for the winning number perhaps? The band is playing a foxtrot. One of the military men takes to the floor with a woman in a red dress; he may be the only one who can dance a foxtrot – it is unlikely the others can, certainly not with those wives. Good-looking in an athletic way like a footballer, he swings the girl around confidently, shooting off authoritative glances in all directions. He must practise them in the mirror every morning.

"Him the Military Governor. You like him?" Words which have me standing on the edge of an old volcano. I am saved by the entrance of the Count, followed dutifully by Parsifal. The Count bows over my hand without kissing it this time. The Canary Countess, coming out of her trance at the arrival of important people, is all ears and eyes now. At a nearby table, a party of the Salvation Navy are enjoying themselves in an unreligious way; two young men with wispy beards are drinking continuously, and one of the women has rejected her home-made uniform for a mini-dress as brief as an ice skater's, and fishnet stockings. They are making a lot of noise. Tasso orders another whisky.

"Remember your ulcers...."

"My ulcers no bother me at all," he says happily.

"Why don't you ask the Canary Countessa to dance?" I suggest, to get him away from the whisky.

He takes up the idea immediately. "Will you dance, madame...?" She dismounts from her barstool cautiously as from a camel, and wiggles coyly after him on to the dance floor. I am feeling rather smug at my ruse when, suddenly, a waiter appears at my elbow, asking me to move my car, as it is in the way of some important person. I glance to where Tasso is dancing with the Countess, holding her at arm's length. What can I do? I can't go onto the dance floor to tell him, "The waiter has asked me to move the car..." But if he sees me disappear there will be hell to pay. The waiter is standing there expectantly, there is nothing for it but to go and move the car as quickly as possible and get back before he notices my absence.

I run down the red carpeted stairs, out into the car park, move the car, run back into the hall, take the lift which brings me to the right level faster than I could run up the stairs. Pushing open the door, I am confronted by the Countessa, preparing to enter it. She looks at me indignantly.

"He dropped me like a hot coal the moment you left the room. Silly girl! Did you think I was taking him away from you?" – as if my absence was some cheap feminine ploy. She is old enough to be my grandmother! Behind her, Tasso's face is dark with suspicion.

"The waiter told me to move the car!" He wants to know which waiter, and checks my story with him. The whisky is working now. Back in the restaurant, the band switches to the 'Irakina', the familiar circle dance. The effect is electric – the military wives take to the floor with confidence, hand in hand, swaying gracefully, executing the subtle steps faultlessly making it look so simple and easy; the athletic Military Governor capering and cavorting, skipping and twirling, shooting off his glances like the rays of Apollo, draws them after him with nothing stronger than a cotton handkerchief.

"Time to go," says Tasso. I am so glad. Down in the hall, three members of the Religions Navy, two men and a woman, are waiting for the mini-bus back to town. He offers them a lift; they accept, and squash themselves into the back seat of the Fiat. In the car, attempts at conversation soon dwindle, a peculiar silence prevails – a silence which has something wrong with it. I feel anxious. He is drunk; something is fermenting. I drive to the harbour where the ship is. He doesn't move from his seat to let them out. I have to. The two men get out, the woman stays in the back seat.

"I'll stay with them," she tells them. They walk away. Then, in her American drawl, I hear her say, "Tasso…what game are we playing?" What does she mean? What game are we playing? I feel as if someone were trying to suffocate me with a plastic bag – I am trying to breathe, and he just coughs the way he does when drunk. "Is she your wife, Tasso?" She knows his name.

"No, I am not his wife! But I have been with him long enough to feel like it! Just get out of my car! It happens to be my car, and I want you out of it." She doesn't move. Neither does he.

"Let's talk this thing out…" she drawls.

"What thing? Just get out of my car." Tasso, slumped in the front seat, says nothing. "And you can take *him* with you." *I'm past caring if they do it – but not in my car. They can do it somewhere else. I want to go home and sleep.*

"Look," she says blandly, "I like you both."

"Americans *always* say that." *God! She doesn't give up easily. She needs sex this badly? In this state he's incapable of it anyway.*

"I'm not American. I'm Canadian…"

"I don't care what you are. Just get out and go!" adding, "I must say you're a great advertisement for your religion."

"I'm not advertising my religion."

"Well, you're succeeding." Suddenly, he gets into the back with her. "Drive around a bit," he mumbles. *Is this happening? Is this reality? What is reality – that one fools oneself all the time? It is three o'clock in the morning, we have had nothing to eat and too much to drink. I thought I had plumbed the depths of this man – is there further to go? Surely I am dreaming this, but I am so tired, I can't wake up, and yet I am more awake than I have ever been.*

"The only place I'm driving around to is the police station!"

Getting into the car, slamming it in gear, I drive around the town, trying to remember the way to the police station Oh, here we are – this will do. I stop in front of an imposing doorway leading into a stone flagged courtyard. I slam on the brakes, jump out, tip the seat forward, grab the woman, who is now lying across his lap. "Come on! Get out!" She looks up, sees the impressive doorway, and panics. She is out of the car like a cat and running down the street, disappears. Phew! He struggles out of the car. "Go after her!"

"You go. I'm going home."

I have the car in gear when he throws himself across the bonnet. *The urge is irresistible – this is how it happens – because men are rotten bastards and Love a dirty word. "We live by admiration, hope and love...." our school motto. What is the use of education? This is my education and I still haven't learned the bloody lesson!*

"Oh, get in!" He does. It is only then I realise – it wasn't the police station at all. Well – it worked. At home I occupy myself in the kitchen – *if he lays a finger on me....* He doesn't, he goes straight to his bed and falls instantly asleep. He won't remember at thing tomorrow – or will pretend he doesn't...

He comes home early. I am in the small room between the front room, and the kitchen. He creeps down the corridor to the kitchen where he thinks I must be. Standing right behind him, I say, "There's only spaghetti for lunch." He nearly jumps out of his skin. "Oh, I was afraid you going..." It takes me by surprise, I hadn't thought of going. It hadn't occurred to me. You can't keep leaving; you can only do it once, and if you come back, there isn't really any point in going again.

"I am very hungry," he says. We eat in silence. He cannot bear silence.

"What happen last night?" he asks tentatively. "I don't remember anything..."

"I expected you to say that."

"Pó-pó! She was for sure a nymphomaniac one."

"Don't blame her! You must have started it." The manhole cover blows off the cesspit.

"What about you? What you doing with that waiter – you go to the car park. You *putana* too!"

"Why don't you accuse me of being a lousy housekeeper – which I am – instead of a *putana*, which *I am not*." I push back my chair to leave the kitchen, but not without a parting shot, "It's a mistake to forgive you *anything*!"

I have been irritated but never feared the 'other women'. I am 'The Other Woman'. It is him and me. So what am I feeling? The tide has gone right out, showing all the old tins, boots, bottles and dead cats on a vast sea of mud – the mud of that one once called Love. The incident is not mentioned again. In fact, I have lost the power of speech. I haven't spoken for a week. I may never speak again.

"Come on, put out the bad things of your head," he says, baffled as a dog. "I have terrible pains on me.... I have so many pains on my body you don't imagine..." This is all to arouse my sympathy. I have none. In the words of one of their songs: *"You have turned my blood black, and my hair white."*

He tries to please me – "I have buy a big new fridge!" He has bought a new fridge – to please me...? He is trying to please me? It's a long time since he tried that. "But we must to wait for it to come from Athens."

I say nothing. I have no voice.

He tries joking. I don't laugh. On Sunday he says, "We make an excursion – drive around a bit to see the country. You like that!" We drive up to the north of the island – "to see what happens there..."

The coastline has acquired a vulgar necklace of hotels. We drive back across the island on a terrible old road twisting among the olives groves, the winter sun probing through the foliage making a luminous green floor as if lit from below. At the sight of a tiny dilapidated little *cafenion* in the middle of nowhere, he says "Oh, stop here. This is the place for us."

A flyblown little place with lopsided chairs and tables; an old man in charge draws water from the well to make the coffee. The yard at the back has a pergola of old grapes, and an orange tree full of oranges. A notice nailed to the trunk reads *'Don't eat - Poisonous'*. Tasso asks how they can be poisonous. The old man laughs. "I put to stop the children stealing them."A woman looks in through the window, curious at the sound of voices. She goes away, returning with her mother and her daughter; their three pairs of eyes walk all over us like flies, studying us as if we were a baffling puzzle, or a work of art. "Where are you from?" they quiz him politely. Tasso says Alexandria, having just told the old man he was from Germany. They look at me. *"Xeni einai?"* – that word for foreigner, pronounced 'zany'.

"She is English," he tells them, adding, "but her mother was a Turk!" He looks around for something to buy, to spend money in the store, but the old wooden shelves, painted a greasy cobalt blue, are empty except for two small tins of tomato paste.

"Give me those two tins," he says.

The old man takes them down. "What will you do with them?"

"Take them home."

The old man looks mystified. "Don't they have tomato where you come from?"

"Bah! I am from here – from the town."

The old man is still puzzled. "They don't have tomato paste in the town?"

It all ends in laughter, the women holding their hands over their mouths. Laughter wells up in me too…. blowing the door off my self-imposed prison. Damn him! He has made me laugh. As we leave they call out: *"Na parte sto kalo."* 'May you go toward the Good… As we get into the car, another old villager wanders up to stare at us – a beautiful old man with fine features, translucent skin, a full silky beige moustache, wearing a big straw hat, a pristine white shirt over his thick sheep-wool vest, holding a pink carnation between his teeth. His eyes are without curiosity, or even the memory of the experience of life, serene as the moon looking at the earth, a return to an innocence perhaps he never had. This *is* the island I came to – the island that seduced me.

I was sitting in the wine shop as usual in the evening, when I saw *her,* the woman from the ship. She appeared in the doorway – but at the sight of me she blew back into the street like a moth. Well! I have never had that effect before. I felt quite pleased with myself.

24.

New Year's Eve. I am surprised when he puts on his best suit and a tie in the evening – always a dangerous sign. And in the wine shop he buys packets of chocolates, a ritual cake bread, and fancy biscuits. He doesn't say what for, and I don't ask. In the car he points in the direction of the harbour.

"Go that way. I want to see something...." As we get to the Harbour gates he points again, "Go in there...."

I stop like a donkey. "What for?"

"The Salvation Navy make a party tonight on board. They looking for me all over town today to invite us."

"I am *not* going on that ship!" I have lost a whole week struggling with that experience.

"They have invite everybody! The Mayor is going, the Head of the Police is going. Look!" he says, pointing to the cars sweeping through the gates. In one of them I recognise Mr and Mrs Dexter, and the figure of her mother in the back.

"You can go alone!"

"You know I don't go without you…"

"I can't trust you!"

"Okay – don't trust me…but I promise on the soul of my mother…" the Greek's most binding oath, "…I don't leave you for a second!"

"What if we meet her?"

"I wouldn't recognise her if I saw her…" No, he was too drunk.

"I would!" I am beginning to waver, rather curious myself. Putting the car into gear, I drive through the gates. He always wins… At the top of the steep gangway we are greeted by a large woman wearing trousers with a broad leather belt around her enormous waist. She is puzzled when he hands her the chocolates, cake bread and biscuits; in Greece you do not go empty-handed to a party. We are passed to a younger woman full of artificial *bonhomie,* who leads us along the decks and corridors of the old

British ferryboat, to what would have been the first-class dining room, where a buffet is set out and chairs arranged against the walls, leaving a large space in the centre. Mrs Dexter, with the white fur cuffs, is already seated and indicates the spare place beside her. I take it. I have never spoken to her before.

"I wouldn't miss this for the world!" she whispers wickedly. I have to admit...now I'm here... I wouldn't either. A tall, slim woman with silver blonde hair, dressed like an air-hostess, glides across the room directly to me, with a welcoming smile so sincerely artificial I don't know what to do with it.

"I am *so glad* you could come!" Is this the 'blondie' one who bothered him much?

"I didn't know I was coming," I say, telling the truth. It gets rid of her. She goes off to get us drinks and doesn't come back. No sign of the 'other' woman, though I keep my eyes open for her.

All sorts of people from the town are here, even Madame Ellie. Just when it is beginning to turn into a boring assembly of people trying to talk to each other in several different languages, an officer, acting as *compere,* announces the entertainment will begin with "Our folksingers". A girl with large teeth and a guitar and two boys sing their way through three American folksongs, mostly off-key. We clap. A fat girl sings a Mexican song, which is better. We applaud her enthusiastically. Tasso annoys me by saying every few minutes "So nice is! Very good." The next to perform is "Our professional opera singer", a tenor with all the vocal and physical mannerisms of an opera singer. Waitresses slouch in and out of the kitchen wearing extremely tight clothes. All have large bosoms, and their trousers look as if they will burst the seams.

The music changes to Greek music. The compere announces, "And now we ask Mr Tassos to dance for us..." Tasso grabs me without looking at me. We go through the motions, he radiating personality, while my face must look like a shoe. The enthusiastic applause is salt on a wound. Suddenly, the attention of all the officers swings toward the door, They rush to form a guard of honour, standing rigidly to attention as a middle-aged man of large build and large face enters, smiling around at everybody like the sun on a pub sign, without there being any geniality in the face at all.

"It's Zeus himself, come down from Mount Olympos..." whispers Mrs Dexter excitedly.

He shakes hands with the mayor and a few others, including Tasso and Mr Dexter, and disappears again.

"They say he made a fortune in South Africa before he invented this racket." Mrs Dexter is unstoppable, her eyes twinkling in her toad-like face. "If I were thirty years younger, I would invent a religion. I would start with an egg. The egg is the most perfect thing there is in shape and content – everything begins with the egg, doesn't it? I'd start there and make up the rest."

She may go mad every seven years, but she seems more sane than most of us tonight. When the general dancing begins, Tasso says, "We get the hell out of here." The female officers beg him to stay. "No...no... we must to go now...." (He doesn't want anybody asking *me* to dance.) As we leave I recognise one of the men who was in the car that night giving me a curious look. I wonder where *she* is? Is she shut up in the bowels of the ship? Or is she simply afraid of me? We are seen off the ship by a young woman in a lace mini-dress, who thanks us for coming. Next day he comes home saying, "You know what? The Religious Navy leave two bottles of nice wine for me at the Bar Greco."

"Don't you drink it! It might have some potion in it!"

"For sure I don't trust that stuff. I sell and get the profit of that bullshit party!"

It makes a good letter for Pooter.

We have got through the portals of Christmas and New Year. It stuck to the rules, being one of the worst.

*

A couple of weeks later, The Salvation Navy has gone! The town is abuzz with dozens of versions of the story. After being allowed to stay here for months, the ship was suddenly given 24 hours to clear off. The engines don't work, so it was tugged ignominiously out of Greek waters. As usual a letter from Pooter supplies the details.

"*I read in the papers that the 'Salvation Navy', as you call it, was ordered out of Greek waters. Apparently they advertised for a couple of engineers to fix the engines. Two Scotsmen flew out, but the moment they got on board their passports were taken away, and they were held as hostages. One of the men managed to escape and went straight to the British Consul, who boarded the boat with the Greek Police to demand the release of the other man, and the return of their passports. Dramatic stuff! The other man said he was subjected to religious brainwashing...I suppose they hoped to convert them so they would have two free engineers on board.*" He goes on to say, "*I wonder how the season will be for you this summer what with the political and economic crisis here, also a fuel shortage. Several of the biggest tourist companies have gone bankrupt. The island may regret putting all its eggs into the touristic basket.*"

25.

Spring! O-spring-a-ling! Orange trees in flower, humming with bees in the noontime. Roses…fireflies…wild strawberries…the ground changing colour like a kaleidoscope from yellow to mauve, to the creamy foam of asphodels floating under the olive trees. The season has begun. What Pooter predicted seems to be true. There are very few tourists – though walking to the wine shop from the car, the shrill voice of a fat young woman screams to her companions, "Where are the bloody toy-litts. I got to do a wee…!"

At the hotel in the evening, there seem to be more staff than tourists; the bar is empty, with only two middle-aged English women sipping their soup silently; only the British can sup soup silently. A stray dog has moved in and is curled up comfortably in one of the new armchairs. When the manager spots him and tries to drive him out, the dog goes straight over to an English woman, who immediately starts cooing "Oh, sweet doggie… luvly doggie… Oh, let him stay – he's so sweet!" The dog looks up at the manager and smiles. The manager, in a rage, goes back behind the reception desk. These stray dogs are more intelligent than people.

The only people to approach the table where Tasso has the pictures spread out are a young couple, who are deaf and dumb. He responds in mime. They buy a picture. As they move away, another English couple approach, presuming it is the artist who is deaf and dumb.

"I like the one with the donkey." Pointing to it, she mouths, "How much?" Tasso continues the dumb show until he has the money in his hand, when he says "Thank you!" Being English they enjoy the joke.

26

I am just reading a letter from Pooter.

"*This uncomfortable business between Greece and Turkey over Cyprus. The press is full of it here. I wonder how much you get to hear about it with no free press and nothing but propaganda…*" When Tasso charges into the wine shop, he calls out, "Hurry! We must to fill up the car with petrol! Greece have declare war on Turkey!" Driving to the petrol station is hectic with cars and scooters flying around bumping into each other as men of all ages respond like lemmings to the call to arms against their ancient enemy, the Turk.

"Drive around a bit, I want to see," he says. The harbour is choked with Hippies with their back packs, bed rolls, and babies. Tourists with cars, trying to get on the ferry boats out of the country, and Greeks trying to get onto the mainland to enlist. Waiters and stewards from the Greek ferries queue up to telephone their villages and families. "Tell her to go to her sister… tell her to go to the village." Excitement and misery. Even the weather has changed – the summer sky is grey; rain, thunder threaten.

At the harbour café, Tasso orders a '*Turkiko*'. The waiter sticks his nose in the air, "We don't serve *Turkiko*." The gritty little coffee they drink has been called a '*Turkiko*' for 400 years. "We only serve *Elleniko*," he says, and brings exactly the same coffee in the tiny cups. At the petrol station, a young man drives in at speed in a high state of excitement, drama and nerves.

"Fill me up! Hurry! I'm off to war!" With the tank filled, the car refuses to start. It doesn't want to go to war. The young man leans his head against the wheel in despair. How can he go to war if his car won't take him? Tasso and the garage attendant push, but nothing happens until, suddenly, the garage man reaches into the car and turns the ignition on.

In the hotels, the waiters have dropped their trays and gone to war. The manager serves behind the bar; the tourists help themselves in the dining room. The instruments abandoned by the band lie wrapped in their casings. The management has dredged up some old records which relate more to wartime Britain than a war between Greece and Turkey. The middle-aged British take to the dance floor, quick-quick-slowing in the foxtrots and circulating blissfully in the waltz. "Oh, it takes you back... doesn't it, Reg?" – as if it were some lost kingdom, a Shangri-La of romantic fulfilment. "I think this is the best holiday we've had – isn't it, Reg?" The shops are emptying as people buy in bulk. Tasso has bought a whole box of long-life milk, "for my ulcers" and, activated by his wartime memories, two bars of soap.

"Why soap?"

"Soap always disappear in wartime..." We rendezvous with the Valkyries, who have just arrived. "*Die Welt ist verrückt*!" they shriek, which I think means 'the world has gone mad'. At home, Tasso listens to the transistor radio playing *bouzouki* music – the national sound of Greece, interrupted by a rasping voice exhorting *'Greeks and Greekesses'* to respond to the country's need to fight *'Oplar to Oplar' (Weapon to weapon)* the Ancient Enemy, and pronounce that the response to the Call to War has been overwhelming.

"If this war continue, we go to Italy and then to England," he says. The idea gives me a headache. I do some yoga breathing, and stand on my head against the door at the end of the passage by the kitchen. Seeing me in this unnatural position, he reacts like a dog.

"What you doing there!"

"It's yoga."

"No...no! I cannot see that" – as if the world were not upside enough. "Get off your head!"

"I'm not off my head – I'm on it." I am discovering I can laugh upside down, which must be a good thing. He doesn't go to work, nobody is working. This is wartime. Instead we drive out to the tavernas at the beach. The place looks like a battleground with the olive trees felled by the bulldozers. Michaeli's tavern has been knocked down.

"He going to make new place more better for the tourists..." They can't make it better. I feel like weeping. Our sweetest hours were performed in the bare cell-like rooms with the creaking bed, the early morning sunlight forcing its fingers around the edge of the shutters. The disillusion of love is bad enough – but when they start taking the scenery away...

I walk along the deserted pebble beach, seeing everything as if for the last time..... the two boats painted in burnt sienna, white, cerulean blue... a sparrow picking up a piece of bread and flying off .... a small goat sitting on a rock under an olive tree, mouth working rhythmically – pause – swallow – he blows out his cheek, the rhythmic chewing begins again. His ear is like a furled leaf, his pale eye outlined in sienna; his repose. This war means nothing to him; his time of slaughter will come. Suddenly I feel immeasurably old, as if there is no such thing as being modern.

Two days later, a cease-fire – not a shot has been fired. The Regime has collapsed. The Colonels had overlooked the fact that they had sold all their ammunition to the Middle-East. The boxes were filled with stones – so the story goes. The Colonels who bankrupted the country are now under lock and key. The exiled politicians are flying back like pigeons to the pigeon house, and the sycophants are busily changing their hats. The country has gone mad with joy; in Athens they are dancing in the streets, and throwing paint at the US Embassy. There are parties in all the hotels to celebrate the Peace and the New Democracy, even though the tourists don't know what it has all been about.

27

The fridge he ordered has arrived – it has taken a month to get here. Helping the men to get it into the house, he leaves off suddenly "Ach! My back!"

He bellows like a cow all night. I have to rub his back with olive oil. He twists himself into so many positions, ending up kneeling on the floor, lying face down across the bed. I get no sleep at all.

In the morning he makes me drive him to the hospital. It isn't easy to get attention in this under-staffed place; it is only 8.30, the doctors don't arrive till ten. "You must wait," says a nurse, sending him to the waiting room where he keeps up an incessant bellowing like a cow in labour, so they cannot ignore him. The only way to get attention. It's animal and it works. They have to find him a bed and a doctor, who listens to his heart. He picks up the packet of tablets on the side table, "Who prescribed these?"

"My doctor…" The doctor mumbles something and goes. "What did he say?"

"Something wrong with my heart…" *His heart? Surely he has a heart like bull?* Having seen the doctor query the tablets he was prescribed, I take the leaflet from the box and read the English instruction, '*not to be taken in the case of ulcers…*'

The doctors ignore me as a foreigner and obviously not related to the patient, but there is one thing I can do – I telephone Antigone, give her his telephone number, relying on her Savage Earth Mother instincts. She rings back in dramatic excitement natural to her.

"Tassos No All Rite! Must to come him in Athens. Petros come with plane tonight, bring him in Athens…You understand?" Yes, I have put the family machinery into action. I drive to the airport to meet the evening flight. Petros is first off the plane, charging into the reception lounge. I take him straight to the hospital. Tasso is moaning fretfully as Petros, bending over him, kisses him, stroking his head as he would a child, more like an anxious father than a brother younger by a decade. Tasso sleeps, Petros leaves. I spread my cushions on the floor and lie down beside the bed. I have a headache, and fall into a dream in which a great black wave seems ready to engulf us. The doctors pronounce him stable enough to fly the next evening with Petros to Athens.

"But we need the car in Athens…" The idea of driving through those mountains alone in my faulty little car is daunting, but at six o'clock I am chugging across the sea on the ferry in the rose-fingered dawn. The sun is just rising as we disembark. The bleak, beautiful, unfriendly mountains loom up in front of me; I drive into them singing, rising to the adventure of the journey with no more insurance than a small icon, a garlic, a piece of fishing net, and a blue bead with an eye on it. Up the mountains, and down into orange groves, tobacco fields – to the sea again on roads 'average to bad', still in process of being made by blasting and bulldozing; directed with waving of arms, down into a gully and up again. The little car behaves like a goat. At a roadside eating house, I am a bloom out of season, a young woman alone driving a car – the only 'zany'.

Darkness comes down – an old dog fox crosses the road in my headlights. My eyelids drooping, I enter Athens with the engine overheating, and cutting out at the traffic lights. It is after midnight when I find Petros' flat; his sleepy wife answers the door. "They are not here – they are at Marina's flat…."

Tired and fed up, I drive around the streets until I recognise the block. The door of the flat is ajar; in the dimly lit hall, Petros greets me with that gesture of exasperated concern.

"Where are you? Tasso have too much pain." He had to find a chemist to get some drug to ease it, and a nurse to give him the injection. "He is sleeping now…" He is tired and anxious, wanting to get off home; he goes.

As I crawl onto the bed beside him, Tasso, doped but not asleep, says, "What take you so long…?" The drug wearing off, he starts groaning; then he sleeps again. I remain awake. At five o'clock, aware of a noise in the hallway, where the light is still burning, I grope my way towards it. A woman is standing there dressed in a vivid emerald green shawl. *Am I hallucinating?* She smiles at me with incredible sweetness, and enters the bedroom where he is, bending over him, stroking him and murmuring to him as to a sick child. He stirs, opens his eyes and says, "Oh, Aphrodite *mou…*" *Aphrodite, the Goddess of Love.* She massages his arm and neck where the pain is; he is as docile as a child under her hands. She gives him an injection and settles him down to sleep again. Smiling at me, she motions me to follow her into the kitchen, where she makes us both a cup of coffee. She explains how the chemist had phoned her to give the injections.

"I was hospital nurse before marry. Now I have children, I make the injections to people in their homes." She brings out of her bag some small cakes. "I bake today," she says, urging me to eat. She is love…all love…and I too become a child again, when life was something to trust.

"Go to sleep now, you will need it," she says, as she lets herself quietly out of the flat.

28

The next day being a public holiday, none of the family come near us, too busy with their own festivities. Alone in this basement flat, like a mini-Hades, I follow him from room to room as, restlessly, he seeks some place where the pain will stop gnawing at him. When he leans his head against the bookcase in the hall, I notice the small photo propped up against the books It is *me*…taken years ago in one of those photographic booths on Victoria Station – *a young woman in love… Was that me?*

"What's that doing there?"

"I worry for you…last night…" Using it as a talisman to bring me in. Has he always kept this photo with him? Only Aphrodite descends to our underworld, swimming down to us like a compassionate dolphin, to give him another injection, and to bring us food from her own kitchen, aware that we have nothing, and cannot go out; all the shops are closed. The idea of coming to Athens was to get him into a hospital, wasn't it? Nobody has thought it through, and there is no doctor involved.

Next day he takes charge of his own destiny, making me drive him to a hospital in the suburbs. At reception he argues his case for admission, as I watch the dismal traffic through the hall – a man suffering a heart attack is rushed through on a trolley, followed by his wife wailing like a distressed cow. Another patient wanders past in his pyjamas, his nose done up in sticking plaster attached by a tube to a bottle held up by a nurse. He peers about mournfully … *he goes…he goes…the Dong with the luminous nose…*Tasso is having difficulty; the clerk, scratching his head, tells him he should go to another hospital. Tasso wants to be in this hospital. He persists until he gets his way, as he always does, and is allotted a bed.

At midnight the hospital goes on strike; the clerk was trying to do him a favour suggesting he go to another hospital. We are trapped. No doctors on duty, only a skeleton staff of nurses who can hand out only minor painkillers. He begins to bellow in agony again. It embarrasses me, but how do you estimate pain that is not your own? The few nurses on duty scurry past like cats with too many kittens to tend. We are without our Goddess of Love, O Aphrodite! Defending their right to strike, the doctors stand around in groups looking aggressive and defensive. Without their white jackets they don't look like doctors anymore, their professional compassion eradicated. Shrill announcements over the tannoy attack the non-striking doctors. "Dr Pappajannis and Dr Hadjimichaili must not be found ANYWHERE IN THIS HOSPITAL!"

Voluntary workers bring round food, but he has too much pain to eat. I have no appetite. Sleep is impossible, the night is long; he wanders from his bed into the corridor. I follow. He sits on a chair, I pull up another in front of him, so he can lean his head against my back while I cradle his arms around my waist. We must look like copulating insects. The lift makes the sound of whales singing. From a radio in the Matron's office pours out one of their vital love songs: "*Den boró na kimithó...pos ponó....pos ponó....pos ponó*" Can't sleep for the pain...the pain...the pain...

The Matron and the doctor, who are defying the strike, discover us in the corridor. They lead him back to his bed, and give him an injection. They do not know what to make of me, but signal me follow them into the corridor again. I wonder what they are going to tell me. The Matron, with motherly concern, takes the initiative, speaking in English. "You will have great trouble with him."

"I've never had anything else!" I say, laughing with relief. Taken by surprise, they laugh too; the matron gives me a womanly hug, and the doctor pats me on the back before moving to the next ward. They have given me the injection I need.

Corridors unswept, hair and cigarette butts gathered in the corners, the lavatories unspeakable, the strikers indifferent and self-righteous.

We are up a gum tree. What are we doing here? My presence by his bed evokes the question mark: am I wife...or what? The mother of a lad with a broken leg says in Greek, "I don't believe it!" In the corridors I am asked if I am his daughter, or if I am at school. My lack of maturity is reflected in their eyes, as I sit like a student reading Tolstoy by the night light in the wall. By their standards I do not have the status of a woman at all. The hospital being out of the centre of the city, the family doesn't come near us, too busy with their own lives. I leave him only to drive back to the flat for a hot bath, and fall sleep on the bed.

A ring at the door wakes me…who knows I am here? I open the door fearfully – and see Aphrodite.

"I was just passing – I wondered if you were here." I tell her about the strike. "I will come back with you. I know some of the doctors in that place. I was working in there before I married…"

The doctors hanging about the hall recognise her immediately and greet her with joy. One of them is prepared to follow her to the ward. He gives Tasso an injection, but her presence alone is enough to calm him. She makes him comfortable, tidies the bed. Having done all she can to help us, she must return to her children before they come home from school. In the morning, Marina turns up; as a Celebrity of Stage and Screen, she sets the place into a buzz and bullies the nurses to find a cleaner to wash the floor, and clear away the rubbish. She brings two doctors to his bedside who put him into a collar to ease the pain.

"He must *stay like that*! That's how he should be," she commands, passing the responsibility on to me.

"Has he ever done anything he should?"

She has no answer, and leaves, scribbling autographs on her way out, convinced she has made a difference.

An hour later he pulls the collar from his neck and throws it across the room, and starts bellowing again.

No sign of the strike ending. We have been here ten days; ten days have ten nights. It is like being stuck on the Trans-Siberian railway in the middle of the Gobi desert. Will it ever move again? I phone Antigone.

"We must get him out of here! He's getting no treatment and the pain is killing him!"

"But he choose to go in that place. Is not easy to get him to another hospital…"

"We can't stay here!"

"Okay, I try…" And she rings off. She appears in the middle of the afternoon, passionately triumphant. Her husband, The General, has used his influence.

"We have find place for him at the Military Hospital! Is best hospital in Athens." *Not surprising under a Military Dictatorship.*

We get him up, bundle him into the lift and out to the car. Under her erratic directions we find the Military Hospital in the centre of Athens. The young doctor who receives us looks at me and says, "I trained at Bart's in London."

Tasso is put in a room with two other patients – a room full of sunshine with a balcony looking over the traffic.

He must have a 'night-sitter', a job for impoverished widows as it was in Dickens' day. The woman looking after the elderly comatose gentleman in the next bed agrees to take on Tasso. It doesn't work, he is too much trouble – all she has to do for the other man is massage his gentlemanly toes. The father of the young man in the third bed, an ugly man with a big mashy face, when he sees me trying to shave Tasso, takes the razor from my hand, performing the task himself with the greatest care. The gentlemanly corpse is replaced by another octogenarian who dozes most of the time but is always hungry when he wakes and wants a cigarette. I light it for him, he takes immense puffs, the smoke pours out of him.

"May the God be always with you," he says graciously for any service. He keeps asking for his trousers. I find them in the cupboard and bring them to him. One of the pockets is lumpy and tied with string on the inside; he feels for this lump – his money – and, reassured, falls asleep. I put the trousers back in the cupboard. Best of all is the young male nurse, Janni, who waltzes in and out of the room like a Pierrot, performing his tasks full of sympathy for the patients.

We seem to have turned the corner but it proves to be a labyrinth as he is moved from Orthopaedic to Pathology. The doctors are saying nothing, except that they must do more tests. Since this is a Military Hospital, I must have a pass to come in and out, and I am not allowed to stay at night.

"He's the most difficult patient," says the doctor from Bart's, wondering what I am doing with this man. "I have given him a sedative that would knock out an ordinary man for three days…it makes him only drowsy." *Tasso is not an ordinary man.* The doctors give their verdict; a tumour the size of an orange in the lung, a metastasis into the neck and shoulder causing the pain; nothing to be done; only a matter of time and that is short.

The family reacts like a nest of ants under attack. As they shout and squabble in their fear and panic, I walk away. I need to be alone, and return to the dust-sheeted underworld of the empty basement flat. A canary on a balcony somewhere is singing a witless aria like a demented soprano. "*Thou'll break my heart thou bonny bird that sings so blithe from yonder twig…thou minds of departed joys….*" If I had a gun I would shoot it. Yes, there were joys, even if they departed – and his death was with us from the first moment. He lived life like someone trying to commit suicide without intending to succeed.

Why have I loved this man? Is it something in me – or something in him? What did we recognise in each other? What should one do with Life – live it tamely, or gather it up into a ball and throw it as far as one can? And who will I be without him? Back at the hospital, his bed is empty – our things have disappeared from the room. It can't have happened that quickly! Turning back to the lift in bewilderment, I meet Petros coming out of it.

"Where is he?"

"He is alright. Marina fix up special cancer clinic, more better – Marina pay. Come, I take you."

We speed through the traffic to a backstreet off a main boulevard where a building like a jerry-built block of flats flashes an illuminated green cross, indicating a private clinic.

The room is like a bedroom in a sleazy hotel. Marina, violently substituting Hope for Despair, is saying, "This is more better, darling! You see – it has private bathroom, everything!" I gaze at the rusty stain from the dripping taps and a hair in the washbasin.

"It's not very clean," I venture, marvelling that *She*, paranoid over cleanliness, hasn't noticed.

"I tell someone to clean up." And Marina breezes off to perform at the theatre. Petros leaves too.

We are alone. No doctor comes. The nurse, a mature, hard-boiled woman, probably with a family to raise, has no tenderness to spare for us. Everywhere is shutting down for the Easter Holiday, the festival of Death and Resurrection. We are trapped again. Is this Vladivostok or Tashkent? As evening falls, a murmur of voices in the street below draws me to the window. People are gathering with lighted candles, a bare black cross is held aloft, a catafalque covered in mauve flowers rests on the shoulders of four men. The singers begin the chant that will haunt the streets for the rest of the evening – the Virgin's lament for her son. The crowd moves off in formation following the catafalque. Good Friday. What's good about it? Well, anyway *they* call it '*Great Friday*', – *Megali Paraskevi*.

The pain returns like an animal gnawing his shoulder. I press the bell to summon the sullen nurse. She shrugs, there is no doctor on duty and she cannot give the strong drugs. She gives him a mild sedative, and goes away to lock herself in the office to sleep. She is not to be called again.

"Phone Antigone! Phone Petros!" The flash of his old fire raises absurd hope. There is a phone by the bed (at least that is provided by the management). I dial Antigone's number. She is angry too.

"Marina do that! She take him away from the best hospital in Athens What I can do? Nothing! The office closing for the Easter… must to wait till after holiday now."

He grabs the phone from me. "I'm going to DIE here…"

She rings off, promising to do her best. In the morning, the General comes bounding into the room looking quite boyish – Stalin must have been a boy once – followed by Petros.

"We can take him back!" He has fixed it. Petros helps me dress our puppet. As the General and Petros, supporting him between them, fumble him into the lift, he keeps saying, "I'm fed up…I'm fed up…" Fed up with the process of dying. Returning to the Military Hospital proves to be a mini-resurrection regarded as a miracle to those who presumed that when he disappeared, he had died. They cross themselves…and throw out their arms to embrace me as well as him. Janni, the young male nurse, sidles into the room mewing like a cat. It should be inappropriate but the comedy is received with joy. He presents Tasso with a little package, an Easter gift of a fluffy chick and a plastic egg cup with a red egg in it. He pins a rose to Tasso's pyjamas.

Great Saturday: Night of the Resurrection; I bring two beeswax candles from the chapel in the courtyard, he wants me to light them on the bedside table. Just before midnight, the priests in embroidered robes take up their position on the steps of the hospital, to intone the liturgy. From the big balcony I look down on a sea of candlelight as people gather, the nurses and doctors in their white coats. The sound of the priests intoning is the sound of bumblebees, suddenly culminating in the great shout: "CHRIST IS RISEN! HE IS RISEN INDEED!" – the affirmation of life over death. Friends and strangers embrace one another in the joy of the moment. I run back to the room where he is, to find one of the candles burned out, the other still alight.

Next morning, "*Xristos anesti!*" (Christ is risen!) says Matron, entering the wards. "*Xronia pollá*! (May you have many years!) *Kalá anastasi*! (Good Ressurection to you!)" – offering the joyous and pitiful greetings of this day to those of her patients who are resurrected after the battle with the night. They return the salutations in perfect trust. "*Xristos anesti!*" says Janni, waltzing in and giving a little pirouette. "*Xristos anesti!*" says the cleaning woman coming to broom around the floor and carry away the detritus. It is all a bit too much for me; I need to get out into the air.

It is a beautiful morning; the Hilton Hotel is just across the road. With sudden resolution, I say, "I'm going to have breakfast at The Hilton!"

"Good idea," he murmurs, "but don't be long…" Spring is in evidence in the trees growing out the pavement, as I wait to cross the road. The wonder of it – that spring can permeate even to the centre of this ugly modern city with its once glorious past. The traffic lights change, offering just enough time to walk briskly across – best not to dawdle, it can lead to instant death. Death isn't bothering me this morning; my mind toys with that inevitability like a child too tired to take an interest. Among the American tourists, I order the full breakfast menu: cereal, eggs and bacon, toast, jam and coffee. I haven't had a proper meal for days. In the ladies' room, I revel in the hot water from the taps, the sweet-smelling soap, then browse through the English books at the bookstand and buy one – another luxury. I feel an inexplicable joy. Is it life asserting itself in me as it drains out of him? Should I feel guilty? I have no reluctance to return to him. I am checked on the threshold of the room by the sight of a young woman by his bed, his daughter. For an awful moment I wonder if the mother is with them and retreat to the corridor with my new book until they've gone, but Antigone appears and, grabbing my arm, says, "Come! I tell them we must to be all together now!"

The daughter by the bed keeps picking invisible bits off his pyjamas. She is 22 now and engaged to be married.

"Have you got pain now, Bábá?" she keeps saying.

He tells her gently to stop asking. "The pain is always there…" His son keeps his distance by the window as if trying to take in the changed image of his father on the bed, but when Tasso calls him, he moves quickly, bending his face close to hear his words, kissing and soothing him. *The child is father to the man*….When they leave, the daughter does not look at me, but the boy pauses and in faltering English, murmurs "Thank you", which stuns me. *He was only five…* The girl's fiancé follows them out of the room – I hadn't noticed him.

When Marina turns up, she tells me, "You must to leave the flat, darling. They will be staying there – you understand."

I go back to the flat, put all my things in the car; but what do I do now? I am not allowed to stay with him in the hospital. Where can I go? I haven't got money for a hotel. I ring Aphrodite; instantly she says, "Come!" Soon I am sitting in her kitchen with her children, being fed on lentil soup.

As his body dissolves, his face gets thinner; he looks as he did when I first knew him. Rather than going away, he seems to be coming back. His eyes are tragic – as when, with no money in his pocket, he danced the poetry of his egotism in the *Zembekiko*.

He urges the nurse pressing on his buttocks to find a new place to put the needle. "Do it gently, *Krissi kopella*...my golden girl..." Restless with pain, he wants to sit up on the side of the bed, leaning his head on my shoulder like a tired child. When the tsunami of pain surges through his flesh and nerves, breaking against his bones, I hold on to him as if we are drowning in a tempestuous sea. I put my hand on the pain; separated from it only by his skin, I cannot feel it. I stay at night now. The Cerberus on the hospital gate barks at me to prove he is doing his duty, but at the same time, with a wink and nod, indicates "Go on...I haven't seen you..." and I slip up the stairs like a cat to the forbidden kitchen.

We are alone in the room; the General has seen to that. I kip on the spare bed. The family pay for the Night Woman, Roula, a rough, cheerful soul. I'm glad of her company and her humour through the long hours of night. Of the other Night Women, she says, "We're all widows – or without men!" with a laugh. She has two children and an invalid aunt of 80 on her back. Brave souls all. In this setting, the boisterous Greek character is channelled into sympathetic interest and involvement in 'the other patient'.

The hand of a stranger caresses my shoulder, "Are you alright, my girl...?" Often taken for a schoolgirl, I accept that I am a pupil in their school of life where everyone vibrates with a unique humanity; no-one seems a stranger – even the banisters on the stairway offer sympathy to my hand.

At the *cafenion* outside the gates, I buy yoghurt and biscuits – sometimes an ouzo with a coffee. The café-owner asks me if I am German. I reply "No!" too tartly. "I'm English!"

"Why you say it like that?" he reprimands me. "Aren't Germans good people too? Look!" He pulls up his shirt sleeve to show a bayonet wound through his bicep. "From the Germans – wartime – but Germans is not all bad. There are good Germans and bad. Good British and bad. Good Greeks and bad. We are all the same."

Indeed I am a pupil in their school of life.

Strange birds fly into our cage. The room is often full of obscure relatives who haven't seen each other for years, talking loudly as they rediscover the threads that bind them to each other. 'Uncle Pete' turns up – having spent 25 years in the States, he expresses his folk wisdom in a Bronx accent: "When they knock on the door yer gotta go…but they makes yer suffer foist." During the day the room is so full of people it is like a party. They bring folk remedies – massage him with spirits, and give him a grey powder from a monastery: a miracle cure. It makes him cough and he needs oxygen after it. Antigone wants to force food down him – "To give him *dynamie!*" – though he is incapable of eating now. I watch with detachment.

While the chatter goes on noisily over and around him, he is still part of life. He whispers to Petros, "Find Dandi. Bring Dandi here." I remember when we came to Athens one time, he was trying to find this friend of his youth, asking for him in the Street of the Tailors. The reaction he got was cagey and no one admitted they knew this man. Two days later, a small, waxy-looking man in a neat black suit, hair discreetly hennaed, stooped as if from a spinal injury, appears in the room and swoops on Tasso like a blackbird, hugging and kissing him, visibly weeping. Tasso stirs, opens his eyes. Recognising the stranger, he whispers, "Dandi!" He comes every day to sit by the bed for hours, though Tasso can hardly speak. When the General and Antigone are in the room, an undefined truce exists between the General and this mysterious little tailor; certainly he is not just a tailor.

"When was the last time you saw Tassos?" the General asks.

"It was 1944. We were both taken in a street sweep by the Germans in Athens and put on the train with the Jews to the death camps. When the train stopped at Thessalonica, the last place in Greece, the people come to the station to give us any food they had. The platform was crowded. Tassos had worked his way round to the open door right behind the guard. It was a cattle truck. When the guard turned to fix somebody, Tassos stepped onto the platform and stood among the people. In that moment the train pulled out of the station! That was the last time I saw *him!*"

indicating the passive figure on the bed. "The bastard got off!" crossing himself.

"And you?"

"I spent the next two years in Dachau." Looking across at me, he suddenly says, "Nobody has told me who she is?" They ignore the question. It seems a good moment to take myself down to the *cafenion*, where I order an ouzo. Turning away from the counter, I find Dandi standing behind me. He has followed me. Placing his hand on the breast of his black suit, and speaking in English, he says, "May I ask you a question – as a brother?" I nod, wondering what he can have to ask me. "Are you married with Tassos?" I shake my head.

"I've been with him a long time though", as if it were more of an achievement.

"Ah!" he nods, appreciating the point. "Tell me something else..." He holds his waxy head on one side like an inquisitive bird. "Have you any 'grievances' with him?" *He knows the man.*

Laughing with surprise, I shake my head, realising, suddenly, that all my grievances have been consumed in the fire of his pain. I try to explain.

"When I came to Greece first and met him...I didn't know anything. He has been my 'University'." It feels right to use Tasso's idiom.

The strange, small man like a waxwork nods his head in wise assent, and insists on paying for my ouzo. He does not order one himself.

"I learn early in life, if I drink I am going to kill somebody." For sure, he is not just a tailor... "If you should need any help – call me. I will come running." And with a courteous bow, he steps into the bright light of the street and disappears.

In the afternoon I go back to the basement flat to sleep a bit; the daughter and her fiancé have gone.

At six o'clock, I return to the hospital. At the reception desk, a young nurse is talking to her boyfriend on the phone. "I can't meet you tonight, Spiro...I've got to stay on – we've got three *going up* tonight." *Going up*? Roula isn't among the Night Women clattering out of the lifts. She rings up to say her old aunt is poorly and she cannot leave her; another Night Woman is found to help me. She sits by him, fanning him, while I doze on the spare bed. I am too tired to think, yet one line of poetry has been in my head all day: *"To cease upon the midnight with no pain..."* Keats? Waking from a shallow sleep, I find Aphrodite bending over me... Aphrodite! In her green shawl just as I saw her that first night. Is she real or am I dreaming? I haven't seen her for days – unable to get to her warm family kitchen among the children, for coffee or a bowl of lentil soup. She goes to him, testing his breathing, feeling his pulse; opening his eyes briefly, his lips murmur, *"Aphrodite..."* She is his kind of woman.

She beckons me to follow her into the corridor where we can speak. "I have had you in my mind all day...I had to come." Holding my hands in hers, anxious for me, she says, "His time is very near – I think *the thread will be cut tonight...*" She uses the word *'Lachesis'*, evoking their ancient daemon, who, at birth, allots each man his portion. She goes. I return to the room where the woman is still fanning him. I lie down and drop off again, my eyelids like heavy metal shutters moving over grains of sand.

Something wakes me sharply – his hands are waving feebly as a dying moth, his breathing rapid and light. The blood seems to be draining away from his features – muscular contractions begin as if he was a rubber puppet being squeezed into hideous grimaces. I hold his hand as the woman fans more frantically, murmurs in little gasps, "Oh, *to telos eniai...*it is the end... *Panayia mou!*" The contractions cease, he is still. I go for a doctor, a young female doctor – *he would appreciate that* – but she orders me to leave the room. Why? I know he is dead. I shake my head. She bends over him, listens to his chest, feels his pulse, pushes up an eyelid revealing the brown of his glossy dog's eye – as bright as in life!

"It is finish..." she says in English, staring at me as if expecting something of me. I am silent. She goes. The Night Woman leaves too. I am alone with him for a moment before the male nurses enter, pushing a trolley. They pounce on the body, ripping off the bedcovers, stripping off his pyjamas. I can't see that, and go to the phone on the landing to ring Petros, glancing up at the clock as I do so. It is three minutes after midnight. *'To cease upon the midnight with no pain.'* Petros says he will come. I sit on the plastic leather settee on the landing. One of the Night Women – her patient asleep – strolls up and down. Scenting drama, she sits down beside me just as Tasso's body is trundled into the lift and disappears.

"Your husband?"

I shake my head. "I wasn't married to him." Why I have to be so honest, I don't know.

"You not married with him! You won't get his money!" is her reaction.

"He hasn't any." At which she loses interest and goes back to her patient. It seems a very long time before I hear Petros's quick steps on the stair.

"I had to phone round the family, you understand," he apologizes. Returning to the empty room, we strip it quickly of all traces of our residence there. Down in the courtyard Antigone, sitting on the steps weeping, drags me down beside her.

"How did he go? What was it like?" I tell her how it was.

"I have never see anybody to die..." she says, shaking her head from side to side, like a melancholy bird trying to dislodge her grief as something inflicted into her skin and bone. Petros is inside dealing with the paperwork. A mortuary attendant comes to ask for the clothes. I have prepared for their custom of dressing the body as for life rather than death, and have had his clothes cleaned: vest, shirt, tie, socks, shoes and the old black corduroy jacket. I get them from the car; the attendant bears them away. The spring night smells so sweet even in the middle of this city; we seem anaesthetized by it, sitting on the steps, while the General marches up and down, flicking his worry beads over his fingers. Antigone looks at me, as the female doctor did.

"You don't crying... You no cry...?"

"The British *never* cry!" the General says proudly, as if it were one of our better qualities.

His body will be flown back to the island for burial, so at five o'clock in the morning, I drive away from the city, rapidly exchanging its artificiality for the open hillsides, where the solitary shepherd watches his sheep and goats in a timeless vacuity of space scented with thyme and sage; and a silence intensified by munch and fart of beast. The sun comes up like a great red orange, and the world looks a fabulous place. I am singing at the top of my voice when the engine boils. Pulling into a garage, the engine haemorrhages all over the cement. The garage man stares at it and shakes his head. "Big problem."

I am stuck. I can't worry. I can't seem to worry about anything. A lovely feeling. I suppose I should tell someone where I am. The garage man allows me to use the phone. I try Antigone. No reply. I get Marina.

"My car's broken down. I'm stuck. I can't get there... I don't know where I am but it must be 200 miles."

"No! No! You must to be there! Take a taxi. I pay – give me to speak with the man." The garage man takes the phone, his face changing as he realises he is talking with the Celebrity Marina, Star of Stage and Screen – a household icon.

"Yes, yes! *Kyria* Marina! She is safe with us. My cousin has a taxi. You can trust us."

When he hands the phone back to me, Marina's voice says, "Make them take you to the police station to fix the price of the taxi – so they don't *skarrak* you...you understand?" *That's Tasso talking...*The Garage man's cousin arrives with his taxi – they take me to the Police station to establish the price per kilometre. I mention the General's name, at which the Police chief bows his head reverently. I am getting the hang of it. *Tasso is here ... I can't see him... but I can feel him.... this is fun ... like the old times... It's all coming back!*

Settled comfortably in the back of the taxi, with nothing to worry about, I feel like Persephone returning from the Underworld. At home for the first time in two months, I wake in the night to find myself holding onto the back of a chair as if it were his hand.

At the cemetery, we enter the broad avenue between the cypress and the sarcophagi, Marina suddenly says, "Darr-ling! Don't come into the church – you understand? Stay a little bit far...Okay?" Is this because I am not his wife? I don't care, but the General says angrily, "Why?" and clamps my arm firmly under his, appointing himself my protector against the members of his own family.

From within the church with the facade of a classical Greek Temple comes the scent of beeswax candles and the bumblebee hum of the priest's incantations. Mourners dressed in black fill the interior in front of the white and gold *iconostasis*. The open coffin, with him in it, stands in the centre.

"You want to go in?" the General says, "I take you!" Neither Marina or Antigone wants to go in. "No! No! I can't see him like that...!" they wail, clinging to the columns like the chorus in a Greek tragedy. I don't want to look on him dead either... until...I see the tip of his nose above the edge of the coffin... It draws me like a magnet across the threshold, igniting a burst of hysterical female weeping at my intrusion.

Concentrating on his nose, I step cautiously as a cat up to the boat-like coffin containing him submerged in flowers except for the shoulders of his black corduroy jacket.

It is *him* – really him, not the perished rubber puppet of two nights ago. *Him*, restored – even to a hint of smile at the corner of the mouth as if to say, "What do you expect?" He looks as if he could leap out of that box and dance a triumphant *Zembekiko!*

Antigone, who has followed me, gasps, "Oh, he is beautiful!" I tuck the rose I am carrying next to his cheek.

Another burst of hysterical weeping follows me out in the bright sunlight. I clap my hand over my mouth to hide the laughter they would not understand. He's done it again! He's got off the Death train! *Le Roi est mort – Long Live the King of the Good Basters...*

The service over, the coffin is closed and borne to the graveside. Mourners have poured into the cemetery – half the town must be here, shopkeepers, café owners, familiar faces all: Costa the Canary, Tomá the Melon head, the lorry driver, the

379

butcher, the baker, his work-mates... all openly weeping as if something of their own lives has been taken from them. *Kyria* Rosa, our landlady, comes up beside me and links her arm in mine. Standing by the graveside, the General speaks the *Mirologia* – the Words of Destiny, extolling Tasso as man, fighter and artist. The clods hammer down on the coffin. It has a hollow sound. *He's not in there... Maybe he's somewhere, but not in that box...no box could contain him...*The crowd begins to drift towards the gate, where the family forms up in a line – the son, the daughter, the brothers and sisters...their husbands and his wife... *the real one.*

I slip through the gate, and stand under a tree. *Kyria* Rosa stays with me. *I can't just push off, can I? I would like just to walk home and come here again tomorrow, early in the morning. That will be good...*

It is with embarrassment I watch the line of mourners, Tomá, Spiro, Costa (the tavern singers), swing toward me; dumb as animals, they press my hand. They are followed by the General, who breaks ranks to plod toward me. Placing his hands on my shoulders, he kisses me formally on both cheeks.

*

Collete has sent a packet of dead roses from Paris. I must take them to him. It is a beautiful morning. I pick the spring flowers from the hedges until I have a nice bunch. Threading my way through the close-packed marble, I stop short at the sight of a woman in black bending over his grave, lighting the oil dip lamp, and turn away in wonder at the Chimera called Love – with its lion's head, goat's body and serpent's tail... '*or any incongruous conception of fancy...*'

...But how many legs does it have?

THE END